Annie O'Neil spent most of her childhood with her leg draped over the family rocking chair and a book in her hand. Novels, baking, and writing too much teenage angst poetry ate up most of her youth. Now Annie splits her time between corralling her husband into helping her with their cows, baking, reading, barrel racing (not really!) and spending some very happy hours at her computer, writing.

Susan Carlisle's love affair with books began in the sixth grade, when she made a bad grade in mathematics. Not allowed to watch TV until she'd brought the grade up, Susan filled her time with books. She turned her love of reading into a passion for writing, and now has over ten Medical Romances published through Mills & Boon. She writes about hot, sexy docs and the strong women who captivate them. Visit SusanCarlisle.com.

Miracles in the Making collection

Risking Her Heart on the Single Dad by Annie O'Neil
The Neonatal Doc's Baby Surprise by Susan Carlisle

Available now

Also by Annie O'Neil

Tempted by Her Single Dad Boss
The Doctor's Marriage for a Month
A Return, a Reunion, a Wedding
Making Christmas Special Again

Also by Susan Carlisle

Nurse to Forever Mum
The Sheikh Doc's Marriage Bargain
Highland Doc's Christmas Rescue
Firefighter's Unexpected Fling

Discover more at millsandboon.co.uk.

RISKING HER HEART ON THE SINGLE DAD

ANNIE O'NEIL

THE NEONATAL DOC'S BABY SURPRISE

SUSAN CARLISLE

MILLS & BOON

First Published in Great Britain 2020
by Mills & Boon, an imprint of HarperCollins*Publishers*
1 London Bridge Street, London, SE1 9GF

ISBN: 978-0-263-27967-2

MIX
Paper from
responsible sources
FSC® C007454

This book is produced from independently certified FSC™ paper
to ensure responsible forest management.
For more information visit www.harpercollins.co.uk/green.

Printed and bound in Spain
by CPI, Barcelona

RISKING HER HEART ON THE SINGLE DAD

ANNIE O'NEIL

MILLS & BOON

This book goes out to all those amazing doctors
who pour their hearts and souls into
making true medical miracles occur.

CHAPTER ONE

KIRRI LOOKED UP at the soaring skyscraper and beamed. *Unbelievable.* Her new workplace for the next six weeks was epically fabulous.

The Medical Innovations Center, from the outside at least, was everything she'd been hoping for. A towering testament to pioneering medicine. Maybe the doctors here would see what her brother couldn't. Dreams *could* become reality if she worked hard enough.

So what if it was pouring down with rain and she looked like a drowned rat? She wasn't here to look hot. She was here to set her brain alight. She was in Atlanta, Georgia, baby!

Ah…spring. Wet and warm. Such a contrast to back home in Sydney, where people were deciding whether or not to turn the central heating on. If everything went according to plan her research would blossom in tandem with the Georgia peaches.

Mmm… She inhaled a big lungful of Georgia air. Totally different from the salt-laced breezes back home. It was more…floral. Jasmine? Honeysuckle? Who knew? She had six weeks to find out. If she ever left the lab, that was. From the brainboxes alleged to be inside it, she was pretty sure she'd have to be dragged out when the research exchange was over.

She tipped her head back further, then opened her eyes

wide against the rain. In this weather, and from this angle, it really did look as if her new office building's rooftop was tickling the heavens. All glass and steel, the ultra-modern building that housed the Piedmont Women and Baby Pavilion screamed trailblazing, forward-thinking, state-of-the-art medicine. It was *her* kind of place. The pinch herself variety.

Still a bit jet-lagged from the long-haul flight, and too excited to sleep, she'd come in early. Sunrise early. And perhaps three entire days early on top of that. She wasn't technically meant to start until Monday—but who needed settling-in time when she was about to embark on a last-ditch attempt to prove to her brother she'd been right all along?

It would be hitting sunset o'clock back home, where her brother was no doubt pounding out furious email after furious email. Or silently fuming even as his genius continued to dazzle their illustrious patient list. So she hadn't strictly cleared the trip with him. Or hung around to see what his reaction to her absence would be.

She'd covered all her bases. Put replacement neonatal surgeons in place—all of them desperate to work with Australia's so-called Baby Whisperer. Being his kid sister was handy sometimes. But at other times—like most of the time—less so. Like right now, for instance.

If she'd thought her chances of getting him to change his mind about pulling the plug on her research had been slim a week ago they'd be non-existent now. Her lab—her broom closet, more like—would remain dark and untouched for the duration of her absence. The type of research she was doing was not the Harborside Fertility and Neonatal Center's jam. But it should be, because bringing healthy babies into the world was.

She resisted the urge to check her phone, wrung out her

hair and swept away another stream of raindrops to gaze at the place that had offered her and her research a lifeline.

She squinted against the increasingly heavy rain as a helicopter with a bright red cross on its underbelly swept in from the mid-level cloud-base and began to descend to the rooftop. Her heart began to pump with that telltale adrenaline that came with any medical emergency.

She'd never admit it to her brother, but the crystal-clear focus that came with performing life-or-death surgery was something she'd find hard to put to the side for the next six weeks. Surgery in the day, research at night. That was her life and she'd always liked it that way.

Right up until Lucius had pulled the plug on her DIY lab.

The invitation to come here and devote herself to research had been all the nudge she'd needed. A chance to make her dreams come true? Hell, yeah!

The helicopter disappeared out of sight as it settled on the roof. Her eyes dipped a smidge to the floor, to her temporary home away from home. *Clever,* she thought. Putting the Piedmont Women and Baby Pavilion on the top floor of the pre-eminent medical facility. Easy access to the roof and the clinic's most critical patients. Everyone must have wanted *that* prime real estate.

Heart, lungs, ears, nose, throat… This building had specialists for everything and everyone. But not a single one of them apart from the Piedmont Women and Baby Pavilion offered fetal and neonatal surgery. Inside its doors she'd be able to tap the brains of some of the world's leading neonatologists. And she couldn't wait.

Her brother would have said that the rainy day was a sign of misery yet to come, but she knew better. Beyond the clouds the Georgia sky would be every bit as blue as Sydney's, and when night fell there would be an entirely new set of stars overhead. Hopefully they were aligned in her favor.

Just as she was about to head into the main reception area a man raced past and bashed into her shoulder.

"Easy there, mate. You won't miss the parade!"

She whirled to face him and in so doing lost her balance. The basher reached out to steady her, one hand holding her upright until he was sure she was all right, the other holding an umbrella aloft.

Oh, my.

He was rather good-looking. Especially if "rather" meant drop-dead gorgeous of the possibly Latin, possibly Clark Kent variety of gorgeous. This was sexy-nerdy on a whole new level.

"I do beg your pardon, ma'am. Are you all right?" Superman asked.

She mumbled something. She wasn't sure what. His fault, really. For being so…*mmm…*

"Ma'am? Is everything okay?"

Kirri opened her mouth but nothing came out. Why couldn't she talk? She was a thirty-seven-year-old highly qualified surgeon, for heaven's sake. She had the power of speech.

She tried again.

Nope. Nothing.

If she hadn't looked into his chocolatey brown eyes and gone all gooey inside she would have been *completely* capable of giving him a piece of her mind for not watching where he was going. It wasn't as if the plaza in front of the medical center was teeming with people.

She would have done that. Told him off. She definitely would. But he was just her type.

Thinking the words gave her a proper slap back into reality. She didn't *have* a type. Not now, anyway. And she was far too busy to date, but…

She would bet actual cold hard cash that Superman, here, had been one of the nerdy kids back in the day. The type who got perfect grades, never got in trouble, was rotten at sports and the opposite sex paid no attention to. A bit like her. The type of nerd who never got asked to dance. She would've danced with him. And gloried in his transformation as he became an adult.

Athletically built with neat ebony-black hair, a speckling of salt and pepper at the temples. Bone structure a model would die for, a cheeky little divot in the center of his chin and those *eyes*. Espresso-brown with hints of gold.

He'd lived. She could see that by the small fan of crinkles arrowing out from his eyes as he narrowed them. Either that or he was using his special X-ray vision to ensure she was all right. Or checking out her bra. Perriwinkle blue lace, if he was interested. Front clasp, if he needed more details.

He blinked. Something quite different from lust was illuminating those flecks of gold.

Recognition.

She didn't know how, or why, but it was as if he saw straight through to her heart. If she'd had properly functioning ovaries they'd be working double-time about now.

And then, in another blink of an eye, he was a stranger again.

He gave a swift apologetic wave, pointed upwards, as if the gesture would explain why he was so distracted, then turned to go.

Fair enough, mate. We've all got things to do. But... nice to meet you.

As if he'd heard her he doubled back, handed her his huge golf umbrella and then, in one of those caramel-rich accents she'd only ever heard on television, said, "My heartfelt apologies. May I offer this as consolation for my rudeness?"

And then he disappeared into the building.

Mercy.

Half of her was tempted to race into the building and get trapped in the lift with him for the rest of the day. But the other half—the half she was far more comfortable with—wanted…no, *needed* to get up to her new lab and get to work. Twenty-four-seven if they'd let her.

She looked at the handle of the umbrella that he'd just been holding, then at the front doors of the building. Tempting. Definitely tempting…

Her phone buzzed in her leather backpack and against her better judgement she tugged it out and looked at the message.

Oh, crud-buckets.

Australia's very own Baby Whisperer was giving her a right telling off, if the full caps message was any indication of its contents.

CAN'T HEAR YOU!!!

She typed her message back, like the kid sister she was, and then, reminding herself that she was a highly respected neonatal surgeon, deleted it and chose the far more mature option of ignoring it altogether.

She gave her shoulders a wriggle to shift some of her confidence from her heart through to her spine. Her father had always told her that aiming high wasn't high enough. Well, if pushing the elevator button to get up to one of the world's most prestigious research and treatment centers was anything to go by, she'd finally done it.

The Piedmont Women and Baby Pavilion was the pinnacle of neonatal care in the Northern Hemisphere. On a par with her own employer, Sydney's Harborside Fertility and Neonatal Center.

The biggest difference was that her big brother wouldn't

be her boss here. Not for the next six weeks. Thanks to the mysteriously enigmatic Dr. Ty Sawyer.

Somehow this premier neonatal surgeon had heard about her research and through one of his colleagues had offered her a lifeline—a research exchange. She'd have six weeks at his clinic and one of his colleagues would have six weeks at theirs at some point a bit further down the road.

The offer had been like receiving a direct hit of oxygen. Forty-two days to launch herself at a lifetime of sibling rivalry and finally prove she'd been right all along. That or go home with her tail between her legs and never hear the end of it from Lucius.

No pressure, then.

At least Lucius was some fifteen thousand miles away. She knew her big brother meant well in steering her away from research and back to full-time surgical practice, but there was something deep within her that needed to be *right.* She could be a forerunner in neonatal intensive care. Artificial womb technology was the key. Even if it *did* sound like science fiction.

So! New country. New clinic. And a once-in-a-lifetime chance to prove to her brother that she wasn't peddling false dreams.

She knew in her gut that she had the scientific clarity to give struggling mothers-to-be genuine hope that one day they could carry a baby to term. Hope and science *could* be bedfellows. Sometimes it just took a few thousand miles' distance from the naysayers to prove it.

She took a step toward the entryway, doing her best to ignore the nerves as they kicked in. There was no time like the present—and the present was now.

"Everything okay, Dr. Sawyer?"

Ty glanced up from the running water at the scrub station and frowned. "Sure. Fine."

He bit off the usual ending, *Why do you ask*?

Amanda, one of his top specialist delivery nurses, didn't miss much, and today was no exception. He was still shaken. Even with a handful of minutes having passed between running into that extraordinary-looking woman outside the clinic and now.

Bright blue eyes that looked as though they were being backlit by Hollywood… Rich auburn rain-soaked hair reaching halfway down her back… Lips the color of a burnished rose… Hip leather jacket… A fluffy, tutu-like skirt in camouflage fabric… And, if he hadn't been mistaken, because he'd been desperately trying to keep his eyes on…well, her eyes, a T-shirt with kangaroos dressed as cheerleaders on it.

The pompoms had been in an awkward position. Awkward for someone trying to maintain eye contact, anyway.

None of which was either here or there—because the one thing he'd definitively noticed was that he'd been attracted to her. And not just in an *oh, she's pretty* sort of way. It had been the sort of attraction that had gripped his vitals and given them a proper shake. A meeting-a-soulmate sort of shake. In other words something he thought he'd never feel again. Not since…

Well, he hadn't thought he'd ever experience that particular sensation again.

Despite his diligent scrubbing, and trying to assume what he hoped was his everyday demeanor, he could feel Amanda's eyes staying on him for a moment longer. And then, when he didn't respond, she went for a change of tack.

"Want me to run you through the details again?"

"If you wouldn't mind."

Details. Surgery. Exactly what he needed to take his mind off those bright blue eyes that had synced with his as if meeting the gaze of a long-lost lover. Madness, considering he'd only had one lover, but…

He scrubbed the thought away. His wife had been his one and only true love. Whatever it was that had happened this morning was clearly a freak occurrence.

He glanced out at the empty OR. The critical care transport team would be rolling in with the patient any second now. He'd seen the helicopter coming in to land and was surprised they weren't in the operating room already. Perhaps something had happened on the helicopter that demanded they take things slowly.

Though he'd virtually memorized all the details of the case Amanda ran him through it again.

Mary Lingford was an expectant mother. She lived just under a hundred miles outside of Atlanta, hence the helicopter ride in. With rush hour traffic starting as early as four a.m., they weren't taking the risk of her being stuck in an ambulance. At forty-three years old she was a high-risk pregnancy. She was twenty-seven weeks pregnant with a baby boy. And the baby, her local hospital had discovered last night, during a routine scan, had a congenital heart defect.

Hypo-plastic left heart syndrome. The most common lethal condition in congenital heart disease. About one in five thousand babies had it. None survived without surgery.

There were still a good thirteen weeks of pregnancy remaining, so Mary's baby needed to stay inside her. But that heart needed fixing. The Piedmont Women and Baby Pavilion was the best place for both of those requirements to be fulfilled.

Ty turned around so the scrub nurse could help him gown up. "Have they done any pre-anesthesia? I want to make sure they've steered clear of teratogenic drugs. Accidentally inducing labor at this point would be a nightmare."

"I called in last night, and an hour ago before they prepared her for the flight. No pre-anesthesia. They're leaving everything up to our team."

Ty smiled. There was never an i left un-dotted or a t left uncrossed on Amanda's watch. Extra-generous in this case, seeing as he'd scheduled the operation for early morning and she most likely would only be observing. She was a specialty delivery nurse. A skill they were hoping they wouldn't need this morning. But it was protocol.

The safety of Ty's patients was paramount. He went where most surgeons refused to go. Directly to the womb.

Amanda nodded toward the operating room, where their patient was being wheeled in. "Looks like they're ready for you."

Good. Ty needed to put his blinkers back on. The blinkers that had seen him through the last few years of his life. Through work and caring for his daughter and his extended family. Those were the three components of his life. None of which included having adrenaline spikes when he laid eyes on a complete stranger.

The telephone rang as he entered the OR. Amanda took the call.

"All right if Dr. West scrubs in?"

Ty looked up in surprise. "She's here already?"

Amanda nodded. "Jet-lagged, apparently. Said she thought it would help her understand the clinic's ethos if she scrubbed into a surgery and saw things from the ground up. Would you like an extra pair of hands?"

He nodded. "Why not?"

How interesting. He knew Dr. West was a surgeon, but from the sounds of her research papers he'd thought she'd be more lab rat. Someone whose world revolved around cell slides, microchips and Petri dishes. But it appeared he'd been wrong.

Good. He'd made a good call. A surgeon who wanted to hit the ground running? He liked her already.

Amanda wrapped up the phone call. After saying hello to his patient, and assuring her that she was in the safest of hands, Ty turned his attention to the anesthetist. Giving the patient the wrong type of drug could induce labor, thereby doubling the risk of administering anesthesia.

"Back home in Oz we try to go as minimal on the anesthesia as possible. Too risky for baby *and* mom."

Everyone turned as a feminine Australian accent filled the operating theater.

Ty's chest constricted as his eyes clashed with the familiar pair of bright blue eyes. Umbrella girl. Right there in the scrub room. Reminding him once again—or his body, at least—that he was still a red-blooded male.

Yessir.

Still vital and responsive, even after five years of certainty that his chances of connecting with a woman on that sort of level had died with his wife.

The woman tore her eyes from his, then gave the rest of the team in the operating theater a quick wave. "G'day, all. Sorry… I know I shouldn't be sticking my nose in before I've been briefed properly, but I presume the goal here is to keep the baby precisely where it is?"

This was Dr. Kirrily West?

Ty couldn't believe it. She wasn't the woman he'd been expecting. Not that he'd seen a photo or anything, but... *seriously?* Umbrella woman? And what was she doing talking about anesthetic before the very stressed patient was even anesthetized?

He gave his patient's shoulder a gentle squeeze and said in a low voice, "We've got a new surgeon scrubbing in but only as an observer. Nothing to worry about."

Mary gave him a silent nod, concern evident in her crinkled brow.

Ty looked back to the scrub room, ready to give this new doctor a piece of his mind.

Kirrily West wasn't wearing her chic biker chick ensemble anymore. She was in a pair of Piedmont scrubs, and making the standard-cut cotton top and trousers look far more interesting to take off than they should.

Why the hell hadn't he looked at her photo before he'd okayed that plane ticket?

No need to be a surgeon to figure *that* one out. He was a busy man, and looks didn't factor when he was considering groundbreaking researchers who might make an invaluable contribution to pre-term fetal welfare.

He caught himself staring instead of chiding as she swept her hair up in one hand, twisted it with the other, then bundled the auburn coil under a blue surgical cap. It was a simple gesture that made it far too easy to imagine many things he shouldn't.

Silky hair... Soft bare skin... A whispered moan...

What an idiot. He should have done that video conference call with her rather than tasking his colleague Mark with the job.

So that what? He could have changed his mind? Decided that a woman with a heart-shaped face and brilliant sapphire eyes that made his heart do strange things wasn't worth his time, despite her obvious genius and passion for neonatal surgical advances?

Science didn't work like that.

He didn't work like that.

Even so… The woman now twirling around for the scrub nurse to do up her surgical gown wasn't at all who he'd been expecting. He'd presumed she'd be… Well, *older* for one thing. Her insight into fetal reconstructive surgery was on a par with much more senior surgeons. Her take on what might be achieved one day in the world of neonatal intensive care was potentially Nobel-prize-winning stuff. Literally life-changing for countless premature babies.

None of which explained why he'd expected an old,

frumpy librarian type. Smart didn't equal unattractive, but…

Oh, this was a disaster.

Kirrily West pressed her freshly gowned elbow to the intercom button again. "Any thoughts on the anesthetic front?"

"Dr. Sawyer?" whispered Mary, reaching for his hand. "Is what she's saying true?"

Right. Though only a handful of seconds had passed, it was a handful too many. *His* operating theater. *His* operation. *His* method of treatment.

He looked at Kirrily West and said pointedly, "As our patient Mary, here, is awake right now, perhaps it would be best if we talk her through just how safe her child will be rather than focus on what hasn't happened."

He didn't know how they did things Down Under, but they did things Southern-style here. It entailed TLC and a whole lot more professionalism and tact for starters.

He addressed his team—and, most importantly, the *patient*. "As ever, Mary, our number one priority is your baby's safety. I'm not saying this is a routine surgery. It isn't. It's specialized. But this is the best place for you to have it and everything has been taken into account. Particularly the anesthetic."

Mary's brow was knitted with worry lines. "But what was that other doctor talking about? Will the anesthetic hurt my baby? I don't want to do this if the surgery is going to induce labor!"

She tried to push herself up from the gurney.

Ty resisted shooting Kirrily West a look—an eyebrows raised look, straight up to his surgical cap, that would make it clear to her that this was *exactly* why precision verbal conduct was every bit as important as precision surgical conduct.

But actions spoke louder than words, so he gave Mary's

hand a reassuring squeeze and a pat. They both knew this was very likely her last chance of having a child, and he sure as hell wasn't about to be the surgeon to let her down.

"Like I said, everything's been taken into account and the protocol is as safe as these things can be. We're going to administer tocolytics. They're drugs designed especially to prevent premature labor. And I've just been told the emergency transport team administered an H-2 antagonist last night, which will also help." He looked Kirrily West straight in the eye. "Thoughts, Doctor?"

CHAPTER TWO

KIRRI GULPED. THIS was *exactly* the sort of thing her brother would have ejected her from his operating theater for. Leaping before she looked.

She called it spontaneous innovation. He called it foolishness. Up until now she'd thought both of them were a little bit right.

How on earth had she not noticed that the patient was still awake?

Easy. She was running on adrenaline and showing off for the hot doctor. At least Dr. Ty Sawyer wasn't there—the surgeon who ran the Piedmont Women and Baby Pavilion. That would have been unrecoverable.

Even so, she had to wonder if she could have made a worse first impression…

Probably not.

That's what happened when she showed off like a teenaged girl, hoping her nerdiness would appeal to his nerdiness, and then maybe—if pigs began to fly—she and Captain Umbrella would live happily ever after…

Struth.

If she hadn't been fully scrubbed up she would have thunked herself on the forehead.

Sheepishly she pushed the intercom again with her elbow. "Still all right if I join you?"

"Observation only," came the crisp reply.

Fair enough.

She'd been too keen to please. Too eager to prove she was worth the investment. And she wasn't just talking about the business class flight over. She was talking about being given access to one of the world's premier research labs, an amazing park-side apartment in the center of Atlanta and six precious weeks away from her brother to give her project one final push before deciding whether or not to give up the ghost.

Fulfilling one dream to make up for the loss of another was the way she'd rolled for the past few years.

Her hands hovered above her flat belly, then dropped to her sides.

Right. Enough of all these feelings.

She dialed back her nerves and entered the operating room. Whoever this doctor was, he wasn't impressed with her. And very likely he had the ear of Ty Sawyer, her benefactor. She had one shot to prove him wrong. Otherwise her packed bags would stay that way.

She stood to the side while Dr. Chocolate Eyes spoke with his patient for a while longer, assuring her that whilst nothing came with a one hundred percent guarantee he would do his best to offer her ninety-nine-point-nine percent. Next he spoke with the anesthetist, then the pair of them together. He was calm, encouraging, and a picture of capability. It took a lot to impress Kirri but she was impressed.

Soon enough he was ready to begin.

Hypo-plastic left heart syndrome was a critical congenital heart defect, and performing the surgery to the letter was the only option. If he didn't fix it now, once the baby was born the left side of his heart would be unable to pump essential oxygen-rich blood to the rest of the body.

"Where would you like me, Doctor...?"

Kirri scanned the small group. There were three women

and three men there. All gowned up. Only one with eyes that made her heart skip a beat. She looked away from him and chose a chap with more gray hair than the others. Could he be Dr. Sawyer?

A nurse nodded at a spot directly across from Dr. Chocolate Eyes. "Dr. Sawyer likes his spare pair of hands here."

Wait. *What?* Dr. Chocolate Eyes was Dr. *Sawyer*?

Oh, this was bad. The turn-around-and-jump-right-back-on-the-plane sort of bad. Why weren't there any pictures of him on the website? Normally this type of surgeons—the so-good-they-were-famous type—had pictures of themselves all over their websites, their literature. How had she managed to pick a camera-shy guy?

She checked herself. A woman who jumped on a plane and went to the other side of the world at the first whiff of a chance to prove her brother wrong should probably research things a bit more thoroughly.

Not that she would've refused the trip even if she'd seen his photo. Plenty of too-good-to-be-true men walked through the doors of their clinic back in Oz. Usually with a gorgeous wife on his arm, seeking the opinion of the Baby Whisperer to get the beloved child she'd put on hold after opting to have her career instead.

Lucky them. Able to put it on hold rather than spend their entire life knowing it would never be an option.

Kirri squished the thoughts away. Worrying about who her brother could and couldn't wave his magic fertility wand over wasn't her remit today. Making a fresh start was.

So... Dr. Chocolate Eyes was her new boss.

Okay. Fine. Just because he made her tummy do all sorts of curious things that other deeply scrumptious men didn't, did not mean she couldn't get a grip and focus.

So she took in a deep breath, calmed herself, and watched as the magic of surgery began.

A few hours later she exhaled.

Watching Ty Sawyer at work was breathtaking. It was like having a special glimpse of one of the world's best artists at work. Skill and finesse all wrapped into one incredibly talented package. No wonder people flocked to his clinic.

With little more than a microscopic glance in her direction, he'd left with his patient and gone to the recovery room. Now he'd returned, wearing a pair of fresh scrubs. Dark green. A nice contrast against his skin. He definitely looked as if he had a splash of Latin in him. It would explain the shiny black hair and thick dark lashes…

Barely meeting her eyes, he gestured that she should follow him.

Okay. She guessed they weren't going to go through the ritual. *How do you do? Nice to meet you. Sorry about earlier.*

Well, he *had* given her an umbrella. Maybe if she gave it back the gesture would melt the frosty atmosphere keeping him two briskly timed paces ahead of her as they virtually race-walked down the corridor to a stairwell.

"How're mum and baby?" she asked his back, then jogged a bit to catch up with him.

"Not too different from when you saw them last. As you saw, the surgery went well. The prognosis looks good. Her son will no doubt have more surgeries ahead of him when he's older…but it's a life saved for now."

She let the words slide into place with the weight they deserved. Easy enough, considering everything he'd said had slipped down her spine like warm, buttery caramel. How was it that the Georgian accent wasn't the world's favorite? She was its newest number one fan. So long as it came out of a certain someone's mouth.

A rather nice mouth, now that she could see it properly because he wasn't wearing his surgical mask. It was full for a man's mouth. Sensual, even. And tipped into a demi-frown that she could just imagine parting with her tongue—

Er...*no*, she couldn't! She could imagine no such thing.

She forced her mind back to more neutral territory as they zipped down the stairwell and opened a door to another corridor. This floor was quieter than the surgical floor above, which had what she liked to think of as the quiet hum of healing. This floor was obviously for the researchers.

Her heart-rate accelerated as she jogged yet again to catch up with Ty Sawyer and an idea struck. "You wouldn't happen to have the fetal echocardiogram, would you? The one they made the diagnosis from?"

He slowed his pace enough so that Kirri didn't have to jog. "It's on the system. Any reason why?"

She shrugged. "I geek out on that kind of stuff."

She threw him a goofy look, then tossed caution to the wind. She'd already made a complete idiot out of herself in front of him, and would very likely be packed off back to Oz by the end of the day, so why not go the whole hog?

"I kind of have a collection."

"Of echocardiograms?"

"Yeah." She risked a bit of a brag. "The earliest HLHS I diagnosed was fifteen weeks."

He gave a low whistle. "Early."

She grinned. Couldn't help it. She was the first to do it as far as she knew. Before that it had been sixteen weeks.

"I know. I think I was lucky. That or I have bionic ears. Anyway, I've got prenatal ultrasounds for pretty much every day of gestation and for all sorts of conditions. I thought it'd be interesting to have a look. Or rather a listen."

"Fine. But first..."

Oh, here it comes. The ticking-off she deserved for stuffing her bloody foot in it back in surgery.

Ty stopped in front of a door, crossed his arms and went epically frowny. "In future, if you scrub in again—and that's conditional—it's important for you to recognize hierarchy. And that begins with me."

Kirri barely contained an eye-roll. Typical male surgeon. Showing the little girl how things were done in the big boys' world. Yeah, she'd messed up—but she did have a few strings to her own bow in the surgical department. Thank goodness she was going to be a lab rat for this six-week stretch. Hot or not, she couldn't deal with being patronized in surgery.

"Right!" Ty clapped his hands, as if relieved the telling off was over, and gave her a quick once-over. The type a general might give a soldier before allowing him out onto the battlefield. "Allow me to show you our lab, Dr. West."

"Crikey. Dr. West's too formal for me!" Kirri laughed, but knew there was a bit of an edge to her narrowed eyes.

Ty had known in an instant he hadn't needed to tell Kirrily West off. Something about the way her eyes had blazed when he'd made his ridiculous "hierarchy" speech told him she was the sort who'd be beating herself up about it for ages without him fanning the flames.

"Call me Kirri," she said pointedly. "Not as awful as Kirrily. I've always thought it sounds a bit like a rash, doesn't it?"

Hardly. More like the trill of a songbird, Ty thought, wishing like hell he hadn't gone all speechy. It wasn't his style. Nothing he was doing around this woman was his style.

"Right!" He clapped his hands again. Too loudly. "Let's get you to work."

Ty mentally kicked himself as he led her into the lab.

Maybe *he* was the one who could do with keeping his mouth shut.

Watching Kirri introduce herself to the team in the research lab was like watching a peach tree break through the floor and blossom right in front of his eyes. Life where he hadn't imagined it possible.

Not that Ty's team weren't amazing. They were. Their hard graft and scientific know-how were at the heart of many a so-called "medical miracle". They were just…well, *quiet*.

"G'day."

She held out her hand and beamed at one of the lab-coat-wearing researchers. Malachy. The older gent was unbelievably intelligent and incredibly shy.

She pumped his hand up and down. "Nice to meet you. I'm Kirri. It's short for Kirrily, but Kirrily sounds a bit girly, doesn't it?" She skimmed her hands along her scrubs, as if she were a tomboy rather than a stand-in for a nineteen-fifties pin-up. "Not exactly girly material, am I?"

She didn't wait for an answer. She just laughed and moved on to the next person as Malachy nodded and gave a dazed smile, clearly as awestruck as Jose before him, who'd reacted in pretty much the same way. Open-jawed. A bit overwhelmed. Not at all under the impression she was a tomboy. Nathan was busily cleaning his specs. Fogged up, most likely.

All sorts of uninvited feelings were careening round Ty's chest as Kirri worked her way round the room, her blue eyes occasionally flicking back, a bit nervously, to meet his. Admiration. Excitement. Disappointment. That last one was just for him, though.

He didn't like it that the one person in the room she was nervous of was him. Sure, she'd made a bit of a hash of things back in the OR, but it wasn't anything that he hadn't been able to fix. There'd been no need for him to go all icy and withdrawn. It definitely wasn't in his nature to be so cool, and he already knew he'd be getting an earful from the surgical nurses about not making her feel more welcome.

Apart from when she was around him, she didn't seem to have a shy bone in her body. She asked people who they were, what projects they were working on, begged permission to read all their papers so that she could be on the same page as everyone else.

If hurricanes were something you could wish for, and came in the form of a beautiful woman who could work a room like a successful ice salesman in Alaska, this was Hurricane Kirrily in action.

Little wonder he'd felt blindsided when she'd swept into his OR with all that vitality. She'd reminded him of how he'd once been. Bursting with enthusiasm. Keen to make not only a good impression but the *best* impression. Feeling the sting when he was put in his place.

She'd come here seeking what *he* had wanted when he and his co-founder had set up the Piedmont Women and Baby Pavilion: a place where imagining the impossible was encouraged.

He stuffed his hand through his short hair and gave the nape of his neck a rough scrub. He'd been wrong to be so curt. To tamp her very clear passion for medicine. It was either envy or attraction that had made him behave like an ass. Or both. Not an easy pill to swallow when there were six more weeks of it to come.

Ty glanced down the corridor toward the stairwell. He had a full roster of patients today, and as everyone was used to him sticking his nose to the grindstone and then haring off late afternoon to meet up with his number one girl, today would be no different.

Except it already was.

He'd handed his umbrella to a complete stranger because he'd felt something he thought he'd never feel again. *Connection.* There'd been something in Kirri's eyes that had touched him. He couldn't put his finger on it, but whatever it was it had felt like hope.

He looked out the window, beyond the leafy presence of Piedmont Park, and pictured his little girl swinging from the climbing frame or whooshing down the slide in her school playground. Tallulah. His six-year-old. Fearless, a powerhouse. *She* had a nickname, too. Lulu. Not that having nicknames meant anything. It was hardly a sign.

"You'll know, sweetheart. It may take a while, but you'll know. And for heaven's sake do something about it when lightning strikes. Our sort of magic rarely comes along twice."

His wife's words hit him straight in the solar plexus. It was the first time in years he'd remembered her saying them at all. He'd played them over and over when she'd first passed away—mostly because the idea that he'd find someone else to love the way he'd loved her had seemed impossible—but, as time had gone on he'd come to believe that she'd been wrong.

He wouldn't find love again. Not like that.

Gemma had been the love of his life. Cancer had taken her just short of five years ago, and the only love he experienced now was the fierce, protective love between a father and a daughter. And the love of his family, of course.

His four sisters and his parents had all but moved in with him after Gemma had died. Gradually they'd left him and Lulu to it, but they were still in and out of each other's homes so often they might as well all live together.

Loving them was enough. More than enough. Had been for the past five years, anyway. He wasn't experiencing a hurricane. Or a sea-change. Just a spring shower with an unexpected twist. Handing a rain-drenched woman an umbrella was hardly the beginning of a journey down the aisle.

"What do you think, Dr. Sawyer?"

Ty looked back into the room and realized half of the researchers in the lab—and, more to the point, Kirri—were staring at him.

"I beg your pardon. What was the question?"

Kirri gave an embarrassed laugh. "See? Didn't I tell you I keep putting my foot in it with the poor man! And now here's me throwing a spotlight on it." She turned to him and explained. "I was telling everyone that I looked like a drowned rat when I met you and you were a real-life Prince Charming."

She bit down on her lip. Hard. As if she hadn't meant to describe the scenario in quite that way.

When he didn't say anything she pressed on. "C'mon. Help me out, here. I'm really digging a hole for myself. You know…?" she prompted gently, a hint of warmth pinking up her cheeks. "With the umbrella? It was the icing on the cake."

"What cake?" Now he was properly confused.

"Getting the offer to join your brain trust for the next six weeks!" She said it as if it were the most obvious answer in the world.

Again he said nothing.

"Right! My chatterbox tendencies clearly need to be curbed." She gave her hands a swift rub. "What do you say someone shows me some desk space so I can find some room for my womb?"

Ty took that as his cue to leave.

Kirri blinked at the empty spot that had been filled by Ty.

Um... Okay...

"Does he always do that?"

"What's that, honey?" asked Gloria, a wonderfully warm African American woman with a slow drawl.

"Disappear."

She had been hoping to apologize for being such a nincompoop in surgery before he left. And for the Prince Charming comment. At this rate she'd have a rather long list.

Gloria batted her hand at the empty doorframe. "Oh, don't you worry about him, honey. He's delighted to have you here—he's just shy."

"That's one way to put it," said one of the men in a white lab coat. Malachy, was it?

"He's not shy—he was just distracted."

Yet another piped up. "He probably got a page. The OR is booked all day today."

Then the conversation took off in all sorts of directions until the entire population of the lab—about eight of them—were staring at the empty doorway in consternated silence. A silence only Gloria seemed brave enough to break.

"Mind you… I've never seen him like *that*."

"Like what?" Kirri was enjoying this more than she should. But getting the low-down on her new boss was a whole jar full of awesome sauce from where *she* was standing.

"Tongue-tied," said Malachy.

Gloria nodded in agreement.

"He isn't exactly a Chatty Kathy at the best of times," piped up another woman, Leigh, as she wheeled her chair over to a row of test tubes. "But it's true. He's normally not so…*mute*." She shrugged, then tipped her head to a microscope. "Maybe he's got a lot on his mind. It's been a busy week. And next week's even crazier, if what Stella was saying is anything to go by."

"Who's Stella?" Kirri asked.

"Surgical nurse," they all answered.

"She was probably in there with you today," one of them tacked on.

Kirri was about to quiz them about the surgeries Ty would be doing when Gloria patted the desk.

"Why don't you put your bag down here and we can take you on a proper tour of the lab. We're all real excited to hear more about your research. And, of course, show you our baby."

Kirri grinned. "You mean the 3D printer?"

Gloria's smile shot from ear to ear. "We didn't think you'd flown round the world just to look into some Petri dish."

Kirri felt an instant camaraderie with the group. Petri dishes had their place in the world of research…but 3D printers? They offered a gateway into modern medicine few things could.

She unshouldered her backpack, looked round the room and grinned. "I can't believe I'm actually here."

"Dr. Sawyer is a champion of innovative medicine," said Nathan. "So, like you said, he's a real knight in shining armor. For this kind of stuff anyway."

He abruptly turned to his lab table and started scribbling down some notes.

Gloria shook her head and laughed. "Don't worry. You'll get used to us all soon enough. C'mon, honey. Why don't we go and get you a cup of coffee or tea or something? And then you can tell me all about this baby grow bag of yours."

Kirri threw back her head and laughed. "That's a brilliant way to describe it. Much better than womb on a chip."

They walked and talked their way out of the lab to a small kitchen area, where some coffee was just being brewed.

"And this has nothing to do with artificial womb technology?" Gloria asked.

"No," Kirri said solidly. "I'm sure you know as well as I do that elements of AWT are mired in all sorts of ethical and moral dilemmas that'll take years, probably decades, to resolve. That's why sticking with the purely biochemical elements of helping premature babies survive seems to be the fastest route to making an impact."

Gloria gave her a sidelong look. "But you're not expecting any sort of major breakthrough over the next few weeks, are you, sugar?"

"Oh, no!" Kirri lied. "I'm just here to spread my wings."

And totally to have a breakthrough.

It was the only way she could garner some attention for her own rather primitive research lab and get some funding back in Oz.

"Good call," Gloria said, pulling mugs down from the cupboard and pouring them both a cup of steaming coffee. "Dr. Sawyer is real supportive of that sort of approach. His specialty is, of course, surgery. But he's a firm believer in investing in innovation."

"Any particular reason why?"

Gloria looked at her as if she was crazy. "He's Dr. Cutting Edge! He got that way by going out on his own. Taking huge risks not many doctors would take. He wants to help folk who can see a reality that other people can't. There's a line a mile long to work in this lab. You're a lucky woman being eagle-eyed by Ty."

Interesting… So Ty was a surgical maverick? Having watched him today, it was clear he was highly trained in classical surgical styles. So much so it made her itch to learn from him. See the fetal surgical world through his eyes.

Gloria handed her a mug. "So. Give me the elevator pitch for this grow bag of yours."

"Well, first of all, I'm stealing that description." Kirri grinned. "Let's see… If it was a longish elevator ride, I suppose it'd go something like this: imagine a 3D printed womblike environment, hosted by a microfluidic cell culture chip that would ultimately serve as a replacement for an incubator."

"Good..." Gloria nodded. "And how would you explain that to the layman?"

Kirri took a sip of hot coffee, thought for a moment, then said, "The baby grow bag will revolutionize survival rates in premature births and help expectant mothers' health."

Gloria gave her a satisfied nod. "I look forward to being a part of that." She lifted her coffee mug to Kirri's and toasted her. "Welcome aboard, Kirri. May your research be fruitful. And don't you pay no mind to Dr. Sawyer. His head is always off and away somewhere. Unless he's in surgery, of course. And then he's your man."

She gave Kirri a little wink, then set off back down the corridor as if she knew a secret she wasn't yet ready to tell.

Her man.

The phrase knocked around her chest along with a strangely weighted sense of longing.

She'd had a man about six years ago. One she'd thought she'd spend the rest of her life with...right up until he'd dropped her like a hot potato.

He'd wanted children. She'd waited too long to tell him she would never be able to give him children of his own. When she finally had it had been as if he'd flicked a switch on his heart and turned glacially cold.

For the first and last time in her life she'd lowered herself to begging. Said she'd do anything to keep the relationship going. Adopt. Foster. IVF or a surrogate. But he'd lashed out and told her she'd *never* be fit to be a parent. Not with her compulsive need to be on a professional par with her brother.

He'd said it as if wanting to be the best was a *bad* thing!

As if being on a par with Lucius was an impossible dream. It had been a cruel comment he had known would speak to the little girl in her who knew she'd never please her father.

She took a sip of scalding coffee and let the sensation burn away the all too familiar waves of emptiness as she headed back to the lab.

No point in worrying about it now. Her role in life was to help other women who *could* have babies. Women who could lead the life she'd always imagined having herself. And the only way she was going to do that and survive was by being at the top of her game.

CHAPTER THREE

THREE DAYS LATER and Kirri was finally opening her eyes at the right time in the morning. The scent of brewing coffee might have had something to do with that.

Coffee makers with a timer. Who knew?

Apart from utterly humiliating herself in front of Ty on day one, she was absolutely loving it here. There was a freedom in not being Lucius West's kid sister that felt positively liberating. Everywhere she went, she was just a girl in the crowd. A chick in a lab coat. No one to prove anything to—except for one deeply gorgeous, dark-eyed doctor.

She had *a lot* to prove to Dr. Ty Sawyer. The man had invested quite a chunk of money in her. In her brain, anyway. Not that he'd exactly been hovering over her in the lab, or anything. She'd barely seen him since Prince Charming-gate. Then again, it had been the weekend. Some people actually had lives.

Some people had someone to go home to.

She shook the thought away and re-centered herself. She wasn't here to flirt. She was here to work.

Speaking of which… She glanced at the bedside clock. Time to get up and get on the road.

She rolled up and out of bed. The beautiful condo the clinic had provided her with was an amazing place to call home for the next few weeks. All glass and steel—a bit like the Medical Innovations Center—the corner apartment offered stunning views of central Atlanta and beyond.

If they wanted the place to act as an advertisement for the sprawling southern city it was working. Beautiful sunrises and sunsets… The lush surroundings of Piedmont Park in the heart of Atlanta…

Not that she'd seen much of the city center yet. She'd spent the weekend making good on her promise to read up on all the lab's projects. It was going to be a fascinating place to work. They were exploring every area of fetal development and beyond, and didn't seem shy of confronting wide-ranging and complicated issues like neonatal abstinence syndrome, fathers' stress in NICUs, oxygen physiology and just about everything else under the rainbow so long as it offered preterm neonates a better chance of survival.

She took a slug of hot coffee, stared out the window toward the clinic and gave a wistful sigh.

No doubt about it. She'd been hit by the "new crush" bucket. Ty Sawyer had certainly made an impact. Literally and figuratively.

What an absolute dill she'd been.

Room for my womb?

What had she been thinking?

Very little, obviously.

Weekend aside, she'd barely seen him since he'd fled the research lab.

Her more practical side told her it was time to shake off that particularly large chip on her shoulder. So what if he hadn't sat down with her to go through her research? It had been three measly days. Not checking up on her showed faith. Belief that she could get on with it on her own. Pragmatism.

Or abject horror that he'd hired her in the first place.

Even so… If the roles had been reversed she was pretty

sure she would've invited him to a barbie, or on a guided tour of Sydney's finest offerings, or at the very least offered him a quick glass of beautiful Aussie wine to break the ice.

Maybe he doesn't want to break the ice. Did you think of that, Kirri?

The scenes of their brief encounters replayed on a loop.

There'd been a flash of something when their eyes had first met. Connection. A crackle of response when their fingers had brushed as he'd handed her the umbrella. The flare of it had blazed again when she'd seen him from the scrub room. Lightning bugs had danced round her belly and she was sure she'd sensed the same in him. But she'd thought the same of her ex. Thought the connection she'd felt zinging between them had meant they could weather any storm.

She put down the coffee and took a slug of ice-cold smoothie.

Delusion juice.

Her brother called it that when she'd appear, bleary-eyed, after another long night in the lab, wielding a green smoothie to be chased up by a double hit of espresso.

"Hitting the delusion juice early, are we?"

Lucius had had a point. He'd had lots of points, actually. Despite the turn of phrase, she'd always known he wasn't being snarky. He wanted her to focus on the job that she had. The one she was paid to do. Neonatal surgery. And she *did* focus on it. When she was doing it. The rest of the time it was all about holing up in the lab she'd crafted out of one of the old store cupboards, trying to tag team all the huge research centers that were also trying to create baby grow bags.

Or, in her brother's words, letting her life pass her by.

Up until the moment she'd boarded the plane to Atlanta her day-to-day existence had pretty much been comprised of surgery to keep her brother happy, research to keep herself happy, and sleep because… Well, that part was obvious.

Eating had happened. The odd night out with colleagues had happened. Dates rarely happened. Which was another problem. Because she didn't just want a child of her own. She wanted the whole nine yards. The doting husband. The cute little house. Nothing fancy. Just room for a barbecue and maybe an apple tree with a bench seat swing. A treehouse for the kids…

She conked her head on the breakfast bar and groaned. Her brother was right. She was on a full dose of delusion juice and showing few signs of recovery.

Creating a properly functioning artificial womb wasn't just a pipe dream. It was a constant reminder of the one thing she didn't have. A womb of her own.

She could joke, and wear tough-girl clothes, and maybe sometimes have one too many tequila shots, but the facts remained the same. Mother Nature had skipped over her when she was doling out baby-making equipment and it scraped her heart raw.

Mayer-Rokitansky-Küster-Hauser syndrome was a rare condition. She'd been born with ovaries, eggs and female hormones, but no womb. No ability to get pregnant. And there was nothing she could do about it. She'd never have a child of her own. There were, of course, womb transplants now, at a handful of hospitals around the world, but at thirty-seven years old, and chronically single, she didn't see the point.

Besides, the break-up with her ex had been so scarring she'd unwittingly begun to fulfill his prophesy. He was right. Her work life had rendered her completely unfit to be a mother.

The only counterbalance was knowing she was trying to help women who weren't in her rather fetching knee-high boots. Women who could *get* pregnant but struggled to carry the pregnancy to term. Hence the need for a baby grow bag, to nurture extremely preterm fetuses.

If she could develop it, it would be the most advanced neonatal incubator in the world. Not to mention that it would take fetal survival to the next level. There were other advantages too. Surgery, for example. Much easier on mother and child because they wouldn't be compromising the mother's life. And, of course, access would be much easier.

But, as with so many of these things, there was a complicated web of medical ethics to navigate and research was still—*ha!*—at the incubating phase. She'd be old and gray and maybe dead before it ever actually happened, so perhaps her brother was right. It was time to give up the delusion juice and start hitting the truth serum. She was a gifted surgeon, and if she really wanted to help she should give more of that gift on a daily basis rather than devoting herself to a pipe dream.

As if her brother had been reading her mind, her phone buzzed with a video call from him. It had been five days since she'd left. Maybe this time he was checking to make sure she was alive rather than detailing the terms of her contract in full capital letters. A contract she was very much breaking by being here in Atlanta.

But dreams were worth breaking a few rules for, right? So she pressed "accept", put on her cheekiest smile and grinned at her brother.

"Hey, Luci!" She always called him Luci when she wanted to make him grumpy.

"Hey, yourself, Maple Top."

Hmm… He was using the term of endearment he'd coined years back, because Kirrily meant leaf. He only ever did it very occasionally. He must want something. She braced herself for a speech.

"How's it going up there?"

Unusual… Chit-chat before laying into her. It was a tactic he'd never used before.

She played along. "Good. The facilities are amazing. Dr. Sawyer's got quite the set-up." She launched into a vivid description of the modern lab, the access she had to all the Piedmont research and how exciting it all was.

"More exciting than down here?"

Was that…? Wait a minute. Was her brother *missing* her?

"No, not at all…" she floundered. Because it was—a little bit. "It's just different. New. Nice to get a fresh perspective on things."

She could almost see the words arrowing straight to Sydney and crashing against her brother's solid stance. He still thought that the only thing she'd gain from coming to Atlanta were some frequent flyer miles.

"Right, well…" He scrubbed his hand through his hair and shook his head. "Thanks for sorting out the roster. See you in a few weeks."

Suddenly she missed her brother like she'd miss a limb. Sure, he was a pain, and they never had deep and heavies or hugged out their differences, but even if he wasn't a cuddly-bear-style big brother he always had her back. This call was proof that, no matter how cross he was with her, he still did.

"Thanks for ringing. I'll be sure and keep you up to date with everything here." Kirri swallowed back the sharp sting of tears, trying to keep her smile bright. He was a good man, her brother. She really needed to push herself hard at the clinic. Prove to him that what she'd done had been worth the risk.

"You take good care, then." He hung up the phone.

Kirri stared at her handset in disbelief. It was possibly one of the longest personal conversations they'd ever had.

Usually just about everything they talked about at length involved the clinic.

Before she had a chance to think about it too much, her phone rang again. Kirri didn't even bother looking at the number and answered playfully, "Well, hello again, stranger."

"Kirri?"

Kirri's cheeks flushed hot pink. What was Ty Sawyer doing on the end of her phone?

"Dr. Sawyer! Apologies. I was just speaking with my brother. Sorry. What can I do you for? For you?"

Stop! Talking!

Ty, unsurprisingly, sounded confused. "We're a surgeon down today. Childcare issues. I was wondering if you might be up for a day in the OR rather than in the research lab?"

Was this an olive branch? Or desperation? Didn't matter. She was going to pounce on the invitation like a hungry cat.

"Absolutely. What sort of surgeries are on the roster?"

He rattled off a few in-utero procedures she'd done before. Nothing wild, but operating on a baby still inside its mother always made life interesting.

"Are you sure you're up for it?" Ty asked.

Hmm… Make microscopic advances in her research or spend all day making magical medicine with Dr. Chocolate Eyes?

"Of course. Definitely. Can't think of anything I'd rather do."

Especially if it got her in Ty's good books again. Even his normal books would be good. Whatever those were.

Ty Sawyer was still very much an enigma to her. And he might stay that way if she didn't start behaving like someone who *didn't* go all fluttery and googly-eyed whenever she was in his presence.

"Any particular time?"

"Whenever you can get here."

"Consider it done."

Kirri flew in and out of the shower, tugged on a lime-green A-line skirt and a T-shirt bedecked with a unicorn jumping over a rainbow and was out the door in a matter of minutes.

Once scrubbed up and in a surgical gown, she felt more grounded. The OR was her "can-do" zone. A place where she felt comfortable. Confident.

But hitting the right note was critical. A day showing the team what she was really made of would set her up perfectly for the next six weeks of research. And perhaps the next six weeks of Ty Sawyer.

Ty had to admit it. He was impressed. Three surgeries down and Kirri seemed indefatigable. She was a precision surgeon. Gifted, even. She approached repairing the most delicate components of a tiny infant's body as naturally as she might approach breathing. She was also excellent with anxious parents. Both the mothers who had to go into surgery and the parents who had to watch their infant children being wheeled down the hall on a gurney. He found those moments tough. Especially as a father himself.

Amanda had been right to push him into asking her to join them in the OR today. Just as well, considering he hadn't exactly given Kirri a warm welcome. Before he'd met her, he'd planned on inviting the visiting doctor to dinner with his family over the weekend. Taking her and Lulu on a cycle tour of the sprawling Piedmont Park. Pointing out the best places for that essential morning cup of coffee.

In short, he'd planned on pushing himself out of his normal mode—recluse—in an effort to get to know the woman behind one of the most exciting medical innovations he'd seen.

And then he'd met her.

The lack of a specialized surgeon this morning had backed him into a corner. Get over himself or cancel the surgeries. He hated leaving patients hanging, so he'd relented and called Kirri, convinced she'd barely make it through one surgery, let alone three. But working with her was like working with an extra set of his own hands. Pure synchronicity.

They often had visiting specialists, and there was always some new little technique to pick up, or a different instrument to try. Sure, surgery was meant to be textbook—but someone had to write those textbooks and Kirri was definitely in that league. Beyond it really. She was the definition of "in a league of her own".

"So who's next?"

Kirri pushed through the OR doors with a fresh surgical gown billowing behind her, looking like a pop star about to dazzle thousands of fans. She was doing that, all right. Even if those fans were an OR full of nurses, anesthetists and surgical students. And, Ty had to admit, one single dad who had been figuring out the best way to tactically avoid her for the next six weeks.

Ty ran her through the case. A six-month-old little girl, Meredith, who had gastro-esophageal reflux. The poor little thing wasn't getting all her nutrients and, more importantly, was in danger of breathing food or drink into her windpipe, which would irritate her lungs or cause infections.

They'd be performing a fundoplication. If things went as smoothly as they had in previous surgeries, the noninvasive procedure should have the little one right as rain in a matter of weeks.

It had been Amanda's idea to call Kirri when Ty's senior partner Mark Latham had called in, unable to come to work. His wife was out on the West Coast, doing some corporate lawyer thing, and one of his little girls was sick. When Amanda had suggested they call Kirri, rather than reschedule all the patients, Ty had balked.

Amanda had pressed. Said it was in the interest of their patients. They all knew that was the easiest way to get him to agree to anything.

It turned out Ty had had absolutely nothing to worry about. Kirri was every bit as knowledgeable, patient, willing to learn and talented at teaching her own deft surgical techniques as her reputation had suggested. She was so relaxed as she conducted the extremely delicate neonatal surgeries that she was even able to chit-chat.

She'd already won over the surgical nurses with her compliments about the facilities, their work ethic, their exactingness and, of course, their scrubs. They had fun scrubs here at the Piedmont Women and Baby Pavilion. Every color of the rainbow and each splashy print singular to the state of Georgia.

"And what do the green scrubs represent? That's the anterior retraction of the left lateral segment of the liver set. Could I get a Babcock clamp, please?" Kirri held out her hand for the device.

The nurse who handed it to her—Stella—answered for the team. "Oh, those are for the state amphibian."

Kirri's eyes flicked up to meet Ty's, and he saw a twinkle of amusement evident, even through her surgical glasses.

"The state amphibian?" she said dryly.

"The green tree frog," Stella explained, without a drop of humor. She took more pride in her home state than most. There wasn't a ball game with the letter G involved that she wasn't cheering for.

"Love it."

Kirri prepared the second incision. A three-millimeter

cut that would disappear just a few weeks after surgery, if all went well.

"So, what are the other state emblems?" Quick eye-flick to Ty. "Suction, please. I'm just about to prepare the second five-millimeter port."

She did it swiftly and efficiently as Stella rattled through Georgia's other state emblems.

"The state bird is the Brown Thrasher. The fish is the Southern Appalachian Brook Trout." She listed a few more. The fruit—peach, obviously—the state flower, the state gem, the state insect… "And our state crop is the peanut, of course."

Kirri laughed. "The peanut?"

"Oh, yes," Stella assured her. "There's even a state monument. Isn't there, Dr. Sawyer?"

Ty threw Stella a look that he hoped communicated the following: *Would you please stop trying to draw me into this conversation? I know what you're doing.*

The nurses—Stella in particular—were on a mission to set him up with near enough every single female who walked through the clinic's doors. All those over twenty-five years old, anyway. Had been for the past year. It was as if they'd all decided that four years was long enough to mourn his wife's passing and it was time for him to pull up his socks and get on with the business of loving again.

As if it were that easy.

"Peanuts…" Kirri gave a happy little sigh. "I've definitely been through my fair share of those. Right, then! Here's the five-millimeter trocar—done. Are you ready to put in the neonatal gastroscope, Doctor?"

Ty nodded, his eyes once again connecting with Kirri's. There was something joyfully infectious about her energy. It was like that yellow brick road to Oz. Alluring, but frightening as well. The great unknown. Loving the same woman from the age of sixteen made the idea of falling for someone new little less than terrifying.

He had his routine. No need to veer from it now, when Hurricane Kirri was going to be back off to Australia in a handful of weeks.

"The next thing you'll be telling me is that there's a state-sanctioned barbecue," Kirri said, and laughed as she lowered her surgical goggles into place.

Everyone gasped. "But there *is*!"

Conversation erupted around the pair of them—Ty and Kirri—about whether dry rub was better or sauced barbecue. Beef or pork. And, of course, the more complicated question of what side orders to choose. Colorful language burst into play when someone said they were considering going vegetarian and were looking for the perfect way to grill an eggplant.

Kirri merrily worked away through the lively debate, with Ty serving as her second set of eyes and hands. And then someone mentioned Chuck's Charcoal Heaven.

Uh-oh. Ty knew where this was heading. He didn't hire the smartest nurses in the country for nothing, but sometimes… Sometimes they got the better of him.

"You go there every Tuesday, don't you, Dr. Sawyer? To Chuck's?"

Ty barely held back his *Oh, no, you don't.* Stella could sound as innocent as a child when she wanted to. Like a child asking if they were possibly *maybe* going to be passing an ice cream store when she knew damn straight that they were.

"They have some lovely barbecue at Chuck's," Stella pressed, clearly intent on making good her self-proclaimed role as his personal cupid. A role he truly wished she would relinquish. If he wanted to go on a date, he'd go on a date.

The unspoken lie gave him a sharp twist of discomfort.

"You'll know when you're ready, darlin'..."

He tipped his head toward Kirri and said. "Perhaps we should give Dr. West a bit more quiet space to conduct her surgery? I doubt the finer points of dry rub or sauce are of interest to her right now."

"Oh, no. Don't stop. It helps me relax."

One glance and it was easy to see she was smiling. Ty knew quite a few surgeons who liked music while they operated. He was a fan of country, himself, but it had been his wife's favorite as well, so for the past five years he'd operated in silence. Detailing Georgia's finest delights as if the entire surgical team were moonlighting for the tourist board was a new one for him.

Curiosity got the better of him. He had to ask. "Talking about barbecued meat *relaxes* you?"

"Not necessarily that topic, per se, but..." Her eyes flicked up to meet his. "This is going to sound ridiculous, but I like the sound of your voice. Your accent maybe. It's comforting."

Her gaze lingered on his eyes for a moment, then went straight back to the surgical screen as if she'd told him she preferred a harmonic scalpel over conventional knot-tying for the finer points of surgery.

Was it time? Time to let go of that protective shield of hurt and loss he'd wrapped himself in when Gemma died?

He heard himself ask, "Do you like barbecue?"

Nice work, Romeo.

Stella threw him an encouraging glance and tacked on a *go ahead* nod. *Get on with it*, her eyes were saying. *We've got your back.*

"I love it—but you've got some tough competition."

"Where?" Stella gasped. "You better not say Texas."

"I think you'll find barbies are a national pastime in Australia," Kirri replied.

"You should take her to Chuck's, Dr. S," Stella said, oh, so casually, her eyes fastidiously glued on the screen, where Kirri was delicately wrapping the upper part of the baby's stomach around the base of her esophagus.

Oh, boy. And here it was. The awkward moment when he did or didn't ask Kirri out.

There'd be hell to pay in the debrief room if he didn't. And a strange new set of emotions to resist if he did.

He liked her. And not just professionally. But he had a little girl to think about. One who'd been asking about other little girls' mommies and what he thought it might be like having a mommy of her own.

He looked across at Kirri. Those blue eyes of hers met his as if she sensed he was trying to work out whether or not she was worthy of barbecue.

It was a much bigger choice than she'd ever know. Brave some barbecue or stay mired in a routine he knew needed changing one day. But…was *this* the day? Was this the woman he would change it for?

Kirri knew a plea for help when she saw one. Ty needed rescuing. She could see it in his eyes. Those shiny, espresso-rich eyes of his were virtually pleading with her to help him. The poor man was clearly being pushed into a set-up. It had happened to her enough times to know one when she saw one.

No matter how scrumptious she thought he was, first and foremost he was her lifeline to those all-important medical breakthroughs she needed to make. And as such she needed to tilt her lance. Or whatever it was knight-esses in shining armor did when they were trying to do good. Turn and run away?

She cleared her throat pointedly. "Don't you worry about me. I can look after myself." She expertly tied off the final internal stitch. "All done. You can remove the camera now, Doctor."

His eyebrows lifted. "Finished?"

She tipped her head toward the screen, where one freshly sutured esophageal passage was on view. "Finished."

"That was fast." Ty began slowly to extract the camera as another member of the surgical team moved into Kirri's place to close up the small incisions.

"It was done to the letter," she said.

"I didn't say otherwise. I was merely commenting on how expedient you are."

"But not at the expense of the patient's welfare."

Ty's eyes hit hers with a flash of light. "I would expect nothing less. Not in my OR, anyway."

Kirri chewed her lip. It was the only way to bite back the snarky comment she would happily have flung at her brother if he'd said that.

Why are your hackles up? Because he doesn't want to date you? You don't want to date him. Or do you? Do you? OMG you do.

Quit having a conversation with yourself and let the man run his OR the way he wants. Get out of your surgical scrubs, get into the lab, make a medical breakthrough then go home and get on with things.

"Would you like to join me for some barbecue tonight?"

Kirri's eyes snapped back to his.

Say something, idiot!

"Um..."

Nice one.

"It's very casual. Beyond informal, in fact. And it wouldn't be just the two of us."

Everything that had been tingling around her nervous system dulled.

Ah. Of course he had a girlfriend. Maybe a wife? She hadn't seen a ring on his finger. Then again...he was a surgeon. Most of the male surgeons she knew didn't bother with rings, what with all the scrubbing up.

"My daughter and I go every Tuesday," Ty said into the yawning silence that was now consuming the operating room.

"Oh!" Kirri flinched at the high pitch of her voice, then managed to squeak, "You have a daughter?"

The knife plunged into her heart.

He had a daughter.

Ty Sawyer knew the precious love between parent and child that she would never know.

She knew it shouldn't hurt. Not anymore. It was as if the pain was built in now. A low-grade ache, reminding her of the relationship she'd lost because of a glitch in her genetics.

"Tallulah."

There was no missing the love in Ty's voice.

"Atlanta's biggest devotee to barbecue."

Ty stepped back from the operating table as the rest of the team silently moved in. Their attention was on the patient, obviously—but it was patently obvious that their ears were glued to the interchange between Ty and Kirri. So much so it felt as if they were bearing witness to a miracle. And it wasn't the miracle of modern-day medicine.

"If you're happy to leave from here, I tend to go straight from work. Six o'clock suit?"

She glanced up at the clock. It was almost three. Enough time to develop a case of the sniffles?

"Perfect."

It wasn't. She didn't want to go out with Ty and his daughter. She was always super-awkward with kids, too bright. She always ended up feeling like a freakish maiden auntie—which she'd also never be because her brother looked about as ready to have babies as her body was. Not at all. Which was weird, considering he adored them, but whatever…

Without so much as a tip about what one wore for "casual barbecue" Ty left the room.

Well, she thought as the rest of the surgical team threw each other a combination of winks and wide-eyed glances, *like it or not—it looks like I have a date.*

Ty tried to focus on the images on his computer screen and couldn't.

After the unbelievably awkward end-of-surgery "Would you like to join me for some barbecue?" incident, Kirri had fled to the research lab and Ty had holed up in his office with imaginary paperwork. Imaginary because he was finding it difficult to focus.

What on earth had he been thinking? Inviting her to eat barbecue with Lulu? A little girl who might easily think he was bringing along a candidate for stepmother. She'd never outright asked him if she'd ever have a new mommy, but he wasn't blind to the way she looked at the mothers at school events. Little girls were built of hopes and dreams. Hopes and dreams he hadn't let himself consider, let alone actualize.

He gave his scalp a short sharp scrub, willing some common sense to fall in. Maybe he could tech talk with her all night. That would put Lulu off the scent of what his body was telling him. He was attracted to Kirri. An attraction that was more than skin-deep.

A couple of hours later—strangely close to six o'clock—Stella tapped on his office door.

"Why, Dr. Sawyer, as I live and breathe. I couldn't find you anywhere. I thought you might've pulled a sickie."

He gave her a wry smile. She knew him well. He far preferred practicing medicine to sitting in his office doing paperwork. It was definitely the last place on anyone's list to look for him. Even so—a *sickie*?

"You know as well as I do that my mother would consider that awfully bad manners. I suppose your mama would too, Stella."

"That she would." Stella leant against the doorframe and smiled. She clearly wasn't through with him yet. "Well, aren't you just full of surprises? Asking our good Dr. West out to join you tonight."

Ty laughed and threw a sideways *get you* look at his cheekiest employee. Not only did she merrily cross the employee-friend line every chance she got, she was also a damn fine pediatric nurse. Being ribbed every now and again was worth each precious minute she treated his high-needs pediatric patients.

The way he saw it, for every life saved they put a bit more light back in the world. Light he needed as much as the next person. Because the day his wife had died near enough all the light had gone with her. And without his little girl… Well, that wasn't a world worth thinking about.

Stella smiled at him, fluffed her afro, then relaxed into an attitude he knew all too well: An *I told you I was right all along* face, quickly followed by a gloating smile.

He tapped his pen on his desk. "Isn't it funny how you just happened to mention barbecue and my nights out? All on a Tuesday, no less."

"Oh, it wasn't me who brought up barbecue. It was Kirri."

"Oh." He gave the back of his neck a rub. *Had* it been? "That's strange."

"Very," said Stella, a contented smile playing on her lips as she handed him a form to sign. "Some might take it as a sign."

Yeah, right. He handed the paper back and she gave him a new one. She had a stack of them and was taking her time.

"I just helped put two and two together, is all."

"If that's what you want to call it, Stella."

"It is." She smiled and made another exchange of papers. "What're you going to wear?"

He looked down at his cotton plaid shirt and khakis. "Dad gear", as his sisters relentlessly mocked. He bought it all online. Easier than actually going shopping.

"Been a while since you dusted off your glad rags, isn't it?"

"For barbecue?" He huffed out a laugh. "I'll wear what I'm wearing, Stella. No need to go black tie."

"Suit yourself."

Stella started humming. This was one of her favorite pastimes. Putting a mirror up to Ty's non-existent social life. She was always "casually" pointing out some lovely single woman she happened to know who was joining a group for tailgating at a ball game, or picnicking in the park—doing anything apart from work, to be honest. She said she wasn't pushing—just putting the invitation out there in case something better didn't come along.

Something better always did. Being with his daughter. She trumped everything. Especially his non-existent dating life.

Stella gave him a once-over and started clicking her tongue.

"What? I don't look that bad, do I?" He looked down at his clothes. Plain old khakis and a dull-colored dad shirt that probably could've done with a run-in with the iron.

Oh, Lord. He cared.

"Oh, wipe that look off your face, Ty. You look fine. I'm just surprised it took you this long to show Kirri some proper hospitality. What with you being a proper Southern gent, and all."

Stella's smile was pure innocence, but he knew what she was saying. *You were being rude because you find her pretty.*

"I was planning on doing it. I just thought if I was going

to show her Atlanta properly she might like something a bit more…" He sought the right word. *Was* there a word?

"Fancy? Classy?" Stella filled in, then instantly dismissed them. "No, sir. Kirri strikes me as a woman who'd be happy wherever, whenever. You just put Lulu in charge, pop a bib on her and have at it. She'll love it. She'll love *you*."

Oh, God. He hoped not.

He glanced across at his computer's screensaver. It was a photo of him pushing Lulu on a baby swing. She was young. Six months old. Laughing and smiling…at her mother.

It was the last time Gemma had felt well enough to join them at the playground.

He swallowed down the bile. Cancer was so cruel. So was widowhood. Five years and counting and he simply hadn't found the knack for it. Didn't know if he ever would. His daughter's sheer joy in life demanded that he live in the present, but there was a huge part of his heart still lodged on that awful day in the oncologist's office.

"Stage Four cervical cancer. Fairly advanced. It's up to you, of course, but we would advise delaying treatment until the baby is delivered, if you'd like to carry the pregnancy to term. But bear in mind doing so could affect your chances of survival."

They'd only just found out she was pregnant. Gemma had never had a chance of long-term survival. She'd chosen their daughter's life over her own.

She'd pushed through her pregnancy, and then nearly one more year—but that had been sheer force of will and probably a bit of blind luck. She'd wanted to see her baby and she had done so.

Saying goodbye after she'd fought so hard to bring life into the world—the life *they'd* created—had been the most painful thing Ty had ever experienced. He wasn't even sure he'd finished saying goodbye, if he were being truly honest. It seemed too final.

He knew some people plastered their homes and workplaces with photos of their deceased spouse. Talked about them all the time. Laughed when they recounted stories of the "good old days". He wasn't up to it. There were pictures in his daughter's room, of course, but none in his. Or elsewhere. Hanging up Gemma's photo would feel like turning her into a shrine.

He knew she wasn't coming back, but he still hadn't figured out the best way to own his deep-seeded love for her and still get on with life. So, while he pushed everything else in his life forward, his personal life circled endlessly in the same listless holding pattern.

"Are you going to take her to the bowling alley as well?" Stella handed him another paper to sign.

"If she's up for it. As you well know, Lulu and I will be going regardless."

His Tuesday nights with Lulu were sacred. Well. Not that sacred. They often had people join them for the triumvirate of barbecue, biscuits and bowling. Family. Aunts, uncles—any number of the fleets of cousins that kept her from feeling like the only child she was. Plenty of folk from the office had come along one time or another too. Never once, though, had he brought a date.

She's isn't a date. She's a colleague.

He thought of the way his body reacted when he was around Kirri. Like one magnet to another.

Stella fanned herself with the rest of the papers and gave him an approving nod.

"What? Why are you looking at me that way?" he asked.

"I'm just proud of you, is all."

"Proud? For what?"

"Putting yourself out there."

He snorted. "I'm taking an employee for some barbecue and biscuits." He gave her back the signed papers. "And that's happening mostly because *you* backed me into a corner."

Stella shook her head, perched herself on the edge of his desk and leant in. "Uh-uh. I didn't back you nowhere. You *wanted* this."

"You'll know..."

Stella wasn't done yet. "Now, Ty, forgive me for butting in where I know you don't want people sticking their noses—but somebody's got to do it and I've given myself the job. I know your heart was broke real bad all those years ago…"

His jaw tightened. Yes, it had been. Smashed into a million tiny pieces, if anyone wanted to know.

Stella put her hand on her heart. "I didn't know your wife as well as you did, obviously, but I knew her well enough to assure you that the one thing your Gemma would've hated would be to see you alone for the rest of your life."

She tutted at him before he could interrupt.

"You are always encouraging people to change. Take risks. Push harder. Dig deeper. Travel…try something new! The only person I don't see doing that in his own life is you."

She held up a hand.

"I'm not talking about work. We all know you're light years ahead of everyone else on that front. I'm talking about here." She tapped her heart. "I know you've got your daughter, and your family are amazing, but I've seen the way you look at her. At Kirri."

She stood up and put her hands out in a *Stop, I'm not done yet* position.

"She's here for six weeks. Have a trial run. That's all I'm saying. No one's asking you to fall in love or elope to the Caribbean, or anything. We just want you to have some fun."

Fun?

Wait a minute…

"We?"

Stella nodded. "All of us. We love you, whether you like it or not, and just like your family we want to see you happy. If a fling with a sexy brainiac from Down Under brings some light back into those eyes of yours I say go for it."

She left before he could say anything.

She needn't have bothered. He was completely and utterly dumbstruck. Have an affair? Just *because*? Merely thinking about holding another woman in his arms felt like betraying his wife's memory.

That familiar resolve set in. *Nope. Wasn't going to happen.* They'd have their barbecue, maybe bowl a few pins and that would be that. In fact he'd do better than that. He'd call in reinforcements. No way was this going to be a date, let alone the start of an affair.

From tomorrow morning it would be work only. End of story.

CHAPTER FOUR

KIRRI FELT LIKE she was being frog-marched to her date. Ty was barreling along with that same crisp take-no-prisoners walk he'd used on their first day after she'd gaffed in the OR. She'd thought today's series of successful surgeries had put them in better stead, but apparently not. It appeared all this so-called Southern hospitality didn't extend as far as the parking lot.

"This is us."

Ty pointed at a comfortable-looking SUV in a rather daring shade of orange. Definitely not the color she would have picked for him.

He caught her funny look and explained. "My daughter picked the color. She said it reminded her of Pippi Longstocking's hair." He gave a *what can you do?* shrug.

It was a micro insight into a man who clearly liked to keep his private life just that. Private.

His eyes lingered for a moment on the car, as if he were seeing it anew, and the hint of a smile appeared. Against her better judgement, a little part of her melted. But she had a very strict rule: *Do not find adorable things fathers say about their daughters adorable.*

The idea of falling in love with a single dad—if he even *was* single—was... *Oof!* It would be inserting herself into a permanent reminder that she would never be enough. Then add on the fact she'd never live up to the ex—because no matter how awful she'd been, she'd produced a child. And, as her own ex's extremely quick marriage to a woman she would never have imagined him marrying, and subsequent rapid-fire arrival of three children proved, love *was* conditional.

So, no, thank you very much Mr. Hot-Maybe-Single-Maybe-Divorced-Dad. You carry on being all cantankerous and edgy. Suits me to a T.

They climbed into the car. Ty maneuvered it out of the parking spot, out of the subterranean carpark and out into the golden early-evening sun.

Her eyes drifted toward his hands on the steering wheel. Still no ring. No divot, even. So definitely not married. Dating or divorced it was, then!

Ty pulled the car onto the freeway with a comment about Chuck's Charcoal Heaven being twenty-odd minutes down the road before clicking on the radio. Excellent. Small talk was out. Less chance of her putting her foot in it.

It was a kids' channel. There was a song on about a penguin going for a swim with a dolphin. She couldn't help it. She cackled.

Ty shot her a look. Either he hadn't been listening or this was his playlist.

"Sorry. Didn't mean to offend. Is this one of your favorites?"

He frowned at the radio, then that soft smile hit again. "My daughter's."

Kirri laughed, then spoke without thinking. "Your daughter seems to wield a lot of power in your household. What else is she in charge of?"

Ty's grip on the wheel had tightened along with his jaw.

The look she received this time was barbed. It delivered a message she knew all too well. The *back off, you're not her parent* look.

She'd clearly overstepped. A blunt reminder of why she avoided lusting after men who had children.

Frustratingly, she felt the sting of tears tease at the back of her throat. Nothing like being put in her place by a kid she'd never met.

The over-familiar lash of self-flagellation whipped into play. *Why* had she made that stupid comment? It wasn't Ty's fault she couldn't have children. Parents were *meant* to be protective. It wasn't her place to comment on how he and his child did things. Not her place at all.

She forced herself into a more useful line of thinking. She should be asking all the usual questions. *What's her name? How old is she? Is her mom meeting us there or are you single and free for a bit of a snog later?*

She axed that last one with a bit of a smirk, but felt her heart sink all the same. Not only did she struggle speaking to parents about their offspring, she *really* struggled making chit-chat with their children. Babies were cool. Before two they couldn't really talk. And over eighteen they were much more difficult to imagine giving birth to. Everything in between: *#itscomplicated.*

Ty moved his hand to the radio to change the channel, then obviously had a change of heart and switched it off entirely.

After a moment's exceedingly awkward silence he gave her a quick glance. "Apologies. I barely notice the music. I tend to let Lulu pick the things she cares about, and I pick the things I care about, and as such my life doesn't often look the way it should for a thirty-nine-year-old man."

She snorted. "There's a look that goes with being thirty-nine? I wish someone had told me that earlier. I've only got two years to figure out what it is!"

His lips twitched into a smile. "Perhaps not, but I suspect it wouldn't involve 'Itsy Bitsy Spider' on a loop. Or bright orange cars."

"Oh, I don't know..." Kirri felt herself warming to the subject. "I'm sure the powers that be would happily make an entire line of orange vehicles because of the fleets of children who adore Pippi Longstocking. As a sort of redhead, you can count me amongst the converted."

She was a Pippi aficionado, so could happily discuss her for hours should the need arise.

"Noted," said Ty, and nodded, that smile of his still playing on his lips.

Mercy, he was sexy when he wasn't frowning, and even then...

"You'll have to forgive me, Kirri. I shouldn't have been short with you. It's not the way I normally treat new colleagues when I take them out for barbecue."

She gasped in fake horror. "You take *all* the new kids in town out for barbecue? And here I was thinking I was special."

His eyes flicked to hers, the gold glints flaring as they connected, then he turned back to the road. *Uh-oh.* She'd possibly gone a bit OTT on the buddy-buddy thing.

He finally spoke. "Only the extra-talented ones who get caught in the rain."

A warm swirl of relief and something else a whole lot saucier twirled through her. *He thought she was talented.* She knew she was talented, but to hear it from Ty felt special. He didn't strike her as a doling out compliments kind of guy. She gave a silent cheer whilst trying her very best to keep her grin contained.

"Why don't you pick a channel?" Ty turned the radio on again.

"You go ahead. Your car. Your tunes."

"No, honestly..."

Ty's voice was laced with that dry humor she was beginning to get used to.

"If Stella hasn't told you already, she will no doubt volunteer the information that I have a tendency to get stuck in my ways."

He gave his jaw a scrub, as if considering whether or not to plump for a bit of spontaneity. He gave a solid nod. Decided.

"Why don't you liven things up? Pick something *you'd* listen to in *your* car."

Now she felt stupid. If he had a girlfriend surely she wouldn't choose kids' radio? Not if she wanted to get a ring on her finger, she wouldn't. But if she was sure of anything about Ty it was that if you wanted him you got a package deal. Any man who bought a bright orange car and listened to penguin songs was a devoted daddy.

She thought of the possibly imaginary girlfriend doing Lulu's hair. Helping her into her jim-jams at night. Reading her a chapter or two of Pippi before turning out the light with a kiss and a murmured, "Sweet dreams." Then she forced herself to stop.

Could loving someone else's child feel the same as loving one of her own?

She looked at Ty's striking profile. He was all strong-jawed, five o'clock shadowed and cheekbone-tastic. His hair was too short to give her the completely insane excuse to brush some of it away from his eyes, but it was tempting.

Who was she kidding? Everything about Ty Sawyer was tempting. She was already wondering about loving a child she'd never met, for heaven's sake!

She turned to look out the window and fuzzed her lips. Falling for him was utterly ridiculous. A pipe dream. Up until now her love life had pretty much consisted of just that. Pipe dreams and delusion juice.

Love had been conditional in her family. Entirely merit-based. *Behave impeccably. Be the captain of the team. Be the best in your class.* It was all she knew. Work and work and prove her worth and still the cuddles from her mother were nothing to look forward to. They were of the weird patting variety that made her feel as if her mother was only doing it because she'd read about it in a manual. And hugs from her father…? Non-existent.

"Go on. Pick a channel, Kirri."

Kirri snapped out of her fug and scanned along the digital options until she landed on a pop music channel.

Ty arched an eyebrow but kept his eyes on the road. "Is this what you listen to back home?"

"It's my guilty pleasure." She sang a few bars, did a couple of silly hand-moves, then sat back in the seat and hummed along until the song ended and another began.

Once again silence fell between them, but this time it felt more…*alive*. Electric, even. The kind of electricity that hummed between two people who were attracted to each other. A turbo-charged frustration.

Half of her wanted to scream, *Pull over now*, jump him and make crazy spontaneous love. The other half wanted to shout at him for being so damn quiet.

Shouldn't he be giving her helpful cues about working at Piedmont? Or, more pressingly, about his daughter? Little pointers about what she was like. Things she liked to talk about. Favorite unicorn. Stuffed toy. Whether or not he was single and why he wasn't spelling out what the arrangements were with his daughter's mom. That sort of thing.

But, no. Just the odd glance that sent her belly into lava lamp mode.

After a few more songs he put on the indicator and left the freeway. "We're just a couple of minutes away now."

"How is your daughter getting there?"

"Oh, my sisters are bringing her. Or my parents. I can't remember. One of them."

Kirri gave a double-take. "You invited your family?"

Hilarious. She'd heard of inviting wingmen along, or at least arranging to get a tactically timed phone call ten minutes in, or in her case faking a page—but inviting his whole family along? That was a new one on her. Then again, perhaps it was genius. Adult buffers right there on site if she went all mealy-mouthed on herself and couldn't talk.

"My parents and my two older sisters will be there. The two younger ones are busy."

"One boy growing up with four sisters? It's a wonder your car isn't pink."

He shot her a glance. "Don't you dare say something like that in front of them."

She gave him a *try me* face.

"Honestly. There is nothing they will not try once a seed is planted. You'll see."

A few minutes later she did.

Ty's family were absolutely wonderful. His parents and his older sisters were indeed there. No girlfriend, fiancée or "family friend". And then there was Lulu. Six years old, the spit of her father and absolutely charming. Lulu Sawyer was officially the first child between two and eighteen to bust Kirri's I-can't-talk-to-you record.

She had a thousand questions about Australia and then some.

"And it's like summer at Christmas?"

"It isn't just *like* summer—it *is* summer!"

"So..." Her little button nose crinkled adorably. "What do you eat after you open your presents?"

Her family weren't much for celebrations, so they usually went to a restaurant—"to give your mother a day off in the kitchen." Her father was simply made of largesse.

She squelched the truth and told Lulu about what other, normal people did. "We have exactly what you have. Turkey and all the trimmings. Others have barbecue. Seafood, usually."

"It sounds amazing. Papa, do you think we should go one day?" Lulu beamed up at him and batted her lashes.

Ah. *Now* she knew why their car was orange.

Ty gave a vague nod, then suddenly became intent on plucking everyone a napkin out of the silver holder.

Half an hour later Kirri was seeing sides of Ty she wouldn't have believed existed. One of America's most innovative surgeons by day, adoring father and much loved son by night. She felt like she was in a sitcom. The really good kind that you wished would never ever end.

The Sawyers were the type of bonkers family she had always dreamed about being a part of. Everyone talked over each other, laughed with each other and very clearly loved one another, despite their different personalities.

Ty was dipping in and out of his role as the strong, silent type, as well as laughing and joking along with his family. But whenever his gaze crept her way it was with all-penetrating looks she was finding harder and harder to read.

She would have thought the sparky hits of connection they'd experienced in the car would disappear once Ty's family absorbed them into the huge booth at Chuck's, but no. They just got sparkier.

"Pass the butter, please."

Zing!

"Would you mind handing the hot sauce over?"

Fizz.

Frisson-laced reminders of that very first time they'd literally crossed paths. Fireworks went off each time their eyes met. Scary, exciting and utterly captivating. He didn't even have to look at her for her tummy to go all flip-floppy with pleasure.

She glanced over and caught Lulu beaming up at him. She bumped the tip of her index finger against his nose in a gesture that clearly meant *I love you, Papa.*

And from the soft smile he unleashed when he tousled

her dark hair and gave her a little half-squeeze Kirri instinctively knew it was his way of saying *I love you, too, Lulu. With all my heart.*

It was the type of bond nothing and no one could ever break. It was the type of love she ached for.

Kirri looked away and focused on Ty's parents—Marina and Henry. They were having a spirited conversation about a local baseball team. In their early seventies, she couldn't imagine a more charming couple. Gracious, fun-loving and completely relaxed. They were, in short, the complete opposite of her own parents.

Before she could stop herself she blurted, "Thank you so much for including me on your night out. This is my first proper Southern meal since I've arrived."

Ty's mother's hands flew to her chest as she gasped. "Well, that's just terrible. Henry? Did you hear that? This poor girl's been here all weekend and not had a proper meal." She clucked and wagged her finger at her son. "Ty, you shoulda told us you had a special guest. We would've made a proper fuss over her."

"She's not spe—"

Kirri bit back a pained grin as Ty all but stuffed his actual foot into his mouth.

"Ty!" His mother swatted at him. "Manners!"

His sisters tsked and his father threw him a questioning look.

They all knew where that sentence had been going.

She's not special.

It was a sentiment that shot her straight back to the way her father had made her feel as he'd goaded Lucius on to higher and higher academic success. Sidelined. Unworthy. Hungry for approval she knew she'd never get. Little wonder, considering her father was straight out of the nineteen-fifties *Distant Father Handbook*. Sexist, not entirely politically correct, and utterly driven to make her brother a "proper man" by tearing him down bit by bit and then sitting back to watch as Lucius gathered the pieces and tried to put himself together again.

"And here's the first of it, Dr. Sawyer."

A server appeared, a big smile on his face, his arms weighted with two platters laden with unctuous looking ribs.

Saved by the barbecue!

The Sawyer family applauded their approval as the server slipped an enormous slab of ribs on the table. Everyone except for Ty. He was still beating himself up about that stupid comment.

She's not special.

Of course Kirri was special. Talented, inquisitive, fun-loving and utterly beautiful, to name just a few reasons.

Special enough to take a risk with his heart?

He grabbed a rib and let the flavor explosion drown out that particular line of thinking. He was happy as he was. Forward-thinking, groundbreaking surgeon at work—steady, reliable, chino-wearing dad the rest of the time. It was Stella's fault for planting that ridiculous seed about having an affair. He checked that thought, too. It wasn't Stella's fault. It was his for giving it air.

"Sure that's enough for you, honey? You're our guest and we want to make sure you feel real special."

Ty's sister Patsy sent him a pointed look as she reached for one of the ribs herself. She was the eldest of his two older sisters, both as warm and welcoming as the next. He'd stupidly been hoping they would do what they normally did whenever they met a single woman—talk about all of the men they could set her up with. But, no. They just kept talking about how fabulous Ty was when he wasn't sticking his foot in it. As if they were in some sort of conspiracy with Stella.

Did everyone want him to start dating? Or did everyone want him to date Kirri?

"This is amazing," Kirri said, a bit of sauce trickling down her wrist. "I don't know if I'll *ever* have enough."

At just that moment she stuck out her tongue to lick the sauce off. Her eyes met Ty's and the statement took on a whole new meaning. Hope, fear, wonder and a thousand more emotions were reflected back at him. What shone through most brightly was that neither of them was on familiar territory and that both of them were feeling the same thing: curiosity…

An energy charge shot straight down to his bootstraps. Stella was right. His sisters were right. It *was* time to take a risk, because for the first time since Gemma had died the *person* was right.

Kirri was completely different from Gemma, but he didn't need to see a grief counsellor to know that searching for the same type of woman to replace his dearly departed wife would only end in tears. How could a man replace his childhood sweetheart? He couldn't. But perhaps he could find it in his heart to love someone completely new. Someone like Kirri.

For the next six weeks, anyway.

Kirri blinked and all the questions in those blue eyes of hers were replaced with a light, bright smile.

Perhaps a fun fling was exactly what the doctor ordered. What was the worst that could happen? She'd say no, they'd get on with their jobs and then she'd go back to Australia? Fine. Then he could slip back into the status quo and go on for another five years without anyone pushing him to leave his comfort zone.

Mind you, if his sisters didn't stop discussing what a heathen he was, the possibility of an actual date might not be an option. He looked across as Kirri's grin widened and his sisters batted comments back and forth.

"Who raised you? A wolf?"

"Don't insult Mama. It's Ty who's the heathen."

"Kirri is a treasure. He's been downright rude, not introducing her to us till now."

"I bet it wasn't even his idea. Was Stella the one who knocked some sense into you?"

"I'll bet it was Winny and Reba."

He knew protesting would only add fuel to the fire. Growing up with four sisters had taught him as much.

Kirri was openly laughing now. "Winny and Reba? Who are they?" She took another piece of corn on the cob from the diminishing pile.

"They're Ty's younger sisters," Ty's father explained for him, seeing as his mouth was full of food. "They're at the local park, watching a couple of our grandkids' baseball games along with their own children. How about you and your family? Is it as big and boisterous as ours?"

Shards of something Ty couldn't put his finger on lanced through Kirri's eyes.

"Nope! It's just me and my brother. We're so busy with work I imagine we'd be pretty terrible at the whole traditional family thing."

"Oh, I doubt that," Henry said. "One glimpse into the eyes of your own child and it's instant love. That kind of love runs deep."

"I'm sure it must."

Kirri flashed another one of those quick smiles of hers that didn't quite light up her eyes, then began to rearrange the food on her plate, nodding and listening politely as his father went on to detail all the aunts and uncles who were also involved in the children's lives. And cousins. There were scores of them.

For heaven's sake... Why were they unfurling the family tree? It was obvious the woman didn't have a big family like theirs. And the more his parents went on about it, the more Ty felt as if they were rubbing salt into a raw wound.

Before he had a chance to cut in, his sister Tammy asked, "Is the family you *do* have as nuts as ours?"

"We definitely don't have traditions like this," Kirri said, her voice a bit too bright, her smile slightly frozen. She gave her head a little shake, then swiftly changed the subject. "Did *you* not have a baseball game today, Lulu?"

His daughter shook her head and beamed up at Ty. "No, ma'am. I never let anything get in the way of barbecue and bowling night."

Ty smiled and gave her a squeeze. He dreaded the day that would change. But, as he'd seen with his older sisters' children, change was inevitable. His little firecracker would discover sport, drama club or—God forbid—boys. There would come a day when she went off to college. Led a life of her own. Then he really would be on his own.

"The barbecue is definitely worth leaving the office for," Kirri said, clearly more at ease now they were off the topic of happy families. "But I've never been bowling, so be gentle on me."

His mother jumped in. "Well, thank goodness my boy's finally learnt some manners and got you out of that stuffy condo of yours."

Ty shot Kirri a quick apologetic grimace. She gave him a soft smile in return. And if ever there was a way of saying *you're forgiven* that smile was it. Pure gold dust.

His mother was on a roll. "If we'd known you were here over the weekend we would've had you over for roast chicken or pie. Fattened you up." She gave Kirri a quick once-over and clicked her tongue. "Don't they feed you right over there in Australia? So willowy!" She said it with a splash of good-humored envy rather than as a chastisement.

Kirri laughed. "They do," she said, then admitted, "But

this is probably the first full meal I've had in months." She held up her hands before everyone could pile in and chastise her. "Back home I work late most nights, so it means I'm not that great a cook."

"What about your mama? Didn't she teach you the basics?"

Kirri's eyes flicked to Ty's. Before her smile and laughter took over he saw what no one else did. His suspicions were right. She hadn't had a happy childhood. And, no. No one had taught her the basics.

"I get by. Nothing a frozen burrito and a microwave can't fix."

"Oh, well, that won't do." Marina Sawyer fixed her steely dark eyes on Ty. "Son? You're to bring this young woman over next time you release her from that clinic of yours and we will have a cooking lesson. Several, if there's time. One every weekend."

She wasn't giving Ty a choice. He shook his head and grinned. If Kirri didn't watch herself his parents would be signing adoption papers by the time her tenure was over. Which wouldn't exactly jive with the whole *why not have a fling with her?* idea—but he was still on the fence about that one, so…

"Very well, then," Marina said decisively. "I recommend we start with peach pie this Saturday. That way we can have it Sunday after church, when Kirri joins us for family lunch."

Ty didn't bother to protest. Not so much because there wasn't any point but because he loved seeing the spark of joy light up in Kirri's eyes.

CHAPTER FIVE

KIRRI'S FIRST INSTINCT had been to protest, but one look at Ty's mother and she'd known Marina wouldn't hear otherwise.

"Don't bother," Ty said to her warmly. "There's no point in resisting. I'll pick you up on Saturday morning."

The look he gave her was entirely different from anything she'd seen from him before. It said, *I've got your back*. It said, *I saw your sadness.* The insight was humbling. Intimate, almost. As if he knew her better than she knew herself.

The man was like a kaleidoscope. Perfectly wonderful one minute, cool and reserved the next, and then, in the blink of an eye, kinder than she could have ever imagined.

"Right, then. That's settled. Now, let's tackle the rest of this food, shall we?" Marina said with a bright smile.

No one dared disagree. They collectively piled in as more baskets and trays appeared at their booth. Biscuits, of course. So fluffy and buttery Kirri could have eaten a dozen. Collared greens. Beans. Coleslaw. And an endless stream of ribs.

It was clear from the familiarity of the waitstaff that Ty hadn't been lying when he said he came here every week. His daughter even had her picture on the wall, from what must have been her fifth birthday, if the candle count was anything to go by.

Kirri ate and smiled and soaked it all up. She'd done a lot in her life but she had never had a happy, talkative, family meal like this. Ty's family were exactly the type she'd dreamt of growing up in. Rambunctious, non-judgmental. *Loving.*

She crushed the thought with terse pragmatism. *You didn't grow up in a family like that. Move on.*

Marina's heritage was, as Kirri had thought of her son, Latin American. She'd passed on her pitch-black hair to all of her children, and as a born-and-bred Georgia girl sounded every bit as southern as Ty did.

Well, Ty's accent was a lot like warm caramel and it did funny things to her tummy…so perhaps a bit different.

Marina was a third-generation Costa Rican, whose grandparents had come over to study English Literature at college and had ended up being asked to stay on as teachers. It was a tradition that seemed to have trickled down the family in a not altogether linear way. Ty's mom had taught biology. One of his sisters taught history.

"Gemma did, too, of course," Ty's mother said.

"Gemma? Is she another one of your daughters?"

Marina's voice dropped in volume as she checked that Ty was still busily discussing the finer points of doing his daughter's hair properly, after a lecture from his sister Patsy. Fishtail, apparently, was best.

"Oh, honey, I thought you knew… Gemma was Ty's wife."

Kirri's tummy lurched. So he *did* have a wife.

"She passed just over five years ago now."

Her breath froze in her throat. *Ty was a widower.* The thought hadn't even occurred to her. And just like that her heart split wide open for the man.

"Cancer," Marina whispered. "She put treatment on hold to have Lulu, here, but a year after she was born it got the better of her."

She popped on a bright smile and offered Kirri a fresh set of napkins, which she took as a sign that Ty was paying attention to them again.

She picked up a rib and began to eat, because it was all she could do not to throw herself across the table, grab Ty's hands in hers and say, *I get why we're connected now. We both know loss. Heartbreaking, bone-deep, soul-destroying loss.*

It made sense. The reason they clicked and sparred. Pain knew pain. Love recognized love. Advance and retreat, then try again. It was how they survived. It was how she hoped to gain the courage to stop herself from retreating and fill that aching void in her heart one day. The void she was so desperately trying to fill with her pioneering inventions.

Could she ever have room in her life for both?

As if reading her mind, Ty gave her a silent nod. He *saw* her. He saw her more than anyone ever had. And instead of making her feel vulnerable, it filled her heart with peace.

A while later Ty's father knocked his hand on the checkered-clothed table to get their attention. "C'mon, everybody. Finish up. We'll have dessert at the ice cream parlor down at the alley."

Kirri smiled at him. Henry was a tall silver-haired gentleman who had the same lean, athletic physique as his son. He ran a corner shop in exactly the same neighborhood he'd grown up in—Hank's. Which had been his father's name before it had been his own. Kirri really liked him. She liked all of them, if she was being honest.

She let her gaze slide once again toward Ty, who was smiling at his daughter as she devoured the remains of her potato salad.

Ty was a widower.

The news had properly rattled her.

She knew people's deepest traumas shaped them. However much she'd love to avoid the fact that she was trying to develop an artificial womb because she didn't have one, she couldn't. She tried on a daily basis, but her research was torture sometimes. The plain truth was that even if she did make that all-important breakthrough it wasn't as if she'd suddenly have a husband and two-point-four children.

Had Ty's loss affected his relationship with medicine? Was it the reason he was so forward-thinking in the OR? Her work was meant to help women experience the joy she knew she could never have. Was he trying to do the same?

He obviously hadn't remarried. So he'd clearly loved Gemma deeply. That or, like her, he'd buried himself in his work. Work that made him face his worst fears every single day. Saving women and the babies they were carrying from possible death. He must regularly operate on women who had discovered they had cancer when they were pregnant. Did it give him joy to know he'd saved lives or was it a daily reminder of the woman he'd never hold in his arms again?

She forced her thoughts away from unraveling a widower's emotional trauma and focused on Ty's family as their banter continued to fly about the table as freely as air. They emptied the final dishes, joshed, joked and teased about enormous appetites and expanding waistlines, but all of it was loving.

There was none of the bite that usually accompanied her own family's dinner table banter. If you could call the conversation the few times they'd all eaten together and actually spoken "banter". No doubt about it. Her family was definitely...*trickier.*

She and Lucius were her parents' only children. Their father was a highly sought-after neurosurgeon and had always been extremely demanding of them in those rare hours he'd spent at home. Demanding of Lucius, anyway.

Her old pops—something she wouldn't ever dream of calling her father to his face—definitely belonged to another era. In his book men had jobs and women had children. Their mother had been a nurse when she'd met their father, and had given it all up to raise their family, but parenting hadn't brought her the joy it brought so many women. As such, she disappeared into books for days at a time, diving into other people's worlds for a bit of escape from her own.

After he'd found out Kirri couldn't have children, her father had pretty much left her to her own devices. Something she was pretty sure Lucius would've loved for himself. There wasn't a single thing he'd done during their childhood that had gone unnoticed. As such, he still rode himself pretty hard. She wondered what he'd have been like if he'd grown up with easygoing parents like Ty's. Happy?

Hmm… She wasn't sure Lucius was the sort who'd ever be happy. Not with his perfectionist drive.

As they prepared to leave the table Marina cleared her throat and nudged her son. "Isn't there anything you'd like to say to our special guest, honey? Something about not inviting her over earlier?"

Ty's exasperated smile for his mother was hilarious. The one he threw *her* made butterflies take flight.

"I apologize for not inviting you over earlier. I humbly beg your pardon."

Swoon!

"It's fine." She waved off his apology and his mother at long last seemed satisfied. "I was jet-lagged and I had a lot of studying to do. I can't believe how many research projects they're doing at Piedmont. It's really impressive. Besides…" She couldn't seem to get her mouth to stop talking. "He gave me his umbrella."

A round of confused looks turned her way.

"It was raining when we first met. He hit me and—"

"He *hit* you?"

"No! No, no—not like that. We were just— We ran into each other, and it was raining, and he gave me his umbrella."

It had been one of the most spontaneously kind things anyone had ever done for her.

His sisters nodded approvingly as they inched out of the booth with Lulu, to go to the ladies' room and wash all the barbecue sauce off their hands.

Both of Ty's parents turned to their son and his father smiled. "He's a good 'un, our boy. Definitely the brainbox of the family. You must be, too, if they flew you all the way over from Australia. Very special indeed."

She saw Ty feign interest in an invisible stain on his shirt to cover up this new variety of embarrassment. Being spoken about as if they were at a parents' meeting or about to go to prom.

It was kind of adorable. A privilege, really, to see this version of him. She felt as if, with his family's help, she'd unearthed an entirely different human being. Perhaps this was why Stella had urged him into having barbecue with her. A chance to show her the man behind the surgical mask.

"You'll have to tell us all about what it is you're researching when we get to the bowling alley," Henry's dad went on.

She smiled and nodded. She'd become good at that. Explaining her desire to help expectant women while leaving out the part about how she hoped it would fill the emotional void in her own soul.

She had a little speech. A brief but impassioned number she'd curated to assure people that she wasn't playing God, that she was simply helping the preemies who struggled to have a proper chance of survival. She often gave it, then ran off to the ladies' room to have a quick weep, a swift face-wash, before returning with a spark in her eye and a smile on her face that didn't let anyone know her heart had just broken all over again.

She wondered if there would be a day when it would ever stop breaking.

Lulu skipped out of the restroom with her aunties in tow and waved when she saw Kirri. Poor little thing. Losing her mother before she'd even had a chance to get to know her.

Kirri's throat grew thick with emotion, then suddenly she realized Ty's parents were still waiting for an answer. "I'm over the moon to be given this opportunity to carry on with my research. And I'd be more than happy to tell you all about it."

Against her better judgement Kirri looked at Ty. Their eyes caught and meshed. That warm, fuzzy feeling that had been working its way through her bloodstream all night flared again.

Ty reached out and with the pad of his thumb wiped something off the corner of her mouth.

"Sauce," he said, his tongue dipping out to swipe a little left on his own full mouth.

Oh, mercy. This was going to be a long night.

Ty sensed Stella's arrival in the staff kitchen before she spoke. He took his time pouring his coffee, giving it a stir, wiping up the ring on the counter. He knew what was lying in wait. An interrogation.

"So!" She pounced the minute he turned round. "How was it?"

"Barbecue at Chuck's is always good. You know that." He took a sip of his coffee, feigning pure naiveté.

"Dr. Sawyer, you know damn straight I'm not talking about Chuck's."

He laughed. Stella wasn't normally this forthright, so it

must have taken all her reserves of patience to wait until this morning to get a full report.

"It was lovely."

"Good. Lovely's good. And did your guest enjoy Chuck's?" Stella blocked the doorway so Ty couldn't get out.

"Very much."

"And did the two of you enjoy your time together?"

"Lulu and I had a ball."

Lulu had actually really taken to Kirri. She'd been a bit shy at first, as she often was with new folk, but once she'd heard Kirri's accent she had suddenly overflowed with questions. She'd even thrown her arms round her waist at the end of the bowling for a spontaneous farewell hug. He might have been wrong, but when Kirri had swept Lulu's hair away from her eyes and wished her goodnight he'd thought her eyes had gone a bit glassy.

He'd never admit it, but his had, too. Up until that moment he'd never imagined his daughter loving another woman as a mother figure. But the way they'd looked at each other... A whole new level of conflict had churned up in him in that instant.

He was an adult. He could look after his own feelings. But not everyone was up to loving a man whose number one priority was his little girl, and he was damned if anyone was going to break his little girl's heart. Least of all a woman whose life was on the other side of the world.

"Dr. Tyson Sawyer," Stella chided. "You know darn straight I wasn't talking about you and Lulu. Though do give that precious little girl of yours a kiss from me. It's been too long." She fixed him with a stern mama bear look. "I was talking about Kirri."

Ty tried to inch his way past her.

"Uh-uh. Not until I hear whether or not you finally offered that poor girl some proper hospitality. And you know what I'm saying by *hospitality.*" She dropped a none-too-subtle wink.

Ty frowned. Talking about his sex-life with Stella was about as weird as it was discussing it with his mother. Something he never wanted to do.

He set the record straight sharpish. "We had a nice time. At least she said so when she got in her cab after bowling."

Stella looked appalled. "You didn't drive her back?"

"Well, no. Lulu needed to get to bed, and Patsy and Tammy were going the other way—"

Stella cut him off. "Wait a minute. Are you telling me you invited your *sisters* along? Oh, Ty…"

Before he could protest that he had hardly set out to woo Kirri, Stella continued.

"Tell me you didn't bring your parents along, too?"

She crossed her arms, clucking her dismay when he said yes.

"So let me get this straight. You bring one of the most beautiful women to ever cross our threshold to barbecue, with practically your whole family, and then you stuff her in a cab at the end of the night without so much as a 'welcome to Georgia' kiss? Son, your wooing skills are *rusty.*" She tsked her disappointment.

The last time he'd asked someone out formally had been when he'd asked Gemma to prom, and they'd already been dating for a year, so… "I guess you *could* say I'm out of practice."

A softness hit Stella's features. "I know, Ty. But you like this girl." She leant in. "In all honesty, I'm proud of you. I didn't think you'd actually go through with it."

"Why?"

She shrugged, checked behind him to make sure there was no one around. "I just thought you might be too stuck in your ways since you lost Gemma."

"I don't think these types of things come with timelines."

Courtesy of his work, he'd met more than enough men in his shoes, and every single one of them had dealt with their loss differently. Married the nanny. Never remarried. Married someone they met on an internet dating site. Devoted themselves to their children. The list went on.

"No, they don't." Stella stepped to the side so he could pass. "But mark my words. When you get a second chance at finding something wonderful you better reach out and take it."

After checking there weren't any emergency medical helicopters due, Kirri pushed through the door to the roof and tilted her head up to the sun.

She'd hit a snag in her research and needed a bit of a breather to clear her mind. It was the type of snag that served as a blunt reminder that the clock was ticking. Six weeks had sounded like ages when she'd jumped on the plane a few days ago. A glut of time.

No hovering big brother, wondering when she was going to get back into surgery. No surgical patients to pull at her heartstrings. Just six long, glorious weeks to deep-dive into the world of her baby grow bag.

Today the time limit loomed with terrifying proximity.

Her phone buzzed in her pocket. She answered it without looking, wincing when she heard her brother's not so dulcet tones.

"When are you coming back?"

"Nice to hear from you, too, brother dear," Kirri snapped.

Why couldn't he be more like Ty was with his sisters? Supportive. Loving.

"When are you coming back?"

"I told you. End of June."

"You'll be too late."

Her heart skipped a beat. "For what?"

"We're putting the 3D ultrasound into the operating theater."

Her shoulders dropped from her ears. *Oh.* So he had bought it after all. It was about as close to *I miss you, please come home* as she'd get from her big brother.

She'd trialed the device before she'd left and done a proper sales pitch for Lucius. He'd done the usual. Leaned against the counter in her lab—he wasn't much of a sitter—stared at her, arms crossed, a perfect poker face giving absolutely nothing away. Normally she was used to it. That time it had infuriated her.

A 3D ultrasound would give them a fast, simple and remarkably detailed way to comprehensively evaluate a patient's uterus. What on earth was there to think about? It wasn't as if the clinic was short on cash.

He'd closed their meeting with a request for her to clear out her lab within the week and "get back to some proper work."

That afternoon she'd received Ty's email about the research exchange. One trip to the embassy, two days of mad phone calls later, she'd been packed and ready to go.

She reminded herself of this before she reached out and grabbed the carrot Lucius was dangling in front of her now.

"I've still got five more weeks here. Five and half, really."

Lucius exploded. "What exactly are you trying to prove, Kirri? That just because some other clinic on the other side of the world is blowing money around like confetti you're going to win the Nobel? You're not. What you're doing is too big for you. You need a team. A university's backing. Along with a hospital, a biochemical lab and a proper human study—which will take decades to organize. Maybe longer. You'll have to fight ethics board after ethics board. Politicians. Religious leaders. What is the point of wasting all of this time when you could be helping women here and now? In *Sydney*."

Tears stung the back of her throat like razors. He definitely knew how to stick the knife in. So much for *I miss you. Please come home. I've bought a new expensive toy for you to play with.*

She wanted to scream at him. Tell him he was wrong. Ask him to offer her the type of support they'd both craved from their father—unconditional. But no words came out.

"Right. Here's the way it's going to go," said Lucius. "You get yourself together. Get on a plane. And come back home."

"And what if I don't? I made a commitment to these people."

"You made a commitment to *me*! And you've broken it." He huffed out a sigh, then tried a more conciliatory tone. "Let's put it this way, Kirri. Your job here is to be a surgeon. And because I don't want you embarrassing Harborside I'll let you see out this ridiculous exercise of yours."

"*Let* me? Instead of what?" she snapped.

"Firing you for insubordination."

Kirri's heart leapt to her throat. Lucius was right. She'd taken advantage of the fact that they were family. If anyone else on their staff had done this they would've been served their walking papers on ice the second they'd stepped on the plane.

Lucius continued. "Top tip? Spend your time there wisely."

"I *am*."

"I'm not talking about the research lab—I'm talking about the operating theater. They're a notch above the rest over there. You could probably learn a few things if you ever pulled your head away from that microscope of yours."

She was sure there was a compliment in there somewhere, but she was hard pressed to find it. Mind you, he hadn't fired her.

She heard him mutter something to someone else. "Gotta go," he clipped. And then the line went dead.

The hot, angry, tears she'd refused to let fall during the phone call streaked down her cheeks. Being here was meant to be liberating. Instead she felt stuck between the exact same rock and hard place she'd been stuck in back in Sydney.

She wasn't a fool. She knew she was climbing just about the steepest research mountain of impossibility there was. She also knew that her research filled those empty hours between the end of a long surgical day and dawn. She didn't want to get lost in boozed-up nights or empty love affairs. She wanted meaningful content in her life, and right now that was her research.

If she had any sort of confidence in her mothering skills she'd adopt a child of her own. More than one. But the truth was—thanks to a certain ex-boyfriend—she *did* doubt her ability to offer the pure, wholesale love a parent should offer a child.

She swept the tears away to make room for more. He had been right. Her parents had set a horrible example and beyond neonatal surgery she had just one solitary interest. Making preemies' lives more viable. What did she know of sugar and spice and everything nice? Let alone snips and snails and puppy dog tails?

Right, then. If that was what she wanted to do she'd best get on with it.

She pulled a tissue out of her pocket, tidied up her make-up the best she could without a mirror, then headed for the stairwell door.

Just as she was about to open it the door whooshed open and Ty filled the doorway. She wobbled on her chunky heels and, just as he had that very first time, he reached out to steady her. Only this time their gazes locked and held.

She knew in an instant that he saw through her watery smile. Straight through to the pain and anguish that served as her fuel. Anguish she ached to share with someone who could give her some perspective. But *this* someone…? She didn't think so.

Ty was exactly the wrong audience for what she knew in her heart. There was no way she was going to have a breakthrough while she was here.

"Sorry," she eventually managed, wriggling back from his comforting touch. "I was just getting some fresh air to see if I could work through a problem." She huffed out a little laugh. "Usually I go and watch someone else do a surgery, but there wasn't anything on the board so I thought some actual fresh air might be a novel idea."

"Great minds." Ty tapped the side of his forehead. "I often come up here when I need to figuratively see the light." He smiled and looked out to the clear blue Georgia sky.

Kirri did a mental sign of the cross, grateful he was pretending not to notice that she was upset.

He closed the door behind him.

"Sorry, I—I was just going to get back to the lab."

He pulled a fresh handkerchief out of his pocket and handed it to her. "You might want to tidy up your mascara a bit before you go."

Ah. How embarrassing.

"I'm not much good as a mirror," Ty said. "But I am pretty good at listening."

Kirri frowned. She wasn't sure if the one man who made her blood boil for all the right reasons was the best person to pour her heart out to. Then again, he was the one who'd invited her here to do her groundbreaking research, and if she wasn't able to do it then she might as well let him know he should save his money for someone else.

The idea of giving it up hit her with another wave of tears to fight. She sniffled and gave him a weak smile, suddenly hugely relieved to have someone who was there to simply listen. "You sure?"

"Absolutely. There should've been an operation on the board. Mine. I just had to cancel it. So…"

He looked out to the skyline and rubbed his hand through his hair. From the shadows crossing through his eyes she could tell why it had been canceled. Something had gone wrong with the patient and it wouldn't be safe.

She reached out and gave his arm a squeeze. "Tough one?"

He nodded. "Very. We lost the baby."

She nodded her head at a bench someone had put at the far end of the roof. "Want to talk about it?"

He laughed. "Don't go trying to turn the tables on me. I'm the one who's supposed to be listening to *you*. Besides, how many men do you know who like to talk it out?"

She gave a casual shrug. She didn't know any. "The smart ones?"

He laughed and began walking toward the bench. She was going to take that as an *I'll try.*

"It was an intrapericardial teratoma."

Kirri inhaled sharply. "Those are rare."

No surprise things had gone the way they had. A tumor on a foetus's heart was often a death sentence. *Too* often.

"Very." Ty nodded, his hand rubbing the back of his neck again. "And, as you probably know, the best way to get that particular type of tumor out is during the fetal period."

It was the only way, really. If the rapidly growing tumor wasn't treated, it was lethal.

"And there was nothing that could be done?"

He raked his hand through his short hair. "Of course there was. But…" He blew some air through his lips, clearly trying to steady his emotions. "If I'm being clinical, we got the referral too late. We tried to drain away some of the fluid yesterday, to prepare for the surgery, but then the mother developed pre-eclampsia, the baby's tumor wanted to keep on growing, and—" He stopped. There was no need to spell it out.

She knew what that meant. Choosing one life to save another. Kirri's heart ached for him. It was one of those situations utterly beyond anyone's control, but when you knew you could have done something if only you'd had more time… Torture was what it was. Torture because if the planets had aligned correctly you might have been able to save a life.

"I'm so sorry. It sounds like you've just endured a not so perfect storm."

"It's almost cruel to come outside and see the sun is still shining." He looked away and cleared his throat. "Anyway, the mother's safe. In Intensive Care, but alive."

The way he said it came with unspoken words: *I feel like I failed her.*

Words escaped her as she tried to hand him back his handkerchief. He wasn't crying, but she hoped he would see it for what it was—a gesture of kindness. Empathy, even. She knew more than most that nothing made a situation like this better. It was just a fact. Life could be cruel sometimes, and doctors confronted those cruelties on a daily basis. Sometimes you could just get on with it. Other times…? Not so much.

He looked at the mascara-smudged handkerchief and laughed. "No, thanks. That's for you." He patted his pocket. "I've got back-ups. Tricks of the trade." He shook his head and sat down heavily. "It's just so tough to convince someone they're lucky when the baby they've been carrying for twenty-four weeks has just died."

"I don't suppose it would help if I say I'm sure you did the best you could."

He gave her a soft, sad smile. "I think you know the answer to that one."

She did. It didn't matter how much logic you applied to certain cases. Some hit you harder than others. And this had clearly been a sledgehammer.

They sat in silence for a few moments, listening to the hum of traffic drifting up from the streets below.

Abruptly Ty hooked his ankle up onto his knee and turned toward her. "This wasn't meant to be about me. We're up here because of you."

She laughed outright at that. "You weren't meant to find me here at all! I was hiding."

"What? From me?" Ty made a scary face that quickly melted into genuine concern. "We're a team here at Piedmont. I know I didn't make the best of impressions when we first met, and we still haven't had a chance to have a proper sit-down and talk through your work here—"

Kirri cut him off. "Don't. Seriously. We caught each other off guard, that was all."

Their eyes meshed and held. Warmth flooded her belly as butterflies took flight. *Oh, boy.* He'd definitely caught her off guard. In more ways than one.

Her brother's words came back to her loud and clear. *"Make good use of your time there."* She was pretty sure he hadn't meant ogling the boss.

She ran her hand through her hair and twisted it into a quick knot, as if the gesture would contain the riot of emotions she was experiencing. She stared at her hands, then finally admitted, "I feel embarrassed for being up here now. What you've gone through today puts my situation into perspective."

His brow crinkled. "What situation are you in?"

She debated telling him about her brother's phone call, but then decided to follow her heart. "I had a bit of a hitch today with an element of the 3D printing."

She waited for him to throw up his hands, as her brother would have, but no. Nothing. He just crinkled his gorgeous forehead a little bit and nodded, waiting for more.

"Okay. So… As you know, I'm using organ-on-a-chip technology—"

"The baby grow bag? Yes. Gloria told me you like her nickname for it."

"I do." She grinned. "Very much. So, it's kind of hybrid between a grow bag and an actual gel-based organ, but anyway… Your 3D printer is the thing that will help me most at this phase."

"In what way?"

"Well, using a 3D printed organ is a step up from the original grow bag concept."

"Was it literally a bag?"

"Pretty much. Much more technical, obviously, but to all intents and purposes it looked like a large, clear zip-bag. Research teams trialing them are using premature lambs. All above board, and absolutely no harm to the lambs, but I'd prefer not to venture into animal testing."

He nodded. "That was one of the reasons I was excited by your research. We heard about the team in Japan doing some incredible work, but we don't really have the resources here to do that kind of research."

"What you do is amazing," Kirri said with feeling.

She pulled her knee up onto the bench and propped her chin on it so she and Ty were face to face. Talking about this kind of thing charged her like nothing else.

"Organ-on-a-chip technology could change the face of medical research. Pure scientific advancement for the betterment of everyone. It's groundbreaking stuff. But it's also in its infancy."

"Ha!" Ty gave her knee a poke. "I see what you did there. In its *infancy*."

They laughed at the silly wordplay, each of them visibly relaxing into nerdy science talk. "Anyway..." Kirri forced herself to be completely honest. "I'm struggling with the hydrodrel."

"The fluid that's meant to act as an artificial placenta?"

"Exactly."

They talked through details for a while. Ty was surprisingly knowledgeable on the subject, and also completely unfazed by what had thrown Kirri into a tailspin.

"Listen..." He gave her shoulder a squeeze. "This all takes time. I hope you're not pressuring yourself to have some sort of earth-shattering breakthrough in the next six weeks?"

She swallowed down a big lump in her throat that said, *That's exactly what I'm doing.*

Ty's hand stayed on her shoulder. "You're here to exchange information with us. Not work yourself to death with worry. We know research takes years. Decades, even."

"Longer sometimes," Kirri said, knowing that decades was exactly the sort of timeline she was facing.

Their gazes caught again. Fire flashed through her as the gold flecks in his dark eyes flared. The rest of the world seemed to fade away as Ty reached out and ran a finger along her cheek.

"We're here to support you. If you take one small step forward, we'll be thrilled. If you don't..." He gave a small shrug. "These things happen."

Kirri couldn't help herself.

She leant in and kissed him.

It was meant to be a short, thank-you-so-much-you're-amazing kiss, but the second her lips touched his it became something else entirely. A soft, magical connection.

Both of them pulled back before it could become anything more, but already she knew they had the answer to one unspoken question. They were attracted to each other. Big-time.

She briskly stood up, gave her face a quick swipe with the handkerchief, then clapped her hands together. “Well, on that note, I think I’d better get back to work!”

Ty nodded. Didn’t move from the bench.

His eyes remained on the space she’d just been in.

Kirri didn’t wait for him to say anything. She fled to the lab, vowing she would take that “one small step forward” in the next five weeks if it was the last thing she did.

It was her only choice. Nothing else would keep that kiss from replaying in her mind.

CHAPTER SIX

"WOW. THE BOARD looks chock-a-block today."

Kirri's voice swept through Ty's nervous system like warm honey. It had been a mere twenty-four hours since that rooftop kiss and since then he'd been struggling to think of her in an entirely professional manner.

Not that he'd been all that brilliant in the lead-up to it, but finally touching her, tasting her… It had been like uncorking a bottle of champagne. There was no chance of closing it again.

Like right now, for example. His eyes were glued to hers as if his life depended on it. It was her eyes or her legs, and neither one was giving him any respite from the flares of temptation surging through him every time their paths crossed. But, hell's teeth. Not one of his employees had ever worn a skirt that showed so little thigh to such excellent effect.

Or maybe he simply hadn't noticed before. Not the way he noticed Kirri. Her lips, her hair, her legs, her waist. He'd catch just a glimpse and heat would arrow straight below his belt buckle.

Kirri, quite simply, lit him up in a way no one had since Gemma, and if this awkward little exchange was anything to go by he needed to make a decision about what to do about it. Ignore it? He'd never been in this scenario before. Or—perhaps more courageously—maybe agree that

Stella was right? His family, too, if the non-stop reminders to bring Kirri along on Saturday for her cooking lesson were anything to go by.

"Dr. Sawyer?" Kirri was looking between him and the tablet he was carrying. "Everything all right?"

"Yes, absolutely. Just—"

Just lost in those sapphire blue eyes of yours again.

Something far too intimate to admit when she was standing crisply before him in a lab coat, all but saluting him.

She'd taken to calling him Dr. Sawyer ever since she'd kissed him. As if that would change the fact he now knew she tasted as sweetly delicate as the light floral perfume she wore. She'd been all sorts of polite since then, in fact, but there was nothing either of them could do about the fact that they'd shared something special.

When she'd kissed him it had been the opposite of a quick peck. They'd exchanged heat and intention in that kiss. As if the universe had orchestrated the whole thing. Ever since then he'd wanted to pull her to him. Explore, taste, touch. But the part of him that had never said goodbye to his wife was keeping him in this holding pattern he didn't know how to escape.

"Well..." Kirri gave him a curious look, then turned to go. "See you later."

He didn't want her to go. She brought a fresh energy to the surgical unit that charged him as much as it did the rest of the staff.

"Do something about it when lightning strikes."

"It's twin-to-twin transfusion syndrome. But with triplets."

Kirri turned back around, eyebrows raised. "Oh?"

Fewer than two dozen hospitals in the US did this particular surgery. Far fewer in Australia. Only a handful of surgeons would have had the privilege to perform laser surgery on triplets.

"Boys. Stage four. Apparently they've tried some more natural routes. Horizontal rest, nutritional supplements and external laser therapy. But nothing's worked."

Her eyes flicked up to the ceiling as she did a quick calculation of her own, then dropped down to meet his. "Amniotic reductions?"

He nodded. "The patient's regular obstetrician has tried it all. But the condition's worsened and the triplets are nearly at twenty-five weeks now."

He tapped on his tablet and showed her the latest scan. She stepped in close enough that he could smell that perfume of hers again. Something sweet and fresh. Jasmine and orange blossom? Grapefruit? His fingers flexed then clenched as he resisted the urge to dip down and inhale from that sweet spot at the base of her neck.

"I see..." Her voice had dropped an octave and her eyes had slipped to half-mast, but they remained linked to his. "Any chance you'll lose one of the babies?"

"Not on *my* watch."

Her tongue swept along her lower lip, unleashing a firestorm of response exactly where he didn't need any blood flow. Not at this precise minute anyway.

Talking another surgeon through a patient's history had never felt like flirting before, but this—teasing out the details of the surgery bit by bit, as if describing the way he was going to make love to her later—was ratcheting up the stakes in an entirely different game.

"The mother's being prepped for surgery now."

He continued to stare into her eyes, willing some sort of invitation to come out of his mouth as naturally as the way she'd leant forward and kissed him.

That was the crazy thing about it. It had been both a surprise and yet completely expected. As if it were the only thing they *could* have done. They'd shared something personal. Felt each other's pain. Soothed the other's sorrow with a soft, perfect kiss. It had been as organic as if they'd known one another for years.

"This sort of magic rarely happens twice."

"Would you like to scrub in?"

She tilted her head to the side and gave her lip a bit of a chew. "I was going to grab some lunch from one of the food trucks outside, then head back to the lab..." She flicked her thumb in the direction of the elevators. "Stella says Friday is always a red-letter day for tacos."

He noticed the light shadows under her eyes. Something told him she been sleeping as much as he had. Minimally. A sense of protectiveness flared in him. Here she was on the other side of the world, where she didn't know a soul, pouring herself into her work as if her life depended on it.

If life had taught him anything, it was that every second of every day was precious, and that some of those precious seconds should be spent outside the office.

His family had made that more than clear after Gemma had died. All he'd wanted to do was work. Give all the other mothers a shot at the motherhood his own wife had missed out on. Slowly, but surely his family had pulled his life into balance. It had started with barbecue and bowling. Perhaps that was what Kirri needed. Someone to look out for her. Remind her that non-stop work never gave a person the balance they needed to see the big picture.

"I'll take you out to eat after." He glanced at his watch. "Grandma Poppy's does a mean chicken and waffle plate."

Kirri gave him a funny look. "That sounds like an odd combination."

"It's a don't-knock-it-till-you-try-it combination. C'mon. Scrub in. We're doing it under local anesthetic. It'll take fifteen...thirty minutes, tops."

He was dangling a carrot and she knew it.

That flash of excitement he'd been hoping for lit up her eyes.

"Go on then. Who needs lunch when there are lives to be saved?"

True to his word, in less than an hour Kirri and Ty were outside of the Piedmont Women and Baby Pavilion, in front of a colorfully decorated food truck, waiting for their lunches.

Kirri was still charged with the adrenaline that came from a successful surgery, even though she'd only been an observer. It had been absolutely fascinating—and so quick! Ty's hands were the type that you'd expect from a gifted surgeon. So *capable*.

Capable of doing a whole lot more than surgery, too, if that single touch of his on the roof was anything to go by.

"Are there any plans to do TTTS laparoscopic surgeries at Harborside?" Ty asked.

He took a sip of his lemonade, then leant against the chunky stone columns that fronted the grand entrance to Piedmont Park.

Kirri took a drink of her icy watermelon juice. "This is amazing."

It was a dodge and she knew it. They would have been able to offer precisely the same surgery if she had stayed at home and followed her brother's course of action: surgery only. She'd been offered the chance to train with one of the specialists at a renowned women's hospital in Melbourne, but she'd been so exhausted from her late nights in the lab that she hadn't made the time.

She covered her unease about the decision with a forced nonchalant shrug. "There are a couple of hospitals in Sydney who do it, so we refer patients on. Sometimes their surgeons come to us, but ideally we'd love for all these innovative surgical procedures to be entirely in-house. It's much easier for the patient."

It was a speech she'd given herself again and again that always ended with the same question: Which patients do you want to help? The ones who need you right now? Or the ones you can help in fifty years' time? The need to pick an answer and dedicate herself to it was tearing her in two.

"That's exactly what we feel here at Piedmont."

The passion in Ty's voice spoke volumes. This was his life's work. His calling. Putting A-list surgeons in place to give his patients—both mother and child—the very best chance of survival. He didn't care if he was the surgeon, though obviously he loved it. His main goal was healthy, happy, unharmed mothers and children.

It was a similar remit at the Harborside Fertility and Neonatal Clinic, but in truth the bulk of its renown came from her brother's "Baby Whisperer" status, and as such most of their clients were there for fertility services before moving on to other hospitals once they'd become pregnant. Unless, of course, there were complications. Complications like those she'd tasked herself with sorting out.

Somewhere, buried under a pile of insecurities, she knew she had her own plaudits, but ever since she'd heard about this line of research back in med school she'd decided the only way to bring true validation to herself as an "incomplete woman" was to move artificial uterus research on to the next level.

"Dr. Sawyer!" Grandma Poppy called them over from the shady spot she'd parked the truck in. "C'mon over here, darlin'. I've got your food ready."

Kirri was relieved for the opportunity to change the conversation to food.

"There are some covered picnic tables over there." Ty nodded to a few tables dotted along the edge of a pretty little pond. "Shall we?"

Kirri took her white to-go box from Grandma Poppy. The tangy scent of tomato and spice wafted up to her.

"You'll want to pick up some napkins, too, honey." Grandma Poppy nodded at Ty, who was collecting a few ketchup packets, then leant down and whispered conspiratorially, "Unless you have another way of getting that sauce off your lips."

Kirri flushed deep red.

"Oh, honey. I've seen the way he looks at you." She gave Kirri a naughty wink. "You make sure you eat those wings of yours real messy."

Kirri could only nod, then run away. She silently followed Ty, who mercifully hadn't heard the exchange.

Of *course* she'd thought about kissing him again. It was one of the reasons she'd burnt the midnight oil in the lab last night. If she'd gone to bed without exhaustion to plummet her into a dreamless sleep she knew fantasy would have been only a few easy blinks of the eye away. And that way danger lay.

She gave Ty a sidelong glance. She wondered if "The Rooftop Incident" was seared at the forefront of his mind as well. Kissing him virtually out of the blue! What had she been *thinking*?

Of his lips, obviously. Or, if she was being kinder to herself, of comforting him. Not that it was her normal modus operandi, but she'd been moved by how deeply he had been affected by his patient's loss, and doubly touched by the generosity of his attitude toward her research. Inviting her to his surgery today and then taking her out for lunch were both thoughtful and generous too. Signs of a man who, against the odds, liked to stop and smell the roses.

After she'd had a few bites of her delicious lunch—a basket loaded with spicy chicken wings, mini-waffles and coleslaw—she asked, "Had you done the TTTS before? With triplets?"

"It was a first for me." Ty picked up his enormous fried chicken salad sandwich and eyed it for the best line of attack. "Kind of fun to do it in front of someone who was so appreciative."

"It was amazing. I really should've taken up an offer I had to learn the technique, but..." She held up her hands. "Time. There never seems to be enough of it."

"I hear you." Ty took a thoughtful bite of his sandwich, then asked, "I've been meaning to ask how you manage to maintain a full surgical load in Sydney as well as do your research."

Her mouth wasn't full, but she swallowed anyway. This was precisely the bone of contention she had with her brother.

She took a risk and told him the truth. "I don't, really."

His brow furrowed. "What do you mean?"

"I do surgery during the day and at night and weekends I do my research." She laughed. "If you knew what my 'lab' looked like you'd howl with laughter."

"Try me."

Ty looked like he meant it, so Kirri told him something she would never tell anyone at home because—well, because reputation was everything to the Wests.

"It's an old storage cupboard."

Ty blinked his surprise but said nothing.

Kirri barreled on. "It's not Lucius's fault. He's so busy with the clinic that research in my area isn't really his thing. As you know, he's the king of all things fertility."

"Yes. Amanda, our top delivery nurse, is really looking forward to doing her exchange there."

"She should be. Did you know they've got a way to select embryos with AI now? It's totally amazing. A game-changer in the IVF world."

Ty nodded, took a bite of his pickle, then said, "It sounds as though your research isn't important to Harborside."

Her heart squeezed tight. It really wasn't. But not for the reasons Ty might think. "Yeah, well… I suppose something's got to take priority."

"Why can't they have equal weight? It's your clinic, too, isn't it?"

"Ha! No! Lucius is the driving force with the clinic. I'm just along for the ride."

Ty looked genuinely shocked. "Is that how you see yourself? As a freeloader?"

"My brother definitely does."

She clamped her hand over her mouth. That wasn't news for public consumption. Especially seeing as Lucius was having one of Ty's staff for an exchange in a few months' time.

Ty shook his head. "I can't believe that. Not with your surgical background."

She backtracked. "He's a true champion of my surgical time. But when it comes to my research all Lucius sees is his kid sister bouncing around in cloud cuckoo land."

"I doubt that."

Kirri snorted. "I wouldn't be so sure." She chewed on her lip for a minute, then said, "He's pulled the plug on it."

Ty stilled for a moment, then asked, "Any particular reason why?"

"He says my goals are unrealistic."

"What *are* your goals?"

To do the impossible. To fill the void that comes from never being able to have a child of my own.

"I want to do surgery half the time and research half the time. But the clinic can't afford that, so I do research on my own time and surgery full-time."

"No breaks?"

"No life to break for," she admitted.

Ty nodded, non-judgmental as ever. He was a very good listener. A part of her wondered if she'd be here if she had actually tried talking to Lucius rather than jumping on the first available plane. The other part knew that the Wests didn't talk. They pushed themselves to excel.

"You know," Ty began, "the reason I go to barbecue and bowling every Tuesday is because my sisters made me."

"No way!" It was difficult to imagine making Ty Sawyer do anything he didn't want to.

"Hand on heart. My sisters can be every bit as overpowering as your brother."

Kirri shook her head in disbelief. "I can't imagine trying to do the same to Lucius. How did they manage it?"

"First of all, my sisters outnumber me," Ty reminded her. "I have to choose my battles tactically."

She let the words settle in her heart. Maybe that was where she'd gone wrong with Lucius. They were both stubborn, and terrible at communicating, so their battles started as flare-ups over tiny things and inevitably ended in stony silences that gnawed on her conscience.

She gave a micro-shrug. "We have our moments, but honestly I'm happy at Harborside."

She wasn't really. Hadn't been for a while. Working for Lucius meant she'd always be the Baby Whisperer's kid sister and now she'd hit a crossroads. It was time to make a decision. Leave Harborside for good to pursue her research, knowing she might fail, or accept what Lucius had said. That she'd make more difference in the here and now in the OR.

It was a huge decision. One she didn't even begin to know how to make.

Kirri gave her head a shake, then said, "Go on—you were saying about your sisters?"

"They saw what I couldn't." His eyes darkened and a muscle in his jaw twitched.

"Which was…?"

"I'd lost perspective on that all-important work-life balance." He cleared his throat, then smiled at her. "Which is why you and I are sitting in the park, in the middle of a work day, having deep fried chicken and syrup-soaked waffles."

Ty took a huge bite of his overflowing sandwich and when he put it down Kirri got the giggles. There was a blob of mayonnaise on his nose and some of Grandma Poppy's Magic Mystery Sauce trickling down his arm.

Kirri hooted with laughter as she handed him the pile of napkins. "We're both going to need a cardiologist after this."

Ty laughed along with her. "Or a nap."

Kirri tipped her head toward the end of the park, where her condo was. "A ten-minute waddle away there's a king-sized bed, lying in wait."

Their eyes caught and synced in a humming electric bond. Her mouth went dry as she realized what she'd done. Invited him to her bed. He must think she was desperate for him. Well, her body definitely was, but that wasn't the point.

A hysteria-edged laugh burbled up and out of her throat along with, "I'm totally kidding!" She swallowed when his eyes stayed glued to hers. "Obviously..." The word came out as a question.

"You do look a bit tired."

Her heart careened around her ribcage. Was he accepting her invitation to bed? She narrowed her eyes. He looked serious. Concerned, actually.

Ah. Not a come-on. Just an observation. She hid the disappointment she hadn't expected to feel.

"It's your fault I want to work all the time." She pointed behind her toward the skyscraper where their offices were. "There are far too many temptations up there."

Ty arched an eyebrow.

Stop using sexy talk when you're describing work, you dill!

Ty's tone was serious. "Don't push yourself too hard. I know the exchange has a time limit, but remember now that you know the team sharing information will be much easier."

Kirri knew her laugh sounded false. "But sharing the 3D printer won't!" She waved off her comment before he could reply. "Honestly. There's nothing for you to worry about. I've just been enjoying playing with your fancy equipment, is all."

"Kirri..." Ty's expression turned completely serious. "I didn't invite you over here to work yourself to death. Yes, the research is important. Everything we do at the clinic is. Life and death sometimes. But there's a balance. Your personal wellbeing is every bit as important as the things you work on."

"Sure." She took a big bite of waffle to stop herself from saying what she really wanted to—which was that there couldn't be balance in her life. *Ever.*

She had always burnt the candle at both ends. Cracked it in half and burnt it at four ends when she could. It was how she'd been programmed. There was no red light at the end of her work day. Green was the only color that mattered if she wanted to make changes. Be someone who'd made a difference. So she was *go, go, go* all the way.

What did it matter if she was a burnt-out husk at the end of the day? It wasn't like she had a child to go home to like Ty did. Her job was to make sure other expectant parents had a baby to go home to. A child to raise. If she could do that, then she would find some balance.

Ty was looking intently at her, those dark eyes of his impossible to read. Was he trying to figure out if she was worth the investment? A workaholic? Or just plain crazy? It was impossible to tell, so she did what she usually did in these situations—carried on talking until she found herself an out.

"In fact, if it's all right, I'd love to be able to work on the weekend. Is the lab open or do I need special keys?"

His expression shifted, as if he'd made a decision. "I'm afraid you aren't going to be free this weekend."

"I'm not?"

"No, ma'am." Ty shook his head and put down the remains of his sandwich. "My mother would never let me hear the end of it if I didn't bring you to your cooking lesson. She's already bought more peaches than you can shake a stick at."

Kirri pinned on a smile. There went her plan to put some space between her and Ty. Then again, if she'd really wanted to do that she wouldn't have scrubbed in on his surgery or be sat here munching on Mama Poppy's finest with him.

"Your mother has got her work cut out for her."

"You're a can't-boil-an-egg type of cook?"

"Can't-boil-water type of cook."

She dragged a fry through a puddle of ketchup, then caught Ty looking a bit more pleased with himself than she might have imagined for someone whose social calendar looked set to be eaten alive by Kirri's inability to cook.

"Are you staying for the lesson?"

His smile broadened. "Wolves couldn't keep me away."

CHAPTER SEVEN

TY GLANCED ACROSS at Lulu. She was merrily singing away along with a song about an elephant and trying to teach Kirri the lyrics. Quite unsuccessfully, if the number of corrections were anything to go by.

Lulu was twisted round in her seat so she could face Kirri, who had insisted on sitting in the back of the car when they'd collected her this morning. "No changes on my account," she'd quipped as she'd jumped into the back.

She looked a bit tense and, if he wasn't mistaken, still quite tired. He would put money on the fact she'd stayed late at the lab, despite his popping his head in about six o'clock last night and securing a promise from her that she'd be leaving soon.

An increasingly familiar flare of protectiveness shot through him. Something was driving Kirri's research beyond the obvious. Apart from her brother, she hadn't mentioned much about her personal life. The few times he'd tried to get her to open up she'd deftly changed the topic. Today he had his secret weapons. His mother and sisters. They could draw blood from a stone.

Not that he was equating Kirri to anything even closely resembling a stone. Far from it. But it pained him to think there was something dark driving her to work the way she did. The type of work they did had to come from a place of joy or it could easily destroy a soul.

"Here we are." Ty pulled his car into the drive of his parents' house, smiling when he saw Kirri's eyes widen. His gut told him bringing her here was a good idea.

"This is beautiful," she whispered, opening the car door and slipping to the ground, her eyes still glued to his parents' colonial-style home.

Lulu, as ever, was already running up onto the porch and through the front door.

"It looks great now," Ty said, unable to keep the pride out of his voice. "But it was definitely a challenge to grow up here."

"What do you mean?" Kirri threw him a look as she waited for him to lock the car and head up the drive to the wide covered porch circling the house.

"When they bought it, it was about as close to a wreck as you can imagine."

"Seriously? And you all moved in straight away?"

He laughed at the memory. "We couldn't wait."

"Why?"

"Before this we lived above Dad's shop in a two-bedroom apartment."

Kirri's hands flew to her chest. "All *seven* of you?"

"Yes, ma'am. My older sisters were in bunk beds, I was in a trundle bed, and Winny and Reba shared a crib. My parents soon decided giving everyone a bit more personal space was a good idea." He smiled up at the house. "They have never shied away from a challenge."

Kirri looked from the house to him, then back at the house. "I'm going to take a wild guess and suggest that you inherited some of that gusto."

Ty smiled. It was the type of compliment people usually reserved for his sisters. "What makes you say that?"

She laughed. "Uh…elite medical practice? First-class

facilities? Triumphant surgeries few other doctors would even think about, let alone try? Not just *anyone* could have done all that. It's impressive. Much like this house."

Before he could say he wouldn't have tried to have any of those things if his life plan hadn't been ripped out from under him, Ty's mother appeared on the porch, along with her two middle-aged bloodhounds Pootle and Piggy. His nieces had named them when they were little, and no one had bothered to override their decision.

"C'mon in, you two." She beckoned them to join her. "There's dozens of peaches waiting to be pitted. Crusts to make. Pies to fill. I told the church I'd be bringing half a dozen over for the youth group, so we'd best get cracking."

Kirri shot Ty a triumphant grin. "Like I said—I don't think the apple fell too far from the tree."

Warmth filled his chest as he watched her jog up to the porch, accept his mother's inevitable bear hug, then be ushered into the house along with the dogs. He'd never really thought of himself being like his family before, but he supposed they were all cut from a similar cloth.

His parents embodied everything he hoped he could offer his own daughter. Constancy. Loyalty. Unwavering love. Up until now he'd never thought that his goals could also involve meeting and possibly loving someone new. The hole in his heart made when Gemma had died had become so enormous he simply couldn't imagine the darkness ever becoming light. But perhaps the light had never gone…perhaps it had just been surrounded by darkness and impossible to see.

He went into the kitchen, where his mother was popping a flowery apron on Kirri and setting her up at the kitchen table with an enormous bag of flour and some butter, alongside some sort of kitchen gadget that was going to whiz it all together.

She was like this with everyone, his mother. "Giving my waifs and strays a bit of love," was how she put it. He'd often wondered how she had room in her heart for them all, but looking at Kirri now, and feeling the heat in his own heart, he began to realize that hearts didn't necessarily push things aside to make room for new love. They grew. Expanded to embrace all the love and joy they could.

His mother looked across at him from the counter and said, "I don't know what you're standing there for, son. Come on and join us."

With a smile on his face, he did just that.

Two hours later Kirri had never felt more relaxed or at home than she did here and now in Marina's kitchen. Ty's mother was gracious, patient, kind, and utterly engaged in everything whirling about her.

Dogs. Cats. Grandchildren racing in in their baseball uniforms, asking for one of the huge discs of chocolate chip cookies in a huge old jar. Her husband wandering through, stealing a peach whilst wondering aloud where all the fishing things had got to. Saying he wanted to take Lulu down to the lake, see if they could catch anything.

There were daughters on the phone. Daughters in the house. Daughters picking up and dropping off yet more grandchildren. Ty asking if they minded as he wandered off to do something out in the shed. He was granted permission on condition that he came back once all the peaches had been sliced.

That had been about an hour earlier, and in that time Marina and Kirri had reduced the pile of peaches from enormous to just a few left.

Marina looked out the window and gave a loving cluck. "That boy of mine… He'd live in that shed if there weren't some women in his life to drag him out of it again. His father's just the same."

Kirri nodded. All this was so different from her own family.

As if cued by her lack of response, Marina asked, "How about your own family? They must be missing you, with you being so far away and all. I don't think I could bear it if any of mine upped stakes and moved out of Atlanta, let alone out of the country."

Kirri's laugh sounded far more forlorn than she'd intended.

"You all right, honey? I haven't made you homesick by bringing it up."

"No," Kirri said solidly. "Not in the slightest. If anything…"

"Yes?" Marina handed her a peach. "If anything…?"

"If anything it's made me wistful. Being here with you like this."

"Wistful? What on earth…? Honey, you must be seeing things. This place is a madhouse."

"It's a lot better than silence."

Marina stopped what she was doing and looked Kirri square in the eye. "I can't imagine you growing up in a silent house. You're so full of life yourself."

"Oh…trust me. It was quiet."

Intimidating was what it had been. Family dinners had usually ended up being interrogations for Lucius. Had he passed this exam? Had he got that extra credit? Had he signed up for this club or that club? Activities that would put him in good stead with the best universities.

The answer had always been yes, but none of it had seemed to matter. No matter what, Lucius hadn't been able to satisfy their father. Neither of them had. It was easier, they'd both learned, to study some more or hide away in their rooms with a book. Escape, as their mother did, into someone else's life.

That was what Kirri wanted to do right now. Escape into this life—but for real. Knowing she couldn't twisted her heart so tight she closed her eyes against the pain.

"Are you all right, honey?"

Kirri forced herself to open her eyes, smile and slice up the peach she was holding. "I'm fine."

"I'm sorry if I dredged up some bad memories. But surely you've got some loved ones back home who are missing your beautiful face?"

Again the ache of losing something she'd never had filled Kirri's chest. Her mother had never once told her she was beautiful.

"My family doesn't really work like that. I always hoped that one day I might—" She stopped herself. Dreaming the impossible was almost as crazy as trying to invent the impossible.

"Go on, honey. Finish what you were saying. Everyone's allowed a few hopes and dreams."

Marina's words felt like a warm embrace. "I'd hoped to have a family of my own one day. Like yours. Big and boisterous and a bit crazy."

Marina got up and pulled her into a hug. "You're welcome to be a part of our big family while you're here, sweetheart. There's always room at our table for one more." She held up a finger and wagged it at her before returning to the peaches. "And once you go, don't you dare forget us."

"Not a chance," Kirri said, selecting another peach and getting to work with a gusto she hadn't felt in ages.

The screen door swung open and in walked Ty, carrying a small wooden birdhouse by the tips of his fingers. It was a gorgeous little thing, painted eggshell-blue.

Kirri breathed a soft *ooh*. "Is this what you do in your spare time?"

"Lulu said she wanted one. I know it's a bit late in the nesting season, but there's never any harm in trying, is there? Even if we're a bit late in the game?"

When his eyes hit hers an explosion of connection punched her in the chest. He had been talking about birds, right? She looked away when she noticed Marina's eyes flicking between the pair of them.

"Ty, honey? Why are you holding that birdbox as if it were made of poison?"

"Wet paint," he explained.

Marina pointed toward the door. "Kirri, run and get some newspapers from the back porch, would you, honey?"

Kirri did as she was asked. As she left the room she heard Marina lower her voice and a swift exchange of conversation. A sneaking suspicion told her it was about her.

When she came back in, Marina smiled up at her and said, "It's decided."

"What is?"

"You and Ty are going out to the bowling alley tonight, after supper."

"Oh?"

"Yes. Lulu and her grandfather are going fishing, and of course if she catches anything she's going to have to learn how to clean it and all that. When they get back, the girls want me to bring Lulu over to play with their kids. Tammy's got a pool—her husband does very well in the plumbing trade—and Lulu does *love* to swim. I've got my quilting group to go to, and Ty's father wants to stock-take down at the store, so that just leaves the two of you with nothing to do but twiddle your thumbs. Ty and I did some blue sky thinking just now and we thought it'd be a good idea for Ty to get you brushed up on your bowling before we all meet next Tuesday for barbecue."

Kirri threw a questioning look at Ty. If he showed even the slightest sign of not wanting to go she'd back out faster than he could say *boo*. But his dark eyes twinkled as he glanced at Marina then shrugged at Kirri. His happy, contented face said one thing: *resistance is futile.*

"I think my mother is making a very long-winded attempt at ensuring I ask you out on the date I said I was going to take you on."

What? Date? That had been his plan all along?

"Oh, Ty, you weren't meant to put it like that," Marina scolded, then turned apologetically to Kirri. "I was trying to make it look more casual, but you looked so sad just now, and whenever I mentioned Ty you brightened up. The pair of you both work so hard, and you haven't had any quality adult time in just about forever, so I thought—"

"Mother!" Ty held up his hands for her to stop, his eyes all crinkled with laugh lines. "I was going to ask her!"

Really? Kirri felt as though she was sixteen all over again. A bit shy, very full of hope, and ridiculously happy.

"Well, you were being a slowpoke, Ty." Marina leant toward Kirri and stage-whispered, "Slow and steady wins the race, but sometimes I question that logic." She turned back to her son. "I'm just looking after Kirri's best interest, is all. And yours. Now, if you *don't* want to go out I'm happy to leave the two of you here with some supper, so you can watch a movie or something. Perhaps Kirri could show you a documentary on Australia?"

"Mama!" Ty was out-and-out laughing now. "We're going out!" He turned to Kirri, his eyes flickering with fun. "That is if you're happy to join me?"

Oh, she was. More than anything she was. But she seemed utterly tongue-tied and unable to say as much.

Then came the moment their eyes connected. And Ty had his *yes*.

Kirri and Ty handed in their shoes and took the bowling shoes from the teenage clerk.

"Date night?" The lad winked at Ty, then said to Kirri, "Be careful. This guy's a demon on the lanes."

What the—? Was everyone in Atlanta intent on setting the two of them up? Not that Kirri was exactly resisting, but…*the bowling alley clerk*?

Ty rolled his eyes at the boy, then pointed toward their lane. "My mother must've called him."

Kirri whipped around and shot the boy a look. He was already busy chatting up some pretty teenage girls.

She looked back at Ty. "Seriously?"

"No!" Ty laughed. "But I wouldn't put it past her."

He gestured to a chair at the top of lane number twenty-three. She sat down and began to put on the colorful bowling shoes.

"You sure you're up for a night out?" he asked.

"Of course—why?" Insecurity flickered in her eyes.

"It's just been a busy day, is all. Don't want to tire you out."

"You're not. Honestly, the day has been completely energizing."

"Well, hats off to you for surviving the Sawyer Clan. It can get a bit OTT for some."

"Don't apologize. They're a whole lot better than *my* insane family," she said with feeling.

She picked up a bowling ball and threw him a quick smile, but he could see the same flash of hurt that had flared when she spoke of her brother.

If there was one thing his family had never made him feel it was pain. Quite the opposite, in fact. His family were the ones he and Gemma had gone to when they'd been to the obstetrician and then the oncologist for that soul-destroying appointment. His parents and sisters were the ones who'd picked him up off the ground when his wife had been buried. They were the foundation of his existence, and it hurt him to see that Kirri didn't have the same.

He made a feeble stab at offering her a bright side. "I'm sure growing up with your brother wasn't nearly as bad as growing up with four sisters."

"Oh…it wasn't so much my brother that was the problem."

For the first time that night she refused to meet his eye. *Ah. Complicated parents.*

She didn't offer any more details. Instead she bounced on the balls of her feet, as if testing her bowling shoes for buoyancy.

"Anyway… As you've no doubt gleaned, Lucius comes with his own set of 'interesting.'" She barked out a mirthless laugh. "He probably would've paid cold hard cash—and a lot of it—to have parents as proud of him as yours are of you."

Now, *that* was strange… "I thought Lucius was Australia's number one—?"

"Baby Whisperer," they finished together.

Kirri scrunched up her nose and finally met his gaze. What he saw in those clear blue eyes of hers was a world of complication. Love, sadness, pain.

"He is. But, honestly, I think he'd rather be called anything *but* the Baby Whisperer." She scuffed at the floor with the toe of her shoe. "I hate it, too, to be honest. No one can 'whisper' babies into existence."

She looked like she was going to say something else, then changed her mind and waved it off.

"Anyway. He's amazing at what he does."

She gave her lower lip a grating with her teeth, making her appear utterly vulnerable. It was all Ty could do not to pull her into his arms and tell her it would be all right.

It was what his family had told him again and again after Gemma had gone. *It'll be all right.* But they were just words, and they hadn't changed what had happened.

But day by day, month by month, year by year…they had eventually proved to be mostly true.

The sun still rose each morning. His daughter was a blossoming testament to his wife's gentle spirit and his own family's fiery drive to pursue happiness above all. And, of course, there was his work. Work which had unexpectedly led him to Kirri.

As embarrassing as it was to have had his mother ask Kirri out for him, the nudge hadn't been ill-judged.

Sometimes he wondered if he used his grief as a cloak for being plain, old-fashioned chicken. He'd never really had to ask anyone out before. Face rejection. Figure out how to shield his daughter to ensure she was the last one who could be hurt by his inevitable false starts on the dating front. So he'd simply closed the door on all of it.

Until now.

Maybe it was still a cowardly attempt at dating—choosing a woman he knew was going to leave. But…how had Stella put it? A trial run? Maybe she was after something short-term, too. A hot, feverish romance the pair of them could lock up safe as a good memory when their lives returned to normal.

Who wanted normal when you could have sublime?

He pulled on his bowling shoes, keeping a casual eye on Kirri as she eyed up the bowling ball rack. She was a beautiful woman. Even in the awful fluorescent lighting of the bowling alley it was impossible to ignore the effect being near her had on him.

If he was being entirely honest, Kirri was awakening all sorts of feelings in him that he didn't know what to do with. Have a fling and consider himself officially cured of the grief that had shrouded his life in the wake of his wife's death? Or lose control and fall in love only to have to say goodbye.

There was always the other option. Do nothing and

stay stuck in the same holding pattern he'd been in for the last five years.

He dismissed the thought. It seemed everyone in his world had long since recognized it was time for a change apart from him. His parents were pushing him toward it, and his sisters. Hell, even Stella at work. And he felt himself become more...*alive*...when he was with Kirri. Something clicked into place there and then. Kirri was definitely the one he should be taking the risk on. Whatever happened it would be worth the fallout.

He watched as she put down the first bowling ball she'd selected, then picked up a sparkly red one instead and gave it a grim nod. As if she planned to use it to blast away the unhappy memories he'd unwittingly brought up. He glanced across to the bar and wondered if he should offer to buy her a beer and sit down and talk instead.

She suddenly jabbed her finger into the air between them. "And don't think just because he's my big brother I'm blowing smoke up his ass or anything. He's a right royal pain and working for him is no walk in the park."

He couldn't help it. He clicked his heels together and saluted. "Yes, ma'am."

He was rewarded with a snort and a giggle that perfectly broke any remaining tension between them.

Ty's chest warmed with a long-forgotten sensation. *Pleasure*. Pleasure at bringing a spark of joy to someone. And not just to any someone. A someone whose arrival had metaphorically crashed into his very set routine and given it a good shake.

Vulnerable and strong. Funny and fierce. What other layers were there to this woman?

Unpeeling them could be one of the most enjoyable things he'd ever done. And there was nothing like a brisk bowling match to literally get the ball rolling.

He gave his hands a quick clap and a rub. "Right! Want to throw a few practice bowls?"

She swept her hand over her bowling ball, then licked her lips. "You sure you're up for playing a maverick like me?"

His eyes stayed glued to her lips as they curved into a teasing smile just ripe for a cheeky kiss.

Instead of breaking the tension that hummed between them, Kirri's sassy approach to bowling only served to heighten them. She threw a few practice runs. All of them pitched straight into the gutter. Ty tried to offer her advice, but each time she leant in to her chosen bowling position he kept going cross-eyed, trying to keep one eye on her technique and the other on the way the fabric of her clothing swept along her curves.

She still had that chic biker girl aesthetic going on. Everything fit her as though it were tailor-made. Her light leather jacket had been casually discarded on a plastic seat by the rack of bowling balls. Figure-hugging jeans with a tactical rip or two swept along her long legs. Her dark auburn hair was free tonight, flowing across her shoulders and down her back to where her waist-skimming T-shirt cinched in then swept out toward her hips.

It was jeans and a T-shirt, really, but on Kirri they oozed attitude and panache. She even made the bowling shoes look cool.

No one's asking you to fall in love or elope...just have fun.

Could he do that after all these years? Just have fun?

He'd married his high school sweetheart. Loved her until the day she'd died. Just as they'd promised one another at the altar during their white wedding. Longer, even. To this day he'd never known another woman's touch.

But he felt vital and alive in a way he'd never experienced before. It was as if a part of him had physically died along with his wife and an entirely brand new part of him had come to life when Kirri arrived.

It was an entirely different sensation from the way he'd felt with Gemma. Loving her had been as natural as breathing. They'd been through all the important firsts together. Had known each other inside out. This—whatever it was he was feeling now—was more raw. An unrefined, unfettered, uncheckable attraction that felt too dangerous to give freedom to and too serendipitous to let the chance for happiness pass him by.

And just like that a core-deep need to sweep his hands along Kirri's waist, hips, curvy ass and anywhere else she'd let him touch her took hold of him. *He wanted her.*

He strode to her spot beside the bowling ball stand, turned her around and cupped his hands on either side of her face. One look told him she was feeling the exact same thing. An instant need not to be in the bowling alley anymore.

And when their lips touched…?

Fire.

CHAPTER EIGHT

KIRRI WAS HUMMING INSIDE. So much so she didn't think she could bear the tension anymore. So she tried one of her least marketable skills: casual chit-chat.

"This is a nice neighborhood."

Ty glanced at Kirri and nodded. He hadn't said a word the entire twenty-minute drive from the bowling alley. Normally she'd be kind of freaked out by this sort of behavior. A crazy mad snog in the middle of bowling alley and then…mute driving. But in Ty's case it was kind of sexy. Like sitting next to a lion before he decided to pounce. No. A panther. Any sort of sexy beast, really. Because whatever it was, it was making her feel more dangerously desirable than she ever had. Taut with pent-up lust.

She pressed her forehead to the window, enjoying the cool of the glass. It *was* actually a nice neighborhood. Not too different from his parents'. Leafy. Beautiful manicured gardens. Wide inviting porches wreathed with flower baskets offsetting beautiful pastel-colored homes. It screamed *family neighborhood.*

"I know it sounds ridiculous, but I didn't expect to see so many traditional houses so close to the city center. For some reason I thought all the old ones would be out in the countryside. There are loads out in the countryside in Oz. I mean, obviously there are some old buildings in Sydney, but… Anyway. I like your neighborhood."

Kirri cringed. She sounded like an idiot. The handful of intimate liaisons she'd had over the years had been little more than fleeting flares of lust. After the Crusher of Dreams had dumped her cold she'd made sure her emotions remained in check. But this…? This felt different.

What she'd felt when they kissed hadn't been the temporary flicker of a lighter's flame. No, this heat burnt brighter. Stronger. To the point where it was driving her to talk pure nonsense, when all she really wanted to do was flip up the SUV's irritatingly wide armrests and start tearing Ty's clothes off. Not safe driving practice, of course, but…*that kiss*!

She hadn't thought he had it in him. Well, she *had* thought he had it in him—she just hadn't thought he had it in him to give to *her*!

He was reserved. Losing his wife would definitely account for that. And brilliant. He had, after all, recognized the merits of her own research. Not to mention he was an adoring father whose family clearly thought the world of him. They had been the ones to push them out the door to the bowling alley after a scrumptious seafood pasta dinner.

And more than any of that? He'd kissed her as though the rest of the world had faded away and the only thing on this great big blue marble they lived on was the two of them.

Her belly fluttered afresh at the thought.

Yes, she wanted to kiss him, all right. Kiss him and rip off that plaid shirt and those walnut-colored chinos of his so she could see what else he had going on beneath that calm, cool exterior of his.

Or… She slipped her hands along her thighs. Perhaps *he* would take the lead. Start slow. Real slow. Just as slowly as his fingers had slipped along her jawline as millimeter by millimeter he'd lowered his full mouth to hers for one of the most sensual kisses she had ever experienced.

It had been an extraordinary combination of tenderness and passion. Far better than the rooftop kiss. It had literally weakened her knees.

A tickling of glittery warmth whispered all the way through to her toes and right back up again, until it took a naughty heated swirl round the magic spot between her thighs.

Before she could travel down memory lane too far, he pulled the car into a driveway in front of a beautiful Victorian house tucked back from the street amongst a nestling of mature oak trees.

"Oh, Ty. It's gorgeous."

His lips tightened for a microsecond. It definitely wasn't the move of a sexy panther about to pounce on his sexy prey.

Then it hit her. This was where he had lived with his wife. It had to be. It was the perfect family home.

The house was two-story, a lush sage-green with white-edged windows, some of which were curved or made of beautiful multi-colored stained glass. There was a sprawling porch dappled with cushioned rocking chairs. It was clearly kept with a loving attention to the details that had no doubt made it shine back in the day when it had been built.

Were they details his wife had put into place?

"It was built in 1891 for a local physician. It even has a turret." Ty spoke mechanically. As if he'd memorized the description the real estate agent had used to lure in buyers.

"How amazing. And…" She hesitated, because she knew what she was going to say would ask more than one question. "How long have you lived here?"

Ty leant forward, looped an arm across the top of his steering wheel and gave the house a long, hard stare. "Just about five years now."

The way he said it tore at her heart. Five years ago—shortly after his wife had passed.

She knew straight away that she wouldn't be going through that beautiful front door where a stained-glass posy of wildflowers was set into the center of the pale blue window. The same eggshell color as the birdbox that was sitting in the back of his car.

No. She wouldn't be walking through that door. Not tonight. Perhaps not ever.

The look in Ty's eyes was such a tangle of confusion it obliterated the taut sensual atmosphere that had been buzzing between them. Which was probably just as well. He was her boss. She was here to focus. Not to— Well. Not to do other things.

She tugged up the zip on her leather jacket and pulled her handbag onto her shoulder.

"If it's all right, I think I'd better get a taxi back," she said just as Ty started to say something else.

They false-started a couple more times, stumbling over their words, talking over each other, until Ty finally held up his hands and said, "I think I owe you an apology."

"What for?"

"Kissing you the way I did and then manhandling you into the car."

She actually laughed. "You didn't *manhandle* me. I was a willing participant."

He arced an eyebrow.

"Seriously?" she said. "Number one: if I'd been scared or unhappy we were in the middle of a bowling alley. Help was just a scream away. Number two: you're practically *made* of honor. Any fool can see that." She tapped a third finger. "More to the point, if you had pulled the car into any vacant lot on the way here I would've happily steamed up the windows with you."

The corners of his mouth twitched. Amused or irked?

It was difficult to gauge his true feelings. Kirri threw tact to the wayside and decided to do what she always did. Put the facts on the table and see what happened.

"Look. I fancied you from the moment I saw you, and it seems maybe you fancied me a little bit, too. But I'm not a relationship girl, and I doubt you're a fling kind of guy, so it's probably best if we nip this in the bud."

The corners of Ty's mouth tipped down. "It's not you—"

"I know." Kirri waved her hands. She knew the speech because she'd given it enough.

My work is my life. I'm not in the right place right now. You deserve someone who can give you the life you deserve.

"Why don't we go up onto that porch of yours and wait for the taxi you're just about to call me?"

At long last that broad, relaxed smile of his peeled his lips apart. "Compromise?"

"Depends. What kind of compromise?"

"We have a drink on the patio. Talk it out."

"I thought big roughty-toughty men like you didn't like to talk things out?"

"You think I'm roughty-toughty?"

"You built a birdbox, didn't you?"

He looked up at the house in front of them. "I rebuilt this house…"

"Well, then. Sounds like we have a good starting point."

"Here you are. Hot tea, as ordered."

Ty handed Kirri the steaming mug, then sat on the brightly cushioned chair next to her.

"And the taxi?"

"I'm more than happy to drive you home. Remember Lulu's staying at her aunt's, so I'm happy to be of service."

More time in an enclosed space with her when he was still buzzing with lust? *What was he thinking?*

Kirri shook her head. "I think going home on my own would be wise."

Ty nodded, pulled out his phone and tapped a few buttons. "It should be here in forty-five minutes to an hour."

She raised her eyebrows.

"There was a baseball game tonight and traffic's a bit heavy."

"Ah." She stared at her tea as if it were a crystal ball that could magic up a taxi straight away.

They sipped their beverages for a few awkward moments.

She'd been straight up with him, so he might as well do the same with her. "You know that attraction thing you were talking about?"

She nodded as she lifted the mug up to her lips, disguising her expression.

"Well, you were right. It went both ways."

Kirri sat up a bit higher in her chair. "Go on."

There was a playful note to her voice, but he knew it was time for honesty. "I've been wondering from the day we met what it would be like to kiss you."

"You found out the other day on the roof."

"I know. And it made me want more."

"You've got a funny of showing it. Not that I'm all that brilliant at personal relations myself," she added hastily.

He laughed softly, rubbing his thumb along the back of her hand. "I suppose the thing is I haven't wondered anything about kissing anyone in a long, long time."

Kirri nodded, then gave him a nervous grin. "You're very good at it, if you don't mind me saying."

He gave the back of his head a scrub, his eyes traveling the length of the porch as he did so. "Can I be honest with you?"

"Please."

"The truth is, when it comes to you I want to do a whole

lot more than kissing. And that's something I haven't done since Gemma passed."

She lifted her eyebrows but said nothing.

"Up until the moment I pulled into the drive my plan was to carry you into the house and tease every thread of fabric off of your body—to do my damnedest to make you feel as hot and bothered as you make *me* feel."

It was a huge admission and, surprisingly, he felt a weight lift off his chest as the words found purchase in another one of Kirri's beautiful smiles.

"What stopped you?"

"Seeing the house."

Kirri gave his hand a soft squeeze but said nothing. She was giving him the time and space to tell his story at his own pace.

"We used to drive past this house all the time, Gemma and I. It was old and crumbling to bits. A lot like my parents' house was when they bought it. Neither of us could bear to see it fall into ruin, so we set our hearts on buying it one day. Well, one day never came, because cancer came first and swallowed up our lives. *Her* life anyway. I was so angry when she was taken. She had less than a year with Lulu. Not anywhere near long enough for Lulu to remember her. But she sacrificed herself so that Lulu could have a rich, full life. I swore then and there that my neonatology practice would change."

"Ah..." Kirri tapped the side of her head. "I wondered what it was."

"What?"

"The thing that gave you the guts to do surgeries others don't."

A hit of gratitude exploded in his chest. He was glad she saw it that way. "Most folk call it insanity."

"Somebody has to be the pioneer." She put on a television announcer voice and intoned, "*He's the surgeon who will go where no man's gone before...* Or woman," she finished off brightly, then tucked her feet under her on the rocking chair seat.

Her expression was bereft of any judgement, just held interest.

"And if that courage is motivated by something emotional I think it clarifies the mission," she said.

Her choice of words piqued his interest. "What do you mean by 'mission'?"

"Well, you'll take calculated risks other people wouldn't dare to because you don't want anyone else to experience the sort of loss you have." She shook her head. "The way I see it, if a surgeon can do something about a problem—fix it—they should. You do that. Anyone who says otherwise is using common sense as a camouflage for their own fear."

Something told him she wasn't talking about his surgeries anymore, but her own research.

"Want to talk about it?" he asked.

She laughed at his echo of her words. "I suppose fair is fair—but you haven't really finished your story."

He took a drink of his tea, then nodded. Fair *was* fair. "The truth is, it feels like I've gone through a sea-change in only a matter of days."

"In what way?"

He traced a finger along her arm. "*You* arrived."

She gave a self-effacing laugh. "That's normally a signal for most men to run for the hills."

He locked her in a serious gaze. "I doubt that. If I were a guessing man, I'd imagine it was the other way round."

She feigned an air of indifference. "I'm just picky."

When their eyes met, a bit of her bravura wilted.

"Too picky, maybe."

Ty shook his head. There was no way he was going to let her take the fall for a step he didn't know how to take.

"Don't do that. You deserve someone special, Kirri. Someone who can devote themselves to your happiness."

The idea that it could be someone else kicked him in the gut. Real hard. Did he have it in him to take this risk? To try, at least?

Kirri's cheeks had pinked up, but she was still shaking her head. "Everyone deserves full and complete love, but some of us take a lot longer to have room in their lives for it. And, of course..." she nodded at him "...some of us know just how high the bar really is and refuse to compromise."

It was a generous thing to say. Acknowledging his wife like that. Especially when he'd all but thrown a bucket of ice on an evening that had been a very obvious prelude to lovemaking. Apart from which, being with Kirri didn't feel like a compromise. It felt like a prize at the end of a long race. A prize that deserved to be cherished.

Ty lifted his mug in a toast. "You are wise beyond your years, young woman."

"Not so young, but I'll take the compliment."

She sniggered, but there was a hint of something he couldn't identify in her expression as she looked away.

Then, abruptly, she put down her mug and said, "I can't have children. That's my thing."

The hollowness and pain in her voice tore at his heart.

"I am *so* sorry." He reached out to take her hand but she shook her head. She didn't want comfort. Not for this.

Quickly, as if she'd made a deal with herself that she just had to blurt it out, she told him she had been born without a womb. MRKH syndrome. There had never been any chance she'd have a child. She'd found out when she was fifteen. The physical anomaly had colored her father's view of her. Put yet more distance between her and her mother. Doubled her drive to be recognized for her medical achievements as much as her brother was for his.

Her research was the only thing that kept her emotionally afloat, because it filled all those empty hours she would have loved to fill with a family of her own. And now her brother was insisting she cease and desist. Said it was destroying her rather than building her up.

She admitted there might be some truth to that. Her honesty was humbling. And the fact she could never have a child of her own and yet had devoted her life to helping others who could was little short of miraculous. Most people in her position would have walked away.

"I imagine loads of people have asked you this, but have you ever thought of—?"

"Adopting?" she finished for him. "No." She huffed out a sigh. "There was an ex… Andrew." She traced her finger along her mug. "I knew he wanted children and stupidly held off telling him I couldn't until it was too late."

"Too late for what?"

"Too late for my heart not to break when he dumped me for precisely that reason. Too late for the accusation that I'd never be a good mother anyway not to dig in and take hold."

Her voice sounded brittle with pain.

Ty's jaw tightened. "What an ass."

"Well…" She shrugged. "He wanted kids of his own. I couldn't give them to him. It may seem closed-minded of him not to have considered having children through another route—adoption, fostering—but ultimately I kept something from him that I shouldn't have. My deception came back and slapped me in the face."

"You shouldn't blame yourself for that."

She hung her head and sighed. "It's not like there's anyone else to blame. I became the person he said I was. Work-obsessed. Emotionally unavailable. Freaked out by kids."

"What? You were brilliant with Lulu and my sister's children."

Again she shrugged. It was still clearly a very raw subject.

She took a sip of her tea, then looked up at him. "I suppose the simple truth is I want what I can't have. That is how life works sometimes, isn't it? Wanting the one solitary thing you can't ever have and destroying everything else in your life in pursuit of the impossible."

Ty couldn't have put it better himself. He'd done his best with Lulu, but he knew that without his family propping him up she wouldn't be the well-rounded happy little girl she was today. His daughter was happy, but he knew she had the odd hit of envy for children who had mothers. A mother would love her in a way he never could because… well…because he was her father. No one could be both. No matter how hard they tried.

His brows tucked together as he took another long gulp of his hot drink. Did he want a wife? Someone to stand by his side and help him raise his daughter?

It was a question he had no capacity to answer in this exact moment, but he felt a closeness to Kirri he hadn't felt with anyone in years, and her honesty moved him to be forthright with her about the here and now.

"I truly did want to pick you up and carry you into this house."

She blinked her surprise. "You don't have to say that."

He took her hand in his, looked her in the eye and said, "I wanted to. Honestly. You are a beautiful, intelligent, sensitive, incredible woman. But when we got here and I saw the house…"

He wasn't sure he should go on, but if Kirri deserved anything it was honesty.

"I think the long and short of it is that the only woman I ever imagined carrying over that threshold was Gemma."

"And I'm not Gemma."

Saying the words felt like a knife in Kirri's heart.

She should have known better. Pulled back sooner. Never left the lab. Or Australia.

She pulled her hand out of Ty's and tucked her knees up under her chin, wrapping her arms around them so that she could look as small as she felt.

Just as she'd thought.

She wasn't good enough.

Not for Ty.

Not for her brother, who wanted to pen her into a surgical corner.

And she hadn't been enough for her father, who had barely acknowledged the fact she'd graduated from med school and made something of herself.

She'd never been enough for the boyfriend she'd known wanted a family one day either.

"I think we'd better check on that taxicab."

"No. Kirri." Ty took her hand back in his and held it. "You've got it wrong. I *did* think that. It was a wobble. A big one. But I didn't waver for the reason you think."

She tugged her hand free again. "What other reason could possibly exist that would make you refuse to enter your house with me when we had driven here for the express purpose of doing—you know—*things*?"

Ty raked a hand through his hair, then seemed to make a decision. He pulled her into his arms, then tipped her chin up so that she was looking him straight in the eye.

"I freaked because I *could* picture carrying you into that house. I *could* picture ripping your clothes off. I freaked because when I kiss you my entire body is alight with fire and I don't ever want it to stop."

She shook her head. This was definitely not the explanation she'd been expecting. "That's a *good* thing, right?"

He tipped his head down to hers, his lips brushing against her mouth as he whispered, "I was scared. Scared right to my marrow. Because you make me feel like a brand-new man and that is one helluva change for a fellow to confront when he's falling for a woman who can't bowl for peanuts."

What little remained of her smile faltered. And then she kissed him. Hard. As if her life depended on it.

He kissed her back with a matching intensity, so perhaps it did. It seemed to at this moment, and that was all that mattered.

Before she could wrap her head around what was happening, she felt one of Ty's strong arms round her waist and the other shift under her buttocks. In one fluid move he lifted her up without a pause for breath. She wrapped her legs round his hips as he walked the pair of them through the front door.

It was a bold decision, and one she knew he wouldn't be taking lightly.

The pounding of their heartbeats synchronized as the door slammed shut behind them.

They made it as far as the stairwell. From there on out it was take no prisoners. Everything that had been pent up in them from that electric first moment of connection was unleashed in a torrent of feverish kisses, erotic caresses and the most delicate of touches.

Her T-shirt was gone in a trice. Then his shirt. Her boots. His jeans. Shoes, panties, boxers, bra—all gone. So that soon enough there was nothing between them but heat and desire.

Ty was everything she'd hoped for in a man and then some. Gentle. Passionate. Completely immersed in sharing with her the most vulnerable and beautiful moments a man and woman could share together.

"I can't get enough of you," he moaned as he dropped soft, seductive kisses along the length of her throat, his tongue flicking out for a swift lick when he hit that sweet dip between her collar bones.

She could feel the strength of his desire against her thighs as she pressed toward him and more than anything she wanted to share with him the ultimate intimacy. This wasn't sweet, slow lovemaking. This was carnal desire at its most divine apex.

She pushed him back so she could look into his face. "You're sure you want this?"

She saw everything in his eyes that she felt in her heart. Certainty.

"More than anything."

She parted her legs and groaned with pleasure as the tip of him, primed with desire, began to dip into the shallows of her essence.

Their groans of pleasure wove together above them as Ty pressed deeper, until in one swift, powerful move he was completely inside her. Never before had she felt so complete. It was as if they had been made for one another.

His rhythm fine-tuned itself to hers. She pressed her hips up to meet him as stroke by fluid stroke they reached a climax as one.

He shifted the pair of them so that they lay on their sides, legs and arms tangled together as Kirri relished the sensations still rippling through her body.

They stayed like that for a while, their breaths steadying, the warmth of their bodies binding them together as tightly as the emotional connection she felt to Ty.

He knew her darkest secret and he'd still made love to her. He'd taken a step into the unknown for her. She'd never felt more treasured in her life than she did at this precise moment.

"What do you say we head upstairs?"

The way he said it left little doubt as to what he had in mind.

"Are you sure? Maybe I should get back to my place so that I'm not here when Lulu gets home."

He gave her a gentle smile and tucked a lock of stray hair behind her ear. "I think my mother and sisters knew what was happening before we did."

"What do you mean?"

"My sister sent a text. She'll be taking Lulu to Sunday school in the morning. We'll meet them at the house for lunch. Unless you have other plans?"

She gave him a playful poke on the chest. "You know jolly well my only plans were to try and break into the lab and hide out there for the rest of the weekend. You and your peach pies gave short shrift to that."

He leant in for a long slow kiss. "Tell me you didn't love it."

She wrapped her arms round him and pressed in close. She'd already shared so much with him. How could she tell him that spending the day with his family had been a dream come true? That tonight had been so much better than any icing on the very best of cakes? It was an entire pastry selection of unimaginable pleasure.

Were there complications?

A mountain's worth.

Things she had yet to tell him?

Ample.

Unknowns to confront, in the form of whether to tell his daughter, the fact that their lives were in different countries, the simple truth that she'd never be able to give him a big family like the one he was part of?

Thousands of them.

Were they worth ignoring in order to enjoy this incredibly perfect bubble of…was it love?

She looked into his eyes and saw nothing but tenderness and compassion in them. She hoped he saw the same. It might not be love yet, but she already knew in her heart that the connection they shared would be something she would cherish forever.

"C'mon, you." He laced his fingers through hers and pulled her up. "How about I cancel that taxi of yours and we head on upstairs for some shut-eye?"

He dropped her a wink. The sort of wink that said they weren't anywhere *near* close to getting to sleep yet. But when they did sleep she knew she would be wrapped tight in his arms. And for that she was willing to let the world and her thousands of questions wait for another day.

CHAPTER NINE

TY STRODE INTO the office with a lightness of step he hadn't felt in years.

It had been three weeks since he and Kirri had been together and about half an hour since he'd seen her last.

His family had embraced her as naturally as if she'd long since been one of their own.

His mother adored giving Kirri cooking lessons. She said her daughters already thought they knew better than her, so it was a genuine delight to have someone who actually listened to her for once.

This last weekend Kirri had insisted Lulu join them, because they had been learning how to make baking powder biscuits. A Southern essential, Marina had explained. Kirri and Lulu had finished the lesson covered in flour, but with huge smiles on their faces. The type of smiles that made him stuff his concerns about what he'd do in a few weeks' time to the back shelf. *Again.*

They'd agreed that circumstances dictated that whatever it was they were doing would only be an affair, but… *damn*…it felt a lot like falling in love. It was just so *natural*. Different from what he'd had with Gemma, but every bit as easy.

He was waiting for one of his sisters to invite him over to fix something, or for his father to take him out on a fishing trip. Both were family code for having "a talk". The type of talk that usually meant they thought whoever was on the receiving end was doing something stupid. But no one had said a word.

Last night Lulu had slept over with her cousins, so Ty had spent the night at Kirri's condo, enjoying the delights of the floor-to-ceiling view in between some rather athletic stints of lovemaking and a picnic of Mama Poppy's finest on the living room floor.

They hadn't told Lulu about the "special time" they shared together, seeing as Kirri would be going home in a few weeks, but he saw the way Lulu shone in Kirri's company. She loved showing off for her. Prancing about doing her dance moves from ballet class, singing her favorite songs, begging Kirri to watch the latest Disney film…

Put plainly, rather than resisting a woman coming into their lives, as Ty had feared, Lulu had taken to Kirri being a part of their family activities with arms wide open. As if she'd been waiting patiently all these years for this very specific flame-haired whirlwind to swirl in and shake up their lives.

Lulu clearly ached to have a woman in their lives. One who was there just for Ty and her. It worried him, because he knew there would come a time in the not too distant future when Kirri would leave, and Lulu wasn't the only one who would struggle to say goodbye.

Despite having agreed to keep their blossoming romance separate from their professional lives, the sly smiles and muffled giggles his staff regularly jiggled with when he wished them a good morning made it clear that the Piedmont grapevine was buzzing with the news that Dr. Sawyer had more than a hint of a spring in his step.

"Good morning, Stella."

As ever, the surgical nurse was waiting for him in the staff kitchen, with his coffee already poured and a list of the day's surgeries.

"Good morning to you, Dr. Sawyer." Her tone spoke volumes. She was the cat who'd got the cream. "I presume you had a lovely weekend?"

"Very." He accepted the coffee and took a long sip. "This is delicious."

"Same as ever, Dr. Sawyer."

He frowned at the mug and took another drink. Madness, he knew, but it felt like he was tasting coffee properly for the first time in years. All foods, really. He was seeing colors more brightly. Smelling the scents of spring with greater pleasure.

It was as if a filter had been lifted on his entire life. A gray, tasteless filter that had fallen into place when Gemma had got sick. It had robbed his life of beauty and, if he were being truly honest, of his natural vitality.

As a doctor, he knew cancer was rarely tactical. Taking out darkness with more darkness, it never took into account the kindness of the soul. The generosity of the person it would be robbing loved ones of. The parent the child would never know…

His wife's words tugged at his heart in a way they never had before.

"You'll know, sweetheart. It may take a while, but you'll know. And for heaven's sake do something about it."

"You look different."

Stella tipped her head forward so that she was looking at him over the rims of her glasses. It was the type of sage look a television psychologist might give to someone who had finally turned a corner.

He didn't bother asking different to what. He knew. He looked as if he'd rejoined the land of the living.

"You going to do something about it?" she asked.

He smiled at her but didn't answer.

His gut churned at the thought of taking Kirri to the airport. He of all people knew how precious time was and how critical it was to make the most of it. He of all people knew the physical, soul-sucking pain of saying goodbye forever.

This time he didn't have to.

If he didn't say something, *do* something, he knew he'd spend the rest of his life wondering if he had let the best thing that had happened to him in the last five years walk right out of his life.

He wanted her to stay as much as he wanted to draw breath. But asking her to do so would be selfish. It would be a huge sacrifice. One he didn't know he could ask her to make. Apart from the complications of the specialized visa she'd needed for the trip, they'd already allocated the clinic's research funding and the all important 3D printer for the next three years. For the foreseeable future, at least, Kirri wouldn't be able to use their labs. Would working on the surgical ward and loving him and Lulu be enough?

He honestly didn't know. But he'd never find out if he didn't ask, and he sure as hell was going to try.

As if she'd followed his entire train of thought, Stella gave him one of her wise owl smiles. "Don't think I'm pushing, but if I were in your shoes I know what I'd do."

She popped on a bright smile.

"Right!" Stella turned toward the door. "Are you going to stand there all day, sipping that cup of coffee like it's honey and nectar, or are you going to get into that scrub room and start saving some babies' lives?"

He smiled and laughed, clapped an arm round Stella's shoulders as they headed toward the surgical unit. "Let's do it. Let's go save some lives."

Kirri pushed back from her microscope and sighed. She was well and truly struggling. As advanced as this 3D cell-structure model was, there were still miles to go before she could get the culture model to mimic the uterus's true cellular properties.

A warm, cuddly sensation swirled through her as she reminded herself that Ty had said not to worry about epic breakthroughs. She wasn't here to score the goals. She was here to be a player in the game.

Trouble was, she still wanted to be the *best* player. It was part of her genetic fabric to push on, no matter how hard the battle.

She tipped her head into her hands and tried to get the facts straight. There were literally so many microscopic factors her mind kept fuzzing with the details.

"Anything I can help with?" asked Gloria, the researcher who was sitting next to her.

"Not unless you can figure out how to create a hydrogel membrane that perfectly mimics the placenta."

Gloria whistled, then shook her head. "That's well out of my sphere of knowledge, girlfriend. You need to be over in Vienna for that sort of action."

"Vienna?"

"Yeah..."

She tugged out the shoulder bag stashed under her desk and rifled through it until she unearthed a magazine that specialized in reporting on medical innovations. She turned it around and tapped the cover story.

"I thought you would've been all over this and packing your bags."

Kirri frowned at the magazine cover.

Scientists make significant breakthrough with artificial placenta model

Gloria handed her the magazine. "If I were you I'd be on the phone to these guys today. How's your German?"

Schlecht, Kirri thought darkly.

Seeing the article made her feel like she'd been ripped in two.

She'd been trying to think of a way to ask Ty about extending her stay here in Atlanta, but what they were doing in Vienna…it was exactly what she'd been looking for professionally for just about forever.

When Gloria turned back to her Petri dishes Kirri began to rapidly scan the article, one word blurring into the next as she read about the hi-tech bio-med team who had made the breakthrough. They were miles ahead of her. Well, a good meter anyway. This sort of research progressed painful millimeter by millimeter, and what they'd achieved was little short of a miracle.

If she'd been feeling more positive she would be congratulating herself on getting as far as she had on her own. They had an entire team and proper funding. She had been pouring her own salary into buying all the necessary equipment herself. It was why coming here to Atlanta had been a godsend. Her brother paid her handsomely, but there was no chance she'd ever be able to buy her own 3D printer.

Words kept popping out at her. *Laser beams. Hydrogel. Biocompatibility.*

When she got to the end of the article she saw that the reason they'd begun their experiment was to explore critical research issues regarding the nutrient exchange between mother and child. Her endgame went much further. The baby grow bag.

Seeing this breakthrough lauded with such acclaim made one thing crystal-clear. If she wanted to make the sorts of strides she believed were possible she needed to go to Vienna.

Her brother's wrath she could deal with.

But the look in Ty's eyes when she told him she'd be tearing this fragile thing they were building in two… The thought churned in her like bile.

She put the article down, her fingers shaking so hard she had to press them to the lab table. Who knew how much truth there was in it? Articles like this surfaced all the time.

Not like this one, they didn't.

She forced herself to look at her work from a different angle. Knowing new things sometimes brought fresh perspective.

An hour later she'd hit a wall.

It was no good. The Austrian team's development had hit her right where it hurt. In the ego. If she'd had their resources, and a whole team dedicated to this one solitary project, she'd be the one on the magazine cover.

If she went to Vienna she could be.

Her heart constricted so hard and fast she pushed away from her desk and left the lab. She needed thinking time.

Without even remembering how she'd got there, she found herself on the surgical floor, looking for the tall, dark-haired brainiac who set her world alight in the opposite way her research did. Balance, happiness, fun…

He has a child.

A child she was falling in love with every bit as much as she was falling for Ty.

It was such unfamiliar territory…and yet she was finally beginning to see how loving a child didn't have to be the complicated web of emotions she'd always made it out to be.

Kirri had kept all children at arm's length because she'd never thought she could love one properly. Ty had clearly seen something in her that believed otherwise and it had given her confidence. Perhaps it was simpler than that. Maybe she and Lulu just clicked. The same way she and Ty had on that first rain-soaked morning.

From the most barren earth comes little grass shoots...

Tingles of anticipation shot through her when she heard his voice around the corner. Her fingers flexed in anticipation of joining him. It hit her that she hadn't felt this fired up about being in the operating theater since… Well, since she'd started researching the baby grow bag.

Boring old facts slammed into her. Surgery was fun right now because she was—honesty check—she was completely giddy with romance. That buzzy, elated feeling wouldn't last forever. If it became love it might, but the way things were on a professional front definitely wouldn't stay the same.

The research lab here was chock-a-block for the next few years and the queue after that was crazy long. She could do surgery fulltime, but would it be enough? More to the point, would she have the strength to step away from the way she defined herself—her work—to have a proper life with Lulu and Ty? Was she brave enough? Humble enough to accept that it wouldn't all be plain sailing? Hopeful enough to know that the rewards would be far better than being on the cover of any magazine? That ignoring Vienna would be worth it even if she might never make her father proud?

She ducked her head into the scrub room and, as she'd hoped, found Ty there, going through the familiar motions. It was almost meditative, watching him. The care he took. Nails, hands, forearms… All scrubbed in preparation for being gowned and masked in order to change a tiny person's life.

She knocked on the doorframe to get his attention. When he turned and saw her that gorgeous smile of his warmed her from the inside out. Saying goodbye to this man was going to be like ripping an organ out of her gut. A vital life-force she'd never known she needed.

"Need an extra pair of hands?"

His eyes sparked as he nodded. "You should definitely scrub in on this one. Keyhole spine repair for a baby with spina bifida."

Adrenaline shot through her. This was cutting-edge stuff. "Amazing! I'd love to be a part of that. Why didn't you tell me?"

"It's Mark's surgery, really. I'm scrubbing in as an extra pair of hands." He gave her a cheeky grin. "I did actually come up to the lab to tell you about it an hour ago, but you looked so serious I thought I'd better leave you to it."

"*Moi?* Serious?"

She jested to cover her nerves. He'd seen her frowning in the wake of reading about the Vienna discovery. Thank goodness he couldn't read minds.

"Deadly," he said, his eyes connecting with hers. They narrowed. "Is everything all right with you? You seem a bit distracted."

Just trying to figure out whether to follow my head to Vienna or my heart to Atlanta.

"Kirri?"

Nuts. He knew something was up. He was getting good at reading her body language. Too good.

Would it be so bad to have someone know you that well? Someone to help you weather the storms?

Her shoulders shifted up to her ears, then dropped heavily. "I am."

He glanced at the OR, where the staff were beginning to enter from the other scrub room. "I've got to get in there, darlin'. You are more than welcome to join us. Whatever it is—I have no doubt everything'll work out for the best."

With every fiber in her being she wanted to believe him. But she'd once believed in Santa Claus.

Was whatever it was they were sharing just a fiction, brought about by her short-term contract, or was this like the spirit of Christmas, which overrode every child's discovery that Santa wasn't real? Eternal, enduring, magic.

* * *

"Can you grab that pile of blankets, please, Kirri?"

Henry pointed at the back of the family's SUV as he and Ty hauled a cool box over to where the family was setting up a picnic.

"Absolutely."

Her gaze caught and snagged on Ty. Her man. Her temporary man, anyway. He was looking tanned and gorgeous and, most of all, completely and utterly relaxed. A far cry from the uptight, speed-walking hunk of sexy Ice King she'd met on that first day. The one whose chink had appeared in the form of an umbrella and glints of gold in his eyes.

Tingles of delight at the memory skittered through her, and then again as she mentally replayed the soft kiss they'd stolen today, before the children had all piled out of their grandparents' house and into the cars.

Part of her had felt like the naughty teenager she'd never had a chance to be. *Thanks, Dad.* The other part of her had felt utterly content in a way she'd never imagined possible.

Nothing had ever felt so natural to her as being part of Ty and Lulu's lives. They were busy. Work, Lulu's numerous activities and plain old life got in the way of loads of "Ty and Kirri" time. But when they had some it was pure gold dust. In all honesty, it was *all* gold dust. One huge hunk of glowing golden nugget.

"Here, let me help you honey."

Ty's sister Tammy bustled in beside her and tugged out the mammoth pile of picnic rugs and homemade quilts that seemed far too beautiful to spread on a grassy field in the park—but that was exactly what they were doing.

"Now that you're part of the posse that pile just keeps getting bigger and bigger."

Instead of taking the comment as a slight, as she might

have a few weeks ago—hypersensitivity being one of her superpowers—Kirri felt well and truly welcomed by it. She was part of a "posse"!

Up until now she'd been used to putting herself to the side at group activities—waiting for the natural pairings to take place and then sticking herself on an edge ready for a quick escape. Not here. And definitely not with the Sawyers running the show. They were all for one and one for all. It felt incredibly enriching to be a part of such a happy family.

She squeezed her eyes against the twist of emotion that inevitably followed any sort of reminder that her time here came with a ticking clock.

"You all right, hon?"

Tammy shifted the stack of quilts to her hip and caught her in a little half-hug.

"Yeah, of course. I just…" She watched as a tumble of cousins and in-laws grabbed picnic baskets, the family dogs and each other, then made their way to the site that Winny had pegged out for them, holding her newborn.

"I just wish my brother could see this. See me." Lucius would think she'd gone clinically insane.

Tammy's brow furrowed. "Why? You have open-air movies in Sydney, don't you?"

"Yes, but—" She'd never been. She doubted Lucius had.

The point was, the Sawyers were doing it as a *family*. And she felt part of that family. Rather than feeling less valued than any of them, because she couldn't have children, she felt valued simply for being *her*. Not that they knew her secret—Ty had honored her request to keep that private—but for the first time in her life she didn't mind if people knew. These people, anyway.

With crystal-clear clarity Kirri knew without a shadow of a doubt that her whole "don't date men with children" rule had been a form of denial. She'd been denying herself a love she'd thought she wasn't worthy of when in actual fact it was a love she *could* give. A love she craved like air.

She'd spent all these years being terrified of failing. Sticking to her workaholic routine as if it were the thing keeping her alive, and not the hopes and dreams she'd stuffed into a cupboard all those years ago when her ex had made her feel valueless.

"Why don't you call him? Your brother?" Tammy nodded at the pocket she knew Kirri kept her phone in. "Do one of those video calls. Show him what a good time you're having. We'll all cheer and wave!"

"Oh…it's about five in the morning at home. Better not."

Five in the morning but her brother would be up, having his first cup of coffee and preparing for another long day at Harborside. She definitely wasn't the only workaholic in the family.

Besides, calling him up when she was having such a brilliant time outside the lab would be like salt in the wound. Proof, if he needed any, that she wasn't prioritizing Harborside above all else. Not to mention the fact he'd feel a thousand shades of awkward with all the kissing and the hugging and the general being in and out of each other's business that Ty's family enjoyed so much. Little wonder, since the pair of them had virtually been raised to be lone wolves…

But…oh, it was lovely here. Her heart felt as though it was healing from wounds she'd never even known she'd endured.

Her father would balk at most of the activities that seemed to bring the Sawyers so much joy. Goofing around with the sprinkler in the back garden. Cheering on the grandchildren at their Little League games as if they were watching the World Series. And, of course, things like tonight. Bundling everyone—seventeen of them in total—

into a virtual motorcade's worth of cars and heading down to Atlantic Station's recently renovated Central Park to watch an open-air movie and eat—a mountain of barbecue, of course.

It was a vivid reminder that perhaps there was a bit more to life than Petri dishes and—she could hardly believe she was even *thinking* this—3D printers.

Which made knowing that her fantasy lab was sitting in Vienna, glowing away like a whole different type of magical kingdom, that much harder. The question was, was it an illusion or the type of magical kingdom where dreams really did come true?

Depends upon what the dream is, you goose. Depends upon what the dream is.

As the cartoon before the main film flickered to life they finally decanted everything from the cars, and the children were soon parked in front of huge banana leaf trays of chicken wings and barbecued ribs.

Her phone rang.

Lucius.

She signaled to Tammy that she'd be back in a moment and took the call. "Hey, Luce. What's up?"

"*Someone* sounds like they're not in a lab preparing to change the world."

The words didn't come laced with venom, but they definitely hit their mark.

She had been slacking—if working regular office hours could officially be called slacking.

A well of frustration balled in her belly. Why didn't she seem to be able to get the balance right?

Because there had been no balance in her old life.

Guilt poured in as she shot a glance toward the downtown area, where her research was sitting all by itself in a darkened lab. It wouldn't exactly be crying itself to sleep at night, but she wasn't here to have jollies out in the park with a family she was going to have to say goodbye to. With a man who'd made her see life from an entirely new angle. She was here to work.

But they were so persuasive!

"The fresh air will do you good!"

"You *must* see a movie in the park—there is the *best* popcorn."

"You've never seen *Singing in the Rain*?"

"Too late! I've booked you a ticket."

That last had been from Ty. He'd run his fingers along her arm as he told her, knowing his touch was all the persuasion she needed.

Lucius didn't wait for a response. "Have you booked your flight yet?"

Her eyes hooked with Ty's across the picnic ground and he waved her over. She signaled that she'd be a minute. He smiled and dropped her a slow wink that sent ripples of approbation through her. Twenty meters away and the man could still give her butterflies. Hell, they didn't even have to be in the same *room* and he gave her butterflies.

Would it be the same if she was on a different continent?

"Kirri?"

"There's one with seats a fortnight from today."

It was a lie. She had booked an open return and hadn't yet checked. And there was also Vienna to consider.

"Right, then. Book it."

She definitely would, but… *Oh, God.* Suddenly the thought of going back to her old life felt like depriving this new self she was discovering of oxygen. It wasn't Lucius's fault. Not at all. And the lure to stay was so much stronger than the amazing sex she was having…although that helped. The truth lay with one incredible man—and his daughter, if she was being completely honest—whom she was falling madly in love with.

Could true love happen that fast? In the blink of an eye?

It certainly felt like it.

But was it a love that could endure distance? Long hours at the lab? A dedication to something outside the family unit?

Living her life without the pressure of having to deliver results in order to be valued had been a revelation. And it was Ty who had made her see that. He had made it clear to her time and again that her research was one hundred percent about getting a fresh perspective. Not about results. He'd even teased her the other night, as he'd dropped some rather scrumptious kisses onto her belly, that if she did come up with a breakthrough he'd have to fire her.

He'd been joking, of course, but the freedom to think and explore, to let her imagination run wild with her project, was all thanks to the amazing man she was staring at right now.

He was hoisting Lulu up onto his back for a quick piggyback ride to the popcorn stall. Her heart ached to be with them. She wanted it all. The love, the work, the emotional rewards of living a rich and colorful tapestry of a life.

"Kirri? Is there a time delay or something on this line?" Lucius was getting impatient now.

"No—sorry. I'm here."

In Atlanta. And so is my heart.

"Good. Book your flight."

"I will." She would.

"And the sooner the better. The locums you hired are chomping at the bit, wondering whether they need to stay or go. And they're not the only ones who are wondering."

"Oh, well…"

She wanted to tell him to book them forever. Hire the best. To say, *You don't need me there. You never did. You were only doing what a big brother does. Care and protect. But I don't need you to look after me anymore, big brother. I need to spread my wings. See what I can do under my own steam.*

"I need a proper answer by the end of the week, Kirri."

Three more days.

She pictured herself back at the beautiful cutting-edge clinic her brother helmed and began to feel the oxygen leaving her lungs. Then she did the same with the lab in Vienna.

She could hardly breathe.

"You'll have your answer," she managed, though she already knew in her heart what she wanted.

Was she brave enough to ask for it?

"Fine." Lucius, as per usual, hung up the phone before she could tell him what she really felt.

I love you. I miss you. I wish we were closer.

And she wasn't just talking about geography. She meant close like Ty was with his sisters. But merely *thinking* of telling Lucius she loved him felt scary. Rejection was such an inbuilt factor in their family life, the idea of admitting she loved him set her stomach churning.

He's had your back all these years. Why would he stop now?

He'd put up with a lot more than any other boss would. And she owed him. She owed him her full commitment back in Sydney at the Harborside Fertility and Women's Neonatal Center.

Ty and Lulu appeared by her side as she pocketed her phone.

Ty gave her a quick squeeze, then slipped his hand into hers as Lulu took her other hand, her arm wrapped round a huge tub of popcorn.

"Everything okay, Kirri? The movie's starting."

Ty's brow furrowed as he tried to read her mood.

"Fine. Just a work call."

He gave her a sharp look. He knew work calls at this time of night only meant one thing. A work call from home.

"Urgent?"

"No," she managed to choke out. "Just a bit of forward-planning."

A flash of dismay lit and then darkened Ty's eyes. He was clever. He knew it had been Lucius and that they'd been talking about her return to Sydney.

"C'mon, Kirri." Lulu tugged at her hand. "I want to sit on your lap when we watch the movie."

Kirri looked down into the little girl's dark eyes—a perfect reflection of her father's—and saw pure, unbridled expectation in them.

Leaving Ty would be one thing, and just thinking about it unleashed a level of pain she didn't know if she could handle. Leaving Lulu would be a whole new brand of heartache. Kirri didn't know if she had it in her to do it.

In just a handful of weeks this chirpy little squirt of a girl had wormed her way into her heart in a way no child ever had. The mere idea of bringing tears to Lulu's eyes filled her with dread. And Kirri knew the pain she felt in her chest only hinted at the true responsibility that came with loving a child.

Did she have what it took to offer the type of commitment to Ty and Lulu they deserved?

Her eyes flitted back to the Medical Innovations Center skyscraper.

Did it have to be a choice?

"If you want to make a name for yourself you have to make choices. Success requires sacrifice."

Her father's voice sent a chilling numbness through her. A personal life or a professional legacy. That's what it seemed to boil down to. She'd dedicated years of her life to her research. Could she give it up for something that didn't come with a guarantee?

Nothing comes with a guarantee, you dill. Not science, not medicine, not love.

She felt the little girl's fingers in her right hand and the strong, caring man's hand in her left.

The time had come to make a decision.

CHAPTER TEN

TY PULLED KIRRI in close to him and whispered, “We have ten more floors, if you’re game…”

Kirri snuggled up close to him and spoke in a low husky voice she’d not heard come out of her throat before. “Game for what, exactly?”

Ty tipped his lips down to meet hers and showed her.

By the time the lift doors opened on the Piedmont Women and Baby Pavilion Kirri knew her mouth looked as though she’d used a glossy plumper on her lips. Kissing the man of your dreams had a way of doing that to a girl.

“See you later for that gastroschisis?”

Kirri nodded. “Absolutely.”

They waved goodbye and Kirri jogged up the stairwell to the research lab. In all honesty she was keen to do any and all the surgeries Ty invited her to. She was loving it in the surgical ward—and not just because Ty was there. For the first time in ages she didn’t feel surgery was something she *had* to do before she was allowed to do what she *wanted* to do.

A few hours into the day the phone rang. It was for Kirri.

When she finished the call her insides were vibrating with conflicting emotions.

“You all right, sugar?” Gloria asked, just as Ty entered the lab.

Her eyes shot to Ty's.

"Everything okay?" he asked.

Kirri nodded dumbly.

Ty was by her side in an instant. "Kirri. Talk to me. Is everything all right?"

"Yes. I…um… That was the research team in Vienna."

"The one you were telling me about?"

She nodded. She'd showed him the article the night before. He'd nodded. Said it looked interesting. Then he'd put it aside as easily as if she'd shown him an article on peach blossom. Interesting, but no earthquakes.

"They want me to go and work with them in Vienna."

Gloria clapped her hands. "I *knew* it was worth it."

Kirri's eyes snapped to hers. "What do you mean?"

"I might've accidentally on purpose forwarded them your résumé. You can thank me later in the form of a strawberry daiquiri. Large."

Gloria clapped again and turned around to her microscope, humming a happy little tune.

"Are you going to take up the offer?" Ty's voice was neutral but his eyes had gone a shade of dark she'd never seen before.

"I told them I need to think about it."

She saw the impact of her words in an instant. Ty was trying to look supportive, but she could see that the last thing he'd thought she'd do was jump on a plane to Vienna. In all honesty she'd thought the same thing, but… It was a chance of a lifetime.

She began to babble on about everything they did. The lab. The number of scientists involved in the project. The biochemists. And the *funding.* Oh, man, the funding was out of this world. No wonder they'd made such leaps. And if she put her research with their research, who knew what would happen?

Too late she realized she might have let her enthusiasm for the Vienna team boil over. "Maybe we could talk about it after work?"

He gave her a curt nod. "I promised Lulu homemade pizza and a movie. Up for that?"

She nodded, unable to say what she really wanted. *Forever and always...*

It was the chance of a lifetime.

But so was what she had with Ty.

She didn't want to choose, but she knew deep in her heart that she had to. A life of intellectual plaudits and groundbreaking medical innovation was what she'd always dreamed of.

She'd also always dreamed of being loved.

Ty was gone before she had a chance to communicate to him what she hoped he already knew. That this was difficult. That she would've already been on the way to the airport if she hadn't met him. But she had. And as such she had a decision to make.

It had been a night filled with the unspoken, and Ty was feeling increasingly agitated.

He didn't want to stop Kirri from following her heart. Couldn't. His entire ethos at the clinic was to inspire and then watch as his staff moved on and grew. But he'd never fallen in love with a person he was meant to set free before.

It tore his heart in two to have to let her go, but hobbling her passion for research was the last thing he was going to do. No relationship could survive that sort of blow.

"C'mon, Kirri!" Lulu ran up the stairs. "It's book at bedtime!"

Ty noted Kirri's hesitation as he headed up the stairs in his daughter's wake. "You're welcome to join us," he told her.

Kirri's brow crinkled. He could almost see the wheels whirling behind her dark blue eyes.

"I don't want to get in the way of any rituals."

He almost laughed. She'd already broken through *that* barrier the day she'd come to Chuck's Charcoal Heaven with them. Bowling. Movie nights. Baseball games. Tonight had been just a simple meal at home and a movie on TV. Even though the tension of her decision had been buzzing between them, the house had felt more like a home than it ever had.

He didn't want that feeling to vanish. He didn't want *her* to vanish. But he would not be held responsible for crushing her dreams.

Lulu appeared at the top of the stairs, brandishing a book. "Kirri! Can you read me my story tonight?"

Kirri's eyes sought Ty's as if seeking permission.

"Maybe Kirri's a bit tired, darlin'."

He hoped not. He needed to talk to her. As they'd left work she'd told him that not only did the center in Vienna want an answer by tomorrow, so did Lucius. And then she'd turned on the radio.

"I want Kirri to read it," Lulu insisted. "She does the kangaroo voice better."

A smile lit up Kirri's face and she put on a goofy voice and bounced up the stairs. "That's because kangaroos are Australian."

"Just like you!"

"That's right!" She reached the top landing. "Just like me."

Her eyes caught with Ty's and in that instant he knew Kirri was in the exact same boat as he was. Desperately trying to make the very best decisions about her future. He saw affection and warmth and maybe even love in those eyes, but there was also that critical hint of reservation.

His heart bashed against his ribcage. He didn't want to let her go. He was a better man when he was with her. A better doctor. A better father. That part had taken some getting used to, but she was amazing with Lulu. Particularly considering how difficult he knew it was for her to be with children.

He went to the bedroom door and watched as Lulu snuggled up to Kirri, who was stretched out alongside her on the butterfly quilt his mother had made for her a couple of years back. She looked perfectly relaxed and Lulu's entire demeanor oozed contentment.

Lulu's index finger was resting atop Kirri's as she traced along the words she was reading, hopping up occasionally when the text shifted from dialogue to *"Boing! Boing! Boing!"*

It was a heartwarming moment he'd never thought he'd experience without feeling the searing pain of grief and loss. It was, of course, the kind of moment he thought he'd be sharing with Gemma. And now he would no longer be sharing them with Kirri.

As painful as it was, he knew it was the right decision. He would encourage her to go.

Kirri glanced up and saw Ty in the doorway. She'd been so engrossed in reading the story she hadn't noticed anything other than Lulu's little fingers resting on her own, and now the weight of her young body as she drifted off to sleep, using Kirri as a pillow.

"Everything all right?" he asked.

Perfect, she mouthed, and then said aloud, "Catch up with you downstairs in a minute?"

Ty nodded with a smile. A knowing smile. He'd had six years of moments like this. This was her first—and, boy, was it out of this world?

She glanced at the bedside table and saw a small framed picture of a woman holding a baby in her arms. Gemma and Lulu, she presumed. Tears stung at the back of her throat as she imagined how heartbreaking it must have been for Gemma to know she'd never have a moment like this. Reading her daughter a story. Having her fall asleep in her arms. Curling into her as if she were the safest person in the world to love.

Behind the picture she saw another photo that had been taped to the wall. It was Ty, Kirri and Lulu, each brandishing a bowling ball on that very first night they'd been out for barbecue. They were all beaming. Especially Lulu, who wasn't looking at the camera. She was looking at Kirri.

She inhaled a bit more of the sweet scent of Lulu's hair as she eased her down into a nest of pillows surrounded by a rainbow of cuddly toys. Not quite ready to leave, she knelt by the bed and stroked her silky dark hair, memorizing the freckles that ran across her little button nose, her cherubic smile and the dimple on her left cheek.

Moments like this felt like they were virtually impossible to give up. No wonder single dads were protective of their little ones. Who'd want to shoulder the burden of breaking their children's hearts by introducing someone into their lives and only to take them away? Ty had taken quite a risk, letting her into their lives like this. It showed a level of courage she wasn't sure *she* possessed.

She ran her fingers through Lulu's hair and knew in that moment that she could definitely love a child who wasn't her own. She could love Lulu. Probably already did. Love was love. Kirri would never have any idea what it would be like to love a child of her own, so why compare the two? Love came in all different forms, didn't it? The love of an idea. A dream. Brotherly love. The love you had for a parent, no matter how unreciprocated or conditional it was.

She thought of the job in Vienna. Was it the final hurdle she must leap to grasp her father's attention? Or would there be another and another, until in the end she would realize it had all been for nothing? Her father—and her mother, come to think of it—truly weren't capable of that type of love. Selfless, generous, unconditional love.

Lulu nestled into her hand, making sweet little-girl sleepy noises as she did so.

Kirri's heart felt as though it were being torn in two.

Maybe it was time to give up the childhood dream of winning her father's approval. Ty's family had accepted Kirri into their lives as easily as they would have welcomed one of their own. Couldn't that be enough?

The only thing she wasn't a thousand percent sure of was…

"Hey, darlin'…"

Ty appeared again in the doorframe. His eyes dropped from hers to his daughter's cheek, nestled in Kirri's hand. His expression was more serious than she'd ever seen it.

"Do you mind if we have a little chat before you go?"

Uh-oh. She'd overstepped.

This was precisely why she'd never let her feelings run away with her before—because now that she'd had a taste of what her dream life could be like bearing the loss of it might be more than she could handle. No amount of research would ever make up for this. For Ty. For Lulu. For the life she now knew she desperately wanted to live.

She followed behind him, her heart in her throat, waiting to hear the words she'd feared hearing all along: *I'm afraid this isn't going to work.*

Ty thought he'd experienced the definition of a hammering heart before now—but, no. He had not. If his heart didn't watch it, it would punch straight through his ribcage and out onto the back porch.

"Everything okay?" Kirri asked as she sat down on the porch swing.

She looked as nervous as he felt.

He sat down on the swing beside her. "Fine. No. That's

not entirely true." He stroked his fingers along her cheek. "I've never been better. Up until about two o'clock this afternoon, that is. Never been better." He heard the emotion in his own voice and forced himself to carry on. "And I think you know the reason why."

"Go on."

Kirri's features had softened with a wash of emotions that made saying what he had to a thousand times harder.

"I think you should go to Vienna." He held up a hand when she opened her mouth. "As you know, we can't offer you ongoing research here. Not the type they can. All I can offer is a post on the surgical ward, which I know isn't where your heart is, so..."

Damn this was hard.

"If you really want to make those strides forward, it seems like Vienna's the best place for you."

His voice sounded like a stranger's. The voice of a man he'd never want to meet.

"Fair enough."

Kirri's voice was barely audible. And it contained traces of a bitterness he hadn't expected to hear.

"It's what you want, isn't it?"

"Of course." She gave a strangled sort of laugh. "I can hardly believe I'm not on a plane right now. I was just... you know...fulfilling the criteria of our contract."

Had he messed up? Got the wrong end of the stick? She'd just seemed so energized when the job offer came through. Jubilant, even.

"Look..." He took both her hands in his. They lay limply in his palms. "We will give you the highest of recommendations, of course. Not that you need them, seeing as you already have the job. I just want you to know that what we've shared outside of the office these past few weeks—"

Something flickered across her eyes that he couldn't

pin down. Before he could put a name to it she blinked and replaced her shocked expression with a bright smile.

"Good!" She pulled her hands out of his, rubbed them on her thighs, then gave them a clap together. "Happy to know I have your professional support."

Ty began to flounder. Had he read her enthusiasm the wrong way? Surely this was what she wanted?

"If it was surgery you were after I'd be offering you a contract in a minute, but Piedmont isn't the best place for you—"

She waved her hands for him to stop. "Please. I get it. You're being very generous." She popped on a very bad German accent. "I love *schnitzel und kuchen*. Vienna vill be amazink!"

She looked anything but happy.

"Kirri, please don't think I'm saying this because I don't believe in you. It's not that at all. You know as well as I do that Piedmont isn't the right place for the type of leaps you're hoping to make. Vienna is—Japan is."

Kirri abruptly stood up. "Yes, well… Lucky for me I like sushi, too." She pulled out her phone and opened the app for a taxi.

A few deeply uncomfortable minutes later it arrived, and without so much as a backward look she disappeared into the night.

Walking up the stairs toward his bedroom, he felt like he was hauling boulders of grief. He'd just said goodbye to the woman he loved. Why did doing the right thing have to come at such a cost?

Lulu appeared in the doorway. "Papa? Has Kirri gone for the night?"

Worse. She'd very likely gone for good.

"I'm afraid so, little one."

Lulu's lower lip quivered. "Has she gone forever?"

Ty looked blindly out toward the street and silently

pulled his daughter into his arms, so she wouldn't see the anguish in his face. Something core-deep told him it *was* forever. And that it was all his fault. He'd just hammered a nail into a coffin he'd built himself.

"You were right. I was wrong!" Kirri shouted at her phone as she haphazardly threw a blouse into her suitcase.

There was no point in packing things nicely because she never wanted to look beautiful for anyone ever again. Not after this fiasco.

How could she have thought Ty loved her?

I think you should go.

The words echoed in a loop in her head. If only there was a way to turn it off.

He wanted her to go.

This felt about a million times worse than when her ex had dumped her all those years ago. Worse because now she knew *exactly* what she was missing. And Lulu! How could he have let her cuddle Lulu like that when he knew he was going to give her the brush-off?

Pure, unadulterated heartbreak. That was what she was feeling.

The only way he could have been more blunt would have been for him to say, *It's all been a mistake. So sorry. My bad! Here's your ticket out of town—now go.*

"G'day, Kirri." Her brother's voice was as dry as ever. "I see someone woke up on the wrong side of the bed."

"Oh, stuff you and your niceties." Kirri wasn't in the mood for witty banter. In fairness, she wasn't in the mood for anything except for crying. Weeping or raging. Those were her two options. So she'd chosen the latter and she was taking it out on her big brother. He was stoic. He could take it.

She threw in a pair of heels she never should have

packed. Fancy nights out on the town. What had she been *thinking*?

"What am I right about?"

"Coming to Piedmont for research."

"Why? I thought I was going to have drag you out of there kicking and screaming."

He was. Right up until the minute she'd figured out Ty didn't love her as much as she loved him.

"It was a set-up," she snapped.

It wasn't, but saying as much made her feel better.

"What? The thing in Piedmont?"

"*Yes*, the thing at Piedmont! What else would we be talking about?"

"Well…"

Lucius's deep voice came across the line as clearly as if he was sitting next to her.

"I was thinking it might be about the reference request I just received from a certain biochemistry clinic in Vienna."

"Oh." She flopped down on the side of the bed. "That."

"Looks like the opportunity of a lifetime."

"It is."

A sob caught in her throat. It was the perfect job offer for an over-emotional, highly charged, heartbroken Australian doctor intent on filling the baby void and now the love void with all-consuming research.

She scooped up a pair of socks from the floor and threw them into her suitcase.

"Kirri, back up. Will you please explain to me, as if I am simpleton, what the hell is going on? I thought you were getting on blue blazes there."

Her heart was breaking. That was what was going on.

"I am. Well, on the surgical floor. Not so much on the research floor, which is why Ty thinks I should go."

He also didn't love her. If he did, he'd hardly be pushing her out the door, would he?

More tears cascaded down her cheeks. She didn't even know why she'd called Lucius. It wasn't like he was going to offer her any advice beyond telling her to come back and get to work. No. This was it. Her future was mapped out. She was going to become a *lederhosen*-wearing science nerd who ate cake for supper. And there'd be a cat. She'd need at least one prescient being in her life to care if she lived or died.

Lucius didn't say anything. Her insides churned with frustration. If she was going to feel awful about this one thing then she wanted to feel awful about everything in her life. Get it all over with.

"Did he say that he thought your research was useless?" Lucius asked.

No. He hadn't.

"He said he thought I should follow my passion elsewhere because this wasn't the place to pursue it."

A thick silence hummed between them.

"Oh, go on! Say it. I know what you're thinking!" she said.

"I don't think you do."

"Well, I do. You're thinking, *Good. Someone else has finally had the guts to tell my sister to stop her research. It's utterly pointless, so she might as well pick up her scalpel and get back to the operating theater, because it's the only thing she's any good for.*"

"I think you might be missing a few critical points here, Kirri."

She glared at the phone. Typical Lucius. Couldn't he simply listen to her rage and then say *There, there, everything's going to be all right*, like Ty would? Well, like Ty would have if she hadn't stormed off and left him to get on with the rest of his life without her.

She sighed and said a conciliatory, "Like what?"

"Well, like the compliments he's given you, for one."

"What compliments? He said he invited me here never expecting me to have a breakthrough."

"Really?"

"Yeah. Really. He expected absolutely nothing of me. Just like Dad."

"Don't compare other people to Dad."

"Why not?"

Lucius's tone darkened. "He's in a league of his own." He took a sharp inhalation, then continued before Kirri could speak. "I think what you're missing is the big picture."

"That's exactly what Ty said!" Kirri interjected.

"If more than one person you trust is telling you the exact same thing, do you think perhaps it's time to slow down and actually listen?"

She started to snap back a retort, then stopped herself.

Trust?

She trusted Lucius and she trusted Ty.

"So what did Ty say to you? Exactly. No embellishments, please."

She saluted at the phone. So many instructions. Then again, he was the first person—the *only* person—she'd thought of calling when her life had crumbled into a million tiny pieces.

"Okay, fine…" She huffed. "Here's *exactly* what he said."

When she'd finished, Lucius intoned, "For someone so smart you can really be clueless sometimes—you know that, Kirri?"

"Well, thank you very much." She sniffed.

"I didn't hear anything in there about you being hopeless, or incapable, or any of the self-flagellating insults you've no doubt heaped upon yourself."

"He said he wanted me to leave."

"He *said*," Lucius replied slowly, "that he wanted you to follow your dreams. He was being supportive."

"How on earth does he know what my dreams are?" she all but bellowed into the phone.

Lucius started laughing.

Kirri's hackles flew up another notch. "This is *not* funny."

Lucius, still laughing, asked, "You're in love with him, aren't you?"

Her heart flew into her throat. "How on earth did you—?"

"Oh, c'mon, Kirri. No one gets that upset when one of the most prestigious physicians in the pediatric world says one teeny-tiny thing they don't like. Does he love you?"

She choked out a no.

Lucius was silent for a minute, then asked, "Did he tell you as much?"

Again, she said no.

"Listen, K… It sounds to me as if he's trying to do everything right by you. Whereas I bulldoze in and tell you to stop your research, *he* says if that's what makes you happy go for it. If that isn't love…"

Kirri mulled it over. Lucius loved her in an overprotective brotherly way. Even though it was annoying, it was strangely comforting. Whereas Ty…

She silently swore.

Ty knew more than anyone that life was for living. He was the last person on earth to stop someone from following their dreams, because he knew everyone only had one life to live.

Her stomach lurched. Could he have told her to pack her bags and leave because he *loved* her?

"Kirri? Are you still there?" Lucius didn't wait for her to answer. "What is it you really want? Is it research?"

No. No, it wasn't. It was to love Ty. Ty and Lulu. And the rest of his huge, wonderfully batty family.

More than that, she wanted to be able to give him a child. A sibling for Lulu. Several, if she could.

But she couldn't. No amount of medical breakthroughs would ever change that one brutal fact.

The thought hit her like a bulldozer.

That was what this was all about. A perverse Gift of the Magi. He was handing her the world he thought she wanted and the one thing she wanted to give him, she couldn't. Was it time to put herself out there? Dare to tell him how she really felt about him?

"I want to be with Ty," she said.

The trial run at admitting the truth felt good.

"I know," Lucius said gently.

"Who made *you* so wise?" She sniffled, and then said, "What on earth am I meant to do about it? He wants me to go to Vienna."

"As your big brother, it's my responsibility to help you see what you can't."

"Which is…?"

"Until you admitted as much you weren't ready to love him. Now it's time to believe in yourself. You're good enough. Just as you are. I know the baby thing kills you, but don't let it define you. You're worth loving. You don't need some hi-tech bells-and-whistles invention to prove you're a good person. You *are* a good person. One of the best."

Kirri felt as though her heart would burst. Her brother thought all those things about her? "But—but you told me you weren't going to let me continue."

"I know. I can be an ass, and I don't always have the best technique for communicating what I really want to say."

"What *do* you really want to say?"

"That I don't care that you were born the way you were.

You're perfect just as you are. The research thing was a bandage for a wound you need to let heal. And you're going to have to find another way to make yourself feel whole."

The way she felt when she was with Ty.

Was giving up her research something she could do and still feel whole?

A fire lit in her belly so hot and fierce she instantly knew the answer. She needed to see Ty—to find out if she was the only who was measuring her personal worth in tandem with her value as a medical innovator.

It didn't matter two beans to her brother. And she knew there was no point in calling her father. He'd always be stuck in his ways, and some wounds… Some wounds were better left as scars that would remind a girl of just how far she'd come.

"So…" Kirri wiped away a few remaining tears. "Does this mean you've had my back all along?"

"Course I have. You're my little sister."

Her heart squeezed tight. Hearing him say that meant the world. "Lucius? Do you think leaving here would make me an idiot?"

"Pretty much."

She laughed. "I can still rely on you for total honesty, then, I see?"

"Always," he said, his voice infused with so much affection she felt as though she were receiving her first ever proper hug from him.

"Lucius?"

"Yes?"

"I love you."

"Love you too, kiddo. Now, go and tell your boyfriend you love him."

She didn't need telling twice.

CHAPTER ELEVEN

TY STOOD OUTSIDE Kirri's door and stared at the huge bouquet of flowers. It was the armload of Australian wildflowers Lulu had helped him select. Was this the right thing? For Kirri, for Lulu, for him?

Damn straight it was.

He moved his hand toward the door.

It opened before he made contact.

Kirri screamed.

Ty winced. "That wasn't quite the reaction I was hoping for."

Kirri pressed her hands to her chest as she composed herself. "Sorry. I wasn't expecting you to be there."

"I need to talk to you."

"Good." She looked him straight in the eye. "I need to talk to *you*."

Ty looked past her shoulder into the bedroom and saw the half-packed bag. His heart plummeted. Talking a headstrong woman into loving you for the rest of her life wasn't a skill he had in his arsenal.

"Packing's going well, I see."

Beautifully observed, Ty. Now, grow a pair! You've operated on twenty-week-old babies still inside their mothers. Tell her how you feel.

Kirri's dark lashes fluttered a moment, and her cheeks pinked up as her blue eyes met his again. She'd been crying. A lot, from the looks of things. She also looked a bit sheepish.

"Um…about that…"

And just like that a ray of hope lit his life up.

The flowers hit the ground. His heart pounded against his chest and in one long-legged stride he was cupping her face in his hands and tasting her sweet dusty-rose lips. Never before had a kiss felt so fortifying.

Her body language spoke volumes. The arm around his waist said *I love you.* Her hand on his heart said, *We are connected.* Her lips tasting and exploring his as if it were their very first kiss said *Never let me go.* He wouldn't. Not ever again. Whatever they needed to do to make this work…find time to explore the possibilities…he would do it.

After they'd held one another for a while she gave him a soft kiss and said, "I guess you've figured out I've struggled with making the right decision."

"It's a *very* big decision."

"Not if you know you're in love with a man in Atlanta."

Ty pulled Kirri close and held her tight. "I love you, too. I just want to do the best by you. Not stifle you with a life you don't want to lead."

Kirri pulled back and looked at him as if he was crazy. "I think we are both suffering from a severe case of getting hold of the wrong end of the stick."

"You were so excited about the research in Vienna. The professional advances you'd be able to make there, Kirri—they'd be huge."

She nodded, her eyes flicking away as she no doubt pictured the high-tech lab there.

"It's a huge decision. Especially when there's a child involved. A child who, by the way, picked out these." He scooped up the flowers and held them out to her with a small bow.

Kirri's eyes filmed over as she pressed her fingers to her mouth.

"Is…?" Ty's heart caught in his throat. "Is Lulu a problem?"

"No! I adore Lulu. She's amazing. But…"

"But…?" Ty's deepest fears turned the heat in his chest to ice in his veins.

"You know I'll never be able to give her a brother or sister—if things go that way."

"My love, I'm going into this with eyes wide open."

"What do you mean by that?"

Ty put the flowers on the breakfast bar, then turned to her. "No one is expecting you to make a final decision right here and now. About any of it. Vienna. Trying things with me. The changes you're facing are huge. Moving country. Continent, even. Loving me. My child."

"In fairness, the loving you and Lulu part is pretty easy," she confessed, with the first hint of a proper smile teasing at the corners of her mouth. "It's the lifestyle changes that go with it that have got me all twisted up inside."

Kirri traced a line down his arm, then pressed her hand to his cheek before she spoke again.

"I'm probably a bit too used to being impetuous. The plus side, I suppose, of having your big brother as your boss. He's relatively flexible about forgiveness."

The warmth in those blue eyes of hers told him something had shifted in her relationship with her brother. In the right direction.

"Not that you aren't flexible," she went on. "But you have Lulu to consider, and—and if you want a sibling for her that's impossible with me."

"Most things aren't entirely impossible," he said.

It was a weighted statement and they both knew it. He was saying he was willing to explore adoption. Fostering.

The possibility that Lulu would be an only child if that suited all three of them.

"But if you want to go to Vienna…you should go."

Her lip quivered. "I'm terrified that letting my research go will make you think less of me. It's how things work in my family. To get attention you have to *do* something. Something valuable. Lucius got the worst of it, being the son and heir and all that, but I always thought—" Her voice broke but she pushed on through. "I thought that if I couldn't give my parents grandchildren, maybe I could give them the kudos of having a daughter who'd achieved something no one else in the world had."

Ty's heart twisted tightly for her. How awful. To think that love came as part of a merit package.

"Kirri, I admire your work. It's incredible. But that's not how I think, darlin'. I love you for *you*. Hell…" He swept a lock of hair away from her cheek. "If you wanted to set up a peach pie stall I'd still love you. Or take bubble baths all day. Don't get me wrong—I'd love to have you on the surgical staff. That's what I can offer you, and I think you'd be a brilliant addition to the team. But…and I may regret saying this… I'd still love you if you chose to stuff my offer in my face and move to Vienna, if you really thought that was what would make you happy. Long-distance relationships can work. Lulu's never been to Vienna. Nor have I."

Kirri looked at him in astonishment. "You'd consider a long-distance relationship?"

"I'd consider anything if it meant giving us more time to figure out what this is between us," Ty said, from the bottom of his heart. "Whatever you choose, know this: I have never once considered your inability to have children as a factor in whether or not I fall in love with you." He gave a self-effacing laugh. "If it makes you feel any better, I haven't been all that sure that anyone would be interested in falling in love with a widower surgeon whose life revolves around his nutty family."

Kirri started laughing. "Are you kidding me? That is one seriously smokin' hot package!"

Their laughter filled the room, replacing the pain they'd shared.

Ty took one of her hands in his and gave the back of it a kiss. "Look, it's up to you what you choose. I know how important your research is to you. But I'd hate to think that you believe what you do for a living defines who you are."

She threw him a quirky look. "Have you been on the phone with my brother?"

"No, but it sounds like we have a similar opinion." He slipped his fingers through her hair and tipped his forehead to hers to give her a soft kiss. "You are amazing. With or without all the wondrous things you do. Your heart, your soul, your generosity. Maybe not so much your bowling..."

She gave him a playful poke in the ribs.

"Kirri, *you* are who I'd love to have in our lives—not your certificates of achievement. But if Lulu isn't a priority for you..." He steadied his voice.

Damn, this was hard.

"Don't," Kirri cut in. "I know Lulu's happiness is paramount. I would never ask you to live life my way, especially if it would compromise her happiness. She's your number one girl." She spoke without envy. And with love in her voice she continued, "Lulu's your world."

"My world has room for you in it, too, Kirri. *And* my family's world. We all love you." He gave a self-effacing laugh. "I think I probably corner the market on loving you the most, but suffice it to say if there's anything I can do or say to convince you to consider being my girl—even if we have to push the boundaries in figuring out how it works—my heart is yours."

Kirri bit down on her lip, her eyes bright with unshed

tears. "It's just all so different to how I imagined finding my happiness."

"Not everything comes in the package we expect," he said.

"You can say that again!"

Kirri laughed and swept away a couple of tears that had lost their battle with gravity. She gave Ty a kiss, filled with gratitude that they were talking. She had spent so much of her life blinkering herself toward her mission to succeed—who knew how much *actual* life she'd missed? Moments like this. Honest, pure, loving moments when, if she was brave enough, she could change her life forever.

She ran her fingertips over Ty's dark stubble and traced her finger along his lips. When she reached the center he kissed them.

You'd be a fool to give this up for pride.

Many other men in his shoes—men with a daughter to protect and care for—would have shown her the door. Booked her airplane ticket themselves. But Ty was a cut above the rest, and he was willing to work with her to find a way for them to live happily together.

"All of this is finally making me realize that the things we *think* we want are not necessarily the best things for us." She leant back on the couch, hearing the astonishment in her own voice as she said, "I had a long talk with my big brooding brother and who knew? He's got a heart the size of Australia and it seems I was the last person to notice."

Ty ran his finger along the back of her hand for a moment, clearly gathering his thoughts. When he did speak, his voice hummed with an intensity she'd never heard from him before.

"As we're spilling our hearts here, you should know I've had my own learning curve to climb. When Gemma died, as you can imagine, my world fell to bits."

Kirri nodded. How could it not have?

"Before she passed I worked with an incredible surgeon as an intern. He knew everything about everything—or so I thought. He liked to do things by the book. *His* book. Safety first was his motto. If you followed the rulebook nothing could go wrong! Was I learning? Absolutely. But I was only learning how to do things *his* way."

Kirri chewed on the inside of her cheek, unsure where this was going.

"Anyway, I was working all the hours God sent. Then Gemma got her diagnosis, Lulu was born, Gemma lost her battle, and for a few months there I was utterly incapable of work. I didn't go in. *Couldn't* go in. The guilt I felt for having devoted myself to the hospital instead of treasuring the time we had together—" His voice caught in his throat but he pushed through. "I know I can't blame myself for not knowing Gemma's life would be so cruelly shortened, but I *can* blame myself for not having prioritized our lives over my work."

Kirri's heart ached to hear the pain in his voice, but something told her he was putting himself through this for a reason. For *her*.

"How did you get through it?" she asked.

He rubbed his thumb along the back of her hand and shot her a soft smile. "My family. A few tough-skinned friends. To be honest, I'd neglected the handful of friends I had left in those final few weeks Gemma and I had. And after she died I didn't want to see anyone. My mentor let me go. No blame there. He had to. Patients don't wait around for a widower to get his act together. In all honesty, if it hadn't been for my mother and sisters I'm sure Lulu wouldn't have heard a human voice for months."

"Oh, Ty. I'm so sorry you had to go through all of that."

He shook his head solidly. "Don't be. I won't say it doesn't hurt that Gemma died. It does, and it probably always will to an extent. But the thing I never expected was to be grateful for the darkness, because the light it has given me in return is something I wouldn't change for the world."

"I'm sorry. I don't understand…"

He brushed the backs of his fingers against her cheek. She so wanted to lean into him. Have him hold her tight. But he was telling her this story for a reason.

"Darlin', can't you see? If Gemma hadn't died, my life very likely would've stayed exactly as it was. I would've carried on with my shifts at the hospital, working for the same mentor. I was happy. We both were. We thought our lives were perfect just as they were. When she died—" he drew in a jagged breath "—I was forced to look at life from a different perspective."

Boy. That had to have been tough. Examining what had obviously been a perfect relationship and then figuring out how to come out of the wreckage after Gemma's death a better man.

Ty continued. "Years later than you I realized just how important it was to make a difference. Not just on a personal level, but on a professional level as well."

"How do you mean?"

"I mean I was living my professional life according to someone else's playbook. I did exactly what my mentor said, never questioning it."

The light began to dawn for Kirri. "We've basically approached life from opposite directions…"

Kirri's personal life had been pure wreckage, so she'd poured herself into forging new frontiers in her professional life, whilst Ty's personal life had been brilliant so he'd seen no need to change what he was doing professionally.

Life had pulled them together from opposite ends of the seesaw. Was now the time to prove they could find the perfect balance?

As if to prove her point, Ty continued. "Think of the lives that have been saved because I decided to look at surgery through my own eyes. Eyes that didn't want to see anyone else having to go through what I had. This is the example I'm trying to set for Lulu. This is why I offer the exchange program. To offer some fresh perspective. Sometimes all it takes is stepping out of your routine to realize whether or not it's working for you."

Kirri's chest filled with a tangle of emotions. She understood what he was saying. All work and no play was making Kirri an unhappy bunny. But was she prepared to drop all those years of hard work—years of wearing her research as a protective shield—to try something new?

"So…you think I *shouldn't* go to Vienna?"

"I'm trying to say this doesn't have to be a black and white scenario. We have options." He looked Kirri square in the eye. "The main question is, do we explore them or stick to what we know?"

Kirri began putting together what her brother had said with what Ty was trying to communicate.

Give this new life a chance.

"What was it that finally clicked for you? When you decided to start the Piedmont Women and Baby Pavilion?"

Ty answered solidly. "No matter what I did, or how I behaved, I wasn't going to get to live the life I thought I would be living with Gemma because there was nothing I could do to bring her back. My only choice was to stop craving what I couldn't have and get busy living the life I had."

The penny dropped—and as it did, the tears began to fall.

Ty pulled her into his arms. "Everything's going to be all right, darlin'. I promise."

"I know!" she sobbed. "It's just so hard."

"What is?"

"Letting go of the crutch I've been holding on to for so long."

"Your research?"

"Yup." She swept away another sheet of welcome tears. Welcome because for the first time they felt healing. "You're absolutely right. I've been avoiding my own life because I've been trying to live the one I'd never have."

She looked into Ty's eyes and saw encouragement and love. He was proof that joy could blossom out of sorrow. That there was life beyond a devastating blow. She had a cornucopia of blessings, and all she had to do was open up her arms and embrace them.

Eventually her breathing steadied. "I can't believe I've been so blind..."

Ty stroked her cheek with his thumb. "I wouldn't say blind. Let's call it 'not entirely focused'."

She giggled and wiped away yet more tears. A shift was happening inside her. One that would change her for the rest of her life if she was brave enough.

"So. What I need to do is live the life I have, knowing I'll never have a child of my own."

He nodded. "As cruel as it is, you won't get that life. You know that."

"I know..." she hiccupped. "I just thought... I thought if I worked hard enough...made a different kind of baby..."

"The baby grow bag?"

She nodded. "I thought if I made that and got my name on a door, or a plaque, or a trophy to put on a shelf, then the hole in me would be filled. But the truth is nothing will fill it. The same way, I suppose, that nothing will ever replace the love you had for Gemma."

"True. But there's no point in looking at the emptiness. What matters is what I *do* have." He went on with a big old smile on his face. "I have Lulu. I have the nuttiest family this side of the Mississippi. And, if you'll have me, I sure as hell would love to have you in my life. Whichever way we can do it. I'd far rather try to make it work than give up now."

She nodded. "I would love that. But on one condition."

Ty's eyes narrowed. He was listening.

Kirri could hardly believe she was hearing the words that came out of her mouth. "Did you mean it about having me on the surgical staff?"

"What about your research?"

"I think I need to let that go."

"I would never ask that of you..."

"I know. But it's time."

A lightness she hadn't expected to feel filled her chest.

"To give it up completely?" Ty looked astonished. Happy. But amazed.

She tipped her head back and forth. "I think what I'd like to do is fly over to Vienna and share my findings with the team, then leave it with them."

There was an edge of doubt in his voice. "If that's what would truly make you happy..."

"You and Lulu make me happy."

Her answer elicited a broad, gorgeous smile. She steadied herself before asking the big question. The one that counted the most.

"Are you one hundred percent sure you'll never resent me for not being able to have a child?"

He shook his head. "Darlin', I never thought I'd fall in love again, let alone have another child. Having you in our lives is miracle enough. I love you exactly the way you are. If having more children had been an issue I never would've taken things as far as they've gone. We have Lulu. We're perfect as we are. A family."

We. A family.

Her heart skipped a beat. "Is adoption something you'd ever consider?" she asked.

Ty brushed his thumb along her cheek. "In all honesty, I hadn't thought of it because I didn't have you. It's not something I'd rule out, though. Or fostering." He dropped a kiss on her forehead. "Listen, there's a whole world of possibilities that can open up for us, but I think we need to do this as clear-eyed as possible. You need to go to Vienna and see what's there, and then we'll get on with living our lives the best we can."

He was right. It was time. Time to trust. Time to love.

CHAPTER TWELVE

"RIGHT, THEN." TY hung up his phone and gave Lulu his best reassuring smile. "He hasn't heard from her since she left for the airport."

Lulu's eyebrows dove together. "But she's coming back, right?"

She was. She'd sent him the itinerary. But he was feeling a bit like his daughter right now. Seeing was believing.

"Lucius said she was." He ruffled his daughter's hair, much to her annoyance. Fair enough. They were both edgy. "Lucius said she was very clear about the fact he should hire a replacement, so..."

"So that means she's coming to Atlanta to stay!" Lulu beamed. "And did you ask the question?"

"I did."

"Did he say yes?"

"He said..." Ty cleared his throat and put on an appalling version of an Australian accent. "It wasn't his place to say yes, and his sister would do as she jolly well pleased."

Lulu clapped her hands. "I'm going to have an uncle who lives Down Under!"

Ty laughed and pulled her into his arms for a quick cuddle, so she wouldn't see the nerves that were tugging his forehead closer to the bridge of his nose.

He and Kirri had agreed not to speak whilst she was in Vienna. It seemed insane now, given the fact he'd told her he wanted nothing more than for her to be in their lives each and every day. But showing her he would support her even if she did suddenly decide she needed to work in Austria had seemed paramount.

He'd been shocked when she'd rung him after a week to say she needed to go to Sydney. They'd tried to talk again, but with the time difference and his work, and childcare demands, their conversations had never got beyond some quick *I'm fine... I love you* chats.

"Not yet, you don't. Right, then, little one. Shall we go get some barbecue?"

Lulu heaved a dramatic sigh. "It's more fun when Kirri's there."

"Only one more sleep until she's back, sweetheart."

And he hoped to God all the sleeps from there on out would be together.

"Okay, Daddy. Let's get this show on the road!"

Lulu marched out of the house and down to the car as if she were in a parade.

He smiled at the doorframe as he locked up. The last time he'd carried Kirri through this door he'd had no idea whether their futures would intertwine or not. The next time he carried her through it he hoped more than anything she'd be wearing a white dress.

Kirri looked at her phone. She was fifteen minutes early, but that didn't mean Ty wouldn't arrive any minute now. It was Tuesday night and that meant only one thing: barbecue, biscuits and bowling.

"Checking your watch every five seconds isn't going to make him come any faster, honey."

Kirri grinned sheepishly at Chuck, and then at the house specialty, a plate of fried green beans with a bit of ranch dip on the side he was slipping onto the checkered-cloth-covered table.

"You trying to give me a heart attack while I wait?" she asked.

Chuck laughed and gave her shoulder a squeeze. "Nah, honey. I'm giving you some extra special soul food to keep that smile on your face. Good to have you back."

"It's good to be here."

She meant it, too. Her week in Vienna had been absolutely amazing. The team there had been astonished at how far she'd come doing research on her own and with limited resources. They'd said if she wanted to stay they'd find a way to make it happen. What had amazed her had been her response.

"No, thank you. I'm busy with a new project now."

A project that involved relocating to Atlanta to see if she could build a new life with a man who'd made her see that she was worth loving just as she was.

She glanced at the doorway, willing him to appear.

"You been away to Australia?" asked Chuck.

She nodded. "And Vienna."

"Vienna!" Chuck looked impressed. "What on earth were you doing there?"

"Finding out that I wanted to live here."

Chuck laughed. "Honey, I coulda told you that the first day you walked in here."

Kirri's eyes widened.

"Oh, don't give me those big ol' blue eyes of yours. He was looking at you the same way you were looking at him. And don't try to deny it. I've been round the block enough to know lovey-dovey looks when they're right in front of me."

Kirri held up her hands with a grin. "Guilty."

He was right. The moment she'd handed her research over to the elite team of scientists in Vienna her heart had told her exactly what she wanted to do. Get on a plane and come back home.

She'd swung by Sydney, to wrap things up there, to sell her apartment. Help Lucius hire a replacement. Give him the big old hug she'd been dying to give him ever since they'd had their heart-to-heart.

And then she'd packed up a few bags and got on a plane.

She crossed her fingers and stared at the door. Just a few more minutes and she'd know if she'd made the right call.

Lulu ran out of the car and into the restaurant the second Ty parked outside of Chuck's. Before he had locked the car door he could hear her sweet little voice whooping, "She's here, she's here, she's *here*!"

Ty's heart bashed against his chest as his keys jammed against the little black box in his pocket. He'd picked it up earlier and had been going to triple-check with Lulu that she was happy for Kirri to come into their lives permanently—but it looked like things were moving ahead of schedule.

He shifted his keys to the other pocket. He didn't want a single thing to get in the way. There had been enough hurdles. Enough wondering. Enough emptiness in his life to know he'd finally found a woman worth taking a risk for.

Kirri and Lulu appeared in the doorway.

"Daddy…?" Lulu was looking at him curiously.

Kirri's eyes were sparkling with the exact same glint of recognition they'd had when they'd very first met. Soulmates.

"How was your trip?" he asked.

Kirri grinned at him. "It was great."

"The I'm-returning-to-Vienna kind of great?"

She slowly shook her head, that smile of hers spreading from ear to ear. "The I'm-returning-to-Atlanta kind of great."

Words failed him. He pulled her into his arms and

hugged her close, her sweet citrusy scent filling the air around them.

He dropped a soft kiss onto her lips. "I love you. I missed you so much it actually hurt. Lulu and I—" He pulled his daughter over by his side and gave her a squeeze. "We didn't really know what to do with ourselves when you were away, so we went shopping. Ring shopping."

Kirri's eyes glossed over with tears as Lulu jumped up and down with excitement. "You did?"

Ty nodded. "We did."

"Do you want to know what I did?" Kirri asked.

The look in her eyes and the warmth in her voice told him he definitely did want to know.

"Lay it on us," he said.

"I packed."

He twirled his finger around. "More information please, darlin'. You're killing me here."

She laughed and gave Lulu's head an affectionate scrub. "I handed over my research and I packed up my apartment in Sydney… To move here. If the offer still stands?"

Ty pulled out the small black box and flicked the lid open so she could see the ring they'd chosen. "Would this answer your question?"

Kirri's hands flew to her mouth. "Oh, Ty! It's amazing."

They all looked at the ring. White gold, with a halo of diamonds around an Australian black opal.

"It's absolutely beautiful."

Ty smiled as Lulu explained. "We went to *all* of the jewelers and said it had to remind you of home."

"Oh, it definitely does."

Kirri held out her hand as Ty slipped the ring onto her finger. It fit perfectly. And when she looked into Ty's eyes she saw nothing but love in them.

"So…can I take that as a yes?" he asked.

"You most definitely can."

Lulu squealed with delight and ran into the restaurant, where they could hear her announcing the happy news that her daddy was going to have a wife.

"You're a hundred percent sure?" Ty asked.

"I've never been more sure of anything," Kirri said, tilting her face up to seal their engagement with another perfect kiss.

* * * * *

THE NEONATAL DOC'S BABY SURPRISE

SUSAN CARLISLE

MILLS & BOON

Thanks for our years of friendship.
Love you, War Eagle!

CHAPTER ONE

AMANDA LONGSTREET PULLED her large suitcase behind her as she exited the Kingsford Smith Airport in Sydney, Australia. The heated air touching her skin put the winter weather of Atlanta, Georgia, well behind her. She enjoyed traveling but she had never gone this far. Twenty-two hours in a small seat flanked by two strangers hadn't been as much fun as she'd envisioned, but still the excitement of coming to Sydney grew within her.

She was counting on the destination making up for the discomforts of the flight. The Piedmont Women and Baby Pavilion, where she worked back in Atlanta, would have probably paid for a first-class ticket for her, but she was too practical to ask. She'd much rather see the money spent on helping a couple wanting a baby.

Making her way across the street to the pick-up area, she remained mindful that in this country they drove on the opposite side of the road. Some people called it the wrong side, but it really wasn't—it was just different. She located the sign for airport pickup and stood beneath it, waiting for her car to arrive.

She scanned the area and harrumphed. Dr. Kirri West had told her Sydney was an amazing city. So far it looked like any other big airport.

Jet lag was no doubt affecting Amanda's attitude. Given a few days, and a chance to explore, she'd surely agree with Kirri's opinion. Right now, all she wanted was to get to her apartment—home for the next six weeks—and crawl into bed.

Still, excitement sizzled in her. She anticipated checking out the city, but only after she'd had some rest and started her job at the clinic. After all, the experience of working at the Harborside Fertility and Neonatal Centre had been the reason she'd come here.

Sighing, she looked up and then down the paved area. *Where was the car?* Her contact at the clinic had said there would be one coming for her. She was past ready for it to arrive.

Patience wasn't her virtue. More than once her mother and friends had told her that her life plan wasn't the be all and end all of existence. That she should lighten up a little.

Even with that advice in mind she'd tucked into her purse a list of things she wanted to do and see in Sydney. As a child, she'd been just as focused on her goals. She had a plan for her life. So far she'd remained on track. In every aspect but one.

Amanda pushed her hair out of her face. Having the chance to work with Kirri had been a real pleasure, but to be under the tutelage of Kirri's brother would only help Amanda rise in her profession. She'd heard enough about Dr. Lucius West from Kirri to know he was a focused and exacting doctor, who had little time for anything but his work. He sounded like a doctor who liked things done by the book. They should get along well.

Where was this car? Was she waiting in the wrong place?

Amanda checked the sign once more. She paced down the sidewalk and then back again, squinting into the sunshine. Had she misunderstood the instructions?

A few minutes later, to her great relief, a black car with the clinic's logo on the door pulled to a stop beside her.

She smiled as the driver climbed out.

"Ms. Longstreet?" A ruddy-faced, heavy-set man came around the back of the car.

"Yes."

"I'm here to pick you up." He pushed a button and popped the trunk lid, taking her luggage.

"I'm glad to see you."

He gave her a brief smile, stowed her suitcase in the trunk, and then opened the passenger door. While she settled in he quickly returned to the driver's seat, and they were soon moving.

She shivered. The air-conditioning blasted cold air. At least it would help keep her awake long enough to get to the apartment.

A swift movement outside the car caught her attention. A blond-haired man with long determined strides was hurrying toward the car. He carried a satchel over one shoulder and pulled along a small overnight bag. His suit jacket was slung over one arm and his tie had been pulled away from his neck. It lay twisted and askew, as if he had done it in frustration.

Her heart jumped.

Dr. Lucius West. She recognized him from her internet research on the Sydney clinic.

He raised his hand and the driver pulled to the curb. After a rapid tap on the front passenger window the driver lowered it. Dr. West glanced at her with tight-lipped agitation. He said to the driver, "I'm Dr. West. I expected you thirty minutes ago. Why are you late?"

Amanda sighed. She was too tired for this drama. Maybe Kirri hadn't been exaggerating about her brother.

"Yes, sir. I was on my way to you." The driver nodded his head toward Amanda. "I had another pickup to make first."

Dr. West didn't wait for the driver to get out and open

the door for him. Instead he deposited his bag in the front seat and joined her in the back. Amanda quickly moved across the seat, fearing that if she didn't he would sit in her lap. The space shrank with him inside. She hadn't expected he'd be such a *large* man.

In addition to that unsettling fact, his pictures hadn't done him justice. He was far better-looking in person. A sliver of silver at his temples in his wavy blond hair shimmered in the sunlight, giving him a distinguished look. One that meshed with his reputation and position. On one of the websites she'd seen he had made the shortlist of most eligible bachelors in Australia. Amanda wasn't surprised. She couldn't help but be awestruck and stare.

"You are…?" he demanded as he settled in, holding his satchel in his lap.

"Amanda Longstreet."

Dr. West studied her for a moment. His eyes were a deep blue, like the ocean, instead of bright blue like his sister's. There were creases at the corners and telltale dark smudges below. Had he been on a flight as long as hers?

"You're American." His words were flat, as if he were determining a diagnosis.

"I am."

Why didn't he recognize her name? Hadn't he been told she was coming?

He continued to study her, as if trying to pull up something that was filed away in his mind.

He nodded slowly. "Ah, yes, I remember now. You're the clinical nurse specialist in the exchange program. Kirri mentioned you."

He *should* remember, since he had been one of the doctors to start it. His clinic and the clinic where she worked were two of the most prestigious and innovative in their care for mother and baby, with a special emphasis on infertility issues. Dr. Lucius West, along with Dr. Sawyer, the head of her clinic, had decided during a conference that a staff exchange to share information would be productive for both clinics. Kirri had come to Atlanta for six weeks and now, it was Amanda's turn.

She gave him her sunniest smile. "Yes, that's me."

He continued to watch her. "I'm Lucius West."

"Yes, I know. You resemble your sister." And she had ogled his picture on the computer screen more than once. "It's nice to meet you."

The opportunity to work with the world-renowned Dr. Lucius West would be the honor of a lifetime. Although Kirri had warned Amanda that her brother could be difficult. She had already started to see signs of that!

"Mmm." His attention remained on the electronic tablet he'd pulled from his satchel. "I'm sorry, I have work to attend to."

"I understand."

She did. He was the head of the clinic and she knew he must have many demands on his time.

A short while later Lucius glanced at the pretty woman huddled in the seat corner with her arms across her chest and her eyes closed. Was she asleep?

He'd forgotten all about the person coming from Atlanta for the staff exchange. It had been mentioned during one of the recent staff meetings, but he'd been checking his emails, only half listening. He'd paid no mind to the date and time of her arrival.

Not that it really mattered, but he had expected a man. Although the gender of the person was of no consequence, since he had little to do with the staff in Labor and Delivery. If he remembered correctly, that was where she would be assigned.

Giving her a closer look, he found her attractive enough, with short brown hair, clear skin and a faint tan. Her figure of full curves instead of bony angles enhanced her appeal. She wore little make-up—but that might be because she'd been on a plane for hours.

Further testimony to how drained she must be feeling was in the dark smudges that shadowed her eyes. Those green eyes which had brightened when she'd realized who he was. All in all she made for an interesting package—if he had been looking for one.

Despite her clear anticipation of working with him, he doubted he'd have much contact with her during her visit. He spent most of his time on the in vitro side of the clinic—not where she would be working. He did follow a few cases from start to finish, but there were many others on the staff who handled ninety-nine percent of the deliveries.

It would be awkward when she woke. He couldn't remember her name…

Amanda. That was it.

He mentally rolled the name around for a second. Had he ever known an Amanda? Not that he could remember.

He looked at her again. Her hair curtained her face. In her sleep she slumped further into the corner, with her chin falling to her chest. She appeared uncomfortable.

Leaning toward her, he eased his arm around her back, pulling her upright with gentleness until her head rested on his shoulder. She released a small sigh and settled against him.

He returned to his electric pad to review his emails.

A stack of work always awaited him. He liked it that way. His work was his life. He had a major part to play in making great medical advances in infertility. Once he'd tried to have a life outside the clinic. But what had that gotten him? A shattered marriage and a disillusioned heart.

Amanda snored softly. Lucius smiled.

He was tired as well. The trip home from Melbourne

after a three-day conference and a return flight delay had been topped off when his ride hadn't been waiting for him. It hadn't left him in the best of humors. Disruption of his timetable was a constant irritation. That must have shown in his manner. He undoubtedly hadn't made a good impression on his visitor.

The driver was making excellent time through the city's afternoon traffic. It wasn't long until he pulled up in front of a small apartment complex in a neighborhood Lucius didn't know well.

"Why are we stopping here?"

"This is where your young lady gets out." The driver looked at him in the rearview mirror.

She wasn't Lucius's young lady. He hadn't had one of those since his ex-wife had walked out on him.

Lucius cupped Amanda's shoulder and shook her. "Amanda, wake up. You're here."

"Uh…?" Long dark lashes fluttered upward.

The action mesmerized him. He hadn't reacted to a woman like this in years. Not since the early years of his relationship with his ex-wife. Amanda's eyes were the green of tree leaves in early spring. And there was a sparkle in them even though she'd just awakened.

"What's wrong?"

Sleep had made her voice a little coarse. Sort of sexy.

He swallowed. That wasn't a thought he should be having about a woman he'd just met.

"Nothing. We're at your place."

Her unfocused gaze met his and he watched as reality dawned on her.

Her cheeks turned pink as she pushed at her silky hair and quickly straightened. "I'm sorry. I didn't mean to fall asleep on you."

"Hey, I've made that flight to America. I know what it takes out of you."

He gave her a sympathetic smile. Now that his sister had moved there permanently he would be going a lot more often.

Amanda returned a weak one. "That doesn't ease my embarrassment."

"No reason to be embarrassed. We're at your apartment."

Lucius opened his door to climb out. Grudgingly, he conceded that her appeal grew with her confusion. Most of the women he met never appeared ruffled, or would never admit they were. He found Amanda's obvious mortification utterly charming.

Not to mention her lovely accent…

Amanda scrambled from the car behind Lucius. The driver had placed her large suitcase on the sidewalk.

Lucius said to him, "I'll be right back. Wait for me." Then he pulled out the handle of her bulky bag and started toward the apartment building.

Stunned that this busy, world-renowned doctor planned to escort her, Amanda just stood there.

He stopped after a couple of steps and looked at her. "Well…?"

"It's not necessary for you to see me to my apartment."

"I was taught that a gentleman doesn't leave a woman stranded on the side of the road." He grinned. "Especially one who has come so far."

Amanda blinked twice. Her first impression of him had been that he was a self-absorbed person, too busy for casual conversation. Yet he'd allowed her to sleep on his shoulder and now he was insisting on carrying her luggage like a bell hop.

Who was the real Dr. Lucius West?

"Surely the driver can help me with that?" She indicated her oversized suitcase.

"I'm sorry," the driver said as he moved back around the car. "I'm not allowed to do more than load and unload the trunk and drive. It's a liability issue."

Amanda looked at Lucius for confirmation.

He nodded.

"Oh, okay…thanks."

She followed Lucius to the apartment building entrance, conscious of the thump-thump of the tiny wheels of her heavy case on the sidewalk.

"Do you have a key, or do you have to call someone?" he asked.

"I have a key. I was sent all the information. I'm in Apartment 203."

She held the glass door open for him to enter. She looked for an elevator, and finding none led the way up the stairs. "Well, at least I'll be getting some exercise," she said.

"Yeah, and you're going to get plenty more of that at the clinic," Lucius drawled behind her.

He must have switched to the carrying handle, because she didn't hear the expected bumping of the luggage as they climbed.

"How far is the clinic from here?"

He placed the bag on the floor in front of the door with the gold numbers 203 tacked to it. "Maybe half a mile?"

"Great. That'll be a nice walk every day."

"I don't know this neighborhood well, but you'll need to be careful about being out at night by yourself. Get a ride with someone or take a taxi on late nights."

Amanda stopped searching through her purse for the door key and met his look. "I'll keep that in mind, but I'm very capable of taking care of myself."

He studied her from head to toe, then brought his gaze back to hers. "If you say so."

She wasn't sure she liked his tone. Thankfully she found the koala bear key chain and pulled it out.

"I see you've already gone native." He nodded toward her hand.

"I couldn't resist. Bought it off the Internet. I was so excited about coming to Australia."

"Is this your first time here?"

"Yes."

Amanda slid the key into the lock, turned the knob and opened the door. This exchange had been a blessing. She'd needed to get away.

It had been only two months since John had left without warning, breaking off their relationship. Before that unforeseen night she'd thought he was the one. Then out of the blue he had announced they were over. His reason being he couldn't compete with her. He'd said she intimidated him.

After that ugly scene she'd decided to put the priority on her career objectives. This trip gave her an opportunity to do just that.

Lucius picked up the bag. Again she waited for him to go first, and he stepped in and placed the luggage on the floor, beside a small sofa that stood in the middle of the room.

Amanda entered slowly, taking in the small but efficient-looking apartment. It consisted of one large room with a beige couch and chair, along with a TV on a stand. A galley kitchen was situated in one corner. She moved further into the room and looked through a door to find the bedroom. The space would be all she needed during her stay.

"I wondered what kind of place the board would put someone up in," Lucius murmured. "I'll have to admit this is about what I expected."

"I'll be comfortable here. I don't have much more than

this in Atlanta." Amanda walked to the kitchen counter and put her purse down. "I'm hoping to spend more time at the clinic than I do here anyway. Thanks for bringing up my case. If I'd had to carry it up, I'd be out of breath. By the way, I'm looking forward to working with you at the clinic."

He extended his hand. "It's been nice to meet you."

She placed her hand in his. A jolt of awareness spurred a quick withdrawal. The second Amanda did so she missed the size, heat and strength of his hold.

"I'm…uh…as I said, I look forward to working with you. I've heard some amazing things about you."

He grinned. "I hope you don't believe *all* my press."

"I imagine at least some of it is true."

Amanda walked toward the door. She needed him to leave so she could reorder her nerves, rattled by their brief contact.

"Thank you again."

"Goodbye, Ms…"

"Longstreet."

"Ms. Longstreet. I hope you enjoy your stay in Sydney."

He closed the door behind him as he left.

For some odd reason it seemed as if all the electricity had left the room with him. Shaking off that odd notion, Amanda carried her luggage into the bedroom. There she found a double bed and a nightstand. Off to the left was a door that led to a small bath.

She left the bag near the bed and returned to the living area. Putting away her clothes could wait. She needed to find a place to buy some food and then she could tend to some other things. After that she'd get a shower and some sleep. Tomorrow would be a big day at the clinic.

Would she see Lucius?

That didn't matter. She wasn't here to dissect and admire Dr. West. Even if he *was* drool-worthy, with his fathomless eyes, sexy grin and square jaw.

Kirri had told Amanda he was brilliant, and everything Amanda had read about him confirmed that. However, Lucius West in person was larger than life.

Enough of that kind of thinking. She needed to get busy.

Seeing a notebook on the kitchen counter, she opened it. Inside she found typed details of places to eat, the closest grocery store, laundry, and drug store, along with general information about the area. She was grateful for it.

Now that she was actually here, in the apartment, she felt more invigorated than when she had first stepped off the airplane. All she'd wanted to do then had been to sleep. After her nap—on Lucius, no less—she wanted to do a little exploring and see if she could pick up some food.

Who knew when she would have another chance? There was no telling what the week ahead might bring. She at least needed to buy breakfast items.

All her life she'd been a Girl Scout type of person. Always prepared. In fact, she was known for it. Many a friend in college had turned to her because they knew she'd have what they needed.

Once her roommate had asked to borrow a stapler. Amanda had directed her to the middle desk drawer, in the back, on the left-hand side.

Her roommate's response after she had located the stapler had been, "How do you *do* that?"

Amanda had answered, "I always put things back where they belong."

That part of her personality hadn't endeared her to her stepfather. Despite her being so prepared, and planning things down to the detail, he hadn't accepted her. No matter what she'd done or how good she had been it had never been enough for him. Yet she was loved by the rest of her family.

After washing her face and brushing her hair, she slipped on a clean set of clothes and put on a pair of sunglasses. She needed to stay up for a little while to get acclimated to the time-change. To help with that she decided to walk around the neighborhood in search of the store she'd read about in the notebook.

Heading outside, she turned west along a tree-lined sidewalk. After a few missteps she soon found the small grocery store, not far down the street. She smiled at the girl behind the counter and went down the first aisle.

Picking up a couple of boxes of macaroni and cheese she could use in an emergency, she added a few more items that she could pop into the microwave. She would have liked to buy a gallon of milk, but that would have been too heavy to carry back with all the other stuff she'd gathered.

If she continued to do this type of shopping she would definitely need a rolling bag to make the transportation easier… And if she wanted a wider choice, like fresh produce, she would have to either rent a car or hire a taxi and go to a larger supermarket.

The thought of renting a car came and went. Her trying to drive in town on the opposite side of the road would be more nerve-racking than beneficial especially when she wasn't familiar with the streets. She'd maybe ask someone to drive her when she became acquainted with more people.

She did know one person. *Yeah, right*. Like she would ask Lucius West to drive her around while she shopped. *That* wasn't going to happen.

With both hands full of heavily loaded plastic bags, Amanda left the store and trudged back to the apartment. She had to admit she might have over-bought, but still she had little choice but to keep walking. Not soon enough for her, she arrived.

Setting the bags on the floor, she collapsed on the couch.

She wouldn't have considered herself out of shape, but after such a long plane ride, and not having rested properly, she'd overdone it by going to the store. She'd learned her lesson.

On autopilot she put the cold groceries away, leaving the others until later. With that done, she took a hot shower and climbed into bed.

Her eyelids lowered. The bed was comfortable enough, but somehow the memory of Lucius's shoulder seemed just as nice.

CHAPTER TWO

THREE MORNINGS LATER, as Lucius walked down the hallway toward the procedure room, he thought of Amanda Long-street. She'd been interrupting his thoughts more often than he wanted to admit. Somehow she had made an indelible impression on him during their brief encounter. But right now he needed to concentrate on his patient. This woman had been trying to have a baby for three years. Nothing so far had proved successful.

As an infertility doctor, he considered hers the type of case he lived for. As a human being, it tore at his heart. He only ever saw women who were desperate for a baby. They either had trouble conceiving or carrying a baby to term. Whichever, his encounters with them invariably in-cluded high emotions.

Because of that he always went in and spoke to his pa-tients, instead of just showing up to do the procedure. They were often nervous and fearful, which might contribute to whether or not the in vitro procedure was successful. The calmer and more confident the woman could be, the better the chance of conception.

Entering the room, where his patient waited on the pro-cedure bed, he walked toward her with a sincere smile and hopefully warm assurance. He noticed his nurse, Lucy, was laying out instruments. Another person standing nearby caught his eye. His smile faded a little as he did a double-take.

Amanda.

She grinned and he nodded.

What was she doing here?

He understood she was a Labor and Delivery nurse. Surely that was where she should be. His role was getting women pregnant. It was what he excelled at, although he always had a hard time figuring out how to describe what he specialized in. Usually he defaulted to a very clinical definition.

He raised his chin and nodded to his nurse, then concentrated on his patient.

When he reached Nancy Davis, the prospective mother-to-be, he placed his hand over hers for a moment. "How're you doing?"

"I'm fine. Just a little nervous is all."

He quickly shook hands with her husband, who stood meekly in the corner.

The woman added with a desperate undertone, "This *has* to work."

"I understand. I know you've been through this a couple of times before, but you don't need to worry. I'll be doing all the work here, and I'm going to try something a little innovative during this procedure. I think it will make a difference. I've had success in the lab with it, and that gives me reason to be optimistic. We're not only going to *hope* this takes—we're going to *believe* it will."

She offered him a weak smile. "I sure hope so, Dr. West."

He did too. "You've taken your medication?"

"Yes. But I really need…" She gave a soft sob.

He didn't doubt her need. Even for him, forty thousand dollars or more each time to try and have a baby was a lot of money. It could even grow into more if there were complications. Like multiple babies…

"We'll get started here in a moment. I'm just going out to wash up and then we'll be ready to go."

He left, and soon returned to find Lucy prepared to proceed. Amanda stood beside the patient, near the end of the table, so they could easily see each other. The two women were talking quietly. Nancy's face was expressive as Amanda spoke.

Lucius approached just as Nancy laughed softly. Apparently Amanda had said something funny. The unease he'd seen on his patient's face earlier had disappeared.

He appreciated what Amanda had done. It was crucially important to this procedure that the patient was relaxed. For some unexplained reason it seemed women were often more likely to conceive when they stopped fixating on becoming pregnant. When they just let go. Amanda was helping with that part of the transfer.

He pulled his rolling chair out, settled on it, and moved to Nancy's feet. "I'll be telling you what's happening every step of the way." He moved closer. "Let me know if you feel any discomfort."

"Okay." Nancy's answer was weak, unsure.

"This shouldn't take more than a few minutes. Then we'll let you sit for a while."

The patient's husband moved closer and took Nancy's hand.

"Just like last time?" Nancy asked.

"Yes."

Lucius removed the long flexible tube that held the embryos from the incubator Lucy had rolled to his side. He literally held this couple's hopes in his hand. If all went well, they would soon have a baby.

"Now, this may feel a little different from last time. The

embryos aren't at body temperature yet. I want your body to warm them to your own natural temperature."

Amanda's soft gasp caught his attention for a second as she stepped back to stand at his shoulder. Was she planning to interrupt? She made no further move. He returned his full attention to the procedure, forgetting everyone and everything but positioning the embryos in just the correct spot.

Moments later he'd finished, and pushed the stool back so he could see Nancy.

"Now, we're going to let you sit quietly for about thirty minutes. Remember you may have breast tenderness, bloating, cramping, or constipation during the next week or so. I want to see you back in two weeks for your pregnancy test."

"Thank you, Dr. West." Nancy looked at her husband and gave him a hopeful smile.

Lucius headed out the door. In the process of removing his gloves and gown he looked back as the door opened. Amanda entered.

"Nurse Longstreet."

"Hello again, Dr. West." Her words were almost as cool as his.

"How're you adjusting to the clinic?"

"Fine. I've met a lot of great people here." She followed him in the removal of her sterile clothing.

"I'm glad to hear it."

Done, he started out the other door of the room.

"Can I have a minute of your time?" she asked suddenly. "I have a couple of questions about the procedure."

"Oh. Like…?" Something about her tone made him think it might be less curiosity and more concern—or, worse, censure.

"I understand it's not protocol to put embryos in until

they're at body temperature, so I was wondering exactly why you felt the need to do it?"

His eyes narrowed and his jaw tightened. He wasn't used to hearing that tone in relation to his work. "And you know about this protocol how…?"

"I've spent the last few days reading your clinic handbook."

Oh. That wasn't the answer he'd expected. "I see you are thorough."

"I try to be." She continued to look at him, as if waiting for an answer to her question.

Lucius shoulders stiffened as he stood straighter. His staff didn't ever question his methods or motives. He was considered by most to be ingenious and successful and his staff followed his lead.

"Do you have concerns about my technique?"

"I'm not exactly concerned about it. It's more like I'm wanting to understand why you did it that way. What if the embryos don't take because of the temperature? Couples invest too much of their life savings, time and emotion in trying to have a baby for you to go rogue. To do something on a hunch."

"Hunch!" He stepped toward her, outraged. "I'll have you know that I've been doing this type of procedure for a long time. There is experience and knowledge behind everything I do. I don't do *hunches*. Couples come to me for one reason and one reason only. They want a baby and I can often make that happen for them."

Amanda's eyes were heated as she glared at him. "I don't mean to hurt your feelings. I'm asking so I can better understand your thought process."

"That wasn't how it sounded to me. It sounded more like you were questioning my ability and my judgement."

"I'm here to learn about the procedures here from conception to delivery. That's all I'm trying to do."

"I appreciate that, but if you're going to question my skills the entire time you're here then this exchange may not work."

He ran this clinic and he wouldn't have anyone—especially an invited guest—questioning his ethics.

"I'm sorry if I've offended you. And I understand your position, Doctor, but that doesn't mean I'm not supposed to learn and gain knowledge. Part of that's asking questions. I can't learn anything from this exchange if I'm not allowed to ask questions."

"Oh, you're allowed to ask questions. What you're *not* allowed to do is question or react to something I say or do in front of a patient. You are also not allowed to imply, via your questioning, that I might have done something wrong."

Ms. Longstreet certainly had gall.

"So the great 'Baby Whisperer'—" she used sarcastic air quotes with her fingers, which made him grind his back teeth "—doesn't have to explain himself regarding following protocol, or answer to anyone when he has done something outside of the norm. Is that what I'm to understand?"

Lucius shifted from mildly irritated to angry. He took a step closer to her and look down his nose. He couldn't help but admire the fact that Amanda didn't move.

"I think you've hit the nail on the head. Isn't that what they say?"

Amanda straightened to her not inconsiderable height, but still only reached to his shoulders, and took a step toward him. Her nose was now an inch or two from his.

"I'm sorry, Doctor, but where I come from the nurses and the doctors are partners. We're all working toward the same result. We get to question what's being done because it's in our patients' best interest. Our doctors' egos have to take a back seat to that."

His lips thinned into a fine line as he glared at her. How

dared she imply that he had less than the best interests for his patients in mind?

"I can assure you that my patients *always* come first."

"I appreciate that. So why do you mind being questioned about how you do something?"

His ire eased a little. "Maybe it's the way you asked me. The tone."

"I didn't realize I had applied any 'tone.'"

She appeared innocent. Lucius stepped back. "I think this conversation has become unproductive. I have work to do."

He left the scrub room and headed down the hallway toward his office. How dared Amanda come into his procedure room for the first time and start interrogating him? Just who did she think she was?

Lucius shook his head. Far more baffling was the fact that he was impressed she had.

An hour later Lucius was still dwelling on his heated conversation with Amanda. Maybe he'd been too rough on her. But Amanda's questions had reminded him too much of his father. He'd always pushed Lucius to explain his decisions, and had questioned his methods so often Lucius had often ended up second-guessing himself.

With his father now in a care home it had been a long time since that had happened. He'd thought he'd outgrown his reaction to having his authority examined. But clearly one small American woman was all it took to bring his youthful insecurities straight back to the surface. He found it infuriating to have his ego on the carpet.

Doctors who did his type of work had to have a strong sense of self-worth—otherwise they would give up. Too often disappointments outweighed celebrations. He lived for the uplifting and exciting times when a woman became pregnant. He needed those to fortify himself against the times when he had to tell a couple the process had failed.

He'd seen the pain and the agony too many times. He thoroughly enjoyed the days he attended the Labor and Delivery Room, to see a couple holding a baby after clinging to that dream for so long. Because of those moments he hated to have his efforts second-guessed.

At one time he'd planned to have children of his own when he married, but he had been young and had thought he had plenty of time. The clinic had just opened and it was doing amazing things with great outcomes. He'd nurtured his work, thinking his wife was happy. Instead she had become steadily disgruntled with his long hours.

Melanie had been left to herself too much.

He'd known she enjoyed the social side of being a doctor's wife, and the perks of being married to a rising star in infertility medicine. He'd believed she'd be satisfied with that for a while, but he'd misjudged the depth of her loneliness.

Even when he'd realized he still hadn't been able to tear himself away from the clinic. And when he'd finally tried to make it work, to make changes in his schedule, her answer had been a firm no. Melanie's parting remark had been that he seemed a lot more interested in giving other people babies then he was in having his own.

That hadn't been true. And yet he hadn't felt Melanie's loss like he should have. He'd decided maybe she was right. He was more married to the clinic than to her. After she'd left, he'd seen a few women on and off, but had never let a relationship get past casual. He'd made his mistake and learned from it. He wouldn't try that again.

There hadn't been enough time then and nor was there now to give to a wife and family. There wasn't time for the attention they deserved. He would need somebody who understood the importance of his work and who didn't demand to have his attention on her full-time. That would be a rare person, indeed. One he didn't have time to search for.

* * *

Amanda remained perplexed about what had gone wrong between her and Lucius. She'd had no idea asking questions would overstep any professional boundary down here. But she was used to protocol being closely followed and she'd only wanted to know why he hadn't stuck to the usual script.

She had been willing to give him the benefit of the doubt. All she'd wanted was to understand the logic behind his decisions.

But apparently she'd overstepped his boundaries in general—personal as well as professional.

She'd done it again. Another man was feeling challenged by her. *Intimidated.* Some of the men she had dated had accused her of being too rigid, too controlling. She hadn't been what they wanted. She was too demanding. Time after time with a man, as soon as she'd let her guard down and allowed her true nature to show, he'd found fault with her character. None had been tactful in their criticism.

After the shock and heartache of her last love interest's rejection, she'd put her dream of finding Mr. Right, getting married and starting a family to one side for a while. Instead she'd turned her concentration on her career goals and put all her energy into achieving them.

That had meant coming here to Harborside and being involved in the amazing work Lucius and his staff were doing in reproduction. The experience would be an important stepping-stone to becoming Director of Nursing at her clinic back home.

Somehow she had to neutralize Lucius's animosity and earn his respect. She had to put them back on the footing they'd been on before he'd left her apartment that first night.

She had no doubt he was a gifted and dedicated doctor. But how could she have known that asking forthright questions about his procedural decisions was off-limits? Come to think of it, he'd become annoyed with her far too quickly. Did that unexpected reaction mean she'd called attention to him doing something he shouldn't? Or was he hyper-sensitive for some other reason?

She shook her head to clear the unanswerable questions away. She'd spend her time learning and gaining all the invaluable experience she could while she was here, and stay out of his way as much as possible.

After he'd left her in a huff she'd gone back to the Labor and Delivery Department. There she'd joined one of the nurses she had met on her first day at the clinic.

Apart from Lucius, everyone on the staff had been friendly, and more than willing to answer her questions. If they didn't know the answer off the top of their head, they'd made an effort to find out.

Now, as Amanda strolled toward her apartment, she found herself continuing to be distracted by her confrontation with Lucius.

The clinic was amazing, and doing some outstanding work—it was everything Kirri had said it was. The only issue Amanda had was with Lucius. Her unintentional professional offense had put a damper on her visit. He had been so kind about taking her luggage up to her apartment, proving her first impression of him wrong. And from that she'd assumed they'd gotten past the initial rough spot of getting acquainted.

Yet here they were.

Kirri was such a charming person Amanda hadn't imagined there'd be any issue with her brother. And when Lucius had made the comment about the exchange not working Amanda had been shocked. She didn't appreciate being threatened. She'd actively campaigned to participate in this exchange and she needed to record it on her résumé as being a successful experience. Lucius's subtle implication that he might send her back to Atlanta in disgrace made her feel sick.

She had to figure out some way to work this out… smooth things over with him. After a night's sleep and a good think she'd form a plan to convince him that she'd respect his professional space in future.

Climbing the stairs, she entered her apartment. She'd bought a few things at the local department store to make the space a little more "hers". A vase with a few flowers now sat on the coffee table. She had also found a couple of inexpensive yellow throw pillows to add to the sofa. The items gave the tiny space some personality. She liked living in Sydney. It would be easy to make it like home.

The next morning, she arose determined to speak to Lucius as soon as she could. She'd tossed and turned all night, rehearsing what she would say. Somehow she needed to get him back on her side.

As soon as she had a free moment at the clinic, she went in search of him. After being directed to his office she discovered he wasn't there. She pulled up the procedure schedule to see if he was doing one. He wasn't. She finally found somebody who told her to check the nursery.

Despite being sure she'd heard the nurse correctly, she couldn't imagine why Lucius would be in the baby nursery. But Amanda didn't argue and went to look.

To her great surprise, she *did* find Lucius there, sitting in a rocking chair holding a sleeping newborn.

Amanda's breath caught in her throat. Her heart softened at the sight of the big man holding the small child so tenderly. He looked at ease, like she hadn't seen him before. As if he had no worries in the world or any concerns about this famous clinic and his part in it.

The man before her now and the man she'd known yesterday were two vastly different people. Never would she have guessed that she would see him like this.

It took her a few moments to compose herself. She stood there enthralled, wanting to take in this perfect example of what was right with the world.

A nurse brushed by her and broke the mood.

Amanda took a couple of steps forward. "Dr. West—Lucius?"

He gave her a preoccupied look.

The fleeting thought that he'd make a good father went through her head. She didn't need to have those types of ideas about Lucius. They weren't going to become friendly enough for her to have that kind of opinion about him. Hadn't Kirri said he was married to his job? So much so his marriage had failed?

"Yes, Nurse Longstreet?"

"I…uh… I was wondering if you had a moment so we could talk?"

"I have a procedure in about twenty minutes."

She looked around. Was that a no? She wasn't giving up. "Maybe I could buy you a cup of coffee?"

"I'm sorry, I don't drink it this time of the day."

He wasn't making this easy for her. "A soft drink?"

One of the babies cried. "As you can see, I'm a little busy here. What do you want to discuss?"

She clasped her hands together and took a step toward him. "I'd really appreciate it if we could talk about what happened yesterday."

He looked toward one of the cribs and nodded his head to the side. "Grab that baby and have a seat."

Amanda scooped the newborn into her arms. A nurse entered, saw Amanda, and stepped out again. Amanda took a seat in the rocking chair across from Lucius. Holding the baby close, she rocked and cooed. The child settled.

"I believe you have a knack for handling babies," he said.

The admiration in his voice warmed her in an unexpected way.

"I can do more than deliver them. And I've held more than one in my time. Including a niece and a nephew."

A shadow entered Lucius's eyes and then was quickly gone. Great—she'd said something else to upset him when she had been trying to gain his trust.

Softly she said, "I thought the babies stayed in the room with their mothers."

"Most of them do, but we take in foundlings without question. This is a safe place for mothers to leave their unwanted babies. And one or two babies belong to mothers who had difficult deliveries and need their rest. That's why we have this many in here right now."

The baby Lucius held let out a gentle sigh.

"I see you have some skill in this area too," said Amanda.

"Thanks. This is a good place to come and decompress."

Lucius needed to decompress? He gave the impression he had everything under control at all times.

She looked around to see if the nurse had returned. "Look, Lucius…um… Dr. West, I want to apologize about yesterday. I didn't intend to question your authority. I certainly would never undermine you in front of a patient. I'm sorry if you felt I had."

"I appreciate that. However, after some thought I believe I might have overreacted to what you asked me."

Amanda struggled to conceal her astonishment. She hadn't expected him to say anything like that.

Lucius continued. "I was raised by a man who constantly questioned what I did. Consequently I don't like to be interrogated about my decisions."

For a moment he frowned, as if confused about what he'd said.

When he didn't continue, she offered, "Thank you for sharing that. Now I understand your negative reaction to my professional curiosity. This exchange program is important to me. I need it to go well."

"Why's that?"

Should she reveal something as personal as her hopes and dreams? But her career plans weren't a secret, and she was too far from home for it to matter if she talked about them.

"I believe coming here is my opportunity to get an important promotion back home. The fact that I'm here watching you perform such innovative procedures, and learning how and why you operate as you do, can only be good for my career. As lofty as it sounds, I want to help hurting women have babies."

"In that we'll always agree."

For some reason that gave Amanda a warm feeling—as if they had found solidarity on this particular point, no matter their personal issues.

The nurse stuck her head in the door. "Dr. West, they're ready for you in the procedure room."

"Please tell them I'm on my way."

He slowly rose and gently laid the baby in a bassinet. He looked at Amanda, still holding the now sleeping infant.

"I'll see to it that you get every opportunity to learn while you're here. Including getting answers to any questions you may have."

"Thank you, Lucius. I'd really appreciate that."

He lifted the child from her arms with practiced ease and lay her in the empty crib.

Amanda stood and Lucius extended his hand.

"Agreed?"

She slipped her hand into his. An electric volt shot through her, as it had the first time he'd clasped her hand. They shook hands.

Too soon, or perhaps not soon enough, he let her hand go and headed for the door leading to the hall.

"See you around," he threw over his broad shoulder with a sincere smile.

He left her feeling muddled in his wake. One minute he had been angry with her and the next he'd acted with understanding and been agreeable.

And he hadn't reacted to the revelation of her career ambitions as she'd expected. What a challenge he had become to understand.

Still befuddled, she checked the sleeping baby before leaving. She liked challenges. Especially intriguing and handsome ones.

The next afternoon in Labor and Delivery, Amanda prepared to help deliver a baby. This one was the result of a second IVF transfer. The mother had conceived the first time, but lost the baby in the first trimester.

The parents-to-be were today equally anxious and excited. Just after Amanda had begun working with couples battling infertility she had learned that these primary emotions were part and package of a clinic atmosphere.

Amanda made a quick review of the mother's medical chart on the computer tablet she held. Excitement bubbled within her. This would be the first time she'd helped with a delivery since coming to Harborside.

The birth of a baby was always exhilarating for the parents, but it was an equal thrill for the delivery staff as well. A new human being coming into the world for parents who had gone the extra mile or more to conceive made these babies extra-special. Nothing compared to the joy of this type of delivery.

Amanda slipped into her gown and gloves as the mother settled herself on the delivery table. Dr. Leah Johannsson, whom she had met on her first day at the clinic, would be handling the delivery. She was a small, soft-spoken woman in her mid-forties, with serious brown eyes. Amanda could understand why she was one of the patients' favorites.

Moments later Dr. Johannsson entered, dressed in gown and gloves as well.

The head nurse had told Amanda there was some anxiety about this birth, since the mother had lost one baby before. She had been on bedrest for the last three months, spending the last two weeks in the clinic's in-care unit. The goal had been to prevent an early birth.

Entering the delivery room, Amanda stepped beside the bed and smiled at the mother. "I'm Amanda Longstreet, a clinical nurse visiting from America. I'm honored to be helping with your delivery today. I look forward to meeting your baby."

"I look forward to meeting Alease too," the mother answered, smiling her happiness.

"What a beautiful name."

"Thanks. We're naming her after my grandmother." The woman winced.

"I think Alease is telling us she thinks it's time to meet her parents." Amanda looked over at the man hovering next to his wife, holding her hand.

The woman sucked in a breath as another pain came.

Amanda stepped back, letting Dr. Johannsson move in next to the bed. "I think this is going to happen sooner rather than later," she said.

Another pain gripped the patient.

"On the next one I want you to push," Dr. Johannsson instructed.

Minutes passed, and then the doctor said, "Don't push. I know you want to, but don't."

Seconds filled with heavy tension ticked by before she said, "*Now* it's time to bear down."

Slowly, little Alease slipped into the world.

The mother sighed and giggled at the same time.

Amanda switched her attention from her to the baby. Her heart caught. Something was wrong. The baby was blue. Not breathing. Limp. A pool of red fell to the floor.

Dr. Johannsson said quietly, “I need some help here.”

The doctor quickly handed the baby to Amanda. The mother was bleeding and the baby was in trouble.

Amanda rushed to the warmer, on her way hitting the emergency button on the wall that would bring additional help. Placing the baby inside the warmer, she dried her and started giving her stimulation with her fingers at the same time. Removing the wet blanket and dropping it to the floor, she quickly tapped the baby’s feet, hoping for a small sound. *Nothing.* She then checked the heart-rate, using two fingers under the base of the umbilical cord.

Sensing more than seeing, Amanda became aware that more people had entered the room.

The heart rate-remained below one hundred and the baby still hadn’t cried. She opened the baby’s airway and reached for an oxygen mask. A large hand was already placing it over the baby’s nose and mouth and giving it a pump.

She glanced up to see Lucius.

Still the baby wasn’t breathing. Amanda quickly checked the airway. Chest compressions were needed.

“You take over the oxygen.”

She didn’t wait for Lucius to respond. Wrapping her hands around the baby, with her thumbs under the center of her chest, she pushed.

“On my count,” she told Lucius. “*One*, two, three,” she recited, like counting for a waltz. “Breathe.”

Lucius pumped the oxygen bag.

“*One*, two, three. Breathe.”

He stayed with the beat she set. They worked for a minute. Then she stopped chest compressions and checked vitals. The baby moved. Amanda felt as if she could finally breathe herself. Lucius removed the oxygen mask. The baby let out a loud cry.

She smiled at Lucius and he returned it. His smile reached his eyes and caused a quiver in her middle.

"Well done, Amanda." His words were soft, and loaded with appreciation.

She nodded before turning her attention to the baby, wrapping her in a blanket and gently pulling a knit cap over the now healthy and pink head. Done, she looked to Dr. Johannsson, who was still working with the mom. She checked the baby's vitals again. Lucius still stood nearby, but didn't hover over them.

"Nurse Longstreet," Dr. Johannsson said, "I believe Mommy and Daddy would like to see their new baby girl now."

Grinning, she carried the baby to the mother and laid her on her chest. They would be allowed to bond for a few minutes and then Amanda would take Alease to NICU for evaluation.

A few tender moments later the mother, with tears in her eyes, looked beyond Amanda and said, "Thank you, Dr. West."

Amanda watched him. Lucius hadn't moved from where he stood near the wall.

He nodded. "You're welcome."

Amanda studied him another moment. He appeared nonchalant, but she could see the moisture in his eyes.

When she turned again, having taken the baby from her mother, he was gone.

Well, well, well. That's twice in a week I've caught a glimpse of Dr. Lucius West's tender side.

CHAPTER THREE

LUCIUS WALKED FROM the parking lot toward all the activity in the beach park. The clinic's annual picnic had been planned for today. All the families who had been helped through the clinic were invited. Many came to show off the children they were so proud of. It had become the best professional day of his entire year and was one he always looked forward to. Even the staff members brought their families.

After the picnic meal there would be contests, like the cutest baby, or the best sandcastle, and games and whatever else the picnic committee had come up with. Then the group picture of the children would be taken. That photo would be blown up and framed, then hung in the lobby of the clinic.

There were families everywhere. Adults stood in groups, talking. Some held small babies while others watched children run up and down the nearby beach. Seeing all the children gave him a sense of accomplishment that came along with the knowledge that he had helped create all this happiness. The sight humbled him.

A number of parents came up to him and thanked him. He had to remind more than one couple that he hadn't done it on his own, and that his excellent staff had been involved as well. For him, it was the way he made his living, but for these parents having a child was a dream come true.

It didn't take him long to tire of their adoration. He just wanted to enjoy the sunny, warm day with happy people at the beach. Seldom did he have a chance to do it. His work came first and taking time off for a social event usually fell pretty low on his list of priorities.

He approached the shelter that was located in a grassy area. A long table had been stationed there. Another table had been left out in the open, so people could eat there. Brightly colored tablecloths covered them. The clinic had provided all the food. He saw a caterer overseeing the meat and shrimp on the barbecue. His mouth watered at the wonderful smell coming from that direction.

A few of his staff mingled under the tent. He spied Amanda, talking to a couple of staff members in the corner. She wore a soft yellow dress that left her shoulders bare. The breeze blew her skirt, highlighting her curves. They were nice ones. She laughed. It reminded him of a church bell on a clear Sunday morning. It rippled through him, leaving peace in its wake. This woman had too much of an effect on him for his liking.

A male staff member placed his hand on her shoulder. Amanda smiled at him. Their friendliness disturbed Lucius. She'd never looked at *him* like that. Maybe he hadn't given her reason to. But that wasn't an area he intended to explore. After all, his days of caring if a woman smiled at him or not were long gone. His work gave him all the emotional satisfaction he needed in his life.

Besides, Amanda was a visiting professional from America. She wouldn't be here for very long and he wasn't interested in a fling, however brief. Even if he was it wouldn't be with someone working at the clinic. When an intimate relationship in the workplace ended it caused too much drama and damage, making the workplace uncomfortable.

If he ever seriously considered becoming involved with

a woman again, he knew their time together would be easy, casual and short. He'd always made it clear to the women he dated that he wasn't interested in perpetuating any "true love" fantasy with them.

He could well understand why men found Amanda interesting. He did. There was nothing more magnetic than a woman who knew who she was and what she wanted. Something about Amanda made him think that was just the case with her. She wasn't the type to depend on a man to make her feel confident. She seemed strong in her own right, could stand on her own two feet, and would dare anyone to say she couldn't. He really liked that about her.

His ex-wife had relied on *him* for her identity. Then one day she hadn't. He hadn't been able too support both her emotional neediness and his commitments at the clinic.

Someone called his name and he turned. Amanda's gaze met his. A primal awareness zipped through him. She smiled, leaving the group she'd been talking to and coming over to join him.

"I'm surprised to see you here. I didn't think this type of event would be your sort of thing," she remarked.

"Where d'you get that idea?"

"Kirri, possibly. She implied you're not very sociable. Maybe just a little bit rigid."

Amanda said it as if she agreed with his sister. Just how much had Kirri talked about him to her?

"Do you always just say whatever comes to your mind?" he asked. "And by the way I'm perfectly sociable." He raised his chin. "When I want to be."

She grinned. "Well, that's nice to know. And, yes, I do always say what I think. How else am I supposed to learn things?"

"And today you've learned what, exactly?"

"That you're sociable despite your unsociable expression." Her smile turned cheeky. "You *can* smile, Doctor. No one will think any less of you."

The woman exasperated him, but he couldn't stop the lift of his lips. "Just so you know, this happens to be my favorite event of the year. It's nice to see how the babies have grown...become children."

Amanda looked at all the teeming activity around them. Her gaze settled on him again. Somehow having her sole attention made him feel special.

"You must be very proud. You certainly have the right to be."

"I'll admit it's nice to see all the families I've helped create. But enough talk about that." He looked at her. "Does the Atlanta clinic have this sort of event?"

"No, but I'm going to recommend they do. It's a wonderful PR opportunity. Plus, it gives the staff a chance to appreciate their good work. Not to mention it's loads of fun."

"Hey, Lucius!" Nancy, his nurse, called to him as she entered the tent. "I'm glad you came."

"I wouldn't miss it." He grinned.

"We're about ready to start serving. You want to say something before we do?" Nancy asked.

"Why don't you do it?" said Lucius. He would rather just remain part of the crowd.

Nancy dared to tug his forearm. "You know they want to hear from *you*. You could at least welcome them."

He glanced at Amanda, who still smiled even while giving him an expectant look, as if she would be disappointed if he didn't do as Nancy requested.

"Okay."

A few minutes later Nancy had seen to it that everyone had gathered close. Lucius proceeded to tell everyone how thankful he was to have them there and say he hoped they enjoyed their day.

Nancy stepped up as he finished. "We need to get the group picture of the children, then we'll eat."

Lucius moved away, sliding off to the side.

"Very inspirational speech, Dr. West."

He recognized Amanda's voice. She stood at his elbow, watching him with unnerving intensity.

"It was more short and sweet than inspirational," he replied.

"You really don't like the limelight, do you?" she asked.

"Not really. You ready to eat?" To his surprise, he found he wanted to talk to her about something other than work.

"Starving."

"Then come on and—let's get something off the barbie before it's all gone." He led her to where the paper plates were stacked and they began filling theirs.

Amanda turned to him. "Do you have someone you're supposed to eat with?"

"No. I was hoping you'd let me join you."

What was he doing? That sounded like he was singling her out. Was he sure he wanted to do that? Yeah, he did. He had become tired of his own company. Amanda made him think, and question his answers. Her wit kept him on his toes. A feat few people could accomplish. What harm would there be in getting to know her better?

"That's my towel over there." She pointed it out on the beach. "The one that looks like the Australian flag."

"Why am I not surprised?"

She grinned. "I bought it yesterday afternoon, knowing I'd need one today. It'll make a good souvenir of my time here in Australia."

He rolled his eyes. Even *he* didn't own anything that patriotic. "I'm sure it will."

"If you'll take my plate, I'll go get us some drinks. What would you like?"

"A soft drink will be fine."

"I'll be there in a sec. Don't eat my food." Amanda left him with a smile on her face.

What he found amazing was the fact that he had one on his face as well. He didn't make a habit of smiling like a silly schoolboy with a crush on the pretty new teacher, but Amanda brought that out in him. Much to his dismay, he was finding everything about her was exhilarating.

Nancy and a couple more staff members joined them, after spreading their own towels and blankets nearby. In one way he was glad to have the distraction from Amanda, but in another he knew he would miss having her undivided attention.

"Amanda," Nancy said, "you've been here a week—tell us what you think about Australia? The clinic? Where you're living?"

"I'm lovin' Australia. Everybody's been so kind."

She glanced at him. Her eyes twinkled. Was she reminding him that all hadn't been smooth between them? That maybe he'd been the exception?

"I really like working at the clinic. Y'all have an exceptional program."

Lucius loved Amanda's drawled out "y'all". Did her accent become stronger when she was aroused? He'd really like to find out…

Lucius choked on his drink.

Everyone focused on him. Amanda studied him with concern. He gave a quick cough to clear his throat.

Amanda continued, "My apartment is nice. I've found a place close by to go for groceries, and a department store for other things about five blocks away. The only thing I'm sad about is that I haven't had a chance yet to see much of the city. I'm planning to do some sightseeing tomorrow. Be a real tourist. I want to see the Sydney Harbor Bridge—from the top—the Opera House at least from the outside, and then maybe go to the zoo. I can't go home without seeing a koala. They're *so* cute."

She sounded like a little girl talking about her favorite doll at Christmas. He found it fascinating that the same woman who went about her job so efficiently and systematically was chatting about sightseeing like an excited child. Who was the real Amanda and why did she fill him with awe every time she was near him?

"You need to visit one of the smaller zoos where you can hold one," one of the staff members said.

Amanda leaned forward. Her eyes wide and bright. "You can do that? Really?"

A male staff member nodded. "Sure. There's a place a few hours out of town where you can. Just take the train."

"I'm gonna have to look that up. Maybe I can go next weekend. Thanks for letting me know. Oh, one more thing. I plan to take a ferry ride across the harbor. See Sydney by water. For us landlocked people in Atlanta, living around this much water is incredible." She paused, looking off toward the ocean. "I might do that this afternoon."

On the tip of Lucius's tongue were the words, *I could show you around*, but he stopped himself saying them by stuffing food in his mouth.

"Have you been to The Strand?" Nancy asked.

"What's that?"

"It's a huge Victorian building full of shops. The building alone is worth seeing. But the shopping is great too."

Lucius groaned, along with a couple of the other males.

Amanda looked at each of them with annoyance, before giving Lucius a pointed glare. "Not *everyone* thinks about work all the time."

Silence fell over the group. Amanda's confusion was plain. His staff would be shocked to hear her speak to him that way. Few people joked with him, or called him out on how he spent his time. That would be no one except his sister, but up until recently she hadn't had much room to talk either.

To get the conversation back on track, Lucius said, "I think it's a beautiful building as well. The stained glass is remarkable on a sunny day."

Amanda relaxed as the others' unease disappeared. But he knew they continued to watch his interaction with Amanda with interest.

He shifted so he could see her more clearly. "You do know there are other things to do around the city that aren't so touristy?"

Amanda straightened, as if his question had been intended to scold her. "Like what?"

He shrugged. "Like going to one of the public ocean pools. They're built right on the ocean. Filled with ocean water. It's an amazing experience to swim in one in the early morning and watch the day come alive."

The others stared at him as if they suddenly had no idea who he was.

"That sounds lovely."

Amanda's voice had turned breathy. It stirred him in ways and places that hadn't been moved in a long time.

"I'm gonna have to do that," she said.

"I'll tell you what—I'll pick you up next Saturday and we'll go for a swim."

He glanced at the others. Their eyes had grown wide and their mouths had become slack. He'd shocked them.

Thankfully one of the staff members down the beach called out, "The games start in fifteen minutes! So finish up your food but leave room for ice cream."

Their little group returned to eating, but occasionally he noticed one or more of them watching him with a smile. Nancy clearly wore a smirk. Thankfully, Amanda seemed oblivious to any undercurrents.

Minutes before they were called to the first game everyone dispersed, leaving him and Amanda alone. He stood and offered his hand to help her up. She studied it for a second and then put her fingers in his. As soon as she got to her feet he released her hand. They placed their trash in a can and walked toward the crowd that was forming.

"I have to oversee the Pie-in-the-Face game," she said. "And I'm still looking for someone to be the face." She gave him a pointed look.

He had no plans to compete in any of the games. He didn't do games. He couldn't think of anything worse than waiting to have whipped cream repeatedly thrown in his face.

Amanda stopped walking and he did too. She continued to look at him. "Will you do it?" she asked. "I think the parents as well as the kids would love it. I know the staff would too."

His eyes narrowed. "What do you mean by that?"

She lifted a shoulder and dropped it. "I believe they think you're a bit of a stuffed shirt. But I know better."

He took off his sunglasses and leaned down so he could see her eyes clearly. "And how do you know that?"

"Because I've seen you in the nursery. You're really a softy under all the bark and gruff."

Lucius threw back his head and laughed. "Ms. Longstreet, I've never met another woman like you."

She smiled. "Is that a good thing or a bad thing?"

"To tell you the truth, I'm not sure yet. But I think today I'd like to prove to my staff how *un*-stuffed my shirt really is."

Amanda's smile grew to a satisfied grin. "I knew you'd do it."

He slipped his glasses back into place. "So sure of yourself, are you?"

Her nose went in the air. "I got you to do something that Nancy said would never happen."

He'd been had. Manipulated. And the worst thing about it was that for some reason he didn't mind at all...

They joined the crowd and for the next hour watched the games. Amanda really got into them. She laughed, clapped and cheered. How animated she became was something to behold. He noticed how many of the staff spoke to her as they passed, or stood next to her in the crowd. She was popular.

Too soon for him, she said, "It's time to get you ready."

They walked over to where a clown doctor had been painted on a board. The face had been cut out.

"We need to get you dressed." Amanda stepped behind the board.

"Dressed?" he asked.

She nodded and reached into a cloth bag on the ground. "Yeah. You'll want to put on a plastic bag to cover your clothes. Come around here." She waved him toward her.

He gave her a dubious look. "You've done this before, haven't you?"

"I have. This was my idea." She shook out a large trash bag and pulled a hole in the end.

"So this was planned for me all along?"

She shrugged. "Raise your arms."

Lucius did as she said. She stood on her toes and reached up to slip the bag over his head. He leaned forward and emerged to find them almost face to face. Amanda stood so close he could clearly smell her over the ocean. Her scent reminded him of the roses his gardener had grown in his back yard. Their gazes met. She had flakes of gold in her beautiful eyes. He could just make out a few freckles over the bridge of her nose.

He leaned forward, then stopped himself. This wasn't the time or the place to kiss her. But he badly wanted to. Instead he met her gaze. "You do know I'm going to get you for this?"

A mischievous grin formed on her lips. "Is that a promise, Dr. West?"

He stepped forward, sandwiching her between himself and the back of the board. Her look dared him. Time ticked by as the air between them became hot and heavy.

"It certainly is," he said at last.

She licked her lips, sending blood straight to his manhood.

"I expect promises to be kept."

The sound of people approaching made him quickly step back. What was he *doing*? He had better sense than to flirt with Amanda—especially in public. But it was so much fun. It had been a long time since he'd felt this alive.

"Let me fix some holes for your arms." She moved to his side and tore another hole in the trash bag. He pushed his hand through.

"I can do the other one." His voice sounded gruffer than he'd intended.

"Okay. I'm going around to the other side and take care of the cream pies. You just stick your face through the hole." She started around the board, then stopped and gave him a wicked grin. "And smile."

Lucius did as she instructed. He looked out at the faces standing before him. Children of every size waited in a line with eager looks on their faces. A small table had been set up nearby. Pie pans filled with white, fluffy whipped cream sat in lines on it. Nancy was working at adding cream from a can to even more pans.

Amanda handed a child of about eight one of the plates. "Now, give it a big throw."

The pie came through the air with cream flying around it, straight toward him. To Lucius's great relief it hit the bottom of the board. He grinned. "Maybe next time."

Another child took his place. His pie hit just to the right side of Lucius's face. This was starting to be fun. Children kept coming. They continued to miss. All he had on his face were a few dollops of cream.

"Since we all seem to be missing Dr. West, we're going to move the throwing line a little closer for the second round," Amanda announced.

The crowd roared and clapped. Lucius growled and glared at Amanda. She just smiled sweetly at him.

The first few children missed again. Then one finally hit the side of his face. The next two managed to get him in the forehead. The next throw hit him square-on. The crowd went wild with laugher and hollering. Before the line was finished his face had been completely covered in cream. He had to blink to keep it out of his eyes.

Not soon enough for him, Amanda announced, "I think Dr. West deserves a hand for being such a good sport."

A big cheer rose to join the applause.

Nancy stepped between him and the crowd. "Thanks for coming to this year's picnic, everyone. See you next year."

Lucius pulled his face back from the hole and started wiping it clean with his hand. Amanda joined him behind the board with a bag in her hand.

He grumbled, "I can't believe I let you talk me into doing that."

She giggled. "You looked so shocked when that first pie hit you in the face."

"It's not funny."

"Yeah, it is."

"I'll show you how funny it is."

He grabbed her and rubbed his cheek against hers, then ran it over her forehead, leaving a large smear of cream. He stopped only long enough to turn his head and do it again. All the time she squealed and squirmed, making the mess greater. With one last pass he scrubbed his nose along hers. Then he suddenly stopped. Looking at her mouth, he licked some cream from the corner and brought his tongue in, tasting the sweet mixture of cream and Amanda.

She stilled. Her look of wonder remained fixed on him.

His gaze met hers. "You taste good," he said.

She ran her finger across his jaw, collecting some more cream. Her eyes glinted suggestively. She stuck it in her mouth and then pulled it out slowly.

Hot blood rushed to below his belt. This thing between them had taken on a life of its own here in broad daylight, on a public beach, in front of his staff. Where children might see.

Not the time or the place. Once again.

He backed away.

Amanda blinked. The mesmerizing sparkle in her eyes disappeared. She reached for her bag and pulled out a roll of paper towels. Pulling some off, she handed them to him. He wiped his face clean, then began pulling the plastic bag over his head.

"Here, let me help you," Amanda said. Seconds later the bag was gone. "You missed a spot. Let me get it for you."

"No."

If she touched him again there would definitely be a show to see.

He lowered his voice. "That's all right. I'm going home after this. I'll clean up there."

Confusion and hurt filled her eyes. "Okay. Thanks for helping out today. You were quite a hit. The kids and parents loved it. And once again you proved you have a soft heart."

"Soft heart?"

"You say that like you think it's a bad thing. I think it makes you very special."

He whipped his head toward her.

She continued cleaning up, not meeting his look.

"I'm sorry I shouldn't have said that. Your secret is

safe with me. You're free to go. Thanks for your help," she added.

"Not a problem."

As he walked away the temptation to ask if she needed a ride home crossed his mind—but did he really want to get involved with Amanda? *No.* And she couldn't really be interested in him either, could she? They lived on two different continents, in different worlds. Right now they worked together, and he had rules. All that could happen between them was a brief, meaningless fling.

He suspected she was the type of woman who wouldn't go for that. Something about Amanda made him think she'd want forever. But he'd traveled that road once and it had ended in a wreck. That wasn't a place he intended to revisit. Nothing but sexual electricity could exist between him and Amanda.

Still, it was hot…and enticing. He still carried the scorch of her touch and the wicked thoughts that had come with her licking that whipped cream off her finger. But acting on those desires would be at best a distraction, at worst possible destruction. He was much better off walking away.

Lucius made it to his car and drove home with the distinct sensation that he was running from something dangerous and desirable, and that he should be scared.

Amanda stood trembling as her blood surged through her. What had she been *thinking* to tease Lucius like that? To act so suggestively and then make such a statement about his personality. Had she lost her mind? She hadn't been thinking or she wouldn't have done it. Now he probably thought she'd been coming on to him.

Ugh.

For a second there she'd been afraid he might kiss her. Worse, she had no doubt she would have let him. That would have been a ten on a scale of one to ten in *wrong.*

She hadn't come halfway around the world to start kissing the head of the Harborside clinic. Her future depended on her being totally professional. She certainly didn't want it to get out that she'd been coming on to the boss. All thought of ever doing so stopped here. *Now.*

She held out her shaking hand. Her body wasn't listening.

She finished gathering the trash with renewed determination. The crowd had thinned, and everyone was making their way to the parking lot. She needed to go home and regroup. Forget about Lucius West and his sexy blue eyes that saw too much, watched her too closely. Becoming involved with Lucius would be a grave mistake—both professionally and personally. She needed to step back, reevaluate what she should do.

Placing her palm to her forehead, she groaned. She'd agreed to go swimming with him next Saturday morning. *Not* a good plan.

Twenty-four hours later she was still mentally bemoaning her attraction to Lucius as she explored the city. She'd spent some time outside the Opera House, studying its amazing architecture. From there she'd found her way to the Harbor Bridge. Now she was climbing it.

A few times she wanted to stop, but she knew it was further to go back down than it was to continue climbing up. Proud of herself for making it to the top, she stood looking out at the beautiful view.

She could only imagine what it would be like to see this scene every day. She wished she had someone to share it with. Lucius came to mind, but she quickly pushed his face away.

Too tired to do more, she returned to her apartment. The ferry ride on the harbor would have to wait for another day. She had several more weekends before she left for home.

By the end of the next day, Sunday, she'd decided that

avoiding Lucius during the next week would the answer to getting out of going swimming with him, and even more importantly would help her avoid any chance of furthering the attraction she felt for him.

Maybe he'd even forget about his offer. Except for that one suggestive moment at the beach, he hadn't acted as if he wanted any more to do with her. In fact, he'd almost run away from her. Whatever those moments had been between them Lucius obviously didn't want any further involvement. Or maybe he feared her for some reason. She couldn't make out what his response meant.

She'd give him an out on his invitation by just not being around. She'd stay close to Labor and Delivery and out of his path. Although she wasn't sure she *wanted* him to forget about it. As contrary as he was, she liked him.

Amanda knew she could always decline his invitation. Say that she had changed her mind. But she really wanted to go. Not only to see the pool but to spend time with Lucius. The only thing keeping her from acting on her attraction was her fear of liking him *too* much. Surely they could just be friends without indulging in their sexual attraction?

She would never have thought the self-important guy who had climbed into the car with her that first day would ever appeal to her. But the Lucius who held babies just to decompress, or the Lucius who had shown up at the beach party she could like—a lot. She'd only known him a week and his merest touch made her body tingle with possibilities.

But she must be careful. More than one man had shown interest in her and then let her down. With Lucius she couldn't afford to make any mistakes. It would matter not only emotionally but career-wise as well. Teasing was one thing—kissing was another.

To her amazement, she made it almost to the end of the week without ever seeing Lucius. But by Thursday afternoon she had Lucius withdrawal symptoms. She even stooped to searching out when he was in the lab or doing a procedure. She learned that he hadn't even been at the clinic because he'd been out of town.

Even so, more than once she nervously looked up, expecting to see him while she worked on helping deliver a baby, because one of the nurses had mentioned he might attend this birth.

All this avoidance kept her on a tightrope of stress. She wasn't sure how much longer she could keep it up.

"Amanda? Dr. West called down and he would like for you to go to his office," one of the nurses announced suddenly.

"Right now?"

Amanda's heart did a flip. *Lucius wanted to see her.* As far as she could tell up till now he'd been avoiding her as well.

She looked down to find her hands shaking. "Please let him know I'm with a patient right now and will be there as soon as I can."

Amanda returned to checking the woman's vitals, thankful she could do it by rote since her mind had gone elsewhere.

Finally finished with the patient, she addressed the other nurse. "I'm off to see Dr. West. Let me know if you need me to come back."

"If there's a problem I'll page you. Don't look so scared." The nurse grinned.

Amanda returned a thin-lipped smile. "I just wish I knew what this was about."

"I've never heard of him biting anyone."

"There's always a first time."

Lucius could nibble on her anytime, she thought, but she was sure that wasn't what he wanted to see her about. Even if she would have enjoyed it.

Making her way to Lucius's office, she walked into the business section of the building. No one sat behind the reception desk. She went to knock on what she thought might be Lucius's office door, but hesitated.

Before she could knock a woman she had been introduced to at the picnic came to the desk.

"Are you looking for Dr. West?" she asked.

"Yes. I was told he wanted to see me."

"You'll find him in the lab. It's hard to tie him to his chair long enough to do any type of paperwork. He loves that lab."

Amanda wasn't surprised.

"It's down the hall." The middle-aged woman pointed. "Turn left and it's the third door on the left."

Amanda followed her directions with trepidation and anticipation. She had no idea what to expect. Her reaction to Lucius reminded her of being next to a fire, feeling toasty and warm but knowing if she stepped too close she could get burnt.

She entered the door marked "Lab." Inside there was a glass wall, and a door made out of the same material. She could see Lucius. He was wearing a white lab coat, seated on a stool, with a large syringe in his hand as he worked on a rack of test tubes.

He looked up when she knocked on the glass. Their gazes met. She'd forgotten what a powerful effect he had on her. A wave of sexual awareness hit her midsection. She stood motionless for a moment.

With a gesture of his hand, he indicated for her to come in, but pointed toward the right. She looked in that direction and found a dressing room. After a nod, she gowned up. Done, she entered through the glass door. It made a swishing sound as the airlock sealed.

For a second, she smiled. She and Lucius were locked in together.

"You wanted to see me?" she said.

He turned toward her. His vivid eyes gave her a searching look. He seemed satisfied with what he saw.

"Yes. I thought you might be interested in something I'm working on. You said you wanted to know about the process from start to finish. Since I'm working in the lab today, I thought it would be a good time to show you."

Her concern at being in his presence quickly became overridden by her eagerness to learn. "I'd love that. Thank you."

"Grab that stool over there and pull it up beside me. I'll explain the process."

His enthusiasm for sharing his work circled each word.

Amanda did as he instructed, but made sure not to sit too close. Even though the temperature had been set low in the lab, she still had to keep a safe distance from Lucius's fire.

He didn't speak loudly. His voice stayed low and smooth, almost reverent, as he explained in detail what he was doing and why.

"I'm working on two different trials. This one is dealing with women who have had cervical cancer and find their ability to reproduce severely compromised."

He went through all the particulars of the trial and his findings so far. "Do you have any questions?" he asked.

Amanda asked them and he patiently answered each one.

"Now, the other trial I'm working on is the use of Kisspeptin-LH compared to hCG. We're seeing great successes there."

Amanda didn't miss the pride in his voice. This man really cared about the work he did.

"My goal, in my lifetime, is to be able to increase our success rate in women having babies by fifty percent."

Amanda's eyes widened. "That is an ambitious goal."

He and his sister Kirri definitely came from the same family. When Kirri had first arrived in Atlanta she'd almost never come out of the lab. What had happened in their lives to make them so driven? It might have been a good thing—but everyone knew what happened if you had too much of a good thing…

Lucius turned earnest. "I know it's a lofty figure, but that's what it'll take for me to consider my work truly successful."

"I think even if you fall a little short you could still consider yourself successful."

"I'll only think I could have done better." His words sounded hard.

"Where did you get such drive?"

Lucius looked at her for a long moment, as if deciding if he wanted to answer or not. He turned to his test tubes once more.

"My father was a demanding man. He made it clear that he was disappointed if I didn't achieve. Failure was something he wouldn't accept."

Amanda nodded. She understood better now. "Kirri told me he was a doctor as well?"

"Yes—and he pretty much didn't leave us any choice except to be doctors as well."

He was still not facing her, and she had to lean in closer to hear him.

"Don't get me wrong—I love what I do. But my resistance to conformity by not following in his specialty has made it difficult at times. Worse, Kirri joined me and not him."

"I'm sure that having a father who required that much from you has helped make you the excellent doctor you are today," she said.

His gaze met hers. "Is that your way of seeing the cup half-full?"

She shrugged. “Better than half-empty. All you have to do is look at those pictures in the lobby to know you were the one who was right.”

That brought a smile to his face.

They spent another thirty minutes discussing the pros and cons of the work he had been doing in the trials. Then, too soon for her, Lucius put down the syringe, rolled the stool back and stood.

“I have a meeting in a few minutes, so that’s it for today.”

They walked out together and dropped their gowns in a barrel before entering the hallway.

“If I don’t see you again, I’ll pick you up at seven Saturday morning,” Lucius said matter-of-factly.

“Do you still want to go?” Her voice shook. She cleared her throat.

“Don’t you?” he asked.

“I just don’t wanna put you out.” Yeah, she *did* want to spend more time with this intriguing man.

“You’re not putting me out. I swim there sometimes.”

“Oh.” So, he wasn’t doing anything special by taking her. “I guess that’s how you stay in such good shape.”

“You think I’m in good shape?” His eyes twinkled.

Her cheeks warmed. Why couldn’t she keep her mouth shout?

She walked away. “What I think is that I’ll be ready at seven.”

CHAPTER FOUR

LUCIUS HAD BEEN taught never to stand a woman up or back out on a date if at all possible. He'd failed miserably on both accounts where his wife had been concerned. More than once he'd taken it for granted that she would be there for him, or be at home regardless of whether or not he'd become caught up in his work. That had certainly contributed to his divorce.

Hoping he had learned from his mistakes, he arrived early to pick up Amanda on Saturday.

Of course the idea of canceling their swimming trip had crossed his mind. Yet his mother's lectures on manners whenever she came out of her book world had won out. So here he was, on this… Whatever it was, he didn't know. But he didn't want to call it a date.

He was well aware of feeling off-kilter, for the first time in a long while, but being around Amanda did that to him. When he'd considered their plans during the past week, he'd still wanted to take Amanda swimming. What he *didn't* want was to be feeling this powerful attraction to her.

Lucius wasn't a long-term relationship person. His failed marriage proved that. His needs, his job, had always come first. His career would always win out. His intense commitment to it made a traditional relationship impossible. In fact his devotion to his work meant his involvement with any woman would only be halfhearted at best. And from what he'd learned about Amanda she was an all-or-nothing person.

Lucius shook his head, trying to send such thoughts flying. Couldn't they be friends? Enjoy each other's company? Maybe share a kiss or two? No, that would never work. He wasn't even going to allow himself a chance to test that theory. It was a bad idea—of that he had no doubt.

What he would do was take Amanda swimming, and then keep his distance.

Feeling totally at a loss—which was a foreign emotion for him—he stood in front of Amanda's door. He prided himself on being master of his domain and in control of every situation. For some reason Amanda managed to make that impossible. He never knew what to expect from her. Their brief encounter at the picnic had more than put him off his normal "arm's length" strategy. Even his wife had never succeeded in derailing him from his established plans.

Amanda challenged him. She'd lured him out of his comfort zone when she had manipulated him into being the face in her pie-throwing contest. And somehow she'd gotten him to suggest she come swimming with him. The most startling realization of all was the fact that he actually enjoyed and even looked forward to their verbal sparring. He could let loose around Amanda like he never had with a woman before. He wasn't sure how she'd succeeded in putting him so much at ease, but she had.

Still, this had to stop—whatever "this" was.

When Amanda had joined him in the lab he had been impressed by how quick she had been to ask questions, along with how informed and thoughtful she was. Her interest hadn't seemed contrived. It had shown in her voice and in the intensity of her eyes. His work excited him and it was refreshing to find someone who shared that same passion. Amanda had seemed to hang on every word he spoke.

His wife hadn't ever done the same, despite having studied nursing. She'd shown no interest in his work. She hadn't wanted to listen to anything regarding what he had strived so hard to accomplish.

He'd finally realized, too late, that she'd gone into the field of medicine solely to find a doctor for a husband. She had been more interested in the social status and the money. As his fame in the world of infertility treatment had grown the more she'd liked it—until she hadn't.

He raised his fist to knock on Amanda's door. Before he could do so, it opened. He stepped back. Amanda stood there with her bag in her hand, wearing some type of flowing dress. Her hair had been pulled back, but several tendrils had come loose to frame her face.

"Hey..." she said uncertainly.

Surprised, he blurted, "How did you know I was here?"

"You're punctual. It's seven o'clock, so I figured you'd already be out here or you soon would be."

"Am I that predictable?" He wasn't sure he liked that idea.

She closed the door behind her. "Not in everything, but in being on time you are. I guess you're ready to go? I am." She started down the stairs. "Am I going to freeze to death, swimming in ocean water this early in the morning?"

Having no choice but to follow her, Lucius hurried down the steps. "You do know that temperatures here have been above thirty-two degrees Celsius and are supposed to go even higher today."

"Thirty-two? That's around ninety degrees Fahrenheit? But that doesn't mean the water is warm."

"I don't want you mad at me when you first get in, because it will be cool, but after you get moving you'll be just fine."

They stepped outside.

"I don't think it'll matter," she said. "I'm really looking forward to it. A pool like that is a novelty to me."

She swung the bag in her hand.

He directed her toward his car.

She came to a halt and studied his midnight-blue two-seater roadster. "I should've known this would be the type of car you'd drive."

Somehow that didn't sound like a compliment. "Is there something wrong with my car?"

It took Amanda a moment to answer as a grin crawled across her face. "Not a single thing. It is *too* sweet. To say that I like it would be an understatement."

Lucius swelled with pride. He opened the passenger door. "Get in and I'll take you for a ride."

"I wanna warn you I may hit you over the head and drive off with it if I get the chance."

Lucius chuckled, somehow feeling lighter. "Of course that would mean you'd be committing a felony."

"I've thought of that." She climbed in and ran a hand along the top of the door. "It would be totally worth it, though."

He closed her door and went around to slide into the driver's seat. "Should I call the police now?"

"I'll try to control myself at least until after I swim. I really want to see this pool."

Lucius started the car and drove away from the curb.

"How often do you go to this pool?" asked Amanda. She had her head back, her eyes closed as the wind blew in her face.

"Whenever I want a change and can take the time to drive there. Otherwise I just swim at home."

"You have a pool at your house?" She rolled her head, looking at him.

"Yeah, but it isn't like the ones fed by the ocean." He

shrugged. "And you agreed to come with me." For some reason that mattered to him. Too much.

Stop. Stop now. Remember the plan. Swim and take her home. No further involvement.

He turned his attention from Amanda to his driving as they passed through the neighborhood and out to the main road. Minutes later he moved onto the coastal road. Soon he pulled into the parking lot beside the competition-size pool. There were only a few other cars there that early in the morning.

Amanda stepped out, gathered her things, and met him at the rear of the car. Together they walked to the gate and went inside. They found a spot on the cement deck and put their belongings down.

Lucius slipped off his shoes and pulled his shirt over his head, leaving him in his swimming trunks. He looked at Amanda and she stared at him. It was like facing danger. His skin heated and his manhood shifted. Coming here with her was a bad idea.

He sharpened his resolve. "Are you going to swim or just watch me?" He needed to get in the cool water before his visceral reaction to her attention became visible. "If you decide to join me, I suggest you remove that dress."

He started for the pool, but not before he saw her come back to reality. He executed a shallow dive into the water. Thankfully, it *was* cool. He needed some help.

When he surfaced, he looked for Amanda. She'd removed her dress, leaving him with a full view of her in a black one-piece that was far sexier than any bikini would have been. The suit showed the cleavage between her full breasts, but only enough to tease him with the thought of what might be hidden. He followed the generous curves to hips that flared, leaving him in no doubt that she was all woman. Her legs were long and shapely, and made more so by the high cut of the suit's leg openings.

This swimming trip had been a bad idea in more ways than one. Amanda played havoc with his libido.

Shaking his head, trying to remove the befuddlement, he called, "Are you coming in?"

"On my way."

Amanda walked toward the steps and Lucius appreciated the subtle muscle movements of her body. *Graceful* would be the way he would describe it. *Sexy.*

He swallowed, bringing his focus back to where it should be. "Keep in mind this is salt water," he said.

Amanda eased down the steps until the water lapped at her waist, then plunged in. She proceeded to do a crawl stroke down the length of the pool.

Lucius joined her, keeping plenty of distance between them. They made another lap back, and then did it again. Amanda was a good swimmer, and she had excellent form.

She finally stopped at the corner of the pool and trod water. He joined her.

"This is absolutely amazing—wonderful." Amanda looked up at the sky. "It's like being in the ocean but *not* being in the ocean."

"I thought you'd like it."

He enjoyed watching her. She seemed to take so much pleasure in life. When was the last time he had stopped long enough to say that about himself?

"This is well hidden from tourists." She looked around. "I'm glad I had a chance to experience it."

"You're a good swimmer."

"Thank you." She continued to study the surrounding area as she said, "I was on the swim team in high school."

"It shows." Her movements through the water had been smooth and flowing.

"What did *you* do in high school?" she asked.

"I went to a boarding school. I was on the debate team."

"That figures."

He twisted his mouth. "Mostly I studied. My job was to make good grades so I could get into medical school."

She splashed at a spot on the wall. "I'd have to say my mom was a little more encouraging than that. I would've done more sport, but my stepfather didn't like paying for extracurricular activities. Specifically where I was concerned."

"Was money a problem?"

He knew she might consider the question rude, but he wanted to know more about her. He'd already told her more about himself than most people knew, and he'd only known her a couple of weeks.

"It had nothing to do with money. He just didn't want to spend it on *me*."

"Why was that?"

The desire to punch something filled him—preferably her stepfather, for treating her that way. His father might have been demanding, and rigid on all occasions, but Lucius and his sister had always known they were wanted.

"You know…the old story. Mother and daughter are a package deal, but he doesn't want the daughter because she reminds him that his wife loved someone else before him."

Amanda was trying to make light of it, but what he'd clearly heard in her voice was hurt.

"It was what it was," she said.

But that didn't make it right.

"Tell me about your father?"

"He died when I was very small. I don't remember him. All I know about him is what my mother has told me and a few pictures I've seen. My stepfather didn't like for my mother to talk about him. Still doesn't."

"How old were you when your mother remarried?"

Why was he asking all these questions? He didn't make a habit of delving into peoples' lives any more than he let them explore his. This wasn't putting the distance between them he'd promised himself he would start creating. Instead he was doing the reverse. He'd better get his act together soon.

"She remarried when I was two, then had my half-brother and sister. My stepfather didn't see me as a part of his responsibility or part of the family. One night I overheard him arguing with my mother about spending *his* money on a prom dress for me. In one way or another he always made it clear he considered me an outsider because I didn't carry his last name."

"Did your mother never consider changing your name to his?"

He groaned in his head. There—he'd done it again. But the draw to know more about her was great.

"I don't think so. She loved my father and wouldn't have dishonored him by doing that. And as I got older I wouldn't have let her. I always refused to be pushed around by my stepfather."

He bit his tongue, but the question got away from him anyway. "Did your half-brother and sister treat you differently?"

"No. We're very close. And they do notice how their father treats me. More than once they've taken up the issue with him for me."

"I'm glad to hear that."

He was. Her childhood must have been hard, yet she seemed to face the world with wonder and excitement.

"Enough serious talk," she said. "We have this wonderful pool to enjoy."

She began swimming again with a little more ferocity than before. Maybe she wasn't as unaffected by her past as she acted. It was as if she were trying to physically shove away those ugly years of being an outsider.

Lucius pushed off the wall and followed her across the pool. They made a few more laps and then Amanda stopped once more beside the wall closest to the ocean. He pulled up and joined her, placing a hand on the side of the pool while she trod water. The sun sparkled on the surface of the water and the ocean splashed against the rocks only feet away, producing a light spray.

Amanda raised her face. It was full of wonderment.

"You know, this really is an amazing place. I *love* Sydney."

Her words were breathy, as if she had swum too hard, and yet there was a kind of reverence to them.

"I'm going to pay close attention to how we get back to my apartment from here so I can come again by myself."

"How about I let you know when I'm coming and bring you along?"

"You would do that?"

That pleasure in her face became more pronounced.

"Sure—why not."

What had made him suggest *that*? He prided himself on his self-control and around Amanda he acted as if he had none. What was happening to him?

Amanda looked as if she was going to say something, but shook her head instead.

Suddenly a wave crashed against the rocks just outside the pool, splashing them. Amanda squealed, wiping water from her face. Seconds later she yelped again and pounced on him, wrapping her arms around his neck, moving her feet as if she wanted to climb him. He had to grip the wall with some force in order not to go under.

Finally Amanda calmed down enough to point as she hung on him. "What's *that*?"

Lucius chuckled. "That's just a baby squid who wanted to join us. He must have been washed over a minute ago."

Amanda's grip eased some, but she didn't let go and her focus remained on the happily swimming sea creature still not far away.

Settling her against him, he felt his mind and body become aware of the luscious woman in his arms. His gaze met hers. She blinked. To his satisfaction her total attention was now fixated on him. His gaze lowered to her slightly parted lips. Dewy drops puddled on her lower one. They looked as pink as the sunrise had been and plush as a pillow.

As bad an idea as he knew it was, he was driven to taste them. To experience them.

His mouth lowered to hers. She immediately joined him in the passion bubbling between them.

Amanda slid down and across him, so they were chest to chest. Her arms remained around his neck. He tightened his arm at her waist. Teasing her mouth with his tongue, he asked for entry and she freely gave it. So sweet, inviting, so enticing and addictive.

Her tongue joined his in a sensual dance.

His manhood lay thick between them.

The sound of someone giggling close by brought him back to where they were. He wasn't exactly a celebrity, but his face was frequently in the papers and on TV.

Reluctantly he broke off the kiss.

Amanda wore a dazed look. "Mmm…"

Her sound of disappointment sent a shot of satisfaction through him. Wow, the woman could kiss. He'd become rocket-hot with nowhere to go.

"We need to take this elsewhere. Families are starting to come in."

He turned her so she fit between him and the wall, protecting her from curious eyes. Seconds later he watched as her eyes cleared.

She peeked over his shoulder. "I…uh…guess we'd better."

He resisted taking her mouth again. Instead he reached

out and cupped the squid, flinging it back over the wall into the ocean. "Thanks, little guy, you made a great wingman."

Amanda giggled and swam away.

He followed more slowly. If being around Amanda had already had him tied in knots, kissing her had sent his mind off into space. He had messed up—big-time. He needed to reaffirm his stance on having nothing to do with her. And after that kiss it would be far more difficult.

As she climbed out of the pool, Lucius took the opportunity to enjoy the view. When she reached their belongings, he called, "Would you mind bringing me my towel?"

She gave him a perplexed look, and then the reason must have dawned on her, because she gave him a mischievous grin. Picking up his towel, she brought it to the side of the pool. "Why, Doctor, do you need me to dry you off?"

Was there anything she wouldn't do or say? He gave a moment's thought to calling her bluff, but knowing Amanda she would do it just to prove a point.

"Thanks for the offer, but maybe later. Just drop it by the steps."

She made a show of letting it slip slowly through her fingers to puddle on the cement.

There wasn't any easy way to cover his arousal, so he made quick work of climbing out of the pool and wrapping the towel around his waist. By the time he turned to Amanda she'd pulled on her flowing dress and had her bag in hand.

"You going to be able to drive, Doc?" A grin still curved her mouth.

"I am—but if you want to, you can." He started toward the car with her beside him.

Amanda's eyebrows went toward her hairline and her eyes widened. "Really?"

"If you'd like to. But I'm not sure a woman who's afraid of a baby squid can handle it."

Turnabout was fair play. He could tease as well.

But something was certainly off with him. He didn't normally tease *anyone*. Kirri would never believe it.

"I can assure you that I can handle it. The squid just surprised me."

He nodded thoughtfully. "Enough that you climbed up me like I was a tree?"

"I did not!"

Lucius chuckled. "Now, you see, it depends on who's the climb*ee* and who's the climb*er*."

"Are you making fun of me?" Amanda glared at him.

"No, I'd never do that." He dangled his car keys between them.

Something really was wrong with him. But he liked it. A lot. Their banter made him feel lighter, somehow.

She grinned and snatched the keys from his hand. A few minutes later they were belted in and Amanda had revved the motor. With a grin at him, she put the car into gear and drove out of the parking lot.

Lucius watched the pure joy on her face as they moved along the windy coast road on their return to the city. He'd never before let anyone else drive his car. His mouth pursed for a moment. Whatever was happening between them, it had to stop here, before it got out of hand.

"For this, I'll fix you breakfast," she announced as she made a turn.

He wasn't sure he should agree to that. But he wouldn't hurt her feelings by telling her no. Maybe he could get out of it diplomatically.

"You cook?"

"Of course I do. I'm a good cook. As good as I am a driver."

She smiled at him.

A smile that reached into his gut and tugged.

He'd been the one to put that happy expression on her

face. The feeling was nice, adding a bit of zeal to his life and, in an odd way, contentment. He enjoyed Amanda's company—even the teasing. With her, some of the weariness of his life seemed to slip away. Come to think of it, he hadn't thought about the clinic, or his work in hours. Surely breakfast together wouldn't hurt anyone?

"You're going to have to give me directions. Good ones. Because I'm driving on a different side of the road and I have to think about that."

"You want me to take over?"

Her chin jutted out and her determined eyes met his for a second. "Not a chance."

"You want to turn left in about a mile."

With a smile on his face he couldn't explain he continued to watch her and give directions for the next fifteen minutes.

Just another hour with Amanda wouldn't matter. How could it?

Amanda loved Lucius's car. Only in her dreams would she ever have thought she'd even get to ride in so fine a car, but to drive it was beyond her imagination.

More than that, she couldn't believe with how much abandon she'd reacted to Lucius's kiss. Worse was the fact she'd jumped into his arms like a silly schoolgirl.

She had been bold. Too bold.

That was an understatement.

She'd even gone so far as to invite him to breakfast.

But Lucius wasn't just some fellow visiting the clinic, or one of the local men who wanted a night out. He was intense, dedicated, serious, driven... The list went on. And she'd been teasing him. Had gone so far as to make fun of his discomfort at the pool when he'd become aroused. Had she lost her mind?

Lucius wasn't the type of man she should be attracted

to. She'd never let anyone close enough to get truly serious—couldn't trust men. They had let her down too many times in her life. Her father had died, her stepfather had never been there for her, and the last guy she'd cared about had ended up being a jerk. She couldn't survive another man disappointing her at this point in her life.

But surely she and Lucius were just friends. Why couldn't they enjoy a swim and breakfast together without it getting complicated?

Maybe because of that kiss…

Perhaps she shouldn't have invited him to eat, but it was too late now.

She drove up the street where she lived. Stunned, she saw several work trucks lined it, right in front of her apartment building. There were people standing around in groups, watching whatever was happening.

"Pull up over there." Lucius pointed to a spot behind one of the trucks. "Then we'll see what's going on."

She did as he said, then handed the keys to Lucius and grabbed her bag, not waiting for him. The first person she came to, she asked, "What's wrong?"

"Fire sprinkler went off."

"Was there a fire?" Lucius asked from beside her.

"No. Just a sprinkler malfunction," the man said. "But it's made a real mess. The building will have to be condemned."

"Condemned? Where am I going to live?" She wasn't speaking to anyone in particular as she walked closer to the apartment building. "I don't know of anyplace this close to the clinic. Not even a hotel."

Lucius had remained beside her. "You can stay at my house until we figure something out."

She stopped and gave him a look of disbelief. "What? I can't *live* with you."

He said in a flat voice, "I said *stay*. I have the space.

It'll at least give you a place for the weekend. A place to regroup. Figure things out."

"I don't know… Let me see if all of this is true."

She kept moving toward her building, dodging all the people. When she reached the front door she saw the man she knew as the apartment supervisor standing there.

"Mr. Kent—what's going on?"

The man looked haggard, and he confirmed what she had been told. "They're going to give us a half an hour to get what we can out of our apartments, then close the entire building up."

Just then a firefighter stepped out of the building and said, "Those who live here can go in for thirty minutes and get what they can. No longer. Please be prepared to show your identification."

Amanda stepped forward. The supervisor vouched for her and she vouched for Lucius when he stated he would be going up with her.

Minutes later, glad she had on shoes that were appropriate for water, she splashed through the front hall and up the stairs. Opening her apartment door, she looked dumbfounded at the soggy mess the apartment had become. She could only imagine what it would smell like when the heat of the day arrived…

"What can I do to help?" Lucius asked from behind her.

She picked up her new pillows, despite them being wet, and pulled them to her chest.

"Amanda, you don't have much time."

Compassion filled his voice, but there was a firmness as well. That was enough to get her moving.

"Tell me what to do." Lucius sounded sterner now.

"There are some plastic bags under the cabinet. Get some and put these pillows and that vase in them. I'll get my clothes."

She went to the bedroom, not waiting on Lucius to respond. She did have an advantage over the other residents in that she didn't live there permanently. Most of what she owned would fit into her suitcase, except what she'd told Lucius to pick up. To her surprise he hadn't argued or said that they were trivial items and should be left behind.

He stood in the doorway. "Is there anything else you want to get?"

"Get those two boxes of macaroni and cheese from the cabinet next to the microwave."

"You can replace those. That's not important." His voice held exasperation.

"I know, but I want them."

She didn't look at him but continued throwing her clothes into her suitcase, willy-nilly. Moments later she closed it. Lucius had returned and he took the case from her, handing her the plastic bags he carried.

"Ready?"

She nodded sadly. The apartment had only been her home for a couple of weeks, but it had been *hers*.

They stomped downstairs, being careful not to slip. Lucius led her back to the car and put her belongings in the trunk. He opened the passenger door and held it until she sat. Then he drove her away in a direction she didn't know.

With it being the weekend, she had no choice but to go with him or go to a hotel. How else would she get to the clinic if she was needed? But why had she let Lucius convince her to go with him so easily?

Because she was weak where he was concerned. And she trusted him. It was something she didn't easily do, yet Lucius had managed to earn her trust quickly.

"You can stay at my place until we figure something else out. I have three spare bedrooms. One is really a suite. You can stay there."

Less than an hour ago she'd been kissing him like there would be no tomorrow. There had been nothing friendly about it. Not that she hadn't enjoyed every second of it. And now she was going to stay at his house.

The idea spelled disaster. At least for her. What if he tried to kiss her again?

Surely she could handle herself like an adult for the weekend? She wasn't a teenage girl who'd been asked by the most popular boy in school to go to the prom. She needed a place to stay. It had been a practical decision. Lucius was just being friendly and supportive. Since she technically worked for him, he probably felt responsible for her.

She wouldn't make more of this invitation than there was. What she needed to do was focus on why she was here in Sydney.

They sat in silence as Lucius drove around the harbor.

"I didn't realize you lived so far from the clinic." She looked out at the sailboats filling the water on this weekend morning.

"Since I was a boy I've been fascinated by my house. When it came on the market I bought it. It's worth the drive."

She enjoyed the view of all the homes by the water. Then they entered another affluent neighborhood, left it, and drove on into one that looked slightly less expensive.

Finally Lucius pulled onto a white graveled driveway. A manicured privacy hedge stood on each side. The drive circled through a well-tended yard of green grass. A sprawling white nineteen-sixties one-story brick house came into view.

Lucius stopped the car in front of double wooden doors. Two large urns holding tall green plants were stationed on either side. Everything was in its place.

"This looks just like a place where you'd live," she said. She loved it immediately. Something about it said *home*.

"I'm not sure that's a compliment… It sounds suspiciously like what you said about my car. I'm clearly a man who holds no surprises."

That certainly wasn't true. Their kiss had proved it.

She licked her lips. "Yeah, but you know I like your car."

"You have made that clear."

His eyes lingered on her mouth. Finally he broke the moment and climbed out. Going to the trunk, he unloaded her things.

"Did your clothes get wet?" he asked.

"They're more like damp."

"We'll get them in the wash right now."

He unlocked the front door and pushed it wide.

"Welcome to my home."

Amanda forced herself not to gasp. The wide and spacious entrance with its high ceiling and gleaming oak floors took her breath away. Ahead was a glass wall that looked out onto a green lawn, and the view of the harbor beyond overtook her amazement at the foyer. She could tell why he liked this house so much. It was a piece of heaven.

Lucius led her down a short hallway that opened into a sunken living room. In it were a couple of brown leather sofa units and a large TV hung on a white brick wall. The understated luxury looked comfortable and very masculine. From here she could clearly see the Opera House and the Sydney Bridge.

"Wow!" The sound rushed from her.

"The laundry is this way."

Lucius moved along another hallway running parallel with the back wall. They were soon in a kitchen that had the same breathtaking view. A small room that branched off it held the washer and the dryer.

"I want to do the pillows first, so they can get as much drying time outside as possible."

Lucius lifted the lid of the washer. "Why're these so important to you?"

"Because I bought them to make the space mine." She shrugged. "I don't know… I just like them." She blinked, trying to keep the moisture filling her eyes at bay. Why was she so upset over an apartment that really wasn't hers?

Lucius must have noticed, because he pulled her into his arms for a hug. She let him. Just for a moment surely it would be okay.

"I know you must be rattled by all this. First a squid and now your apartment…"

She pulled back. "Don't you dare make fun of me!"

"I'm not. I promise." He pulled her back to his chest, then let her go. "I tell you what—why don't I find you something dry to wear so you can get out of that bathing suit? Then I'll show you your bedroom and I'll cook you breakfast—or lunch. Whichever you prefer. Then you can just hang around here and watch TV, swim or sleep. I'm sure things will look better in an hour or two."

She didn't want to agree but it all sounded wonderful. A hot bath, dry clothes and time for a think would be great. Having someone take care of her for a change had its appeal. She didn't usually allow that. Most of the men she'd dated complained she could be too independent.

"Okay, point me in the right direction."

Lucius led her back across the house to the other side of the living room. He opened a door, revealing a spacious room with another view of the harbor. A large bed with a striped bedspread took center-stage. A sitting area lay off to one side, and it included a small TV.

He'd seemed to imply earlier that the suite would be more like a maid's quarters. It turned out to be much nicer and spacious than that. She could get used to staying here—but she wouldn't.

"The bathroom is through that door. Take your time. I'll leave you some clothes on the bed."

Amanda sighed. She'd have a tough time leaving this place to go live in a hotel—or anywhere else for that matter.

"I hope you'll be comfortable here."

"Are you kidding? This is amazing. I don't know how you go to work every day when you could stay here and just *be*."

Could she do that? Just *be* for the next couple of days? Could she live harmoniously with him and the sexual tension that sizzled between them whenever they were near each other? Would it grow to become more than she could resist? Especially since all she had to do was look at Lucius to think of their kiss in the pool and his noticeable reaction to it. She'd seen the thickness of his manhood before he'd covered himself.

"I admit the view did have a lot to do with me buying the house. But it's only really nice if you have somebody to share it with."

"I'll be glad to share it with you. Anytime. Like I said, it's amazing."

That had sounded more suggestive that it should have…

"Then today we'll enjoy it together," he said.

And with that promise he left her.

There was a real chance she'd agreed to enter the lion's den. If she didn't keep her wits about her she would get bitten.

CHAPTER FIVE

LUCIUS WONDERED IF his feelings resembled those of a soldier who had invited the enemy into his camp. Not that he considered Amanda his *enemy*, as such. It was more he was unsure of what to expect. The problem was his attraction to her. He'd tried not to be, yet he had failed miserably.

Still, she was homeless. He had the room, so it had seemed logical and gentlemanly to ask her if she wanted to stay with him for the time being. Unsure about the situation, but in a strange country, Amanda hadn't put up much resistance to his suggestion.

While she remained under his roof he must keep his hands to himself, despite his desire to grab her, kiss her and haul her off to his bed. He couldn't remember being this infatuated with a woman—ever. Their kiss had assured him that there was something special between them.

Not even his wife had held the type of lure for him that Amanda did. Maybe that was because he knew she'd soon be leaving. That there would be no long-term commitment. He'd failed miserably at his marriage and had no intention of doing that again. Nothing about him had changed to make him think he'd be any different from how he had been the first time around. He wouldn't put any woman through that kind of agony.

He'd accepted what his job would require, what his world would look like, when he'd become a doctor. He had been raised to believe that was how he should live, knowing his priorities. Success had brought even more demands on him, but he did good in the world and that was important. Last Saturday's picnic had proved that.

Because of his responsibilities he couldn't promise Amanda anything, but did that mean they couldn't enjoy each other's company before she left, though? They liked each other, had their work in common, and were both fond of swimming. There was also their witty conversation and the fun they had together.

Fun? No one had ever accused him of being a *fun* person. He was rather surprised he was even capable of it. But Amanda made him happy. When was the last time he'd been able to say that?

Would she agree to a fling or just want to remain friends? He couldn't ever offer more than that.

Lucius had almost finished preparing breakfast when Amanda came into the kitchen. He had to reinforce his resolution when she came near, freshly showered and with pink cheeks. She wore one of his T-shirts and a pair of his shorts that were far too big for her. He guessed she wore nothing beneath them, which did absolutely nothing to tamp down his desire.

Amanda sniffed the air. "That smells wonderful."

She did too.

"Hey, how're you feeling?" he asked.

"Better. Just hungry."

He moved the pan off the hot stove. "That's good. It's ready. I went with making breakfast, since I'm a little better at cooking that than I am the other meals of the day."

She giggled.

The sound did something to Lucius in an area of his chest he didn't recognize.

"I could've fixed it."

He inhaled her scent, storing it in his memory. "I've

got it. I'll give you a chance to prove you're a good cook another time."

"I could do supper tonight." She sounded eager.

"I thought we'd order in Chinese and watch a movie. It'd be a lot less work."

Amanda stepped around him. "But I—"

"No argument. You rest today and then we'll see about tomorrow."

"You *do* know you can't tell me what to do outside of work?"

There was strength in her words, but a note of playfulness as well. Although one thing he had learned early on was that Amanda didn't like taking orders outside the clinic.

"I do know that. Now, if you wish, *please* pick up your plate and take it outside to the table by the pool and breakfast will be served."

"That's more like it."

Amanda, with a huge smile on her face, took the plate he had just filled with food. She led the way out the door. He followed with his own plate.

"This is very decadent." Amanda placed the plate on the table.

"I've never thought of it like that." He hadn't. This was simply the way he lived his life.

"That's because you're used to having a pool in the side yard and a beautiful view of the harbor. Living in Atlanta, among a lot of high-rise buildings and with the coast hours away, I never eat in a place like this."

"Still, I wouldn't describe it as decadent..."

"Look at this." She waved her hand around. "Even the plants are perfect."

"If it'll make you feel more comfortable I'll throw a few napkins in among them."

Laughter burst from Amanda. Lucius joined in. It felt

so good to laugh. He'd not known enough of that in his life. He intended to enjoy it while he could.

Amanda settled down to giggles and worked words in around them. "I'm sorry. I'm being a poor guest. It's just that I'm so impressed. You have a lovely home."

"Thank you. Now, what would you like to drink? I only have coffee, tea, and water until I call in my grocery list."

"You have your groceries delivered, don't you?"

"Yes. Is that a problem?"

She pressed her lips together, as if she was making an effort not to grin. "Nope. Hot tea sounds perfect."

"I'll be right back. Go ahead and eat so it won't get cold."

It had been a long time since he'd been a host. He rarely had company, and when he did it was usually a business gathering and he hired a catering service to handle the food. He found it refreshing to show hospitality personally.

This morning he was doing all types of things out of the ordinary for him.

Returning to Amanda, he found her sitting in her chair with her head back and her eyes closed. She straightened as he approached. He placed their drinks on the table.

"I'm sorry. Again, I'm not being much of a guest if I go to sleep on you."

"No problem. You've had an unusual few hours and swimming can tire you as well. After you eat your breakfast feel free to take a nap."

"I have to admit that cushioned lounger looks inviting…" She looked past him toward the pool.

He picked up his fork. "It's all yours. I have paperwork that I need to attend to."

She started on her food when he did. "Do you work all the time?"

He hadn't thought about it, but now that he did he realized he *did* work much of the time. That was what he knew—it had been the example his father had set for him.

"A good deal of it, yes."

"You *do* know that it's okay to take time off as well? It'll make you a better doctor."

Lucius studied her for a moment. "Is that your prescription for a problem I don't know that I have? I'm used to using my time constructively."

His family measured success by how busy they were. They believed in producing results.

"I'm sorry. The way you live your life isn't my business." She returned to her meal.

They continued to eat in silence.

Amanda cleared her plate and placed her fork down.

"Why don't you go on and get that nap?" Lucius said.

"I can't leave you with the dishes—you cooked."

"Don't worry about them."

"Then that lounger is calling me. Breakfast was great, thank you."

"My pleasure. Just be sure that you don't get too much sun." He started gathering the dishes.

"I understand about the Australian sun. I'll get my sunscreen and a hat."

Sometime later he looked out the kitchen window to see Amanda settled on the lounger. She looked relaxed. What would it hurt if he joined her for a while? Work could wait…

He frowned. If he wasn't careful she would corrupt him.

Amanda woke to the sound of soft snores beside her. She looked to her right to see Lucius lying on the lounger next to her. He wore no shirt and dark sunglasses covered his eyes. She studied him. He was a handsome man, with his tanned body, square jaw, and wavy hair that begged to be touched. The temptation to run her hand through it almost overcame her.

He was a combination of toughness and sensitivity. She'd seen for herself this large man holding a tiny baby with such tenderness. He tried so hard not to show that side of himself, yet she'd seen it again today when she'd lost her apartment. He'd been really sweet and understanding, treating her like a queen.

She'd better get her defense shields up if she was going to keep some space between them. The enigma he was had a powerful pull on her. One she feared would hurt her when it was time for her to leave. She couldn't stand another heartache.

Amanda shifted on the cushions. The slight difference in his breathing told her Lucius had woken, yet he remained still.

"Amanda, are you watching me?" His voice had turned gravelly from sleep and sounded super-sexy.

She shivered. What would it be like to hear it in her ear as he entered her?

She cleared her throat. *Whoa,* her imagination was working overtime.

"Uh…yes. I've been thinking that maybe we should have some ground rules while I'm staying here."

"Ground rules?" His tone was now cautious and suspicious. "Like no staring at me while I sleep?"

Heat that had nothing to do with the Australian sun filled her cheeks. She licked her lips. "That one could be added."

"I don't care if you look at me. I find it flattering."

He still hadn't turned in her direction, but she could see a hint of a smile on his mouth.

She needed to bring this conversation back to where it belonged. "I was thinking more like if I'm going to stay here, even for a little while, we need to have an understanding. After that kiss…"

"You didn't like it?" His voice held a teasing note.

Heat rushed through her. "I didn't say that."

Lucius rolled toward her. "Then you *did* like it?"

"I just don't think it should happen again." She had quickly lost control of this discussion.

"Why not?" He still watched her.

"Uh… I just think that sort of stuff will confuse things." This wasn't going well at all. "I don't want us to get uncomfortable with each other. I think we need to keep this friendly and uncomplicated. What happened at the pool doesn't need to be repeated."

She couldn't see his blue eyes for the dark sunglasses, but she could easily imagine them snapping.

"Let's forget the ground rules all except one," he said.

"Lucius, hear me out—"

"Look, I'm attracted to you, but I'm not going to do anything you don't agree with. It's as simple as that. If you want more than just us being 'friendly,' as you put it, you only have to say the word. It's all up to you. If you don't, I'll learn to live with it. Now, does that ease your mind?"

Amanda swallowed. For some reason Lucius's attitude left her bereft. It was as if the idea of remaining friends with her or not didn't matter to him one way or another. Here she was, struggling to keep her distance for both their sakes, and he was acting flippant about it.

"Okay…" Even to her own ears it sounded weak.

Lucius nodded and settled back on the lounger.

Silence hung between them. It didn't feel friendly. If anything, their discussion had escalated the tension between them. She glanced at Lucius. His arms rested over his waist and his ankles were crossed as if all was well with his world. Meanwhile hers whirled with turmoil.

She looked out over the harbor at the boats and the ferries moving across the water. Somehow it eased her nerves. Being in Australia, even with Lucius, was good for her. Life back home had been all about work and proving herself for too long. Here she sat, in this time and place, just enjoying the warmth of the sun.

Sometime later Lucius stood. “Okay, enough sun. Time to go in.”

Amanda started to argue but knew he was right. She didn’t need to burn. She followed him inside.

“Make yourself at home in the kitchen. I’ve got work to do. I’ll see you later.” Lucius left her without a backward glance.

Amanda went to her room and caught up on some reading, then quietly prepared herself a sandwich for lunch. She thought about doing one for Lucius too, but she didn’t know him well enough to know what he preferred, or even if he ate anything at lunchtime, so she decided to let it go.

The sun had started to go down when he came to her open door and stopped. “Hey, I was just getting ready to call for some Chinese. You still good with that?”

“That’ll be great.”

Amanda wanted to groan. Her response had sounded far too eager. But she’d not seen him since the morning and in an odd way she’d missed him. The air seemed less electrified with him not around. Lucius gave her chills, but in a good way.

Ooh, she needed to stop those kinds of thoughts. She was in Sydney to *work*, not to start a relationship with a man, and certainly not with one with such a high profile.

“You won’t require the movie to be a chick flick, will you?”

She put an indignant note in her voice. “I like other movies as well.”

“Good to know. I’ll go call for the Chinese. I’ll let you know when it’s here.” He turned and left.

The evening soon developed into a nice one. They agreed on a *Bourne* movie, and she took one couch and he the other. Lucius had surround sound, so watching the movie resembled being at a real theater. It turned out he even had automatic drapes installed over the huge windows. When they were closed darkness surrounded them, like being in a cave.

Amanda tried to get caught up in the movie but she couldn't seem to get beyond the knowledge that the sexy man who had kissed her like there was no tomorrow sat only feet away.

Her attention kept drifting Lucius's way. A couple of times he caught her looking at him and raised a brow, before his attention returned to the movie. In a way, it made her mad. Here she was, with her nerves in knots and firing overtime, and Lucius sat there as cool as could be. It was wrong. It made her want to rattle his cage.

Before she went to bed, she opened the door to the patio off her room and stepped outside. The lights of Sydney reflected off the harbor. The Opera House looked like full white sails and the bridge twinkled in the velvet of the night. The sound of splashing drew her attention to the pool. Apparently Lucius was swimming. Hadn't he gotten enough exercise that morning or was he swimming for another reason?

Maybe he hadn't been as unaffected by her presence as he had acted. She discovered she really liked that idea.

Lucius woke with a jolt to sounds coming from the kitchen. Someone was in there.

Amanda.

He should've realized that right away, since he'd spent most of the night trying to forget she was sleeping just on the other side of the house.

He'd swum and swum, hoping exhaustion would take

him after spending the evening watching a movie with her just a few steps away. Done with his swim, he'd taken a shower—a cold one—and still his body hadn't settled down. He'd tossed and turned into the wee hours of the morning before he'd finally found some rest.

He'd taken a big risk by inviting her into his home. The problem was he hadn't thought it through well enough. Hell, he hadn't thought *at all*. He'd just opened his mouth and the words had come out. There had been no consideration about what it would do to his mind or his body to have her so close twenty-four-seven.

He was a man who had accepted his solitude long ago, but it hadn't taken Amanda long to disrupt it. She made him want things that had long lain dormant and should remain that way. The sooner she was out of his house the better.

Normally he rose early, but thoughts of Amanda had managed to get his life out of sync. Even something as simple as a night's sleep had become problematic. But her pull on him had to ease sometime, surely? Maybe he would be able to get beyond this—whatever "this" was—if he kissed her again. Just once more.

But he had made a promise. One that he would honor even though it might be the death of him.

He climbed out of bed and pulled on shorts and a T-shirt, then headed for the kitchen. Amanda stood at the counter with her back to him. His first instinct was to slip up behind her and kiss her neck. But as enticing as the thought might be, he held himself in check. He might regret being a gentleman but…

Amanda looked over her shoulder as she continued to butter bread. "Mornin'."

He loved her accent, and the sound of her voice when she dropped the last letter of a word. Somehow hearing it made having to get out of bed something to look forward to.

"Good morning."

"I hope I didn't wake you? I'm making toast and eggs. Want some?"

"Yes, I do. I'm hungry."

His gaze met hers and held. Did she realize it was her he was hungry for?

"I'll have it ready in a few minutes."

It had been a long time since he'd woken to find a woman in his kitchen. He found he liked it. Having someone else in the house was nice. Or was it having *Amanda* there?

How had he let his thoughts, imagination and libido get so out of hand? Hadn't it been just yesterday morning when he had planned to put some distance between them?

Yeah, that had been before that kiss that had left him dreaming of more and before he'd brought her home with him. He was a gentleman, not a monk.

Amanda glanced at him. "Did you sleep well?"

He couldn't answer that honestly, so he gave up and lied. "I did."

"Good. I wanted to ask you about how close the ferry port is to here." She continued to work.

"I'll be glad to drive you anywhere you need to go."

She'd already started shaking her head. "No, I want to ride the ferry. See the city and the surrounding area from the water."

"I've not been on the ferry since I was a boy."

"Then you should come too."

Amanda smiled at him as if it was the perfect solution to a problem he hadn't been aware he had.

Lucius knew he should say no, but he couldn't think of a good reason not to go.

"Okay. While you finish breakfast I'll check the ferry schedule."

"Sounds like a plan." She picked up an egg and broke it over a bowl.

A couple of hours later they were on their way out the front door, Amanda almost bouncing with enthusiasm. Lucius followed with a lot less excitement. He knew he was quickly moving out of his comfort zone and creating more problems for himself.

"How far is it to the ferry port?" she wanted to know.

"I guess about a half a mile."

"It's a nice day—let's walk. The weather report said it wasn't going to rain until later tonight."

He twisted his mouth, lowered his chin and looked at her in amazement. "You listened to the weather report?"

"Yeah, I turned on the radio while I was dressing. Where I come from during the spring and summer we have rain almost every day, so you have to plan."

"I really don't mind driving." He hadn't walked any distance in years.

"I like to walk. It lets you see things you wouldn't when you're riding by. I want to really *see* the neighborhood."

"All right."

Lucius figured he wasn't going to win the argument. From the sound of it she had already made her mind up. He'd quickly learned that she had a tendency to do that.

Strolling down the driveway, they soon reached the sidewalk. They passed a few people. A couple jogged by while others walked their dogs. To his astonishment Amanda spoke to everyone. After their initial surprise they returned her greeting.

"Why do you do that?" he asked.

"What?" Amanda asked over her shoulder as she looked through the gateway of a house.

"Speak to everyone?"

She shrugged and joined him again. "Just being friendly, I guess. It's what we do at home. We make eye contact when we come up to someone and then we speak. I thought everyone did it."

He grinned. "You're shocking my neighbors."

Her eyes widened and she cocked her head to the side in surprise. "Really? Should I stop?"

"No, they'll recover. It sounds like a nice habit to have."

She grinned. "I guess it's a Southern thing."

"I thought maybe you were going to tell me it was an Amanda thing." He found there were a number of things he considered special about her.

"I wasn't gonna say that." She glanced over her shoulder at him.

"Gonna? I like the way you phrase things. Your accent and the slow way you speak. Somehow it's soothing."

"Thank you. But I don't want you to think because I talk slow I think slow."

They turned a corner.

"I would never make that mistake," he said. "You're one of the most intelligent people I know."

"Why, Dr. West, I do believe you're trying to charm me. Thank you. I consider that high praise coming from you," she said in a distracted voice as she studied the house they were passing. "The houses around here are amazing. Everyone takes such meticulous care of them and their lawns."

"Here I was thinking you were super-impressed just with my house."

She grabbed his forearm. "Oh, I am. I really am. It's close to perfect."

"I might have fished for that compliment, but I'll take it."

He liked hearing that Amanda admired his home. He

wanted her to like it. And that really was somewhere he didn't need to go. He would never offer another woman a permanent place in his life *or* his home. No, he wouldn't do that to himself or to the woman. He would only end up disappointing her, and that was something he never wanted to do again.

They took another turn and he could see the ferry port up ahead. He rarely used public transportation of any kind. The ferry would be as much a novelty for him as for Amanda.

He paid for their tickets and they walked on.

Amanda led him upstairs. "I want a good spot."

He looked around. Few people were on board. It was Sunday morning and not as busy as it would be on a weekday, when people were traveling to work.

"I don't think that'll be a problem," he said.

"I think you're making fun of me again."

He grinned. "I'd never do that."

Amanda gave his arm a light swat. "I know you would."

The ferry moved out into the harbor. As it did so they stood in silence for a while, just looking around them.

"This is really amazing," Amanda said, as much to the wind as she did to him. "We have nothing like this close to where I live. I do have a friend who lives on a houseboat on one of the lakes nearby, though."

Lucius crossed his arms and leaned on the rail. "I'm not sure that would be a great place to be during a storm."

"You're probably right. Do you ever take the ferry to work?"

"No, I can't take that kind of time. I can be there much faster driving."

"I think it would be a lovely way to start the day—riding across the water, then walking to work. Relaxing before the craziness of the day starts."

That had never occurred to Lucius. He rose every morning thinking about what he had to do that day. He didn't have time for a leisurely trip to work. Or at least he'd never thought he had.

"That might pose a problem, since babies aren't known for waiting around on ferries."

"That would be the case for me, but less for you. You schedule your procedures."

She had him there. "So, what're we going to do when we get to the other side?" he asked.

Amanda giggled.

"What's so funny?" It had sounded like a reasonable question to him.

"That just made me think of an old joke."

"What joke?"

"You know the one. Why did the chicken cross the road? To get to the other side!"

He chuckled. "I get it. We're riding the ferry to get to the other side."

"Yes, but I'd like to go to that mall, the Strand, and see the stained-glass I've heard about. You're welcome to come with me."

He hadn't been there since he was a boy. His mother had taken him and his sister. His father had had little time for such outings. Even if he had the mall would have been the last place his father would have agreed to go. He was more of a museum kind of person.

Why *shouldn't* Lucius go with Amanda? The seminar notes he had to prepare for the medical conference next month could wait. He'd been doing things out of character since he'd met Amanda, so what would one more matter?

"If you don't mind me tagging along?"

"I'd like to have you join me."

She gave him a bright smile.

Suddenly his day seemed more cheerful.

The time went by surprisingly fast.

After they'd exited the ferry they strolled along the brick walk surrounding the harbor and then started toward the Strand. It was great fun to watch Amanda's face light up as she experienced the city for the first time.

At the mall, she looked up at the stained-glass ceiling in delight. "It's awesome."

Lucius couldn't help but smile. "You sure are using that word often."

"I guess I am. I think most of the things in Australia are amazing."

His chest area warmed when her eyes drifted to him. He didn't know if she was truly including him, but he hoped she was. He liked to think Amanda was flirting with him.

"How about lunch while we're here?"

They found a small café with tables and chairs outside the front door. There they ate their sandwiches. Afterward they walked back toward the ferry port.

As they passed a small grocery store Amanda grabbed his arm. "I need to go in here for a few minutes. I want to get some things for that supper I promised you."

"Why don't you wait and I'll have them delivered?"

She shook her head. "It's just one or two things. And I like to pick out my own produce."

"Okay."

Lucius followed her in. He hadn't been in a grocery store in years.

Amanda grabbed a plastic basket and started down the narrow aisle. She picked out a bundle of asparagus, some eggs, and located a package of brownie mix.

"I'd get some ice cream but it wouldn't make it home."

He took the basket from her. "I already have some at home."

"That figures," she said.

He placed the basket on the bench to check out. "How's that?"

She grinned. "You're a man. Most men consider ice cream a staple."

"I'm not sure I like being lumped in with 'most' men, but I do like ice cream."

She insisted on paying. Then she said, "I'm ready to go home now."

Amanda calling his place "home" left another warm feeling in his chest.

He frowned. In a few weeks she would be going back to America. He must be desperate for female attention to be acting like a giddy schoolboy with his first crush.

Lucius took the bags from her as they left the store.

"I like being able to get my groceries and walk home," she said. "We do too much driving where I live."

They made it to the ferry just as it was docking. This time they rode on the inside. They talked some, but also sat in silence. As they were getting off he took the bags once more. Amanda put up a small argument but soon relented.

At the house, she insisted she'd put their purchases away. He went to his office to check for messages.

It had been an amazing day. Exploring the city with Amanda had been fun. Instead of being tired from the exercise he felt invigorated. He'd seen his home city through different eyes.

In future he would make time to have more days like this one.

It just wouldn't be with Amanda.

Amanda placed a pan of water on the stove. When had she last cooked dinner for a man? It had been a long time. She found it satisfying. It gave her a sense of being needed.

That was something she had always wanted but rarely felt. On the selfish side, and deep down, she acknowledged that had been part of the reason she'd gone into nursing. There she was definitely needed.

But, regardless of how nice it felt, she shouldn't get used to preparing Lucius's meals. Doing so was temporary, a onetime thing, and nothing more. They'd had a lovely day together, but just as friends. That was the way it should be.

Right now she trusted no man not to hurt her. She wanted forever. So far no man had offered her that. Lucius hadn't given any indication he'd ever be that man, so why have all these unrealistic thoughts about him? His friendship would have to be enough.

He had offered to barbecue the steaks while she worked inside on the rest of the meal. She was happy to have his help. He came in as she finished mixing the brownies.

"The steaks will be done in a few minutes." He grabbed a platter.

"That'll be about the time I have everything else ready. Do you think it's too hot for us to eat outside?"

"We'll be fine under the umbrella."

"Great. I'm jealous of where you get to spend your time. I'm trying to soak up all I can before I have to leave."

He smiled. "You're welcome to it."

A quarter of an hour later Amanda had everything together. She'd set the table and was now carrying out a plate of asparagus and a bowl of macaroni and cheese.

Lucius waited at the table with the steaks nearby. "Looks good." He took the bowl from her and placed it on the table. He gave it an unconvinced look.

She narrowed her eyes. "You're surprised?"

"Let's just say it's unexpected."

"I think that's a diplomatic way of dodging my question. May I fix you a plate?"

"Please." He handed her his plate and she placed a scoop of macaroni and cheese on it along with a bundle of asparagus.

She passed him her own empty plate. "Steak, please."

Lucius forked one piece of meat onto her plate and the other onto his. Amanda added portions of the rest of the food to hers, sat down, and pushed the basket of rolls toward Lucius. He took one.

She watched as Lucius initially moved his macaroni and cheese around, as if still unsure. Finally he placed a forkful in his mouth and chewed.

"Not bad. Better than I thought it would be." He sounded surprised.

She snorted in amusement.

"That was a sort of praise." His gaze met hers sheepishly. "In all sincerity, thank you for taking the time to prepare us dinner."

She grinned, feeling vindicated. "It's my pleasure. Tell me, have you always lived in Sydney?"

"Yes, originally just outside of the city on a private estate. How about you? Are you originally from Atlanta?"

"No, my stepfather's job moved us all around the country. We were in Atlanta when he retired, so I've lived there the longest. I ended up going to college there and then taking a job."

"You like it?"

She shrugged. "It's been a good place to live, but I have to admit of all the places I've been I love Sydney the best. The beauty, the people… I like everything about it."

Lucius focused on cutting a slice of tender, juicy steak. "That's nice to know. I think Kirri feels the same way about Atlanta."

"I think she'd feel that way about any place Ty was." Amanda took a bread roll.

"I guess you're right."

He sounded as if he didn't understand that kind of devotion.

They spent the rest of the meal talking about what they had done that day, the kind of music they liked, and comparing other favorite things. When they were done they carried their dishes inside and cleaned up the kitchen.

Amanda took the brownies out of the oven and turned it off. "I'll just get dessert together. I'm going to eat mine outside, so I can watch the sunset. I'd be glad to bring yours to your office."

"I can't join you?" He sounded hurt.

"Sure you can. I just thought you'd have work to do, a movie to watch… I don't want you to feel you have to entertain me."

She liked the idea of Lucius spending time with her too much.

"Would you like me to move a couple of chairs closer to the water?"

"You're starting to know me too well. That would be perfect."

Amanda pulled a couple of small plates out of the cabinet.

"I don't think it's possible to know all about you," said Lucius as he headed toward the outside door.

Amanda carried out two plates of brownie with scoops of ice cream on top and joined Lucius, who had just placed the second chair beside the first. She handed him a plate and they both sat down.

Lucius released a loud sigh of approval after his first bite. "This may be the best dessert I've had in years."

The sound of his spoon scraping over the empty china plate came a few minutes later.

"You want some more?" she asked.

"No." His tone was regretful. "But it was delicious."

He put the plate down between them and leaned back with another sigh. She followed his lead and did the same. They said nothing as the sun, now a bright orange circle on the horizon, slowly disappeared. The only light came from the city and it didn't completely reach them.

They sat in silence for a while. And her mind was more on Lucius than the view as she finally stood up to go back inside.

His fingers were gentle as they wrapped around her wrist. "Stay a little longer. This is nice."

That was the last thing she had expected him to say. She assumed he'd want to get back to his work.

"Okay." She sat down again.

Lucius's fingers trailed across her skin and then they were gone. Amanda immediately missed their heat.

They sat there not talking for a long time, until she couldn't stand the electricity that was popping between them any longer. She wanted him to touch her. Didn't want him to touch her. He'd said it was up to her. It was a gentlemanly concept, but in reality it put all the pressure on her. Her mind said, *Don't go there!* while her disloyal body yelled, *You want him!*

Amanda stood abruptly. "I really should go in now. I need to prepare for work tomorrow. What time should I be ready in the morning?"

"Around eight will be fine." There was an unsure note in his voice, as if she had surprised him.

"I'll be ready."

She headed for her bedroom, not daring to look at Lucius for fear she would turn back and hurl herself at him.

CHAPTER SIX

THE FLASH OF lightning shook Lucius awake and the sound of thunder made him sit up. The wind swooshed around the corner of the house as fat drops of rain hit the window. He needed to get the chairs he'd left near the water secured. He should have brought them in earlier, but his mind had been filled with Amanda instead of outdoor furniture.

The wind shook the window. He shouldn't linger. The pool umbrella needed lowering as well. If he didn't move fast he'd have to fish it out of the pool in the morning. Worse, the chairs might be in the harbor and gone forever, or busted on the rocks.

Jerking on his shorts, he hurried outside through the kitchen door, flipping on a floodlight as he went.

He cranked down the umbrella, pulled it out of the center hole in the table and laid it beside the house, where it would be secure. The rain was beating down now, and rolled off his shoulders.

On bare feet he loped toward the harbor. Picking up a chair, he started toward the patio. He was halfway there when Amanda passed him, going in the other direction.

"Go inside!" he yelled over the weather.

She didn't slow down. He wasn't sure if she hadn't heard him or if she was just ignoring him. Lucius suspected the latter.

Placing the chair on the patio, he went after her. She

was moving slowly across the yard struggling to carry a heavy chair. When he got to her, he took one arm of the chair and together they raced to the patio.

He glanced at Amanda. She was soaked as well. On the patio, they dropped the chair on its legs and ran for the kitchen door.

Inside, Lucius slammed the door behind them. Amanda's hair hung in rainy ropes around her face. Tiny beads of water perched on the ends of her eyelashes. Her eyes were wide and her gaze lay squarely on his chest. She licked the moisture from her lips.

He should have been chilled, standing there wet in the air-conditioning, but instead his body heated rapidly. His manhood stirred. Amanda's thin nightgown was stuck to her body, highlighting her full breasts and generous hips and leaving him in no doubt of her femininity. Her legs were long enough to circle his waist. The neon blue polish on her toes made the corner of his mouth twitch upward. Amanda was sexy in every sense of the word.

She shivered.

The movement brought him back to reality. She had less body mass than he and must be freezing.

Grabbing her hand, he said, "Come with me."

Amanda didn't argue. Another flash of lightning lit the way as he led her to his room. Her soft hiss found his ears as he pulled her through the door, but she didn't resist. Moments later they were in his bathroom. Heading straight to the shower, he opened the door and turned the water to hot.

"Strip."

She looked at him dumbfounded, not moving.

As steam built in the shower he placed his hand on her back and gave her a gentle nudge. "Get warm."

She stepped in and he closed the door.

"There'll be a towel hanging within reach out here when

you're done," he called as he pulled one of the towels off the rack and began drying his hair.

Lucius glanced at the shower. He needed to get out of here. He'd made a promise, after all.

As he walked out of the bathroom he continued to dry off. Going to his dresser, Lucius pulled out a dry pair of shorts and quickly changed clothes. He needed to get Amanda back on her side of the house as soon as possible.

The bathroom door opened. Amanda stood there with the bright light as a backdrop. A towel concealed her body where she held it in place. What little he'd managed to do to ease his longing was lost in a moment. His heart thumped and his manhood grew in hard, hot desire.

Her gaze caught his and then flickered to his chest before traveling downward. Her mouth formed a small O. He could only guess that she'd seen his rigid length, which must be clearly visible behind the flimsy material of his shorts.

Amanda took a slow, hesitant step toward him that soon turned to a bolder one. She stopped just inches before she could touch him. Lucius didn't move. His breaths had turned rapid and shallow. His body tightened almost in pain with his effort not to reach for her. This must be her decision.

She rose on her toes and pressed her lips against his. One of her hands came to his shoulder, branding his bare skin. Her tongue teased his bottom lip. She nipped at it, then soothed the spot with the tip of her tongue. He opened his mouth and joined her in exploration. The kiss grew deep as she stepped closer, squeezing his hardened length between them.

Lucius wanted her badly. Had wanted her for days. Still, he needed to know she understood where this was going.

He broke the kiss and stepped back so he could see her clearly. "Just to be clear, what are you telling me, Amanda?"

Her voice was husky and very sexy as she said, "I'd have thought a man with your intelligence would know."

His look never wavered from hers. "But that doesn't mean I don't want to hear it."

She let go of the towel. "Dr. Lucius West, I want you to take me to your bed."

That was all the invitation he required.

He pulled her against him, felt her lips soft and full beneath his. Amanda met his ardor with equal abandon. Her arms circled his neck. As they tightened her breasts brushed his chest. His manhood jerked. He'd dreamed of a moment like this. Thoughts of what might happen between them had kept him awake over the last few days. Yet those imagined touches hadn't been anything like what was happening to him now. This was far more wonderful.

Her mouth opened and his tongue invaded. She tasted honey-sweet, with a nectar all her own. His hands found her waist, skimmed over her bare hips and moved down to cup her behind.

Amanda's hands moved to his shoulders. Her fingertips kneaded his skin, then traveled along his upper arm. They brushed over his ribs and down to his waist. Her hands rested there, then pulled him closer before they found the waistband of his shorts. A finger traced the line of it before her hand slipped beneath the material. Her other hand followed suit, and moments later she'd pushed his shorts down.

His mouth left hers to place kisses along her cheek and then nuzzle behind her ear. Amanda's soft giggle made his chest swell.

His shorts at his feet, he stepped out of them, rotated her and walked her backward to his bed. There, he turned and sat down, pulling Amanda between his legs. Her hands rested on the top of his shoulders.

Lucius looked up at her. Even with her hair mussed from

where his hands had run through it she looked beautiful. Their gazes met and held. Amanda's eyes were bright with curiosity, and maybe a touch of apprehension.

"I want to admire you." Cupping her cheek, Lucius brought her lips to his.

She released a soft sigh, then kissed him in return.

His hand ran down her hips and pulled her closer before he broke contact. His attention moved to the globes of her breasts, which were full and luscious. Her nipples were extended, begging for his attention. Lifting a breast, he appreciated its weight for a moment, then kissed the curve before slipping his mouth over her tip.

Amanda rewarded him with a shiver.

"Shh...easy... You're so amazing I just want to admire you. Taste you."

He moved to the other breast, caressing it until Amanda's fingers moved through his hair and held him closer. Her groan of pleasure vibrated through him.

Then slowly her hands returned to his shoulders. She pushed him until he lay back on the bed. "It's my turn now," she said.

Lucius watched as she climbed up beside him. She ran her hands over his chest, pausing for a second to brush her palm over the hair at its center. His nerves were electrified. He caressed her from her waist to hip. Her skin was so perfect, silky-smooth.

Amanda stopped her movements and turned her attention to his lips. Using her index finger, she followed the line of his bottom lip with great care. When she did the same to the seam of his mouth he took the tip of the finger into his mouth and bit it gently. She removed it slowly before leaning down and kissing him.

Lucius joined in the heated meeting of lips, pulling her across him. The lightning flashed and the thunder rolled and the rain pounded against the window. It reminded him of the turmoil going on in his body.

He'd been aware of Amanda's passion regarding her work, even her excitement in seeing and learning new things during their sightseeing. He'd hoped those emotions would extend to the bedroom, but what she was doing to him now had gone light years beyond his most sensual dreams.

Nothing he'd shared with another woman had had him as conscious of his breathing, or the sensitivity of his skin, nor had created such an uncontrollable drive in him to take her. Everything about him burned with life, all because Amanda was kissing and touching him. She had opened a door he feared he would never be able to close or would never want to.

Lucius rolled her over on the bed. He watched her eyes heat and her lips part as his palm brushed a nipple. Her look widened with anticipation as his hand traveled to her stomach and rested there before he moved it lower. Her hiss of sensual awareness rippled through him.

"One of the things I like the best about you is that I never have to guess what you like or don't like. You definitely like this..." Lucius ran his fingers between her legs once more.

"Mmm..."

"Will you open for me?"

Her legs relaxed. Seconds later he slipped his finger into her hot, wet center. Amanda lifted her hips and moaned. The sound flowed through him. His manhood throbbed. As he moved his finger in and out of her he placed kisses on her stomach, breasts and mouth.

Minutes later her back bowed and her hips rose, seconds before she shattered and whimpered, "Lucius..."

Languidly she settled on the bed with a soft sigh. Male

satisfaction filled Lucius's chest at the look of rapture he'd placed on Amanda's face.

He watched her eyes flutter open. "I need you," he said.

A sexy invitation formed on her lips. "I'm right here."

Lucius shifted away and reached inside the bedside drawer. He removed a package. Finished covering himself, he settled over Amanda, his manhood finding her center as his lips took hers.

Her legs parted and her arms came around his neck. Lucius entered her, then pulled back. At her sound of protest he pushed forward, and pulled away again. Amanda's legs circled his hips, tightened, letting him know clearly what she wanted. He had no problem with accommodating her.

He plunged deep, filling her, and then stilled. Her heat surrounded him, held him tight, caressing him. His kiss deepened as he began to move again.

Seconds later Amanda joined him, eagerly matching his rhythm. Too soon his passion spilled, and a groan came from deep within him just as a matching cry came from her.

Lucius sank to the bed, being careful not to crush her. They remained tangled together as they caught their breath.

Something about being with Amanda seemed all too right…

Amanda slowly came out of a perfect combination of sleep and warmth. Lucius lay on his stomach with his arm thrown across her middle.

Her eyes widened. What had she done? She'd slept with Lucius! That hadn't been her best idea. Yet he'd been so tempting, standing there in the kitchen with water dripping off his head and his chest bare.

He'd caught her with her mouth still gaping when he'd pulled her into his bathroom. Her surprise had turned to shock when he had all but stuffed her into the shower. She could recognize sexual hunger in a man, and it had been written all over Lucius's face.

As she'd stood under a hot shower that had done nothing to ease the want in her she'd become angry. When she wanted something she went after it. And right then, irrational and impractical as it might be, she'd wanted Lucius. Wanted to meet his challenge.

Determined, she'd stepped out of the shower, dried her hair in a towel and walked into his room, daring him to break down that wall she'd made him erect. She still couldn't believe she'd dropped her towel and stood naked in front of the most handsome man she knew. Yet she'd found the courage to do it.

What she'd shared with Lucius had been beyond anything she'd ever had with a man before. A generous lover, Lucius had known all the right spots to taste and touch. She'd never felt more glorious or wanted than when he'd been loving her.

She looked at him now, all strong and sensual man. Outside the storm had passed, but one grew within her and hovered like humidity on a hot day. She wanted his kisses again—and more. She needed his loving.

But she couldn't. It just wouldn't be wise. It would be too easy to want more and more from him. For as long as she could have it. And her experience told her that wouldn't be for very long.

Carefully lifting his arm, she slowly slid out from under it, then moved across the bed and off it. She headed for the door, with her own room as her intended destination.

"Where're you going?"

She jerked to a stop and turned. Lucius lay on his side with his head propped on his hand. His full attention rested on her.

"I'm going to my bed. I thought you might want to sleep by yourself."

He raised a brow. "What made you think that?"

"I don't—"

Lucius sat up and the sheet dropped to his waist leaving her with a lovely view of his chest.

"Running away, Amanda?"

She bit her upper lip. "I don't run from anything."

He waved her over. "So come back here, then."

Lucius wanted her again. It showed clearly in his eyes. But for how long? That was the crucial question, but right now that didn't seem to matter. The heat, the hunger, the promise of heaven was being offered. Just waiting for her to take it. She wouldn't let that go—yet.

His look made her bold. She strolled back to the bed. "And where exactly do you want me?"

"Right here." He patted the bed beside him.

"What if I want to be elsewhere?"

The flicker of desire in his eyes had grown to a flame as she'd walked naked toward him. She planned to stoke and stroke it into a brush fire of need.

"That's your prerogative. I'll never make you do something you don't want to."

Her heart swelled. Lucius was a good man. Too few people had a chance to see that side of him. She'd been privileged to do so, was honored he'd shared it with her.

Climbing on the bed, she straddled his hips. His eyes widened. With a smile of satisfaction she noted that Lucius's manhood had come alive. She leaned over him, holding his hands above his head as she offered her breasts to him. He sucked a nipple into his mouth. Her core clenched. He moved to the other breast, his tongue circling her nipple then licking it.

She pulled away just far enough so he couldn't reach her and looked down at him.

"Amanda…?" He watched her intently.

"Mmm…?"

"Don't tease me." Lucius's words were gruff.

She brushed against his length with her center. "Who's teasing?"

At his soft growl she smiled, then rose and slowly slipped onto his iron-hard length.

She wiggled with a sigh of satisfaction.

"Amanda!" he said, with an edge of warning.

She giggled, then lifted herself until she almost no longer held him. At his sob of complaint she completely surrounded him. She offered him her breasts once more, which he eagerly took. She rose and fell along with him as he feasted. Her insides tightened and twisted. She kissed him with desperation, wanting these sweet sensations to go on and on.

Lucius joined her in the ebb and flow of motion and soon they found their pleasure in unison.

Amanda fell forward on his chest and rested there. Lucius slowly caressed her back. She soon drifted off to sleep.

Lucius might have thought that starting a work morning with someone else around would be awkward, but with Amanda it was pleasant. He would have liked to shower with her, but he was confident that would have made them late for work. Keeping his hands off Amanda would have been impossible.

They had woken much too late anyway, and she'd hurried off to her room to dress.

He already missed her.

She'd been a lavish lover—and bold. He liked that the most about her. He shouldn't have been surprised. When she'd climbed over his hips and taken him he'd almost lost it. His wife and the women who had come after her wouldn't have dared to show their desire or what they wanted so openly.

Amanda made his life in and out of bed exciting. His

days seemed a lot livelier because of her. Something he hadn't even realized he'd been missing.

But this was exactly what he'd promised himself he wouldn't let happen. Amanda was a temporary fling, just like those other women had been, but somehow, with her, it seemed different. More real.

But he'd never intended for things between them to go this far. Even if it felt like something more, he couldn't offer her anything beyond the here and now. He wasn't the guy for her long-term.

At the clinic, they both went their own ways. As much as he would have liked to kiss her, he managed to refrain.

He went about his day with a smile on his face. More than one person commented on how happy he appeared to be.

It wasn't until his secretary notified him that Amanda was there to see him that he questioned his growing feelings for her. The idea of spending time with her sent a blast of pleasure through him. And, oddly, it wasn't all to do with the idea of them being in bed together again. He liked her; it was that simple.

"Please tell her to come in," Lucius said, trying to sound cooler than he felt.

"Hey." Amanda closed the door behind her and walked toward his desk. "I just wanted to let you know that I'm moving to a hotel tonight. Staff Resources is putting me up in one. They couldn't find another apartment on such short notice, so I have to settle for a hotel."

A knot formed in the center of his chest. He'd believed she'd be staying with him again after last night. He knew it was for the best that she was moving out, but he still didn't like the plan.

"I see."

"Can you take me there this afternoon, or should I get someone else to?"

The smile he'd been wearing when she'd come in had been wiped away. Amanda was acting as if it didn't matter that she wouldn't be going home with him after work. Had last night meant so little to her?

Lucius stepped around the desk, going toward her. He took one of her hands, playing with her fingertips. "You know you're welcome at my place for as long as you wish. After all, you *do* like my house, my pool and my view. And I hope me…"

A look of sadness came over her face. "Lucius, I don't think me staying at your home is such a good idea."

"Why's that?"

"It can't end well. We don't want the same things out of life. We're literally from different sides of the world."

He wouldn't force her. She was right. Last night should remain just what it had been—a nice interlude he would remember fondly.

"I can drive you to get your belongings and then take you on to the hotel."

"Thanks, Lucius. I appreciate it."

She left without further discussion.

He stood there, trying to figure out why he didn't like anything about this arrangement. He should be pleased she was leaving his house before he became too used to her being there. In truth, he already was.

Far too soon for him, he was dropping Amanda off at the hotel. He helped her up to the room with her bag and her pillows. Carrying them around for her had fast become a habit. This time he wasn't enjoying it at all.

"Well, it isn't so bad." Amanda stood at the window. "Not the view you have, but you can't have everything."

Lucius stopped himself from saying what rested on the tip of his tongue. She was welcome to his view if she wanted it. Instead he settled for, "Have you had dinner?"

"Uh… I have a long day tomorrow, and I didn't—"

"Didn't sleep much last night," he finished flatly.

"Yes." Amanda looked at the floor, then at him. "Lucius, I want you to know that our time together was special to me, but we can't continue."

Pursing his lips, he nodded and moved toward the door. He wasn't staying around for more of those types of platitudes. Not when he wanted to take her in his arms and make her admit that last night deserved better than this casual brush-off.

"I agree."

"I'll see you around the clinic."

"I guess so."

He'd wanted short and sweet? That was exactly what he'd gotten.

He closed the door behind him. He wouldn't beg her for more. He'd begged his ex-wife to stay and he'd promised himself he'd never do that again. It had been like a kick in the teeth when she hadn't.

It was two days later when he finally saw Amanda again. He'd hungered for her. Had missed her teasing, his meals with her, even the easy silences they'd had together.

She had just presented a case study from her clinic in Atlanta. She'd been clear and precise in her presentation, answering questions without hesitation and with authority. He had been impressed with her medical knowledge and skill. Everything about her said she was a topnotch nurse, particularly her intelligence and sensitivity. All those attributes he had appreciated both in and out of bed.

Those thoughts were better kept to himself. Now that he'd had some time away from her, he understood her decision to move to the hotel had been for the best. He wasn't a good risk in the relationship department. As a husband, he'd certainly done a poor job.

As people left the room he stayed back, hoping to speak

to her. He might agree with their sleeping arrangements, but that didn't mean he wasn't still drawn to Amanda.

He was speaking to someone else when she finally came up beside him. The other person left and he turned to her.

She grinned at him, and the cloud hanging over him lifted.

"I hear the 'Baby Whisperer' has struck again. Congratulations."

"What?"

"The woman you did IVF on the first week I was here has had a positive pregnancy test."

"Yes. I saw the chart. I'm pleased."

He wanted her to talk to him about something personal, but this was better than nothing. He'd so quickly gone from keeping his distance from her to needing interaction with her daily. She'd flipped his world around and he wanted it righted again.

She studied him a moment—seeing too much, he feared. "You don't look pleased."

"I am. I *am.* We just have to be cautious, because you never know when something will go wrong. This is her third attempt. I'm being cautiously optimistic."

"She has an excellent doctor. I'm sure it'll go well. I'm sorry I won't be here to follow her case."

That's right, Amanda will be going home in a few weeks.

"I'll see that Nancy keeps you posted."

"Thank you for that."

An awkwardness settled between them as they looked at each other.

She broke the silence. "I…uh…better go. We have a delivery brewing."

Lucius nodded. But as soon as she walked away, he wanted to ask her back.

To his own surprise, he called, "Amanda?"

She turned. A small smile formed on her lips and questions filled her eyes. "Yes?"

He stepped closer, so that no one else could hear. "Would you like to have dinner with me Saturday evening? I have tickets to a jazz concert at the Opera House."

"They do jazz at the Opera House?" Amazement filled her voice.

"They do. It's a multi-purpose building."

"I learn something new every day… I'd love to go."

Would she love to because she would go to the Opera House with anyone or because *he'd* asked her? His heart jumped with happiness. It didn't matter. At least he would have a chance to spend more time with her.

"Then I'll pick you up at your hotel around seven."

"I'll be ready. I'm looking forward to it."

He was also. Far too much. Maybe he shouldn't have asked her, but he hadn't been able to help himself. If he could just spend a little more time with Amanda then possibly he would be able to get her out of his system. Surely they could spend a night out together as just friends?

With far more eagerness than he should feel he made reservations for dinner at a restaurant on the water, within walking distance of the Opera House. It had been some time since he'd been on a date and he feared his skills might be lacking. It had been a long time since he'd tried to woo a woman…

Amanda was waiting in the hotel lobby when he arrived. Her hair had been pulled away from her face on one side. Her lips were covered in a light pink lipstick that perfectly matched the dress she wore. On her feet were pretty but sensible shoes, with bows on the top. She looked fresh, wholesome, and completely lovely.

His heart fluttered and he had to sternly remind his manhood to behave.

The tension in his chest increased as he walked toward

her. A smile came to her lips. Had he just been punched in the gut? Could she be as glad to see him as he was her?

He took one of her hands in his, lightly holding her fingers. "You look splendid."

"Thank you. I didn't bring anything with me appropriate for the Opera House, so I did a little shopping this afternoon."

"You look perfect. This is for you." He handed her a single white rose. "I thought it might brighten your room. I know you have a vase."

She smelled the flower. "So nice… Do I have time to put it in water?"

He nodded. "We'll take the time."

They went up to her room and she quickly took care of the rose.

He looked around. "I don't see your pillows."

She gave him a sheepish look. "Somehow they didn't belong here."

"Are you comfortable?" It wasn't a room *he'd* want to spend weeks in.

Amanda glanced around, her lips curling. "I'm fine. Of course it doesn't have your view."

"You're always welcome at my house," Lucius added in a teasing tone, but really he wished she *would* return. The house had lost its light without her presence.

She turned her back, sitting the vase on her bedside table. Then she said, "I'm ready."

Lucius had found a parking lot that was near the restaurant and close enough for them to walk to the Opera House. He'd requested a table by the water, knowing Amanda would especially like that. He wasn't disappointed.

"Oh, this is wonderful!" She sounded awed.

He had been trying to make a good impression. She acted as if he were succeeding. "I hoped you'd like it."

She smiled. "It'll be a wonderful memory to take home."

They ate dinner, making small talk about what had happened during the week.

"I went to the ocean swimming pool this morning," Amanda announced.

"Did you see your friend the squid?"

She grinned. "I didn't—but I did keep an eye out for him."

She laughed. He loved the sound. It made him want to join her.

Finally they had worked their way back to the friendly, comfortable spot they had once had. The one he'd missed so much.

Too soon for him, it was time to leave for the concert. He hated to break the spell.

They strolled to the Opera House, not touching but staying close. As they walked up the steps to the building he took her elbow, glad for the excuse to touch her. He'd wanted to do so all night. It had been too long since he had. He'd missed the silky smoothness of her skin. Just the brief contact now reminded him of the feel of her under his hand as he ran it over her bare hip.

Shaking his head slightly, he refocused.

After they had found their places Amanda said, "These are amazing seats. Front center. When I go to a concert it's usually the back corner."

He chuckled. "It pays to be a supporter of the Opera House. First chance at tickets is a perk."

"That figures."

"You always say that about me. As if I'm a stereotype." Lucius didn't like the idea that she grouped him with other people. He wanted to stand out in Amanda's mind. Although why it mattered so much to him he had no idea.

She turned so he could see her face clearly, then placed a hand briefly on his thigh. "I can assure you that you're not a stereotype. You're a special man in ways you don't let many people see. And I'm honored because I have."

That statement was an ego-builder. Not since his father had told Lucius he'd done a good job when he'd finished first in his medical school class had he felt this good.

"Thank you."

She smiled, settled in her seat again and opened her program. "I didn't know you were a jazz aficionado."

"I think it has less to do with that and more with the fact I can get good tickets. But I do like it. My father had us listen to jazz when we were children, so I guess I picked it up. My ex-wife thought it made us look good to come to jazz concerts."

A moment went by before Amanda said, "Will you tell me about her?"

This wasn't a conversation he particularly wanted to have, yet there wasn't some big secret about what had happened between them. He'd been a lousy husband.

"We thought we were in love, only we weren't. But I guess any divorced couple can say that."

"How long were you married?"

"Three years. Three years too many, if you ask her."

"So what happened?" Amanda turned so that she faced him again.

"I was working long hours. Getting the clinic started. Busy making a name for myself. I left her alone too much. Most of the downfall was my fault."

Amanda placed her hand on his arm. "I'm not an expert in marriage, but as I understand it, it takes two to make it work."

"Maybe so. But to hear her tell it I was more interested in seeing that other women had babies than I was in coming home to make my own. What I really think is that we just weren't suited. She was a social climber and I cared nothing for that world. I did spend a great deal of time away from her, but she didn't make it very appealing to come home."

"It sounds like you put each other out of your misery by divorcing."

"Yes, but it was still a failure on my part. One I've promised myself I'll never repeat. My work will always come first. Not just because it's important, but because it's who I am."

Silence fell and Amanda broke it. "Yet you're here with me tonight?"

Hmm, so he was. He'd have to give that some thought.

The sound of musicians tuning up turned their attention to the stage.

During the second song Amanda leaned close and whispered, "This is wonderful."

He took her hand and held it. She didn't resist. Instead she intertwined her fingers with his.

The concert ended too soon for Lucius. He could have spent hours just sitting there, holding her hand and listening to good music. That sense of wellbeing he'd never had with his ex-wife he'd found with Amanda, in so many different ways.

But what was he doing? Where was he going with this? Was he planning to ask her to marry him?

That wouldn't happen. His job demanded too much from him. Long hours at the clinic and going away to the conferences, both home and abroad, that came around frequently didn't make for a good marriage.

To become involved with him wouldn't be fair to Amanda. She probably wanted children, a family, a stable home life. He couldn't offer her that. The sense of loss left a sick feeling in his gut. Amanda deserved better than the little he could give her.

Resigned to what his future would look like, he took

Amanda back to the hotel. In reality, he wanted to take her home to his bed. But he knew it had to be this way.

He walked her to the hotel elevators. Kissing her on the cheek, he said, "Goodnight."

"Thank you, Lucius, for a lovely evening."

"You're welcome. I'll see you at the clinic."

With a feeling that was pulling him down like cement shoes, he walked away.

Amanda rode up to her room, carrying a sadness as heavy as a bucket of rocks. The way Lucius had left her with such finality tore at her heart. She didn't like it. It wasn't right. Even though she'd been the one to push him away, she didn't want this canyon developing between them.

She'd take him for as long as she could have him. If that was just for a few weeks, so be it. She'd deal with her heartache when she went home. Most of her life she'd felt unwanted by one person or another, and to have Lucius want her so badly was exciting. It made her feel alive.

Before she'd even reached her floor she'd already pushed the button to go back down to the foyer.

She'd missed what they'd had together. Five mornings of waking up alone without Lucius's strong body next to her was enough. She ached to have those moments back, to share more time with him. Why be lonely when she had another choice?

There were still three more weeks before she left. Lucius still wanted her. It had been clearly showing in his eyes all night. If she could have that for just a little while longer why not grasp it? Lucius might not want her forever, but she accepted that.

She had the man behind the hotel desk call her a cab. The nearer she got to Lucius's house the more nervous she became. What if he had changed his mind about wanting her? She might live to regret this impulsive action.

The car pulled into the drive and she saw a dark house. Was Lucius not home yet? Had he already gone to bed? Had he gone out elsewhere after leaving her?

She couldn't stop now—she had to find out.

Amanda stood at the door, ready to ring the bell, and then the cab driver called out to her.

"Lady, I have another pick-up. I have to go."

With that, he left her.

She rang the doorbell, then looked down the drive.

Was the ferry still running this late at night?

There was no answer. She rang again.

Had she misjudged Lucius's signals? Those touches? Kisses? Their night together? Their evening together?

Coming here had been a mistake. She turned to leave.

Her heart jumped when the porch light flicked on and the door opened.

"Amanda?" Lucius stood there, in shorts riding low on his hips.

With a gulp, she forced the knot in her throat down. "You said I could come see your view anytime."

CHAPTER SEVEN

AMANDA BREATHED A sigh of relief and felt her blood hum through her veins as Lucius reached out and tugged her into the house.

"You should have said you were interested in my view before I left. I would've brought you home with me."

"The way I see it, you left me behind."

"Aw… Since you're here, I'll make it up to you. Come on."

His hand tightened on hers as he led her toward the back of the house.

"Why're all the lights off?"

"I was sitting outside."

Did that mean something significant?

"In the dark?"

"Yes. I was looking across the harbor, wishing you were here."

He opened the door to the patio.

Her heart went pitter-pat. He'd been missing her.

"You were?"

"I was feeling sorry for myself."

On the patio, she took the chair he offered. He pulled his own chair close before he sat. Taking her hand, he held it, gently brushing the pad of his thumb over the top of it. They stayed that way for a long time. The moment was too perfect.

Amanda looked off into the distance at the beauty of the harbor. "I've missed this view. It's so pretty."

"I feel the same way."

His tone made her look at him. Lucius watched her, not the harbor. Even in the cool air her cheeks heated at the expression in his eyes.

"I'm glad you came to join me. I've missed you."

She squeezed his hand. "You saw me just an hour ago—and at the clinic before that."

"I did, but it wasn't the same. If I could have pulled you into a closet and kissed you senseless I would have."

She giggled. "That would have been fun. The respectable Dr. Lucius West having the hots for the visiting nurse. There would've been such a scandal!"

"If you had agreed I wouldn't have cared." His voice turned raspy. "Stay with me, Amanda."

"Tonight?"

He brought her hand to his mouth, turned it over and kissed her palm. "For as long as you want."

Amanda's heart swelled. *This* was what it was like to have a man truly desire her. The fact that it was Lucius made it extra-special.

Lucius stood and led her through the kitchen into his bedroom, stopping beside the bed. There he brought her into his arms. His kiss was slow, tender, unlike the hurried fevered ones of before. This one said, *I care about you... I have longed for you...you matter to me.*

Amanda drank in the joyous unknown feeling. She'd been searching for this connection all her life. She didn't want to fall in love with Lucius, shouldn't take a chance on her heart being broken. Yet she was halfway in love with him already. It would kill her when she had to leave, but she couldn't give up this sublime moment—or any others that might happen between them.

"This pink dress..." Lucius skimmed his hands over her

waist. "It looks amazing on you, but I've thought about taking it off you all evening."

Heat pooled between her legs. She lifted her arms above her head in invitation.

Going down on a knee, Lucius placed his hands just below the hem of her dress and deliberately ran his hands up the outside of her thighs. She tingled with anticipation. He stood and finished stripping the clothing from her. He let it drop to the floor.

"Lovely..."

The word whispered across her shoulders as he pushed her bra straps away and kissed the skin beneath. Her breathing became heavy. "You say the nicest things."

He kissed the top of one of her exposed breasts as he worked the clasp of her bra open. "I'm sure that's not true. I have an entire staff that might disagree with you."

"They don't know you like I do."

Her bra joined her dress on the floor. He sighed deeply. "I have missed you. Your beauty."

Amanda shivered as his index finger caressed her breast, moved to the nipple. She reached for him, but he went down on his knee again and kissed her belly button. Looping his fingers in either side of her panties, he pushed them down.

He kissed her mound. Her fingers gripped his shoulders. "Lucius..."

He stood and lifted her against him, letting the whole length of her body glide down him. "You feel so good."

She tugged, then shoved his pants to the floor. Moving to the bed, they fell on it together. Lucius's lips found hers as they became a tangle of passion.

Sweet, satiated hours later, Lucius lay quietly in the early morning with a softly sleeping Amanda in his arms. He had been missing moments like this all his life. The darkness had disappeared with the brightness of Amanda. It couldn't last longer than a few weeks, but he'd make the most of it while he could.

Before she'd shown up on his doorstep he'd been sitting on his patio, thinking about what Amanda might be doing on the other side of the harbor. Now she lay here, in his arms.

He'd been shocked and elated when he'd opened the door and seen that she stood there. He'd tried to play it cool, not wanting to scare her off, while all he'd really wanted to do was to sweep her up into his arms and not let her go.

Rain tapped against the window. It was supposed to rain all day. He snuggled Amanda closer. He couldn't think of a better place to spend the day than in bed with her.

She wiggled against him. His manhood sprang to life.

"It's raining…" she said, more as a statement than a question.

"It is."

Amanda rolled to face him. She stroked his chest and purred, "What do you think we should do today to keep busy?"

"I was thinking of just staying right where we are."

In the past he would have never suggested such an idea. He would have gone to the clinic, made good use of his time.

"That sounds wonderful. But I do hope you mean the whole house and not just in bed, because I could use a shower and something to eat."

He kissed her. "I think that can be arranged. You shower with me and I'll help with breakfast."

"I'm going to need to get my clothes from the hotel."

He fondled her breast, making the nipple stand to attention. "You won't need them today. We'll get up early tomorrow morning and stop by the hotel on our way to the clinic. I miss those pillows."

She giggled and ran her hand over his growing manhood. "Sounds like a plan."

Amanda smiled as she watched Lucius do another lap of the pool. These last few days had been pure bliss.

The routine had been easy to get used to. Their days started with her waking up in Lucius's bed. His arms were always around her, as if he had pulled her to him in his sleep. More often than not they shared a shower before eating breakfast together, and then Lucius drove them to work.

He would give her a quick kiss before exiting the car. They weren't trying to keep their relationship a secret, but they weren't advertising it either.

Occasionally their paths crossed at the clinic. Lucius would give her a heated look that promised something wonderful that evening. And more than once he'd caught her staring at him during a meeting. With each of those interactions she'd left with a tingle of eagerness for more time alone with him.

She'd never felt more desired, more appreciated.

In her experience, men didn't want her. Her father, as irrational as it was, had made her feel unwanted because he'd died. Her stepfather had made it clear she wasn't welcome because she damaged his perfect family picture. Then there had been her boyfriends, who had left her because they hadn't been able to handle her being so driven. The worst had been her last boyfriend, who had destroyed her by making her believe he'd actually loved her.

Being with Lucius had wiped all those negative feelings away and replaced them with precious ones.

She remained painfully aware that what they had wouldn't last. But a girl could dream, couldn't she? And the idea of that dream was sweet enough that she could accept the consequences of a reality without Lucius.

She'd just have to live on the memories. With this staff exchange on her résumé she would focus on her career and try to put her hopes and dreams of more into a box in her mind, bringing the memories out on days when she felt less than wanted.

The first part of the week at the clinic had been slower than usual, with only one baby delivery. Neither she nor Lucius had been needed after-hours.

When she joined him in the car at the end of each day he would immediately grab her hand and pull her to him for a kiss.

The feeling of being the focus of his desire was heady. He acted as if he couldn't get enough of her. After a lifetime of not being enough, or feeling as if she stood on the outside watching a play she'd never be a part of, she felt as if she'd found heaven.

Each evening Lucius would offer to take her to dinner but she always declined, wanting to cook a simple meal for them, eat on the patio with him and hold hands as the sun went down. Then, best of all, she would go to bed with Lucius. There, he was a generous and attentive lover. Her satisfaction seemed as important to him as his own and he never failed to make her feel desired.

On Thursday morning Dr. Johannsson stepped into the room where Amanda had just finished seeing a patient.

"Amanda, I think you might like to attend the examination of my next patient. It's an out of the ordinary case. It's also one we'll be discussing this afternoon during the patient conference."

"That sounds intriguing."

She followed the doctor to the exam room down the hall. Outside of it, Dr. Johannsson stopped.

"This is a forty-year-old woman who is borderline hypertensive and who had an ectopic pregnancy after the last IVF done by Dr. West a year ago. She presented with mild ovarian hyperstimulation syndrome, but that cleared up in six days. She's here requesting to be considered for IVF again."

"How early did the OHSS start?" Amanda asked.

"During the second round of shots."

Amanda nodded. This woman didn't sound like a great candidate for another course of IVF.

Dr. Johannsson's lips pursed. "To complicate the matters further, she has an inverted uterus."

This was indeed a case worth paying attention to.

She and Dr. Johannsson entered the room. On the examination table waited a woman with faultless make-up and hair. Everything about her said she came from an affluent background. A man in business attire stood beside her.

"Hello, Mrs. Moore… Mr. Moore. It's nice to see you." Dr. Johannsson moved toward the couple. "I'd like for you to meet Amanda Longstreet. She's a nurse visiting from America."

Amanda nodded. "It's nice to meet you both."

"Amanda is going to see to your vitals, Mrs. Moore," Dr. Johannsson said, before she started asking both the Moores some questions.

Removing the stethoscope from her neck, Amanda listened to the woman's heart-rate and respirations. All sounded well. She went on to check her pulse points, then her blood pressure. It registered in the high normal range.

Mr. Moore left the room and Dr. Johannsson pulled on plastic gloves and took a seat on the stool at the end of the exam table. "Now, let's see how you're doing."

Amanda assisted as the doctor went about her examination.

Soon she pushed back. "Mrs. Moore, I'd like Nurse Longstreet to examine you as well. Will that be okay?"

The woman nodded.

Pulling on gloves, Amanda took her position. Finished, she stood and removed her gloves. "Mrs. Moore, would you mind if I pushed on your abdomen? It won't take but a moment."

"That's fine," the woman agreed.

Amanda started palpating the area below her belly button. "Please let me know if it hurts anywhere. I understand you've had some pain in the past?"

"Yes."

Amanda stepped back so that she could see Mrs. Moore's face. "How about now?"

"I'm doing okay."

"Good. Thank you for letting me examine you." Amanda smiled at the woman.

Dr. Johannsson said, "You may sit up now, Mrs. Moore. I'll look over your lab work and test results and get back to you soon. It has been good to see you again."

Back in the hall, Dr. Johannsson turned to Amanda. "Amanda, would you mind presenting this case at the patient conference this afternoon? I've had something come up."

"I'll be glad to."

Amanda's second thought was she would be doing so in front of Lucius. It mattered to her that he be proud of her.

Lucius took the last seat on the front row, facing the screen in the conference room, which was arranged in theater-style. The patient meeting had already been called to order. He looked around the room for Amanda. He located her on the right side, one row up. She sat with a group of Labor and Delivery nurses.

The best he could tell, from what had been said and the actions of other staff members when she was around, Amanda had meshed with the rest of the team as if she had been there for years. They not only seemed to like her, but they admired her work ethic and her knowledge. She would be an asset to the clinic if she decided to stay.

The idea sent excitement through him. But that wasn't something he and Amanda had discussed or the clinic had offered. She had long-term plans at her clinic in Atlanta, didn't she? What made him think she'd even consider staying in Sydney?

He looked at her for long enough that she turned and met his gaze. Lucius smiled and she returned it. It was empowering to have a woman show openly how she felt about him. He appreciated the unfamiliar feeling…treasured it.

Over the last few weeks his life had changed drastically for the better—because of her. He'd started to appreciate his life outside of the clinic. Everything no longer revolved around his work. He now looked forward to going home. There was someone to share it with him. And in a strange, unexpected way, it made coming to work nicer too. He had even started keeping regular hours.

He had been lonely. Before Amanda he would never have admitted that. Now he could see it clearly.

He was very conscious of the fact she would return to America soon. That remained his emotional safety net. He surely couldn't mess things up in such a short time? He could be what she needed for at least a few more weeks, couldn't he? He'd not done well in his marriage, but that had been over a much longer amount of time. Whatever this was, he was glad he had it with Amanda.

The colleague who was running the meeting stood and announced, "Amanda Longstreet will be presenting for Dr. Johannsson today."

Amanda stepped forward and took the clicker from him. A slide appeared on the screen with medical data and Amanda started to speak. "This is Mrs. Moore. Dr. Johannsson and I saw her today in the clinic…"

She went on to share the history of the patient.

He loved her voice. The slow enunciation of her words and her dropping of letters he found delightful. In truth, he couldn't get enough of it—especially when she drew out his name when she reached her climax. Even as she stood now, in front of a group of people, speaking with authority and familiarity on her subject, he still loved the cadence of her speech.

He glanced around to find everyone's attention on her. Amanda had a way about her that made people listen attentively.

"Today, after a thorough examination, I found scarring on her vaginal wall and also a golf-ball-sized fibroid. It's Dr. Johannsson's recommendation that Mrs. Moore not be considered for further IVF."

Lucius sat straighter. He'd done Mrs. Moore's first IVF. "I don't agree," he said.

Amanda turned to face him and he saw she had that look on her face. The one she'd worn when she'd dug in about his patient during her first week there.

"Why's that?" Amanda demanded.

He sat forward. "I've had success with a new procedure that she would be a prime candidate for."

Amanda frowned. "Despite the fact she had OHSS?"

"That was a mild case. There's no reason to suspect that will happen again."

The other staff members around them faded away. The room had come down to him and her.

"And the ectopic pregnancy?"

He came back with, "That's not unusual in the practice of IVF."

"Agreed—but she lost three babies before coming to us."

Lucius liked her statement of ownership about the clinic, but he still couldn't agree with her about the case.

"There's also the issue of her inverted uterus," she added.

Lucius leaned back in his chair, crossing his arms over his chest. "We deal with those all the time too."

"Yes, but not along with all the other negatives going against her. Based on the normal guidelines, she isn't a good candidate." Amanda glared at him.

Judging by the thinness of her lips, she had worked herself up to feeling angry.

"She is just the kind of woman we should be helping," he continued in an even tone. "Women come to us for the opportunity to have a baby. We should offer that whenever we can. And I believe I have the skills to do it."

"I'm not questioning that. What I do know is Labor and Delivery. A woman who has already had issues has a much higher chance of losing her baby and experiencing difficulties during delivery. It isn't just about implanting a baby, but carrying it to term, and a healthy birth, and having a healthy mother afterward. There are protocols in place for a reason. At my clinic in Atlanta Mrs. Moore would *not* be a good candidate and would be told so."

Lucius took a moment before he spoke. "Based on my scientific knowledge and experience, I still believe she can be helped."

"I disagree." Amanda's tone held a stinging note. "Emotional and financial well-being are important as well. Sometimes saying no is being compassionate. It isn't always about furthering medical success."

Lucius flinched. She might as well have said he was only interested in promoting his own success.

Her words hung in the air between them. An audible sound of surprise echoed around the room. She'd dared to contradict him in front of other medical staff.

Was he really that dogmatic in his beliefs and actions? Until that moment he'd have said he was unquestionably focused on the whole patient. Maybe some of his ego had been involved—or at least his drive to wipe out infertility might make it look so. But was that realistic?

Whichever it was, Amanda had made him step back and think.

The doctor in charge of the meeting came to stand beside Amanda. The room came alive again.

"I'm sure Dr. Johannsson will have further data on this issue. We'll revisit this patient next week."

When the meeting broke up a group of nurses surrounded Amanda. Lucius overheard one of them say, "I can't believe you talked to Dr. West that way. *No one* does that."

He couldn't hear Amanda's response, but he would have liked to. Did his staff really think he was that inflexible?

Lucius left before speaking to Amanda and headed for his office. What was his evening with her going to be like after that heated discussion?

An hour later, as he walked toward the car, he received a text from Amanda. She had to stay late for a delivery. She told him she would get a taxi home. He offered to come get her, but she insisted it wouldn't be necessary.

Lucius drove out of the parking lot, restless at not having Amanda with him.

He didn't like thinking she might be angry with him. At the end of his marriage his wife had been mad at him more times than not. It had soon begun not to matter to him. But the idea that Amanda was unhappy because of him caused him worry. Which surprised him. It had snuck up on him how important she had become.

With Amanda not home, he had a sandwich for dinner, did some laps in the pool, and then chose to watch TV in the living room. His bedroom wasn't very inviting without Amanda there. He had it bad.

Sometime in the night he heard the door to the bedroom across the house close softly. The shower came on.

Maybe she didn't want to wake him by taking a shower in his bathroom. He went to his bed and waited, giving her a few minutes to join him.

Fifteen minutes went by and Amanda didn't show.

Concerned about her, and equally worried that she might still be angry with him, Lucius crossed the house. He opened the door to the bedroom to find Amanda in bed, already asleep. She probably hadn't wanted to wake him. She must be exhausted.

He eased into bed beside her. Amanda opened her eyes and snuggled against him.

"I thought you'd want me to sleep over here since I disagreed with you in public today," she murmured.

"No disagreement will ever make me not want you in my bed."

Had she been sent to her room as a child, when she'd disagreed with her stepfather? What made her think he wouldn't want her?

"I like the sound of that."

She settled close with a sigh, and soon her breathing evened out into sleep again.

Amanda woke still snuggled against Lucius's chest. She didn't like fighting with him. She'd been disappointed that they hadn't agreed on the case, but she appreciated that they were each their own person. At least he hadn't demeaned her, or shot down her point of view—instead he'd offered his own calmly and methodically.

"Hey..." Lucius's fingers started caressing her hip.

She smiled. "Hey, yourself. You look mighty serious for so early in the morning."

"I don't like fighting with you."

He'd told her he and his wife had done it often. She didn't want any of that in their relationship.

"I don't like fighting with you either. Not to start another one, but I just want you to know I do believe in your skills." She grinned at him. "I also know the 'Baby Whisperer' can't possibly help everyone."

"I don't like that term. What I do, science backs up. I'm just a doctor looking for a way to help as many people as I can."

She cupped his face. "I realize that. You're humbler than people know, and you have integrity, but with our jobs there comes a certain amount of pride as well. I think sometimes you get too wrapped up in the idea you must help every woman have a baby. That's a byproduct of your big heart."

"In there somewhere was a compliment—I'm sure of it. I'd hate to debate with you all the time."

Amanda grinned. "I'll tell you what—why don't we agree to disagree, and celebrate when we do agree?"

"Especially when it's after business hours. I don't like fighting with you. But I sure would enjoy making up." He moved to kiss her.

She stopped him with a push against his chest, before running for the bathroom.

"Are you okay?" Lucius called from the bed.

"I must've eaten something that didn't agree with me last night. We had some food brought in. I'm allergic to spinach—there must have been some in the dip."

She heaved again.

"What can I do to help you?" Lucius stood at the door, concern clear on his face.

"I'll be fine."

She was holding her stomach.

"I think you should stay home today. You're pale. And if you do have something contagious we don't need you spreading it. A good rest over the weekend should be the ticket."

She leaned over the toilet once more.

Lucius pulled a washcloth from the cabinet, wet it and placed it over her forehead. He held it there while she retched again. Afterward, he gently wiped her face and mouth.

He helped her to stand on weak knees. Then put a hand on her back and steadied her as she returned to bed. He tucked her in.

"You sleep. I'll give the clinic a call to let them know we both won't be coming in today."

"Aren't you afraid they'll ask questions? I thought we didn't want anyone to know."

Rather gruffly he said, "I don't care who knows I'm seeing you."

"Thanks for taking care of me."

He gave her a kiss on the forehead. "I'll get crackers and some tea for you."

She tugged on his fingers as he started to leave her. "When was the last time you called in and said you weren't coming to work?"

He looked down at her. "Not ever that I remember."

Amanda's heart swelled with tenderness for him. "That was my guess. We'll be the talk of the clinic!"

Lucius couldn't have been more attentive the entire day. He'd even gone out to a café when she'd said she believed she might eat some chicken noodle soup. She'd wanted to go to the table in the kitchen to eat, but he'd insisted he would bring her a tray. They had shared the simple meal in her bed.

Late in the afternoon, she woke from a nap to find Lucius reading in a chair nearby.

"You do know I'm not dying? In fact, I feel much better."

"I'm glad you do, but it hasn't hurt for you to take it easy for a day."

"Maybe not—but I'm certainly not used to doing so.

What I'd like to do right now is cuddle up next to you and watch a good movie. I'll even let you pick one out if you want to."

"How very generous of you, since you usually have a strong opinion on what we should view." He came to lie beside her with his head propped on his hand, a smile on his face.

"So what you're saying is that you don't care for a woman with an opinion?"

He brushed a lock of hair off her cheek. "I actually appreciate all your opinions."

"Except when I disagree with you—like yesterday?"

He picked up her hand. "Let's not revisit that. We've already made an agreement which I plan to honor."

That evening she encouraged him to go for a swim, so he'd stop hovering. It was sweet, but she felt fine now. And on Saturday Amanda felt well enough to take a walk around the neighborhood in the afternoon, although that morning she'd been under the weather again—but not sick enough to run for the bathroom.

As they walked Lucius held her hand. More than once he was the first to speak to the people they passed.

That evening he prepared dinner, insisting that she hadn't recovered enough to be "messing around in the kitchen". He proudly produced macaroni and cheese and sliced tomato. She sat watching him, enjoying the capable movements she recognized from seeing him at work in the clinic.

He truly was an amazing man. She would miss him desperately when she left.

On Sunday she still wasn't feeling a hundred percent, but she dealt with it. Despite being cooped up at the house most of the time, she found the time had flown by. She couldn't seem to get enough of Lucius. Having him all to herself was intoxicating. She had a driving need to soak up as much of him as she could, while she still had the opportunity.

That afternoon, Lucius said, "I'd like to take you somewhere special next weekend."

His fingers played with hers as they lounged next to each other after a swim in the pool.

"That sounds like fun. Where will we go?"

"I want it to be a surprise."

The words were said almost as if he were thinking out loud.

"That sounds interesting. Any place will be great since I haven't seen much but the city."

"Then I'll make arrangements. Would you prefer to leave after work on Friday or early Saturday morning?"

"I can be ready to go on Friday. Now you have my curiosity up."

She rolled toward him and moved across the small space between them. She ran her leg up his, caressing him as she snuggled close, kissing his neck.

"Is there any chance that I can convince you to tell me where we're going?"

He chuckled, bringing his arm around her and pulling her across his chest. "I don't think so, but I do like the idea of you trying."

CHAPTER EIGHT

Lucius didn't know when he had laughed more than he had during the last week. Amanda had taken finding out where they were going as a full-scale mission that would rival any military maneuver. He'd endured questions like, "What clothes should I pack?" "Will it be hot or cold?" "How far away are we going?" "Are we driving or flying?" "Do I need an evening dress?"

To everything he had simply answered yes.

As her frustration rose and his determination to surprise her became firmer, she turned to trying to get her own way in bed. They'd had sex in ways he'd only dreamed of. To say he was a thoroughly satisfied man would be an understatement.

She'd even stooped to teasing him at work.

And then one day during lunch, late in the week, she came to his office and locked the door behind her.

He looked up from behind his desk. "Amanda? Is something wrong?"

"Yeah, I want to talk to you."

"Is there a problem?" He pushed back from the desk.

She came toward him with a look of purpose on her face. "Yes, there is."

His concern built and he stood up. "Is someone hurt?"

"Someone is *going* to be hurt." She circled the desk.

"I'm not following you." He was truly confused now.

"You'll need to sit down for this."

She gave him a light shove in the center of his chest with her palm. Placing her hands on the arms of his chair, she leaned in, her nose almost touching his.

"Don't you think there's something you should tell me?"

Lucius grinned. He understood now.

"I don't know of anything..."

A smile still on his face, he looked away from her, as if giving it a lot of thought.

She kissed him. It was deep, wet and hot—and best of all it was endless.

He went rock-hard instantly. The woman was going to kill him—worse, make him useless to anyone but her.

Amanda straddled him, her center firmly against his throbbing need as she continued to kiss him until he was mindless.

"Is there something you want to tell me *now*?"

And make this heaven stop? "No..."

She stood up then, glaring at him with a teasing twist to her lips. "Ooh, you make me so mad."

He grabbed her around the waist and pulled her back to him. "Oh, no, you don't. You can't come in here, teasing me, and then think you can just leave me like this."

He pushed at her elastic-waisted scrub pants.

"Lucius, we can't. This is your office."

But despite her half-hearted protest she'd already stepped out of her clogs and pants.

"So..."

He touched her heated valley, slipped a finger into her wet center. A soft *"Oh..."* fell from her lips before she closed her eyes and her head fell back. A few minutes later, when her knees buckled, he brought her up to him, kissing her to keep her from screaming.

He whispered against her ear. "Undo my pants, Amanda, I need to be inside you."

Her hands shook but she managed to do as he'd requested. He didn't have to tell her what to do next. She straddled him, sliding down until she'd taken all of him.

If someone had asked him what paradise was he'd have said that moment. All too soon finished.

He sat there still inside her for a while. It felt almost as wonderful as what they had just been doing.

The ring of his desk phone brought them back to reality. Amanda started to move but he held her in place.

He picked up the phone. "Yes?"

"They're waiting on you in the IVF room," his secretary said, with a note of curiosity in her voice.

"Tell them I'm on my way." He hung up.

Amanda buried her face in his shoulder. "She knows..."

Lucius chuckled.

Amanda gave him a slap to the shoulder. "It's not funny."

"Maybe not. But it's not like we don't talk about sex around here regularly. We could tell her we were conducting an experiment."

Amanda smirked, then scooted off his lap and turned to pick up her pants. He ran his palm across her behind. She slapped it away. He grinned, closing his pants as he watched her finish gathering her things.

"How am I going to face her?" Her cheeks were a bright pink.

He took her by the shoulders. "Honey, settle down. If it'll make you happy I'll send her on an errand, then you can slip away."

"You'd do that?"

"I'd do anything for you."

That made him pause for a moment, a little shaken. He found he truly meant it.

"Give me time to get to the IVF room, then I'll call her

and have her bring me a file. You go on into the bathroom and get yourself cleaned up." He gave her a quick kiss.

She clutched her clothes to her and headed for the bathroom off his office.

"By the way—you're welcome in my office anytime."

Her eyes twinkled at him. "I might come back if you tell me where we're going on the weekend."

Lucius barked a laugh and opened the door. His secretary wore a knowing smile but he didn't care one bit. He was happy.

Amanda looked forward to Friday with gladness and sadness. Gladness because she and Lucius would be leaving for some place unknown, and sadness because she'd enjoyed their week of teasing—especially their time in his office. It had been embarrassing, seeing the meaningful smiles she'd received afterward, but so worth it.

She woke Friday morning with another queasy stomach, but it soon passed. She hadn't eaten much the night before, and she put it down to being hungry. She soon pushed it aside in her excitement over the coming weekend.

After much pleading she had gotten out of Lucius just enough to know she should take a nice dress, a swimsuit and some casual clothes. Which wasn't much different from what she would have packed if he had told her nothing.

He could be such a stubborn man.

She almost danced into the clinic. No one had ever taken the time or cared enough to surprise her with anything. Her mother might have wanted to, but her stepfather would have never allowed it. None of her boyfriends had ever tried.

Lucius made her feel special and she would appreciate all that she could get with him. The hours until they left couldn't pass fast enough for her.

After she'd seen her last patient, she all but ran to Lucius's car. He'd texted that he would meet her there. She swung open the door and hopped in, giving him a quick kiss.

He grinned back at her. "You ready?"

"Yes. Are you going to tell me where we're going *now*?" She buckled herself in.

"Nope."

"Aw, come on Lucius. I'll know when we get there."

"Then you can wait."

He drove out of the parking lot.

"You're so mean."

She knew she sounded like a child on Christmas Eve, who wasn't allowed to open her present until the next day.

"That's not what you were saying last night." He gave her a mischievous grin.

She huffed, crossed her arms across her chest and looked out the window. She liked this laid-back Lucius. To think she'd once thought of him as a stuffed shirt…

The next thing she knew the car had stopped and it had turned dark. Lucius stood outside, talking to a blue-vested uniformed porter. The man was busy removing their luggage from the trunk of the car.

Lucius opened her door. "Hey—you want to get out and see where we are?"

"You're *so* funny."

He grinned. She loved his happy face.

"I was beginning to wonder if you even cared, since you slept all the way here."

That was another thing that was odd about the way she felt. She was more sleepy than usual…

"Where are we?"

"The Central Coast Resort."

He said it as if that would explain everything to her.

She looked around. The building was a low modern

one, nestled among lush greenery. Everything about it, from the opulent orange flowers in the lobby to the elegant woman behind the reception desk, screamed luxury. The wide lobby had been decorated in contemporary furnishings and a blue color scheme.

She and Lucius were escorted to a bungalow, where their luggage had already been placed. It consisted of a spacious living area, a bedroom through a door to the right, and a patio that looked out toward the ocean. Amanda couldn't see it, but she could hear the soothing sound of waves rolling in.

After their escort had left, Lucius turned to her. "I thought we'd just eat dinner here, since it's so late."

"That sounds nice." She looked back at him from the patio door. "Lucius, this place is amazing."

"I hoped you'd like it. A number of my acquaintances have mentioned they've been here and said I should come."

She smiled. He hadn't brought a woman here before. That made the visit extra-special for her. And yet it also remained another reminder that they came from different worlds. Never could she afford to stay in a place like this. And she certainly hadn't been raised with this type of extravagance.

Their dinner was a quiet affair on the patio. Despite her nap, Amanda was looking forward to bed. She requested that they leave the doors open, so she could hear the waves. Their lovemaking that night—and for her that was what it had become—was slow and tender. Even Lucius seemed to want it to go on forever.

Saturday morning, she woke and stretched wide across the bed. Lucius stood at the patio door with a cup of coffee in his hand. She took a few moments to admire his broad back, his slim hips and solid legs. This would be a memory she would hold close.

He turned. "How long have you been awake?"

"Long enough to enjoy the view." She smiled.

He walked toward her. "You're always trying to be funny."

"Trying? I'm insulted. I think I'm always *being* funny." She let the sheet drop just enough to show one breast.

He came to her side of the bed, within touching distance. "So, what would you like to do today?"

"I was thinking I'd like to take a long walk on the beach with you and then come back and attack your body." She ran her fingers down his arm.

"Now, *that* sounds like a plan. How about a couple's massage after that?"

Amanda stretched sinuously. Lucius's eyes flamed, his focus clearly on her breasts that were now fully exposed. She smiled again.

Lucius deliberately set his coffee cup down on the bedside table. His hands went to either side of her hips as he leant over her. Her heartbeat revved up, as it did every time Lucius looked at her with desire.

"But I think we'll change up the plan a little… Bed first, walk second."

She giggled. "Do you intend to feed me somewhere in this plan?"

"I can…" Lucius's lips found hers.

Amanda welcomed him with open arms.

The day was turning out more splendidly than she could have imagined.

At a knock on the door, Lucius climbed out of bed, quickly pulled on shorts and soon returned with a push-tray loaded with toast, fruit and cheese, along with tea and coffee. Again they ate at the table on the patio.

"This is wonderful. The view is almost as nice as yours. You're spoiling me."

He looked pleased with himself. "That was my intention."

"You keep this up and I'll never leave."

Why had she said that? She'd promised herself she wouldn't think about anything but the here and now.

"About that… Have you ever thought of staying here? Working at the clinic? We don't have openings often, but we could always make room for someone with your skills."

Lucius wanted her to stay for her nursing abilities? He didn't want her to stay for him? That hurt. Took the edge off her happiness.

"I already have a good position in Atlanta. There's one position coming open soon that I've been working for years to be qualified for. With this exchange, I should be considered."

"Maybe we can rework things at the clinic so that you could have a position equal to it—or even better."

Still he wasn't offering himself as part of the deal. "What are you really asking?" she demanded.

He sighed. "I'm going to miss you."

She laid her hand over his, resting on the table. "And I'm going to miss you more than I can say. Maybe we'll see each other at a conference sometime. The world is a small place in our field."

"I'd like that."

"I would too."

Sadly, she didn't think that would happen. But right now, her attention should be directed at soaking up as much of Lucius as she could.

Lucius was all too aware of the fact that Amanda would be leaving soon. It clouded his thoughts—especially when he wasn't with her. He'd brought her to the resort so they could focus on each other, not to think about the clinic, their patients or being called away. He refused to let their conversation earlier in the day put a damper on the rest of their time together this weekend.

He'd offered her a job hoping it would entice her to stay in Sydney. Something was telling him she wanted to stay and his gut feeling was rarely wrong.

So why wouldn't Amanda consider a job with him?

They could continue what they had started and see it out to the end. Maybe they would come out on the other side as good friends who had done some remarkable medical work together.

Or could they work out a geographical compromise? But they couldn't live further apart, and right now, it appeared an impossibility. He had his work here and she had her dreams elsewhere.

Why couldn't he be one of those?

Other than that one issue over a patient, he and Amanda were highly compatible. They certainly were in bed. But what if he couldn't sustain a good relationship with her outside of bed? His risk of failure was too great to jeopardize Amanda's happiness. For right now, he must just concentrate on having her remember him with happiness.

They'd gone to the spa for their massages. Having one wasn't his usual idea of time well spent, but he'd enjoyed his mostly because Amanda had been near. The smile on her face afterward had been worth the effort. He'd also made arrangements for her to have a facial, and her fingernails and toes done.

When she'd claimed he'd already spent too much on her, he'd pulled her into a hug. "You work hard and you deserve for someone to do something nice for you. I can do that."

Amanda had gazed at him as if he'd just told the moon to move out of its orbit for her.

"We'll dine out tonight," he said now. "Wear your pink dress—or go to the boutique and get something new. Charge it to the bungalow."

She all but glowed with pleasure.

This was what it felt like to please a woman. He'd spent

years not making his sister or his ex-wife happy. It was self-confidence-building to know he pleased Amanda.

They were dressed for dinner and ready to leave their bungalow later when he pulled out the box that held a bracelet with pink diamonds all the way around it. He was worried that it might send the wrong message, but when he'd seen it, it had reminded him of Amanda. Confident that her practical side wouldn't allow her to buy a new dress, and she would be wearing the pink one for their dinner, he'd bought the bracelet.

"I have something for you."

"Lucius, I don't need anything more. Today has been wonderful. I've never been more pampered." She waved her newly painted nails.

"I saw this and thought of you." He opened the box.

She gasped. "Oh, Lucius, it's beautiful. You shouldn't have."

"Why not?"

She really didn't expect him to do nice things for her. The women he'd had experience with had all but demanded it.

"Because I don't usually go anywhere I'd wear something so fine." She lightly fingered the stones.

"I'll tell you what—wear it tonight, and if you don't want it after that I'll return it."

She kissed him. "It's not that I don't want it. It's lovely. No one has ever given me something so splendid. But because of that I'm doing a poor job of being grateful."

He brought her near him again and kissed her. "I promise it isn't too nice for you."

Her eyes sparkled with moisture, and he came close to telling her they would be staying here in the bungalow for the evening—but this weekend wasn't about him.

They had their meal at one of the restaurants at the resort. Lucius noticed that Amanda touched the bracelet a few times. Her liking his choice made something around the area of his heart glow.

After dinner, they danced. He was so out of practice his efforts reminded him of when he'd been an adolescent at a mandatory dance and he'd have rather have been in his dorm room reading. But Amanda encouraged him. Being with her made almost anything easier.

By the time they returned to the bungalow it had started raining. It was a slow and steady fall.

Amanda opened the door to the patio. "I love the sound of rain."

She started to close it but he said, "Leave it." Then he lit a candle at the bedside and went to stand behind her, wrapping his arms around her.

She snuggled back against him. They stood like that for a long time, both deep in their own thoughts. Finally he undressed her, except for the bracelet, and carried her to bed. Their gazes held as he removed his own clothing.

He made slow love to her by the light of the flickering flame and to the sound of gentle rain.

They spent another lazy morning together the next day. And after eating a late breakfast they headed back toward Sydney. Just outside of Mardi, Lucius turned off the main road.

Amanda perked up in her seat. "Where're we going?"

"You'll see."

"Is this another one of your surprises?" She gave him a pointed look.

He smiled as she touched her bracelet again. "I think you'll like this one the best."

"I don't think that's possible. The weekend has already been perfect. *You've* been perfect." She ran her hand down his thigh.

He clasped her hand and brought it to his mouth for a kiss.

Soon he turned at a sign that read "Billabong Park."

"Are we going to a zoo?" Amanda leaned forward, searching out the window. She almost hummed with excitement.

"We are. I thought you'd like to see some of our native animals. And the nice thing about this zoo is that many of the animals roam free, so you can touch them."

"This is so exciting!"

Lucius wasn't sure it was. He hadn't been to a zoo in years. Since he was a child. Even then it had been with a school group.

They held hands as they strolled along the paved walkways. They saw birds, crocodiles, kangaroos—and snakes. Amanda didn't want to spend much time with them, and that was fine with him. He'd saved the best for last.

"We need to go right up here." He led her toward a small shed.

"Why? I don't think there is anything up this way." Amanda searched the area.

"Trust me."

She squeezed his hand. "Always."

The word seemed to hold more weight than just her trusting in what direction he was taking her in.

As they reached the small building a woman wearing the park's uniform stepped out, holding a koala bear.

"Look! A koala! Isn't he cute?"

"Would you like to hold him?" the woman asked.

"*Can* I?" Amanda looked at Lucius.

"Sure you can. Didn't you say that day at the beach party that you wanted to hold a koala bear?"

"You remembered?" She seemed surprised.

"I remember everything about you."

She beamed at him. "I think that's the nicest thing anyone has ever said to me."

Amanda had managed to embarrass him, and he didn't embarrass easily.

"Go on and hold the animal."

Walking over to the woman, Amanda took the koala in her hands. It perched on her arm, with its head above her shoulder. Amanda's smile went from ear to ear. She spoke quietly to the animal, petting it softly.

It took Lucius a moment to realize his smile had grown as broad as Amanda's. He was enjoying her joy.

He knew that people believed he didn't smile enough. Kirri especially complained about it. What would she think if she saw him now? He probably looked like a clown…

Amanda carefully handed the animal back to the zoo worker and re-joined him. She wrapped her hand around one of his forearms, came up on her toes and kissed him on the cheek.

"You brought me here just for that. Thank you."

This woman had him wrapped around her little finger. He knew he'd never be the same again. It would take him a long time to recover from Amanda.

He kissed her forehead. "The zoo was on our way home."

"Say what you want, Dr. West, but I know you're one special guy."

They arrived home just before dark. And as Lucius prepared for bed his phone rang. The nurse on the phone told him he was needed at the clinic. He hated to leave Amanda but they were already back to reality. And for him that meant his work.

"Amanda?"

"In here," she called from the bathroom.

"I need to go check on something at the clinic. I won't be long."

"Do you need my help?" She put her arm around his waist as they walked to the front door.

"No. I'll be back soon." He gave her a quick kiss and hurried to the car.

As he drove out of the drive Amanda stood on the front porch. He knew she would be waiting for him to return. Yeah, it would be difficult when she left.

Five days, six hours, and forty-two minutes from now...

Amanda woke to feel a flipping sensation in her stomach. Her hand pressed on her middle. A question had been niggling at her. The answer lay just beyond what she wanted to believe, to accept.

It couldn't be morning sickness.

Why couldn't it? She and Lucius had certainly made love often enough.

But they'd used protection.

She groaned. They'd missed a few times when the heat of the moment had overcome them—including that very first night they'd spent together. Still, she couldn't accept it.

Yet she hadn't been herself for over a week. Feeling unwell from eating something bad wouldn't have gone on this long. And she would've recovered from a virus by now as well.

It was time she faced reality. Reality being she needed to take a pregnancy test.

She'd anticipated it would be easy to do so in a fertility clinic, but it turned out to be more complicated than she'd have believed. The clinic had been particularly busy for a Monday, and she hadn't been able to find a time when she was alone in the supply room to pick up a test, or a moment long enough for her to get away unnoticed.

She couldn't afford any speculation about what she was doing. Even though it had become pretty much common knowledge that she and Lucius were seeing each other.

When the word had gotten out they had both taken some

good-natured teasing, but that had soon died down. Even with this acceptance of their relationship Lucius deserved to know before anyone else if she was pregnant. That was if the test came back positive. She still wasn't confident that it would.

She'd administered hundreds of these tests during her career. None had been this hard to manage. Could it be because this one was the first she'd ever done on herself?

During lunch she went to the supply room, acting like a secret agent on an assignment. There she pulled a test out of the plastic box where they were stored, stuffing it in her pocket. On second thought she grabbed another. Being doubly sure wouldn't be a bad idea.

She succeeded in making it to a private bathroom in the back of Labor and Delivery without being seen. Briefly she'd considered going to Lucius's office bathroom—but what if he came in and started asking questions? She wasn't exactly known for her poker face.

Her hand shook as she removed the cellophane wrapper. She had to do this correctly. A false result would be more than she could stand.

She reviewed the directions as if she'd never read them before, then took the collection cup and caught her urine. Moments later she took an eyedropper and placed some of it in the required slot. Gradually a line appeared.

Her heart dropped in sadness as a negative sign showed, but seconds later it turned into a positive.

She was having a baby!

It would have been a lie if she'd said she wasn't elated.

A baby. Lucius's baby.

How would he feel about it? Would he be as happy as she was?

This baby would completely complicate her life.

Yes, but what joy it would bring.

She would have the precious baby she'd always dreamed of. Would he or she have beautiful blue eyes like its father?

Not wanting to shake Lucius's world from the bottom up without being absolutely sure, she took the other test. She smiled. Positive again.

Now the question was how she would tell Lucius…

She suspected he wouldn't be thrilled. But she was certain he would come around. Be as happy as her about it.

Amanda met him that evening at his car, as usual. At first their conversation revolved around the interesting patients they'd seen that day. But what she really wanted to do was shout out that she was pregnant. Still, she had to do it at the right time. While they were driving in traffic wasn't it.

A couple of times Lucius had to repeat what he'd said because she hadn't been listening. Her mind was rapidly moving through scenarios of how to tell him. She finally came to the conclusion that she'd have to treat it like a plastic bandage and just rip it off. Not hesitate further.

But the right time didn't come.

They prepared dinner together. She liked this time in their day the best. Lucius would keep her company in the kitchen. He seemed content. She had the idea he hadn't always been that way.

Still she couldn't say anything.

After dinner Lucius suggested a walk around the neighborhood. They held hands as they strolled. For a man who had not done it before she'd come to stay with him, he acted now as if he enjoyed greeting his neighbors. Amanda took a moment to dream of pushing a baby stroller along as they went.

They were getting ready for bed when Lucius came out of the bathroom and found her staring off into space.

"Is something wrong? Did something happen I need to know about?" he asked.

Concern laced his voice as he approached her.

Her hand covered her middle and she took a deep breath. “I’m pregnant.”

CHAPTER NINE

"HOW DID *THAT* HAPPEN?" Lucius glared at her.

The question would have been laughable if it hadn't been for the seriousness of the circumstances. He was a doctor who specialized in pregnancy. They were two adult professionals who should have been more careful.

"I think you're smart enough to figure that out," said Amanda.

"This isn't the time for your attempts at humor," he snapped.

He paced across the room.

"Of course I know *how* it happened. *When* is more like the right question."

Amanda gave him a pointed look. "That answer would be any day for the last three weeks and more often than not more than once. Take your pick."

Lucius had the good grace to look abashed. "Okay. Let's forget how and when and work on what we're going to do."

"That's not hard. I'm going to have it. Raise him or her and love him or her."

Lucius sounded much more unhappy about the baby than she'd anticipated.

"Amanda, I'm not father material. I certainly had no real example growing up. I'm not good husband material either. As a parent… I just don't think I'm what a child needs."

Her stomach turned sick and it had nothing to do with the baby.

Did he not recognize that all any child needed was love? She'd seen him with the babies at the clinic. He had what it took if he'd just trust himself.

"If that's how you feel then I'll do it by myself."

Lucius ran both hands through his hair. "Of course I'll provide for you both."

How like Lucius to think of practical considerations when all she and the baby needed was the intangible—his love.

"I don't want your money." Her words held bite.

He huffed. "What are we going to do...?"

Gone was the self-assured professional who seemed always to know his next move. They were talking in a circle now. As far as she was concerned there was no "we".

"*We're* not going to do anything. *I'm* going home on Saturday and I'll have a baby eight months later."

Lucius's face paled. He walked across the room and back.

They could have been so good together.

But once again they were on different sides of an issue. One that involved their lives. Their baby. Their future.

Lucius stopped pacing as her phone rang. It didn't do that often.

"I'm sorry, but I've got to get this," she told him. Into the phone, she said, "Hello? Yes, this is Amanda. I'll be there in fifteen minutes."

She hung up and stood. Her stomach took that moment to waver and crash. Grabbing the edge of the bed, she steadied herself.

Lucius hurried to her, fear in his eyes. "Are you okay?"

She raised her hand. "I'm fine. I just stood up too quickly, that's all. I've got to go to the clinic. Dr. Johannsson has tonight off and is out of town. Dr. Theodore was supposed to be on call but he has been in a car accident and doesn't know how long he'll be. Dr. Maxwell is on his way in, but he was at his beach house. A woman who's expecting triplets has chosen now to start having some trouble. I've got to go oversee things until a doctor can get there. I may need you to scrub in too."

Soon they were in the car on their way to the clinic. Lucius's hands gripped the steering wheel as he drove as fast as he safely could. He glanced at Amanda. She was speaking into her phone as she held a hand over her middle. Already her instincts were to protect their baby.

He knew he hadn't handled the last thirty minutes as well as he should have. But he couldn't believe he would soon be a father. *A father.* He glanced at Amanda. She'd be a good mother. She was all that was fine and decent in the world. She'd certainly made a difference in *his* life.

Now that the idea had had time to sink in he felt pride fill him. But despite that he still had no confidence he could be what Amanda and the baby needed for the long haul.

He had zero parenting skills. They had never been demonstrated on him. His father had had his work and his mother her books. He and Kirri had just been in the way. To think he might be husband material was laughable. He'd already proved he wasn't good at that. But what he *could* do was make sure they were financially cared for, regardless of whether or not Amanda wanted him to.

Less than half an hour later they were hurrying into Labor and Delivery. They headed straight to the locker room, where they changed into scrubs.

Amanda had spent the entire drive on her phone, talking to the nurses already in the labor area. From her tone of voice, the case sounded worse than expected.

As they scrubbed in Amanda said, "Dr. Maxwell is still a good thirty minutes out. The patient is showing signs of pre-eclampsia. One of the babies is already in distress. You're going to have to do a C-section. That baby isn't going to make it if you don't. May not even then. The patient is on her way to the OR now."

She pushed through the swinging door, using her hip. "I'll see you in there."

She didn't wait for him to respond.

When he arrived in the OR some of the nurses were draping the woman for surgery. Machines blinked and the constant swish of three heart monitors filled the air.

Amanda was busy doing an examination with a vaginal stethoscope. Judging by the thin-lipped look of concentration on her face, the situation had turned dire.

He nodded to the woman's husband, who stood beside his wife, gripping her hand. Fear shadowed his face.

"Sir, I'm sorry, but you'll need to step out of the room now. When the babies are here and your wife is stable we'll let you return," Lucius said.

The man looked relieved to escape. A nurse led him out and returned.

Amanda finished her exam and he picked up a scalpel. "I'll do the section and then see to the patient. The babies are all yours."

She nodded. "I'll be ready. I want the one that's struggling first."

Lucius went to work. In less than five minutes Amanda handed off a tiny blue newborn to one of the other nurses in the room. He lifted the next one out and passed it to Amanda. She gave it to another waiting nurse. The last one was difficult. He had to do some maneuvering to get the baby out. Done, he handed the third one off.

A machine sounded the alarm.

"BP going down," his surgical nurse announced.

"Amanda, I'm going to need you over here."

He had to stop the bleeding or the mother would die.

Almost immediately Amanda stood beside him.

"Remove the placenta. I'll start massaging."

He had to do what the uterus was failing to do. With any luck uterine atony would soon kick in.

Amanda did as he said, then started pushing on the mother's abdomen.

"Blood pressure rising," the nurse declared.

The bleeding had slowed, but not stopped. He couldn't stop yet.

"Keep going. We've got to get this hemorrhaging completely under control. Get two units of whole blood started, STAT."

Amanda took the blood from the nurse who'd brought it to the table. With speed and efficiency she soon had it locked into the IV and running into the patient. She came to stand beside him and began mopping up the blood in the cavity.

Not soon enough for him, the nurse stated, "BP stable. Vitals stable."

He relaxed his shoulders.

"If you have this under control now I'll go speak to the father. I'm sure he needs a Valium by now."

Amanda moved toward the door and started pulling off her gloves.

Lucius had no doubt that if he were in the man's place he'd need one too. If he was with Amanda when their baby was born he was sure he'd feel the same way.

His chest constricted. He wouldn't be there. She'd be half a world away. He could only hope someone as dedicated as she was would be there to help her.

He finished stitching up the mother, refusing to let his mind wander further. If he did, he feared he might never be able to look at himself in the mirror again.

Half an hour later he handed off the care of the mother

to Dr. Maxwell, who had finally arrived. Then Lucius went in search of Amanda.

He found her in the nursery, holding one of the babies he'd just delivered. There was an angelic expression on her face as she looked at the child. He was sure that look and many more like it would be on her face when their own baby arrived. But he wouldn't see any of them.

Fortifying himself, he stood in the doorway. "Amanda, are you ready to go home?"

His heart gasped with pain when she didn't look at him.

"I'll meet you at the car," she said.

"Okay."

He walked away, conscious of the fact that they still had a difficult conversation ahead of them. But he hadn't changed his mind and he suspected Amanda hadn't either.

It had been a long time since Amanda had felt so tired. This pregnancy was already zapping her energy. To compound it, it had been an emotional discussion with Lucius and a difficult delivery afterward. She was done in. All she wanted was a hot shower and bed.

As she walked down the front hall of Lucius's home she made a left turn into the guest suite. Things weren't settled enough between them for her to think he'd want her in his bed.

"Goodnight. I'll see you tomorrow. Feel free to go into the clinic without me. I'll call a taxi."

Lucius made no response. She'd have been surprised if she was awake enough to hear it even if he had.

The next morning she woke to sunshine. It was late in the morning. She gazed out the window at the harbor, already teeming with activity. She would miss it. But not as much as she would Lucius.

She sighed. For the next four days she would focus on

making good memories. Her hand went to her middle. She had something to look forward to with or without Lucius.

Moisture filled her eyes but she blinked it away.

Was he still here at home? She wasn't ready to face him. If she did she might fall apart and beg him—for what? To stay? For them to find a way to make it work? For him to love her?

The house remained quiet. Undoubtedly Lucius had already left. She needed to go to work as well.

She looked at the bedside table to see crackers and a glass of soda waiting. A sad smile came to her lips. Even though things weren't good between them Lucius was still concerned about her.

On her way to the bathroom she noticed the head indentation on the other pillow. Had Lucius slept there too last night?

Unsure what to make of that, she knew her heart couldn't help but feel encouraged.

An hour later, at the clinic, she knocked on Lucius's office door since his assistant was not behind her desk. Amanda wasn't confident of her welcome, but they needed to talk—even if it was just about living arrangements.

"Come in."

Lucius looked up in surprise when she entered. He stood, but stayed behind his desk. Uncertainty the size of an iceberg loomed between them. She hated that. Had it only been last week that he'd sent her over the moon with just the touch of his hands in this very room?

How quickly life changed.

"I just wanted to let you know I've made arrangements to move back to the hotel this evening."

He looked stricken, and then panicked, as if he had never considered the possibility of her moving out. His fingers gripped the front edge of his desk.

"I wish you wouldn't do that," he said. "You'll only

be here a few more nights and I think we can survive those under the same roof together." He came around the desk, his hand outstretched. "Amanda, I want us to remain friends. After all we'll have a child together."

"I want us to be friends as well, but I don't want to make you uncomfortable in your own home."

She didn't want to go. Truth be known, she'd like to stay with him forever.

"You won't. I'd like you to stay. Please."

Once again she found herself agreeing to something she wasn't completely sure about. "All right. Thank you."

He opened his mouth and then closed it, as if he wanted to say more but wasn't sure how to begin. The self-assured doctor wasn't acting that way today.

A few moments later he asked, "Could we talk tonight?"

"Sure."

Her heart fell. She wouldn't be looking forward to that discussion. They could chat about anything he wanted, but her mind was already made up about the baby and what she would accept from him.

Nothing less than his love.

For her, a baby shouldn't be a way to receive love, but a product of love.

That evening, after dinner, Lucius found himself standing over Amanda like a thundercloud ready to pour rain. That hadn't been his intention. He'd wanted them to find a compromise that they could live with—really one that *he* could live with. And so far Amanda had shot down all his suggestions.

Right now, she was watching him calmly from the sofa. She wasn't going to change her mind about her plans. At this rate all he would have when she left was a path worn in his hardwood floor from the number of times he'd walked back and forth in frustration.

The stubborn woman hadn't moved an inch. She wanted something he was incapable of giving.

After another trip across the room he flopped down to the sofa cushions. He could hear his father saying, *"Pull yourself together, son. West men don't act like that."* Lucius stood up again. He would give it one more shot.

"Stay here. You like it here. I'll share my view with you for as long as you want. We'll make a spot at the clinic for you."

Her gaze remained fixed on him. "Is that all you're offering?"

"I don't know what you mean..."

"I'm not surprised." She shook her head. Her mouth formed a sad smile. "It's not going to work between us. You're sorry about the baby and you feel responsible. I didn't plan this but I'm happy about it."

He glared at her. Here he was, twisting in the wind. In an odd way he suspected his world was coming apart, but he didn't understand how to stop it imploding. He needed to get control back. Amanda sat there coolly telling him that she'd be having his baby thousands of miles away from him and he just had to deal with it.

"Don't worry, Lucius. We'll both be fine."

He forced himself to sit down again, his fingers biting into the sofa cushions. *Without him?* She couldn't have hurt him more if she'd physically punched him.

"I'll let you know when it's born."

"Will that be by mail, email or text?" he spat.

Amanda flinched and turned away from him. Her voice sounded flat when she said, "I'll call the minute I can. I'd never keep you from knowing about your child. If I'd wanted to do that I wouldn't have told you in the first place."

Something gripped his heart and squeezed, making his chest physically hurt. He might believe he wasn't husband material, and he suspected he wouldn't be any better as a father, but he wanted to know his child. He cared. More than she knew. More than he wanted to show.

He waited until she looked at him. "You can't keep my child from me. He or she *will* know its father."

"I would never do that." Her words sounded sincere but still her eyes remained anxious.

Lucius ran his hand through his hair. "I know. I'm just not thinking right these days."

She turned toward him and reached out a hand, but didn't touch him. "How much you see your child will be totally up to you."

"I wish you would reconsider staying here." He wouldn't continue to beg.

She gave him a pleading look. "I don't want to argue with you, but you can't control everything."

Lucius jumped to his feet. "I'm not *trying* to control everything!"

"Right. You control the clinic. Your work. You tried to control Kirri but she broke away—and she had to go all the way to Atlanta to do it. You even try to control your emotions. You're running scared, out of control, and you can't stand it."

He jerked as if she had actually hit him.

Continuing as if she'd been banking the words for a while now, and had finally opened the vault door, she said, "Your childhood with your father has affected how you see the world, and it isn't always correct. Still, it's understandable. You've had a failed marriage when you were raised to believe that failure wasn't an option. Yet sometimes things happen in life that we don't always plan."

She placed her hand over her stomach.

"Sometimes we just don't make the right choices and it ends badly. That's called life. Some things are out of our control. That doesn't mean we shouldn't try again. Or that we should consider ourselves failures."

Lucius glared down at her, his hands on his hips. "What are you saying? Are you saying you think we ought to get married? If that will keep you from leaving, then that's what we'll do."

She stood, went to the window and looked out blankly, her shoulders slumped. "That's a proposal that any woman would be *dying* to hear. Thanks, Lucius, but *no,* thanks."

"I'm sorry—I did that all wrong." He started to go to her but then held himself in check.

Amanda shook her head, still not looking at him. "I don't think you know what you want clearly enough that you should be involving me or this baby."

That hurt—especially coming from her. It sounded too final.

He couldn't help but fight back. "Don't start psychoanalyzing me."

She turned to face him. "I'm not. I'm just stating how I see it. I've made a decision to go home at the end of the week. I'll let you know when the baby is born. You're welcome to see the baby whenever you choose. That is totally up to you. I want this child. I can support it. You need to figure out how involved you want to be and then cut yourself some slack. It might come as a surprise to you to realize that you *are* father material. That's something I already know."

"How do you know that?" He watched her closely.

"I've told you this before. I've seen you with the babies. Tough guy that you are, you go to the nursery to hold the babies when you need some downtime. Guess what? Your secret is out. You're an old softy."

She said it with complete confidence. Stated it as fact. He couldn't have done the same.

"But that doesn't mean anything."

"It's a darn good start. We didn't intend to make a baby. It happened. I won't call it a mistake. I love this baby already. That's why I can't stay here and be your mistress, or have you provide me with a job or a roof over my head. I have pride too, Lucius."

"If you ask me, you have too much," he murmured.

He could have kicked himself. The moment he made the statement he knew he'd said the wrong thing. But now he had to back it up. If not to get it off his chest then for her own good.

"You've become too accustomed to being self-sufficient. You can't see that maybe you could use my help. You think men are either incapable of being what you need or that they will disappoint you, so you never let them get close enough to prove you wrong."

She turned to face him. "That's not—"

"You think we're all your stepfather. Wanting a pretty picture that doesn't include you. You push us all away because you think we're going to leave you anyway."

"I do not!"

"Sure you do. You're doing it right now. I'm not measuring up to the mark you've set so you're leaving. Not even considering other options. At least stay a little while longer and let's see if we can figure out a better way than you and the baby being thousands of miles away from me. Have a little trust in me. In *us*."

"Would you want me to stay if it weren't for the baby? Part of our relationship was built on the fact it would be short-lived. I was part of a package deal when my mother married my stepfather. It didn't work out well for me. It won't be that way again—not for me or my child. You only want me to stay because of the baby. That's not a good enough reason for me."

"So we're back to me marrying you, are we?"

"I've never even mentioned marriage! You're the one

that keeps bringing it up. But, while we're on the subject, you and I both know it would have never have come up as an option if I hadn't gotten pregnant."

With her head held high she started toward the guest suite.

"I think I've had enough talking for one day. Goodnight."

Lucius stood speechless. He wanted to follow her, but now wasn't the time.

He had a lot of thinking to do. A long hard swim was what he needed…

Amanda lay in the dark bedroom with the door open, listening to the water splash as Lucius swam lap after lap in the pool. It sounded as if he were swimming for his life.

Why couldn't he understand that she had been trying to tell him something important? That she wanted his love. Not the job, the view, or to live in Sydney, but him. For a man who prided himself on his intelligence, he'd missed the point where she was concerned.

Sometime later the door to the hall opened and then softly closed. Seconds later the mattress dipped and Lucius gathered her into his arms. Her body had become used to having him close, longed for him.

Hadn't he told her weeks ago that under his roof they would share the same bed regardless of any disagreement between them? It wasn't a good idea, but she couldn't send him away.

"Lucius," she said, so softly it was a whisper.

"Shh… Go to sleep."

He brought her close and she rested her head on his shoulder. She waited, anticipating he'd make love to her, but he made no move to do so. He'd placed another row of bricks on the wall he had started building between them.

With a deep, dejected exhalation she closed her eyes, but didn't find sleep for a long time.

Lucius was gone when she woke the next morning. A plate of crackers and a glass of bubbly soda sat on the bedside table.

A while later Amanda got dressed for work and joined him in the kitchen.

Lucius sat drinking his coffee and staring off into space. He looked as miserable as she felt. His hair was tousled, as if he'd been running his fingers through it. Her fingers itched to touch it, to smooth it into place, but she wasn't sure he would allow it.

She would miss Lucius so badly.

She'd feared some of the antagonism from their discussion the night before might bleed over into the morning but it seemed that by mutual tacit agreement they'd decided that being civil over the next few days would be the answer. No tension filled the room, but instead something much worse hovered over them: the melancholy mist of hopelessness.

"Thank you for the crackers. They do make a difference." She gave him a weak smile.

"You're welcome. I hate that you don't feel well."

His eyes had lost their shine. *She* hated that.

Taking a bite of her toast, she said, "It's just part of the process."

"I sort of feel guilty."

There was that soft heart of his she loved so much.

A genuine smile came to her lips. "Don't. If it's any help, I think morning sickness is well worth the outcome. I'll meet you at the car in a few minutes."

The rest of their days together went much the same way. They lived as roommates, with that brick wall between them growing ever higher. Except at night, when it turned into glass and Lucius came to her bed.

Yet the wall still remained.

More than once she questioned if she was doing the right thing by leaving. Why couldn't she stay? After all, he'd offered her everything she'd ever dreamed of—everything but his love. And in time maybe that would come.

Lucius was a good man. He would be there for her and their child. Couldn't that be enough for her?

But what if she stayed and in time he decided he didn't want her? Other men had. What if Lucius decided she was too opinionated, too driven, too demanding? She still wanted a successful career, and she was still that person who stood up to him, questioned him. Could Lucius accept that?

Worse, what if he decided he no longer wanted her and started seeing another woman? Could she stand being close enough to see that happen?

By then their child might have gotten to know Lucius well, and she wouldn't be able to return to America without ripping her child away from its father, causing untold misery for everyone.

The what-ifs continued to whirl around in her mind. The only answer that came back as a sure thing was that Lucius hadn't said anything about loving her. If they'd loved each other she knew they would be able to work anything out. Without love between them she didn't see any hope for them.

They didn't discuss the future, even though she remained hyper-aware that she would be leaving soon. The breach between them widened, as if he were already slowly breaking away from her. How big would it become when she returned to America?

By Friday she felt sick—and it had nothing to do with being pregnant. Tomorrow morning she would get on a plane and fly out of Lucius's city—out of his life and out of his arms.

Only with a fortitude she hadn't known she possessed did Amanda keep moving forward at work, smiling at all the right times and saying all the right things.

That evening the clinic staff had a going-away party for her. It just punctuated the fact that her time with Lucius had come to an end. She glanced at him. He didn't look like he was in a partying mood either. In fact, he appeared as if he would rather be anywhere but there. He'd spent most of the last hour leaning against a wall with a drink in his hand, glaring at her.

All the clinic staff came to speak to her, and many of them she hugged. To a few she promised to stay in touch. She knew she wouldn't. If she was going to survive she'd have to make a clean cut of it or she'd never get over Lucius. She would never do that anyway.

When one of the men hugged her she noticed that Lucius moved away from the wall and stood ramrod-straight. For a second she feared he might even grab the guy and yank him away from her. She broke the embrace and turned to another person waiting to talk to her.

After the party, Lucius helped her carry her going-away presents to the car.

"You've really made an impression on my clinic staff. I won't be the only one to miss you."

"Lucius, please don't. It's hard enough as it is..."

They drove home with a silence filling the car as deep as the ocean that would soon be between them. They went their separate ways in the front hallway without a word.

She finished packing, then ate a simple meal while watching through the kitchen window as Lucius swam. Finished with her meal, she showered and went to bed. There, she lay tense and wide awake. Would he come to her tonight?

Her heart pounded as the door opened. Moments later Lucius put his arms around her. Amanda turned and ran her fingers over his chest. She couldn't believe she was going to bare her soul, but she couldn't leave without telling him what she wanted.

"Lucius, I need you to love me."

That was all the invitation he seemed to need before his mouth found hers. But she was looking for love from his heart, not just from his body. He still didn't understand—or didn't want to.

The next morning Lucius drove her to the airport. They said nothing on the ride there. Everything had been said already.

She insisted he drop her off at the curb. He took her suitcase out of the trunk and placed it beside her. Their gazes met. Could he see the pain and disappointment in hers? Her chest constricted, as if the world was pressing down on her. She fought for air.

Surely these feelings would pass with time?

A great deal of it, she feared.

"Goodbye, Amanda. I'll be expecting your call."

Lucius's voice held no emotion at all. That brick wall had gone way too high. They had become strangers.

"Bye, Lucius. I've enjoyed my visit Down Under and I wish you a happy life."

She walked off as her heart exploded into a thousand pain-filled pieces.

CHAPTER TEN

WITH A FORCE of will that Amanda hadn't known she possessed, she took the handle of her suitcase and started toward the airport doors. Every fiber of her being wanted to turn and run back into Lucius's open arms. The problem was that his arms wouldn't be open. He didn't want her for forever and she wouldn't settle for less. She and the baby deserved love, not obligation.

Lucius cared for her, and even for this baby too, but he feared he wouldn't be enough for them. She didn't care if he wasn't perfect. She just needed his love. He couldn't bring himself to say it, but she believed he did love her in his own way. He just didn't recognize it, and she couldn't stay on the chance that he might one day comprehend it. If he hadn't figured it out over the last few days there was a real chance he never would.

When she got to the airline desk she learned she'd been upgraded to First Class. She would have a seat that turned into a bed for her return flight. She had no doubt that Lucius was responsible for making those arrangements. He continued to take care of her.

She held her tears in check until she found her seat on the plane. There she let them go.

She'd found a real home and friends in Sydney. It tore her heart out to leave. Even the staff at the clinic had begged her to stay, or at least come back for a visit. She'd promised to come if she had a chance. She couldn't guarantee that would happen. Returning to Lucius's clinic would be too painful.

His outlook on life had been shaped by his parents and by his broken marriage. He'd thrown himself into his work. Facts and figures were always right or wrong, black or white, and they required no sentiment. He'd even treated his sister as more of a test experiment than a sibling relationship. Emotionally, he was as inexperienced as the newborn babies she helped to deliver.

And she couldn't accept what Lucius had offered because of her own background. Settling for what looked like love? She wasn't willing to do that. The pain of leaving him would never be as great as staying and knowing he didn't love her the way she loved him. She wasn't willing to live every day hoping she would hear those three special words and never have them uttered.

More than one person on the plane was giving her a concerned look. The steward asked if she was all right. Pushing a tear away from her cheek, she assured him that she was.

Exhausted and emotionally drained, she went to sleep. When she woke there was a cup of soda and some crackers next to her. Her eyes watered again. Lucius must have left special instructions.

When the steward came by again he said, "Congratulations on the baby."

"How did you know?"

He grinned and nodded toward the crackers. "The breakfast of a mother-to-be."

The one shining diamond in this entire mess between her and Lucius was the baby. It was time she focused on it and not on what couldn't be. Wallowing in negatives wasn't what she needed to do. What she should be grateful for was the precious life inside her.

She landed in Atlanta and took a taxi to her apartment. It seemed like she'd been gone for years instead of only a few weeks. In an odd way, despite all her personal items, it was like she'd left her home thousands of miles away below the equator.

Sitting on her couch, she pulled a pillow to her chest and let the tears go again. She'd had to leave the pillows she'd bought in Sydney behind, because they hadn't fitted in her luggage. They were still on her bed at Lucius's house. Would he throw them out now that she was gone?

The diamond bracelet she had intended to leave behind, but in the end she hadn't been able to bring herself to do so. It was safely tucked in her purse. When the baby grew up, if it was a daughter, she would give it to her—or, if it was a son, to him, for his wife.

She had to get a grip. There was mail to go through, food to buy, her suitcase to unpack and she needed to call her family. Sitting around floundering in her own pain wasn't going to get her anywhere.

Monday morning, she stepped off the elevator on the fifth floor of the Medical Innovations Center and entered the Piedmont Women and Baby Pavilion. She went stock-still when the first person she saw was Kirri West—now Sawyer.

Amanda hadn't thought it through that she would still be working with Lucius's sister. It was difficult enough that they favored each other physically, but what if Kirri talked about him or he came for a visit?

Amanda's stomach swirled and she gripped the counter and closed her eyes.

"Hey, come sit down..."

It was Kirri's voice. Amanda knew that accent. Heard a deeper one like it in her dreams each night.

Kirri gripped her arm and led her to an exam room.

"You okay? I don't usually have people going weak in the knees when they see me." Kirri grinned.

A gorgeous woman, Amanda was sure that Kirri received plenty of wolf whistles when her husband, Dr. Ty Sawyer wasn't around to fend them off.

"You aren't the problem. A combination of jetlag, too little breakfast, the humidity and the Atlanta traffic are more like it."

Amanda moved to sit up. Her stomach chose that moment to revolt.

"Pan."

Kirri quickly handed her a kidney-shaped plastic pan. When Amanda was more herself Kirri asked, "Did you bring one of our bugs home from Australia?"

Amanda had brought something home, but it wasn't an illness. Still, she wasn't prepared to tell Kirri she was pregnant by her brother. That seemed like something that Lucius should share with his sister.

"I'm fine. Give me a few minutes and I'll get it together. I guess I was afraid no one would notice I'd been gone so I had to make a scene."

"We noticed you were gone. I hear we're lucky to get you back because they wanted to keep you in Sydney. I want to hear all about your trip, what you learned, and if my brother is still whispering babies into existence. How about lunch one day soon?"

"Sure. That sounds great." Amanda hoped it wouldn't be soon.

Kirri's phone rang. She answered and told the person on the other end she would be there in a minute. "I've got to go. You get something to eat—and go slow today, until you get your system back on Georgia time."

"Will do."

With relief Amanda watched Kirri leave, then took a few minutes to gather herself and start her day again.

After that unimpressive first day back at work she got up the next morning early enough to eat and drink something. Lucius had always seen to it, but now it was her responsibility.

Amanda managed to avoid Kirri. She just wasn't ready to talk about her time in Australia—especially with Lucius's sister. When other people asked her how her trip had been she gave them a brief description of the clinic, stating that it was brilliant and innovative and that Sydney was beautiful.

It wasn't until one day when she had been assigned an early-morning delivery that she saw Kirri again, other than brief passes in the hall. Kirri had been asked to consult on the case.

As bad luck would have it, Amanda's stomach chose then to flip. Running late, she'd not had a chance to eat before coming into work that morning.

"I'm sorry," she said to the room in general, and ran for the door.

A few minutes later Kirri came into the staff locker room, where Amanda sat on the bench after coming out of the bathroom. Amanda wanted to groan.

"I'm starting to think either I make you sick or we need to run some tests."

Amanda looked at her and shook her head. "There's no need. I know what's wrong."

Kirri's eyes held compassion. "Would you like to tell me?"

That would be a resounding *no*—but Amanda wasn't going to take out her disappointment in Lucius on his sister.

"I'm pregnant."

Kirri continued to watch her. "I'm guessing this happened while you were in Sydney. Is it anybody I know?"

Amanda groaned out loud this time. "Yeah, rather well. It's your brother."

Kirri squealed and clapped her hands. "I'm going to be an auntie! Lucius did tell me over the phone that he thought you were an exceptional nurse, and bright. That's about as high praise as Lucius is capable of. But I had no idea you were seeing each other. He knows about the baby?"

"He does. I found out a few days before I left. I told him." Amanda looked at the floor.

Kirri gasped. Her voice held disbelief when she asked, "And he let you go?"

"He didn't want to. But he didn't make the right offer for me to stay."

"I see."

And somehow Amanda thought she did.

"Why am I not surprised?" Kirri shook her head.

"I'd like to keep this between us, if that's okay," said Amanda. "I'm not ready to tell the entire clinic yet. I'm still trying to adjust to the idea myself."

Kirri nodded. "I understand."

"I'd also prefer that you don't discuss it with Lucius. He's made his decision and I've made mine."

And she wasn't happy about either one.

Kirri placed her arm on Amanda's shoulder. "You love him, don't you?"

Amanda met eyes so like Lucius's. "Very much."

Neither of them said anything for a few minutes.

"I'll honor your wishes for as long as I can. After all, this is my niece or nephew too. I may have to say something—especially if the parents are too hardheaded to get their acts together."

Kirri gave Amanda's shoulders a squeeze.

"When Lucius loves it's deeply and completely. He'll protect those he loves to his dying breath. The problem is he has a difficult time expressing that love outside of actions."

Kirri paused just long enough for Amanda to look at her. "Sometimes even *I* have to meet him more than halfway. Think about that."

That weekend Amanda met her mother at a café in Virginia Highlands. It was one of Amanda's favorite neighborhoods. In a way, it reminded her of Lucius's neighborhood. The homes were older here, and had been refurbished. There was a warmness and friendliness about the area that relaxed her. She needed that today.

Her mother was already waiting at a table when Amanda arrived. She rose and gave Amanda a tight hug and kiss. "It's so good to see you, honey. It has been too long. How was your trip to Australia?"

That was all that it took to bring tears to her eyes.

Her mother reached across the table and took her hand. "Tell me."

Amanda did. Every detail. And felt better for it.

Her mother smiled. "So I'm going to be a grandmother."

Amanda's hand automatically went to her middle, which it often did these days. "That seems to be the case."

They had finished their meal when Amanda said, "Can I ask you something?"

The waitress refilled their glasses and left.

"Of course, honey."

Amanda didn't want to make things uncomfortable between them, but she had to know. Therefore she had to ask. She should've done it long ago.

"Why has my stepfather never loved me?"

Her mother hissed and her face looked stricken, then unbearably sad. "I'm so sorry you've felt that way. I guess some of it has been my fault."

How could it have been her mother's doing? She'd never been anything but loving.

"He does love you, but he has a poor way of showing it. I know you saw him as differentiating between how he felt about you and your brother and sister, but it wasn't as wide a gap as you believe. At one time, when you were little, you would climb in his lap and you were very close—and then, as if a light had been turned off, you refused to have anything to do with him. From then on the distance between you just grew. He tried really hard for a time to reconcile with you. I encouraged him, but didn't push, and the rift just got wider."

"I heard you arguing over my prom dress. He didn't want to buy it." Amanda fiddled with her napkin corner then looked at her mother.

Her lips had formed a thin line. "He wanted you to have a more expensive dress and I said we couldn't afford it."

Amanda was heartsick. "Is that really true?"

"Of course it is."

"Mom, you should have sat me down and straightened me out. Not let me act that way toward him."

"Honey, I don't think it was as bad as you think it was. Some of it we put down to you being a kid, and then a normal hormonal teenager. You were always such a determined girl. It was hard to change your mind once you got a thought in your head. We just had to wait it out until you figured it out differently."

"Like right now?"

Had she been the same way with Lucius? Had she made up her mind and disregarded everything he'd said and felt about the situation?

Her mother gave her a wry smile and shrugged.

Amanda couldn't have been more mortified and disappointed in herself. She'd been so unfair to her stepfather and it appeared she had been doing it most of her life.

"Do you think he'll accept my apology after so many years?"

"Honey, I know he will. It's never too late to tell someone you're sorry and that you care about them."

Later that evening as Amanda tossed and turned, begging for sleep, the memory of Lucius's face when she'd left him at the airport kept running through her mind.

Her heart squeezed. He'd been hurting. A man who never seemed lost for words had said nothing. He knew his own mind—of that she had no doubt—but she wasn't sure he knew his own heart. Even then she'd wanted to reach out and soothe that look off his face.

Amanda rolled over and pulled a pillow to her, wishing it was Lucius. She missed his warmth and the gentle heaviness of his arm which had always been around her. The one that made her feel wanted, as if she belonged.

A sob escaped her.

Tired of crying herself to sleep, she revisited her mother's words. She'd been completely wrong about her stepfather. How had she spent so many years being so mistaken? Why hadn't she seen what was around her? She and her stepfather had both suffered for so long unnecessarily. Worse, she'd let their relationship color all the others she'd had—especially the one with Lucius.

How he must hate her. She'd left pregnant with his child, promising him nothing but a phone call after it was born. What kind of person was she to leave the man she loved that way? She should have done better than that. Given him a few more weeks to think about how he felt. But she hadn't done that, had she? She'd made up her mind and that was that.

Would Lucius accept her apology? Could he possibly feel the same way about her as she did him? Was he just afraid to say it?

She been so dogmatic about returning to America she hadn't given him a chance. She'd chosen her reality instead of seeing it for what it was.

Based on what Kirri said, Lucius showed his love in actions rather than words. Through those she had no doubt she'd been cherished by Lucius. She knew what it was like to live under his protection. Even when he'd tried to check out emotionally he'd still come to her bed each night. He'd only held her until she'd asked for more. Even on the day she'd left he'd placed soda and crackers beside her bed in the morning.

Lucius had offered her everything, but had stopped short of saying he loved her. Was Kirri right? Was it just too difficult for him to do? Had Amanda pushed him away like she'd done her stepfather?

Maybe Lucius had been right when he had accused her of being so afraid of abandonment she'd never opened herself up enough to give a man a true chance.

That would stop now. She planned to go after what she wanted—Lucius, a father for her child, and a chance at happiness.

Lucius left the airport confident that letting Amanda go was the right thing to do. He wasn't the man she needed to build her life around. Or the man who should be the father to their child. He could never give her all that she needed or deserved. His time, affections and support would always be dictated by outside forces.

That was who he was and how he lived his life. If he tried to make a stronger commitment he knew it would end in disaster. He cared too much for Amanda and the baby to have them depend on him and him let them down. He had to accept that Amanda and his baby were lost to him forever.

Returning to his house, he didn't make it any further than Amanda's bedroom door. Disgusted with himself, he looked at the bed. Each night he'd gone to her like a junkie, looking for his next fix, unable to stay away. They had made love for the last time with such tenderness and now the bed mocked him. It was made up and neat, like their relationship should have been, and yet it hadn't happened that way. Instead what had been between them had become messy, storm-blown and painful.

In the center of the bedspread were Amanda's two pillows—the ones that she'd insisted she bring with her after she'd had to move out of the apartment. To him they represented the finality of their break. She'd left them behind like she'd left him behind.

Lucius turned and stalked down the hall, went out to his car and drove off. He drove and drove and drove. The destination didn't matter. What he desperately wanted to do was forget.

It had turned dark when he pulled into a small hotel on some highway and rented a room for the night.

He couldn't face his house again. And fear filled him that he might feel the same about the clinic. Even the city had changed for him. Amanda, and memories of her, being with her, had colored his world. He just had to wait until the memories of her burned away like a morning fog and cleared his mind.

His greatest fear was that it might never happen.

Still, he had the weekend to recover. He'd have no choice but to move on come Monday. There was the clinic to run and his research to see about. As a gifted, mature adult he needed to get on with his life. Amanda had gone and he needed to accept that. Learn to live with it.

Late the next evening he returned to his house. It didn't have the same appeal to him as it once had. During the time Amanda had been there the house had become a home. He'd liked it that way. Wanted it back.

This time as he passed her bedroom he closed the door. Maybe if he didn't look at the bed every time he came and went it would be easier. He had no doubt he was making excuses. The door being closed wouldn't remove Amanda from his mind.

He went to his office and checked his messages with the hope that there would be one from her. There were none.

Thankfully the next week was so busy he even managed a few hours of not letting Amanda creep into his thoughts. He found that the only time she remained completely out of his mind was when he saw his patients. His lab work was suffering the most. Being in a room all alone just made matters worse. It gave him too much time to think, and the processes were too much by rote.

He finally gave up one day, totally disgusted.

This had to stop.

His staff had started to give him odd looks. They would quit talking when he walked up. Or whisper when they didn't think he was around. More than one looked as if they were too scared to approach him.

His world was crumbling around him and he didn't know how to glue it back together.

In a strange way, he was frightening himself. He wasn't eating, he slept on a sofa or in one of the extra bedrooms—if he slept at all. He dreaded going to work and he hated being at home. He was in a black place and he saw no light.

The weekend loomed large and dark before him. Because of that he decided he might as well visit his father. He couldn't make it any worse.

Saturday morning Lucius drove the hour and a half to an exclusive nursing home on the north side of the city. He recognized that he was only going to see his father out of obligation and not devotion.

The man who had been such a demanding figure in Lucius's life had deteriorated in body but his mind remained sharp. When he entered his father's room the nurse sitting at his bedside stood and nodded, then left them alone. His father leaned against the headboard propped up by pillows with his eyes closed. The TV was turned down low, as if it were just background noise.

"Hello, Father."

The old man opened his eyes slowly. "Lucius."

"How have you been?" Lucius took a seat in the chair.

"About the same. I'm stuck in here."

Until that moment Lucius hadn't realized that anything in particular had brought him there today. "Did you love my mother?" he asked suddenly.

His father blinked. His watery old eyes met Lucius's gaze. "Not the way I should have."

"Why?"

"Because I didn't know how to be a good doctor and a husband and father at the same time. It's my greatest regret."

That statement was like a direct punch to Lucius's chest.

"I did great things as a doctor but I pushed my wife and family away in the process. By the time I realized that it was too late. Your mother was in her own world, you'd become a man too much like me, and Kirri..." He shook his head and sighed.

Lucius stared at his father. This conversation was the furthest from anything he'd ever expected to have with his father.

"Work doesn't keep you warm at night, or give you a smile in the morning, or visit you when you become an old man," his father murmured, and then he drifted off to sleep again.

Lucius sat there contemplating what he'd just learned. The foundations of his life had just been shaken.

Had he followed too closely in his father's footsteps? Not only professionally but in his personal life as well? His father had failed in the family arena, certainly, and had made choices that Lucius didn't want to repeat.

Did he drive all the women in his life away like his father had? Lucius had done that with his first wife by not being there, and now he'd driven Amanda and his baby away as well. Did he want to one day find himself lying in a bed alone, wishing he had done better?

Was he really that self-obsessed? A man who couldn't see what he had before him?

What if another man came into Amanda's life? He would become her lover and the baby's father.

Lucius gripped the arm of the chair until his knuckles turned white. He couldn't stay on that train of thought. It hurt too much.

He had always believed part of his and his ex-wife's problems had been because she wasn't involved in his world. Apparently he'd been wrong. Even with Amanda, who understood his work, he had disagreed, but they had managed to get through it. Their relationship had mattered enough to her for them to fight, make up and move on.

Amanda had asked for his help when she delivered another woman's babies, but she wouldn't ask him for help with their own. What did that say about him? Had he really made her think she was that unwanted, or that he cared so little about her and the baby? What if she had trouble delivering, like the mother with the triplets, and he wasn't there? What if Amanda had a difficult pregnancy and he wasn't around to help? She was already having bad morning sickness.

It was his job to care for and protect her and their child. That was what a loving relationship should be about. Caring for each other. And she was thousands of miles away because he couldn't say he loved her.

Did he? He realized he did. Very much.

Had he been so focused on his own shortcomings that he'd been too afraid to express his love?

She'd asked him to love her in bed that last night. And he had, but not as she'd really wanted him to. She'd needed to hear him say the words. To know she was wanted, needed and precious to him. To be told that not just physically, but to hear it said out loud to the world.

Amanda was his chance at real love. A way to change his past. Make his life better. He understood that now. She'd been an outsider growing up. Had given part of herself to people all her professional life and they had all let her down. She wanted to be loved for who she was, not because she carried his baby. To be loved for herself.

And what had he offered her? A move to another country. Giving up the job she'd worked so hard for. Sleeping in his bed with no promises from him and giving up her pride. What kind of egotistical fool must he have sounded like?

He wanted to rebuild his life—with Amanda by his side.

Scooting back on the examination table, Amanda prepared for her first prenatal appointment. She fidgeted with excitement, and yet sadness surrounded her because Lucius wasn't there. If things had been different they would be sharing this moment.

She had no doubt he would be an attentive father and she intended to give him that chance. In two days she would fly back to Australia. She planned to take him up on his offer of a job.

He didn't deserve for her to take his child so far away from him. If Lucius still wanted her at his house and in his bed she would accept that too. She understood who he was. He'd showed her he cared through his actions. From all she'd seen, she had been well loved.

The obstetrician finished her exam. "I pronounce you fit to fly. And I understand you'll be getting the best care there is in Australia. We'll miss you here. Now, I have a few more lines on the chart to fill out and then you can get dressed."

There was some type of commotion going on in the hall. Amanda glanced at the door.

The door swung open just as the obstetrician asked, "Would you like to include the father's name on the chart?"

Lucius stalked in. "Yes, she would. Dr. Lucius West."

"Lucius!" The word came out on a cloud of shock and joy. Her heart fluttered. What was he doing there? Did she dare to hope he'd come after her?

He stepped to her side and took her hand. It wasn't what she'd expected him to do. She'd anticipated him going straight into doctor mode.

Instead he demanded of the other doctor, "How is she?"

With a slight smile on her face the obstetrician answered, "It's nice to finally meet you, Dr. West."

Lucius nodded, but his eyes never left Amanda. It was as if he were drinking her in. Somehow wanting to absorb her, adoring her. It was a rather wonderful feeling.

The obstetrician continued, "She's in perfect health. She's free to fly."

"You're sure?" Lucius sounded anxious. "Fly?" His face took on a look of confusion.

"Amanda, I'm done here. You may dress now." The doctor smiled and left the room, leaving her and Lucius alone.

"What are you doing here?" She scooted to the end of the exam table, preparing to get down. She needed clothes on to handle this conversation.

Lucius offered her his hand. She took it and climbed from the table. Covering herself the best she could with the paper wrap, and without saying a word, she hurried behind the screen.

"Lucius, why are you here?" she asked again.

"I came for my heart."

He sounded as if he was standing just on the other side of the curtain. So close but still so far away.

Fear filled her. Was he sick?

"What's wrong with your heart?"

"You have it. I can't breathe or think or live or work without you."

Amanda's breath caught. Did he mean what she hoped he did?

"Are you dressed yet?" His voice was rough and still so close.

"Not completely."

The curtain was whipped back. "I like you better without clothes on anyway."

Lucius took her into his arms, pulling her to him and kissing her like he would never let her go. Amanda had found heaven. She ran her hands over his shoulders and cupped his face, frantically returning his kisses.

Finally he pulled his head back just enough so she could see his beautiful eyes.

"I love you, Amanda. I love you."

"And I love you, with all my heart."

A quick knock on the door made them look that way. Amanda pulled the paper sheet around her and stood behind Lucius as Kirri stepped in.

"I heard a buzz that there was a famous Australian doctor causing a scene down here. I had to come see who it might be. Imagine my surprise to learn it's just my brother."

She came over and gave him a tight hug and a kiss on the cheek.

"Hey, Amanda. I'm glad to see this blockhead finally came around. I was going to give him one more week, then I was going to break my promise and have a talk with him."

Amanda couldn't do anything but stand there, stunned.

"Tomorrow night you'll both be expected at my house for dinner. The family will be there."

Kirri made it sound like being with the Sawyer side of her family was like a recipe for happiness and she wanted to share it.

"See you then." She went out the door, singing, "I'm going to be an auntie… I'm going to be auntie…"

Lucius and Amanda laughed. It felt so good to do it again. All the laughter had been sucked out of her life since she'd left Lucius.

He kissed her again. "Finish getting your clothes on. We need to talk somewhere with some privacy."

Amanda pulled on her clothes as Lucius waited by the door, watching her. Her hands shook at his intense stare that flickered with desire. She'd missed him all the way to her soul.

Lucius did a fine job of driving to her apartment. To her mind he was exceptional at everything.

They walked hand in hand to the elevator. As the doors closed he took her into his arms and kissed her. It was a kiss of craving, and yet a new element had been added. An element of tenderness, a promise, and the gift of all of Lucius's heart. It was as if two cells in Lucius's lab that had been free-floating had found each other, forming a perfect match.

Inside her place, Lucius looked around. "I like your apartment. It's very you."

She huffed. "It has no view like yours."

"What it has is you. That makes all the difference." He took her hand and led her to the sofa. "We should talk."

She sat. He took a spot far enough away that he could face her while holding both of her hands. "Amanda, I've been an idiot. I'm sorry. When you left anything that was good, right and wonderful in my life went with you. I was even going to let my child be raised thousands of miles away because I wasn't man enough to say how I felt. I do love you. With all my heart."

"Lucius—"

"Let me finish. I've waited too long to say this and I

won't let it sit any longer. I've always believed certain things about myself and what I should do, who I should be. Because of those, and a failed marriage that had more to do with being a failure at marriage than love, I didn't think my life could be any different than it was. Then along came you, with your teasing, your smile…" he squeezed her hands "…and your bright outlook on life. And I saw it could be amazing. The only problem was, I was afraid. Gut-wrenchingly afraid. What if I loved you and you didn't love me back? Or I lost that love?"

"That would never happen." Her heart hurt for the pain he'd been through.

"I couldn't and can't live without you. You are my life. You are what makes the sun shine in the morning and the moon bright at night for me. I have a few things I want to make clear. If it comes down to a choice between you and the baby, I will always pick you. If it's between you and me, I'll save you. If I have to give up the clinic to be with you, I will. If it is between you and medicine, I choose you. If it means living in Atlanta to have you, then that's what I'll do. I want *you*."

She threw her arms around him, moisture filling her eyes. "I want you too. And now it's my turn to express how I feel." She stood and tugged on his hand. "That can better be done in my bedroom."

Lucius grinned and followed her.

She stopped beside the bed. "I've missed you so much…" She began unbuttoning his shirt.

"Are you sure this is okay? I don't want to hurt the baby."

Amanda giggled. "Lucius, you're the smartest and most educated man I know—you know better than that."

"That may be true, but being a man in love with the woman carrying his child trumps all that knowledge."

"Dr. Lucius West, if you don't start taking my clothes off I'm going to hurt you."

She kissed him even while her hands went to his belt buckle.

Later that evening Lucius held Amanda in his arms as they lay in bed talking, and then kissing, then talking some more. This was what was truly important in life. He'd found real contentment for the first time. Amanda would always be by his side and his strongest supporter. Nothing else would ever matter. All the past had been washed away and he finally had a new start.

"I went to see my father the other day."

She turned so she could look at him. "And what happened?"

"To my surprise, a great deal. He told me that he'd learned too late that work isn't everything. That he had regrets where his family was concerned. That he wished he'd done some things differently. He made me see the light, so to speak."

"I'm really thankful for that." She kissed his shoulder.

"It's too late for my father and me to be close, but I'm going make sure my child knows I love him or her and that I'll be proud of them no matter what."

"I have no doubt you will. You make me feel very loved. I've had a revelation of my own. I had lunch with my mother and I learned that my stepfather isn't the person I thought. He cared about me but I just pushed him away—to a point from which it was hard to come back. I went for a visit this last weekend and apologized to him."

"That couldn't have been easy. I should have been there with you."

She kissed him. "You really are a nice guy."

"Don't sound so surprised." He grinned and ran his fingers over her ribs.

"I'm not—I promise. With my stepfather I managed. We hugged. Things aren't perfect, but at least in the future I'll be trying to meet him halfway."

"That's all anyone can ask. Hey, I meant to ask you… where are you flying to?"

"Sydney."

"Sydney?"

She laughed. "Yes—you know…where you live. I was coming back to you."

His eyes widened with wonder. "You were?"

"I was. I decided that even though you hadn't *said* you loved me you had already shown me you did in so many ways. That it wasn't fair to ask you to be someone you aren't."

His eyes twinkled. "So I wasted this trip?"

"I can make it worth your trouble." Amanda slid over and up him, giving him a deep, wet kiss.

Lucius's arms went around her. Yeah, he would be glad he'd gone to the trouble.

As they lay satiated, sometime later, Lucius placed his hand over the place where his baby grew, protected by Amanda.

"I brought you a stuffed koala bear. It's in my bag. You should have seen the looks I got as I came through Customs."

"I think I'll share it with the baby." She placed her hand over his. "I've already gotten what I really want from Australia."

Lucius kissed her behind the ear. "Would you like a girl or a boy?"

"I don't care. I just want him or her to be healthy and to have your blue eyes." She giggled. "The 'Baby Whisperer' strikes again."

"This time I'll proudly accept the title." He placed his lips against her ear. "I was just wondering if you would consider becoming Mrs. Lucius West? I love you from here to eternity and I always will."

She kissed him. "I would love to be your wife. That, and your love, and our baby, is all I'll ever need."

* * * * *

COMING SOON!

We really hope you enjoyed reading this book. If you're looking for more romance, be sure to head to the shops when new books are available on

Thursday 16th April

To see which titles are coming soon, please visit

millsandboon.co.uk/nextmonth

MILLS & BOON

Coming next month

UNLOCKING THE EX-ARMY DOC'S HEART
Juliette Hyland

Rafe's phone continued to ding. Apparently, a late-night ice cream post was popular. He ignored it, but the world invaded their private heaven with each buzz.

—I also want you. The real Rafe. The swing dancer, who has a midnight sweet tooth and gets cold easily. Not the persona that makes an algorithm happy. Annie swallowed the words as she spun her pint to him and grabbed his. "My turn for the chocolate."

A smile pulled at Rafe's lips. Lifting his spoon, he laughed, "I don't want cookie dough. *En garde*, Annie."

Giggling, she defended the chocolate from the swipes of his spoon as he dove for the pint. This was belonging. Laughing over ice cream, late at night, with no audience. How could she make him understand?

Finally, she pushed it to the middle of the table. "Guess I can share." The bottom of the pint appeared too quickly, and Annie waved away Rafe's offer to let her have the final bite. Looking at the clock, she reluctantly pushed away from the table. *If she didn't leave now...* "Thanks for keeping me company. We have a full schedule tomorrow. I think we both need some sleep."

Annie's fingers brushed his as they reached for the empty ice cream containers at the same time. Lightning flashed between them, and Annie didn't care about the buzz of the phone, or anything else. She just wanted, needed, to know how he kissed.

"Rafe," ignoring the tension racing through her belly,

she leaned forward. He tasted of chocolate, heat and summer. Her heart gasped at the tender way his mouth shifted under hers, accepting her exploration. If she took his hand, he'd come with her to bed. The thought excited her before panic rushed into its place.

Stepping away she stared at him, "I—"

Rafe placed a finger against her lips. "Don't apologize. Please."

Pursing her lips, she grabbed the containers, holding them before her, an empty sugar wall between her and temptation. "I wasn't going to apologize." Annie held her breath, wishing she had the courage to ask him to follow her, and hating the uncertainty that kept the words buried.

Rafe soft lips brushed her cheek, "I'll see you tomorrow."

His words held a promise and an escape.

Continue reading
UNLOCKING THE EX-ARMY DOC'S HEART
Juliette Hyland

Available next month
www.millsandboon.co.uk